# THE *un*FINISHED LINE

## JEN LYON

*The Unfinished Line*

First Published in October 2024

Copyright © 2024 Jen Lyon

ISBN: 979-8-9877320-9-0 (paperback)



Published by Doss About Publishing

Edited by Margaret Hulings

Cover design by Mary Wright

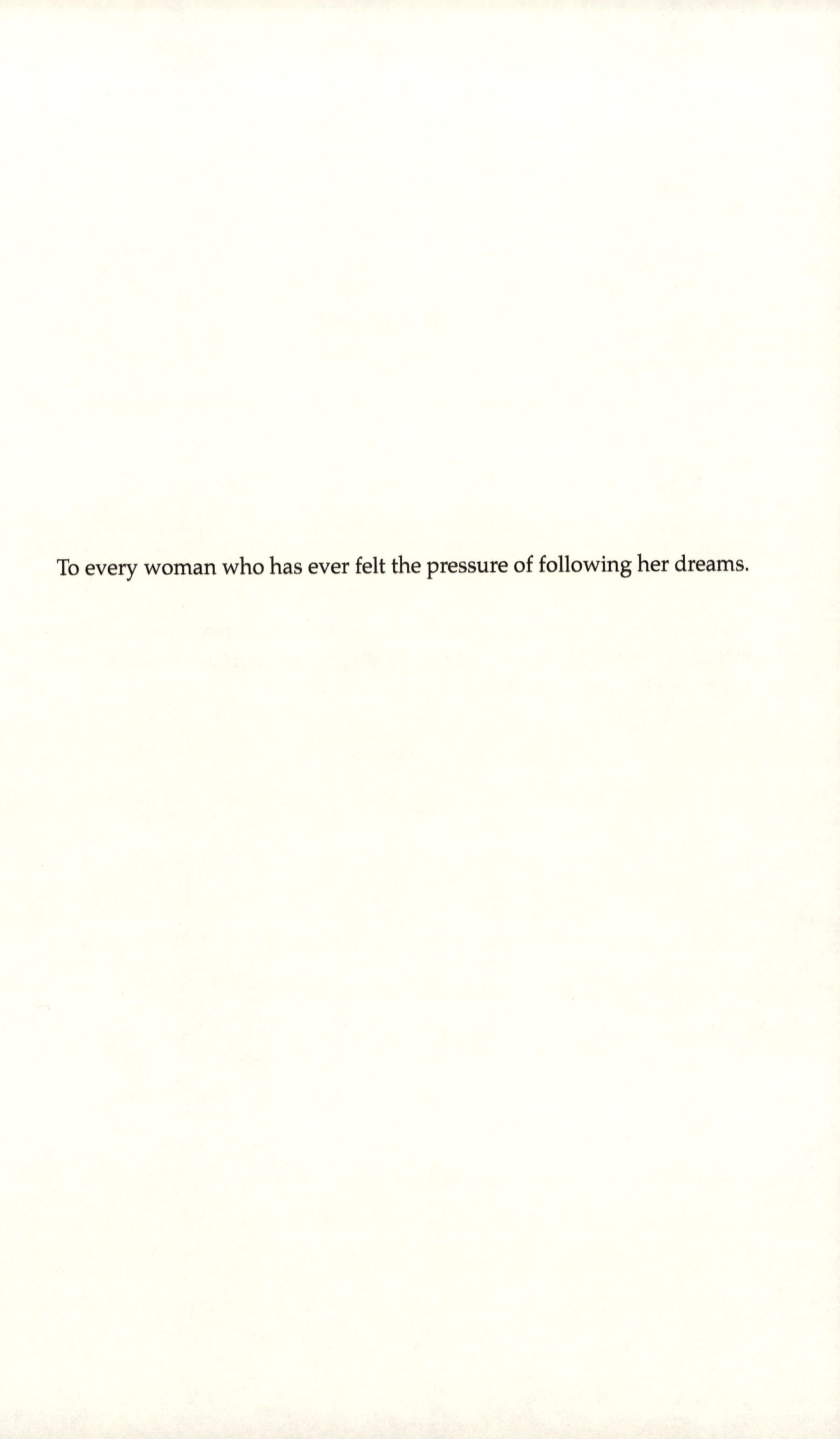

To every woman who has ever felt the pressure of following her dreams.

# Scene 1

The first time I met Dillon Sinclair, I almost killed her.

I was driving back to the hotel from Dani's picture-perfect, postcard wedding. It had been exquisite—exceeding even Dani's standards—but despite being the Maid of Honor, I hadn't been able to focus on my best friend's fairytale ceremony.

Not since I got the call.

*The call*, as I'd later come to think of it when joking around with my studio friends, lamenting our early days of audition-after-audition-after-fruitless-dead-end-humiliating-audition. The call that changed my life. The call everyone in the business was waiting for. Hoping for. The one that, somehow, by the grace of the Gods of Show Business, astonishingly came to me.

But it wasn't just the call that turned my universe on its axis. It was hours after that. Long after the lavish sunset ceremony on Honokalani Beach, and the romantic, poetic vows of *I Do*. After the toasting and roasting, and the barefoot dancing in the shimmering black sand.

I'd made it part way up the winding two-lane highway—the famous *Road to Hana* with its majestic, panoramic views. It was pitch black out, and though I'd driven the stretch of road from the resort to the small, private cove with Dani half a dozen times over the last three days, the turns were still unfamiliar to me. Especially now that I made the trip alone. I drove slowly and praised myself on having limited my wine consumption to the single glass I'd sipped throughout the reception—a feat not easily achieved as I sat in anxiety all evening waiting to make my Maid of Honor speech.

*This must be a breeze for you, Kameryn*, Dani's mother snipped the previous morning, while I anguished in silence over my handful of notes. It felt impossible to sum up the two-decade friendship I'd shared with her daughter—a bond established over wetting our pants in the sandbox on the first day of preschool.

*Speeches must be second nature to you by now.* Snide. Condescending, as ever.

How little she knew me, after all these years. And how much less she even cared. I would always just be Dani's 'farmgirl friend.' Never mind that my mother's occupation as a professional horse trainer didn't exactly constitute a 'farm.' To her, I was just the girl who'd lived outside the city limits of their upper-class suburban district, bussed-in to their fancy schools. It would never make any difference how successful—how accoladed—I ever was in my career. Even when news broke about my upcoming role. It wouldn't matter. I'd never be one of them. My friendship would never be worthy of Darlene Hallwell's perfect little girl.

But none of that was where my mind was as I plugged the little four-cylinder Wrangler along the coastal highway. I was still thinking about Aaron's call; the edge to his voice, usually so calm, so collected, but this time percolating with excitement. He'd been my agent for five years—representing me since the day after my eighteenth birthday—and never once, in all the phone calls we'd shared, had he ever called me Kam.

"Kam!" He'd spoken over the top of my hello. "I've just heard from Universal!"

There was something in the sentence, something in his atypical familiarity, that snatched any response I might have given from my lips.

He'd continued. "It's a go, Kam. It's a go!"

I was afraid I'd misunderstood. I couldn't even hear the inquiry of my clarification over the thundering of my heart.

But I heard his response, his laugh brimming with a buoyant giddiness that snuck through his baritone voice. "This is it, kid. This is *it*. Do you have any idea what this is going to do for you? Hell, for *me*?! This isn't one of Netflix's Top Ten streamers. You hit this one out of the park, Kameryn Kingsbury. Buckle up, because we've got one hell of a ride ahead."

I knew what he meant. I just never imagined it could happen. Not once in the eight months I'd been auditioning for the role did I remotely think there'd be a chance in a million years they'd ever want me. Even when they said they wanted a newcomer, I still figured they'd ultimately settle on a big name. I had so few notable credits. Indie stuff and commercials, a couple appearances on daytime TV. My biggest claim to fame was my two Disney voiceovers. I wasn't the A-lister they'd be seeking.

Only, it turned out they weren't blowing smoke. They hadn't wanted a household headliner. They really did want to cast the lead as an unknown. A no one. A nothing.

And to the desks at Universal, I was exactly that. A clean slate. A blank page.

The project itself held all the weight they needed. *Sand Seekers* was projected to be the next Harry Potter. Star Wars. Twilight. The Hunger Games. It drew the same type of cult attraction, the same fanatic followers eagerly awaiting their obsession to be magnified on the silver screen.

I knew all this, because I'd daydreamed about the role. I fantasized about the call from Aaron, despite knowing in the back of my mind it was never going to happen. I imagined I'd say something clever, something casual. Pretend I knew I'd land the part all along.

*Fake it 'til you make it.*

In the end, I'd never managed to string together more than two coherent syllables at a time.

"Of course, you already know, but mum's the word, Kameryn. Not a breath of this until the green flag is waved." Aaron had at last returned to his succinct, all-business state.

I managed a yes. I might have thrown in a *sir*. And then the call was over, leaving me swaying beside a palm tree a hundred feet from the crystal blue cove where Dani's ceremony was about to start.

Replaying the phone call over and over, I wound around the dark highway, wondering how I would ever manage to keep it secret until everything was settled. It could be weeks. Months, even. Until at last someone from the studio would slip a name to TMZ, pretending the story'd been scooped, and then cash in off the free publicity. Only then could I call Dani—call Carter—maybe even call my mom—and tell them the news. Assure them the headlines were true.

But until then, that cat was locked securely in a bag.

I reached to turn off the radio. It wasn't even Halloween yet and the latest pop edition of Mele Kalikimaka was blaring on the local station, pounding its upbeat chords through my over-taxed brain. I just wanted quiet after hours of being surrounded by the Hallwells, and Dani's two hundred destination wedding guests.

I found the knob on the unfamiliar center console and stabbed it to *off*. Finally, silence.

As I looked up, there was a flash of metal in my headlights. A streamlined frame bent over handlebars. A brief blinking red.

I heard the brakes squeal as I nosed the rented Jeep Wrangler away from the shoulder, clipping the rear tire of the cyclist with the edge of my bumper. There was the dull, nauseating sound of a body hitting my hood. A scream from a second cyclist who narrowly avoided the collision.

And that was how I almost killed Dillon Sinclair.

I guess *almost killed* is a touch of exaggeration. But hey, I'm an actress, over-the-top is my life.

In reality, Dillon was up on her feet, cussing at me before I'd even managed to open my door. But I didn't know that yet. For the second time that evening, my soul levitated out of my body and left my heart a slamming, lurching mess. Only, unlike its earlier cardiovascular circus after hanging up with Aaron, this time, there was no jubilation to its acrobatics. I was frozen in terror. Frozen with my hand on the plastic door handle, shaking from head to toe.

I'd just hit someone on the Road to Hana. I'd just fucking run over someone on the best night of my life.

"Open your Goddamn door, ya wanker!"

This was not the cyclist I had hit. This was the second rider, a tall, wiry, furious man. In my state of shock, I could hardly comprehend his words through the rage of his English accent.

"I—I'm sorry! I'm so sorry!" It was all I could think to say.

He yanked open the door and I automatically began to stagger out, before realizing I hadn't put the Jeep in park.

*Idiot.* I ground the shifter to *P* and slithered out of the driver's seat, my legs shaking so hard they nearly gave out beneath me. I glanced around, expecting to see a bloody hump in the street in the dark.

But no, the person I'd hit—it was a woman, I discovered—was standing beside the shadowed frame of her mangled bike, cursing a hailstorm of insults that stung with each staccato word. She, too, had an accent, though it was more subtle. I wasn't certain where to place it, and at the time, her origin of nationality was the least of my considerations.

The cyclist was silhouetted in the headlamp of the Jeep, the tight skins of her riding gear frayed from hip to elbow, covered in road rash glistening the same color as the flashing taillight from her damaged rear wheel. She cussed again before looking up at me, a trickle of blood dribbling down her lip to her chin.

But—holy hell—she was *alive*. Thank God for the smallest of favors.

"I'm so sorry." I didn't ask if she was okay. I'd just hit her and flung her over the hood of my SUV. The question seemed banal. "I didn't see you on the turn."

"Then your damned eyes weren't on the road." She spit a mouthful of blood and wiped at the gravel embedded in her forearm, the hard line of her jaw clenching with pain. "Fuck," she spit again, but this was directed at the ruin of her bike. "Just fuck!"

I stood transfixed with a thousand-yard stare, my brain abandoning me completely. I didn't know the protocol for this situation. I'd never had so much as a parking ticket. Did I call the cops? Did we exchange insurance information? Was I going to jail? There was no *fake it 'til you make it* on this one.

"I'll buy you a new bike."

Why did the stupidest things come out of my mouth at the worst times?

She looked up at me as if I'd spoken gibberish. Before she could say anything, her riding partner laughed—a bitter, angry bark of a sound that turned my legs from unsteady to positively unstable.

"You couldn't afford to replace her bar tape, ya bloody muppet! That bike costs more than your car. Do you know who the fuck she is?!"

Why my first response was to bristle at the question, to grow defensive, I have no clue. It wasn't like I was in any position to pull the good ol' *but do you know who **I** am?* I mean, come on, I wasn't exactly Margot Robbie. And somehow, *do you know who I am **going** to be* lost some of its weighted impact. Besides—I'd just run the woman over. It didn't matter who I was.

"No." I said instead. Was it pertinent? Was running over Lance Armstrong worse than running over the Weekend Warrior out for their Sunday spin?

"You just hit Dillon Fucking Sinclair, ya knob!"

If he expected the revelation to strike fear in my heart, I'm afraid he was bound to be woefully disappointed. The name meant nothing to me.

"Should I call an ambulance?" It finally dawned on me that was probably the first thing I should have offered.

The woman's head snapped up, her eyes silver in the headlights. "You think they're going to fix my bike?"

There was such a loathing level of sarcasm behind the question, such disgusted disdain, I felt my cheeks color. I felt like a child, standing there, uncertain what to say. To do. This wasn't something that could easily disappear. Not like the way Dani's dad's wallet had vanished those photos from her 21st birthday.

At least I wasn't drunk. And she wasn't dead. But what did it matter? When the press got a hold of it, they'd have a field day. No one would care that it had just been an accident. Hollywood was always at fault in these situations.

I swallowed. I wanted to call Dani—she'd know what to do. But it was her wedding night. No way in hell was I calling her. Besides: *Throw money at it.* That's all she'd say. That's what she'd done her whole life. It was her solution to everything. Cash made anything bad go away. But you had to have enough cash to do that. And my last name wasn't Hallwell.

"Can I give you a ride?"

"Nah, I think I'll pass." The woman bent and lifted her bike, the flashing red of her taillight still blinking in time with the pounding of my heart. The front wheel was misshapen and the handlebars crooked, disallowing the bike to be rolled forward. Instead, she heaved it onto her back, unable to hide the grimace from the effort.

"Sinc—" the man tried to stop her, but she brushed him off.

"Leave it, Kyle."

He turned to me. "You should be charged with reckless driving, ya little—"

"She's just a daft tourist. Let her be." She shouldered the bike into a more comfortable position and started walking down the side of the road.

"At least let me give you a ride," I tried again.

She didn't turn back. "Thanks, but I've seen how you drive." There was no humor in her tone.

# Scene 2

Dillon didn't stay for the medal ceremony or after party, instead slipping back to the hotel alone. She emptied the resort's ice bin into the jacuzzi-sized bathtub and proceeded to soak away her frustrations in the frigid water.

It was the first time she hadn't finished top ten in longer than she could remember.

She hadn't expected to win the Hamoa Beach standard. Not after getting sent arse over tits over the hood of a car two days earlier.

But it wasn't a satisfactory excuse. She'd been fit enough to compete, and as the current number-one-ranked professional triathlete in the world, coming in thirteenth out of a lousy field of forty—in a race that wasn't even sanctioned—wasn't acceptable. Borrowed bike or not. Car or no car.

But whatever. It was water under the bridge. She could lick her wounded pride over the rest of offseason, and apply her focus to winning the races that actually mattered—continuing to do whatever it took to make it clear to *British Triathlon* that, even at twenty-eight, she was still their leading contender to bring home a gold medal. The Los Angeles Olympics were three years away. Her previous wins of bronze and silver weren't enough to show for a lifetime of dedication to a sport that had taken more from her than it had ever given.

Wincing as she dragged herself out of the tub, she paused in the mirror to take a brief assessment of the state of her body: pruned road rash from ankle to shoulder, bruising along her ribs, swelling from hip to clavicle. She had to hand it to herself—just the fact that she'd managed to swim, bike, and run in that condition was no walk in the park.

She leaned closer to the mirror, examining the start of a black eye. As if the damage from the bike accident hadn't been enough, she'd been kicked in the face by another competitor at the beginning of the swim. It was definitely going to turn color.

All said, maybe finishing thirteenth wasn't so bad after all.

Without bothering to grab the towel folded into a fancy origami sea turtle, she gingerly pulled on a pair of running shorts and top, and left a puddle of footprints as she crossed the bungalow to the balcony. There, a hot tub steamed into the balmy autumn air, the panoramic view dissolving into the sleepy island coastline.

At least her sponsors hadn't skimped on the accommodations.

Her coach, Alistair, would have scolded her for going straight from an ice bath to the heat of the jet-streamed water, but he was seventy-two hundred miles away, back in London. Which meant she could do damn well as she pleased.

There hadn't even been enough time for the stiffness of her muscles to thaw before a pounding at her hotel door echoed to the balcony. She didn't bother with an acknowledgment, knowing it was Kyle, who would let himself in without any indication she desired company.

"Well, not floating belly up, I see," he strolled to the railing and leaned over the side, sucking in the ocean breeze as if he hadn't been born in the coastal town of Withernsea.

Dillon rolled her eyes. She knew he was only half kidding. It was true, she took losing harder than she should. She always had.

*Show me a good loser and I'll show you a loser*, Henrik had instilled in her.

*Henrik.*

Her first coach.

The person she detested most in all the world.

She pushed the thought aside. What did it matter what he had ever said?

Kyle turned to face her. "Don't be so hard on yourself, Sinc. It's not like you DNFed."

*DNF—did not finish*. Never in her pro career had she dropped from a race. It simply wasn't an option.

"Shut you! You're only going on because you coursed a decent time."

"Decent?" he grinned, more than eager to talk about his own race results. "Fourth out of seventy-four—"

"One placing shy of a meaningful check," Dillon pointed out, disbelieving how anyone could be thrilled with falling just short of the podium. If she'd missed a top-three payout by thirty seconds, she'd be outraged at her performance. This was their profession, after all. Their livelihood.

But he was Kyle Wood. Nothing ruffled him. Nothing got in the way of his love of the race. Win or no win. Big check, little check, no check. He simply rolled with the punches. First or last, he'd find a reason to pat his back all the way home to Yorkshire.

"Don't you worry, duck—I'll wave to you from the podium in Los Angeles while you're sitting in the cheap seats."

"In your wildest fantasy," Dillon splashed a palmful of water at him. They both knew, of the two of them, she was the more accomplished athlete. Kyle was a strong competitor, but he held none of the accolades of Dillon's illustrious career. World titles. Cup championships. Course records. It never stopped them from taking the piss out of one another, however, a habit formed since the day they'd met more than a decade earlier.

"Oh yeah?" Kyle kicked off his flip flops. "I'm not the one who came in thirteenth place, beat by a bunch of village locals, in little more than a fun run."

Before she'd worked out a rebuttal, Kyle launched his pencil-thin frame into the hot tub, sending a tidal wave of water over the top of Dillon.

"Arsehole!"

"All day, every day," he flashed a knavish grin, shaking out his dripping hair like a wet dog.

"Isn't there some party you should be at, trying to convince one of the local girls you're Prince William's long lost cousin?"

"You're just jealous my disinherited royal act is bound to snag me a shag. Which is a whole lot better than you're going to do looking like Freddy Krueger." He nodded toward the gruesome length of mangled skin visible along her forearm.

"Rubbish—I guarantee any girl of your choosing would still rather go home with me."

"Care to bet today's winnings? Oh, wait," he wagged a dark eyebrow, "that's right, you didn't earn a paycheck. I made enough to spot you a tenner if you want?" He yelped as her heel connected with his shin, but the good nature of his teasing faded when he caught sight of her ribcage. "Jesus, Sinc. Are you sure you shouldn't have that looked at?"

Dillon yanked her shirt down, covering the Jeep Wrangler hood-induced bruising.

"For what? Some quack to pound me full of percs and tell me to kick up my feet for a while?" She lifted herself onto the ledge of the hot tub, determined to downplay the reality her entire body felt like she'd been pummeled by a sledgehammer. "Hard pass."

"Would some time off really be that bad?" Kyle hopped up beside her. "You could go home, have yourself a little holiday, be ready for the beginning of the season—"

"Don't be twp. I've got Key West in three weeks. Sydney after that. I'm not about to go home and mope around for the winter." The last thing she wanted to do was fly back to the grey skies of London and sit around her empty flat. She wasn't a believer in an offseason, preferring to race all year long. It kept her head in the game. Kept her sharp. She'd see her mam and Seren soon enough when she headed to Wales for Christmas. For now, she just needed to turn her focus to Key West. A race she knew she could win.

"You know, a little rest never killed anyone." He lugged himself to his feet.

Dillon could tell from his grimace she wasn't the only one feeling the wear and tear on her body. A career in endurance racing wasn't for the faint of heart. Not with what they put themselves through. Willingly.

"Oh," he turned from where he stood dripping at the railing, "speaking of killing someone—I saw that little twit by the pool. She must be staying here."

"Who?"

"The bint who ran you over. I gave her another piece of my mind. Scared her into believing you were going to make a complaint."

"That girl?" Dillon's head snapped up. "What the fuck, Kyle?" They'd been over it half a dozen times. He wanted her to call the authorities. *For what,* Dillon wanted to know. She hadn't been driving recklessly. She hadn't been soused. She'd just been a careless holiday-maker. It wasn't the first time Dillon had been clipped on the road. It probably wouldn't be the last.

"She could have killed you, for fuck's sake!"

She knew it was his guilty conscience driving his choler. He'd been the one who wanted to go on a cooldown ride along the winding highway. She'd insisted it was too late—too dark. She'd been right.

"Well, she didn't—so come off it!"

"I heard the receptionist say she was an actress or something—here from Hollywood. You never know, maybe she really could afford to buy you a new bike. Not much of an actress, however, if you ask me—when I told her you were going to bring a claim, she looked like she was going to cry."

"You made her cry? You can be such a bastard, Kyle—!"

"And you're suddenly the Queen of Forgiveness? How's the view up there on your high horse, Mother Teresa? Next thing I know, you'll be calling the little numpty, apologizing to her for denting her car, and asking her to dinner."

"It'd be better than listening to you whinge about it, that's for certain." She popped to her feet, regretful of the sudden motion. "Don't you have a shag to find?" she asked over her shoulder, disappearing into the bungalow.

When he had gone and the serenity of her afternoon resumed, Dillon lay on the tile floor, sharing the space with the centipedes and geckos. She worked a massage gun deep into the muscles of her calves, still annoyed by Kyle's intrusion. It was just like him, sticking his nose where it didn't belong. Why he'd had to start some unnecessary drama with that stupid girl—he just never could manage to keep his mouth shut.

Tossing the percussion gun aside, she hoisted herself onto the bed, and picked up the phone receiver.

Fuck Kyle and his meddling.

She dialed the front desk, fishing out a pen and notepad from the bedside table drawer.

The woman who answered greeted her with too much enthusiasm. She was a big fan, she'd told her the day she checked in, offering her a coy smile. *A big, big fan.*

Dillon schooled her voice into what she hoped was something equally chipper.

"Hiya, Mikala! Can you do me a favor?"

# Scene 3

The shrill blast of the bedside telephone made me jump, losing my grip on the mug of green tea I'd brewed, shattering the cup and its contents across the kitchenette tile. I stood stunned, staring at the mess I'd managed to make, before the phone rang again, causing me to wince once more.

I'd been on edge all afternoon—ever since my encounter with that prick by the pool—and my nerves were running full tilt. No one I knew would call me on the hotel landline. Dani and Tom were on their island-hopping honeymoon, Dani's mother, Darlene, had blessedly left for California earlier in the morning, and anyone back home would reach me by my cell. I had extended my stay two nights in Hana, determined to use the extra days to unwind before climbing back onto the Hollywood hamster wheel.

The phone continued to ring as I considered my options:

1. Yank the spiral phone line from the wall.

2. Lock myself in the bathroom and take a second shower, hoping the caller would grow tired of trying to reach me by the time I reconditioned my hair.

3. Pick it up and deal with whatever was on the other end of the line.

I realized—at twenty-three years old—there was really only one option that made sense. And so, treading carefully across the debris of tea and glass, I seized the coiled cord and gave it a solid jerk. It didn't budge. The phone kept ringing.

*Shit.*

Considering the last thing my hair needed in the island humidity was another round of conditioning, I resigned myself to pulling on my big girl panties and swiped the receiver from its cradle.

"Hello?"

"Hi. Is this Kameryn?"

It wasn't like the voice was overly familiar. I'd only heard it once before, and mainly through a plethora of curses and insults flung my direction. But I recognized it immediately all the same. Given that her boyfriend had spent five solid minutes threatening me as I toweled off from my morning swim, it was fair to say the collision on the highway a couple days earlier hadn't been far from my mind.

My first instinct was to hang up. I wasn't up for another round of you're-a-fucking-loser-and-screwed-up-some-silly-race from her after I'd just gotten it from him. However, I also didn't want to make things worse than they already were—not when I was aware of all the publicity I was about to receive. It would be better if I could get this handled on the down low. Which meant keeping my auto insurance out of it.

"Look," I started, deciding I'd try Dani's approach at life, "I'm really sorry about the other night. I get it—it's an expensive bike. Like I said, I'll buy you a new one." The words hurt even as they left my mouth. I'd looked up racing bikes after the confrontation at the pool, and the nicer ones did indeed cost as much as my second-hand car. I didn't have that kind of money on hand. Until I got my first advance for *Sand Seekers*, I was living on a shoestring budget, so if I had to fork over cash, I'd literally have to sell my car. But fine. Whatever it took to put this in my rearview mirror.

"A new bike, yeah?"

She sounded more amused than anything else, which I quickly took an affront to. There was nothing about this I found funny. Especially if I was soon to be taking public transportation to the studio. Wouldn't that just be the way to start my Hollywood blockbuster career?

*And arriving now, Kameryn Kingsbury, ten minutes late off the Red Line subway.*

"Yeah. But if that isn't enough, and you're wanting to press charges, I really feel it's best if you spoke directly to my attorney." The attorney I didn't have. And the one I *definitely* could not afford.

She laughed, and I dug my toenails into the throw rug running alongside the bed.

"Is that an American thing, or just a Hollywood thing—threatening to call your solicitor?"

*Fuck me.* So she knew I came from Hollywood. She'd already been digging around.

"If you're just calling to—"

She cut me off. "I don't need you to buy me a new bike—my sponsor will handle that—and I've no interest in bringing charges, so calm your tits, will you?"

I was thrown by the implication she didn't want anything from me. "Then, uh…"

Apparently, she understood my confusion. "I was only calling to apologize about Kyle. He can get carried away sometimes."

"Oh." I uncurled my toes from the carpet. Despite what a douche bag her boyfriend had been, it didn't feel right that she was apologizing. I was the one who'd hit her, after all. "I—um, it's fine, really. I mean, he must have been really scared for you…"

"Nah," she saved me from my rambling, "he can just be a real arsehole. But listen—instead of blathering on, and talk of lawyers and all that tosh, why don't you meet me for a pint? We can shake hands on it, call it a day, and go our way. I owe you that much for Kyle's bullshit and you owe me as much for introducing me to the hood of your car."

"I…" I wasn't sure what to say. She didn't owe me anything, and I, well, getting a drink with the woman I'd run over seemed… odd. I half wondered if she was playing a joke on me. If she'd convince me to meet her somewhere, and then have a good laugh with her boyfriend while I stood around looking like an idiot waiting for her to arrive.

But it didn't seem like it. There was a directness to her—a candidness that didn't feel contrived. If she was pulling a fast one, she was a better actress than I'd ever be.

"Okay," I said tentatively. "Where?"

Two hours later, I found myself waiting by the trickling fountain in front of the hotel lobby, where a blanket of water irises covered the black pond. I was twenty minutes early, and felt antsy, shifting from foot to foot, fiddling with my keys. Why had I agreed to this? What if she brought that asshole with her? How would I politely excuse myself and tell her I'd changed my mind?

Five minutes before our allotted meeting time, I finally decided to bail. I was going to get back to my room and call her, apologizing that something had come up and I couldn't make it. But before I could make my getaway, she came strolling up the footpath from the seaside bungalow suites that fell way out of my price range.

"Alright," she greeted, one hand lifted in a half wave, the other still stuffed into the pocket of her baggy black joggers, her bright coral sneakers scuffing along the asphalt, "how are we?"

Without her cussing at me, I found I liked the lilt of her accent. It was subtle, different. English, maybe, but I wasn't sure. I offered a wave in return, trying not to stare at the purple bruising and scabbed gravel rash her white tank top left on display.

"Hi." I forced myself to look away from the mess I'd made of her arm and cringed when I saw she also had a pretty rank black eye.

Smiling at my alarm, she jerked her thumb toward her face. "Sorry, but you don't get credit for this one. Hazard of the job, I'm afraid."

I nodded. Whatever that meant.

She stuck out her hand. "Dillon Sinclair."

"Kam." I faltered. "Kameryn." As I shook her hand, I became overtly aware of my sweaty palms. I don't know why I was so nervous. Maybe it was a reaction to her easy confidence. The way she assessed me behind her placid gaze.

"Well, Kam-Kameryn," her smile lifted at only one corner of her mouth, dimples appearing, "mind if we take your ride?"

I hadn't really expected we'd be going anywhere. There was a bar at the resort—the kind with thirty-dollar cocktails for a bobbing slice of pineapple and a splash of bottom-shelf liquor. But she was alone, with no jerk-of-a-boyfriend in sight, so I decided I didn't mind. "Sure." It took me a beat too long to realize she was waiting for me to hand her my keys. "Oh," I said, placing them reluctantly in her palm. "It's a rental."

*God, I was stupid. Of course she knew it was a rental.* Ninety-percent of this island was driving a rental.

"I'll be certain not to hit anyone." She winked, closing her fingers around the fob, and then we were in my Jeep, cruising down Hana Highway, and unbeknownst to me I was just beginning to experience the tip of the iceberg that was the wild adventure of Dillon Sinclair.

We turned south, away from the small town of Hana and the few restaurants dotting the northern stretch of road heading toward Kahului. I figured we were heading for Mokae Cove—I'd seen a tiny restaurant on the way to Dani's ceremony—but we drove straight past the turn-off without so much as a glance at the hand-carved Huli Huli sign. I wasn't an expert on the local geography, but I'd been pretty certain the chicken shack was the last bit of civilization before the multi-hour backroad trek to Kula. The longer we wound around the bumpy road—away from the resort—the more I began to wonder if, with my impeccable luck, I'd somehow managed to run over the only serial killer cyclist on Maui. Leave it to me to make it simple for her to drive me to an isolated beach and extract her revenge.

But if she was a psychopath, she was one who appeared to have a great sense of dry humor, and an affability that managed to put everything about the evening at ease. I guess if I was going to die by homicide, this wasn't the worst way to go.

We didn't chat much. I learned quickly she wasn't one for small talk, and I somehow managed to keep myself from prattling on, a habit I had when nervous. Despite working in entertainment, I had a tendency to be shy, but for some reason, my timidity dwindled as the Jeep bounced along the coastal highway. Part of it was the complete carefreeness about her, the way she seemed so comfortable in her own skin. She wasn't looking to impress me—or even befriend me, as far as I could tell—which was so different than everyone I met in Hollywood. The nature of my career meant the circles I traveled in tended to always be looking for an opportunity. A leg up. A favor. An *in*. We all wanted something from each other—and in turn, were willing to kiss ass, to brown-nose, to lay it on thick, pretending to be whoever we thought the other person wanted to see.

That wasn't Dillon. She appeared to live at face value. And regardless of my earlier concerns that she might be luring me to my death, I found myself settling in for the drive, content with her explanation that she 'knew a tidy place' but it was 'off the beaten path.' So we drove on, the windows rolled down, her humming to the radio as we cruised along the vistas overlooking the endless stretch of Pacific Ocean.

"Now then," said Dillon, breaking our companionable silence as she suddenly turned off the highway onto a single-lane road heading toward the sea, "bloke in here can waffle on forever, but he's an alright guy. The nosh is fair, but the view makes the drive worthwhile, promise."

"How'd you ever come across this place?" I ventured to ask as she parked in front of a ramshackle hut that looked as if it may have already been past its golden era when King Pi'ilani conquered the island in the sixteenth century. There was no sign, no other cars in the narrow strip of dirt serving as a parking lot, and no indication anyone living had graced its threshold in the last four hundred years.

"I've run here a time or two."

She'd *run* here? I didn't know exactly how far we'd driven, but we'd been on the road well over half an hour. I wouldn't have made it a quarter of the hilly distance on a bike, let alone on foot. It explained a bit of how incredibly fit she was.

Before I could comment, the cockeyed door was thrown open, and the massive figure of a heavily tattooed man filled the entire threshold.

"Aloha, makamaka!" he greeted Dillon, his round face lighting with a Cheshire grin. "Back so soon?" His eyes flicked to me as we passed into the cramped dining room.

Dillon led the way toward a curtain of fake flowers, holding them aside to allow me to step onto a small lanai while keeping up an easy banter with the chatty man. I could feel her gaze on me, waiting for my reaction.

She'd said the view was worth the drive, and I imagined pretty much every inch of the landscape running alongside the highway would fit that bill—but this was something different. Beyond the pair of humidity-dampened tables, the expanse of a horseshoe bay extended below the cliffside. The black sand of the shore had turned almost iridescent in the last rays of the amber sun, and the turquoise water looked as if it had caught fire, haloed in the scattering hues of virescent foliage surrounding the tranquil cove.

The entirety of the picturesque scene was, for lack of a better word, breathtaking.

Catching my expression, the corners of her mouth twitched in the hint of a smile, before she returned her attention to the animated Hawaiian.

There was no menu. I was given the choice of vegetarian or non-vegetarian—I played it safe with vegetarian—and when, at last, the man was on his way to the kitchen, she turned to me and propped her elbows on the table.

"Worth it?" She tilted her chin in the direction of the setting sun.

"Worth it," I confirmed, picking up a frosty bottle of Koko Brown. I sipped the ale as she peeled the edge of her label.

Behind us, somewhere off in the kitchen, the cheerful sound of baritone humming floated over the sizzle of a frying pan.

"So," she settled back in the plastic chair, "Kyle overheard the woman at the front desk say you were an actress?"

*Overheard.* So she hadn't been researching me. Maybe her boyfriend really had been blowing smoke up my ass about her wanting to press charges.

I hiked a casual shoulder, waiting for what always followed: *What have you been in?* But for once, it didn't come. Which on any other occasion would have been a relief. I'd always hated the question because I didn't have an exciting answer. Tonight, however, I wanted her to ask. I wasn't sure why. It wasn't like I'd have anything different to tell her. I couldn't mention *Sand Seekers*, and I certainly wasn't going to query whether she'd ever noticed the brunette in the *Pantene Pro V* commercial, or the pair of legs selling *Gillette Venus* razors. Nor did I imagine she'd be wowed by my Disney voiceovers—my biggest claim to fame being a singing, dancing purple dragon. Still, I guess I hoped she'd be intrigued. I think her lack of interest made me want to impress her.

But instead of asking anything about my career, she worked on another corner of her untouched beer bottle label. "And what brings you to the sleepy town of Hana?"

At least this was an easy answer. I gave her the CliffsNotes on Dani's wedding, and my supporting role as Maid of Honor.

She arched an eyebrow, her lips toying with a smirk. "So the nose-bleed heels and that little pink number aren't your usual Friday night island go-to, then?"

Heat flooded my cheeks, despite the evening breeze. Dani and her damned pale peach satin bridesmaid dresses. It hadn't dawned on me until then how stupid I must have looked, standing on the side of the road, tottering in stilettos, the drying flowers of my lei broadcasting my status as a hokey tourist.

But I wasn't about to let her get my goat. I could give as good as I got. So, using the blush to my advantage, I plastered on my best embarrassed expression. "Oh." I cast my eyes to the table. "I'd actual-ly already changed at the reception."

I glanced up in just enough time to enjoy the satisfaction of her horror at the blunder, before I lost the battle with my own sly smile. It took her a beat to realize she'd been had, and when she did, she laughed, her face brightening.

"Well played." She flicked a sugar packet in my direction, missing me by a mile, and slung her lean body back into the chair, drawing one leg to her chest and resting her chin atop her knee. "You've got jokes, Kam-Kameryn."

She asked a few more questions—was it my first time in Hawaii? *No.* Did I like Hollywood? *That answer changed daily—sometimes hourly.* When was I heading home? *Wednesday.*

While this last answer should have triggered a flurry of excitement —thoughts of sealing the deal on *Sand Seekers*, attending the first reading, beginning on-set rehearsals, and all the ways my life was about to explode as I ventured into the world of a colossal major motion picture—those considerations didn't immediately come to mind. Instead, I found myself fixated on the leg she'd hugged to her chest, wondering why I'd never realized calves could be so alluring. The concept seemed bizarre. I mean, I'd done that entire *Gillette* razor commercial and certainly never found any of my fellow actors' legs sexy. I tried to picture Carter's calves. They were hairy. That was as far as that thought process got me.

She caught me staring, and I reddened again, this time without any witty comeback to save my bacon.

"So what do you do?" I rushed through the inquiry, trying to turn the attention anywhere other than my ridiculous gawking.

Her lips never lost their lingering smile. "Me?" She shrugged. "I swim a little. Bike a lot. Run more than I want to."

*So she was a triathlete.* It made sense, then, her insane physique. I lived in Hollywood—every person I knew had a personal trainer, a strength coach, a yoga instructor and nutrition specialist. But this woman's fitness was on a whole different level. It also explained the funky tan lines from her wetsuit and goggles.

"So not an MMA fighter, then?" I gestured at her eye.

"Nah. That's for the weak. Why limit yourself to getting knocked around in a ring when you can get mowed over while you cycle?"

My face must have fallen, because she rolled her eyes and waved a flippant hand through the air, disregarding my immediate contrition.

"Bad jest." Unfolding herself from the chair, she picked up her unsipped beer, but never raised it to her lips. "Do me a favor and forget the other night. An accident's an accident. That's why I rang you. I didn't want you hanging onto it. Honest."

I was a little taken aback by her sudden sincerity, all sense of her underlying teasing absent. It made me feel even worse about the angry scarlet abrasions etched across her skin. But for the sake of the light-ness of the evening, I tried to turn the tone in a different direction.

"Well—it looks like somebody one-upped me, anyway." I forced what almost passed as a laugh, motioning toward her shiner.

"Yeah, well, a heel to the face will get you every time." Her smile returned. "Still out-swam her by a few hundred meters."

"Is that what your boyfriend does, too?" I don't know why I felt the need to bring him up. He was the last thing I wanted to talk about.

Her smile vanished, replaced by a look of total confusion.

"My boyfriend?" She set her beer down. "Wha—oh." Her laugh, low, easy, perfectly complementary to her laid-back persona, sang across the lanai. "You mean Kyle?" She squinted, the fine lines of a life lived in the sun creasing the corners of her eyes. "Tell me," she held my gaze in something that felt like a challenge, "do I really look like the kind of girl that would be interested in a plonker like Kyle?"

"I…" My response faltered as I tried to catch her drift, and when I did, I spiraled into the abyss of complete idiocy. How oblivious could I really be? I mean, I lived less than two miles from West Hollywood, which was practically the gay capital of the world, and I'd grown up a stone's throw from San Francisco. But the thought just hadn't occurred to me.

"Oh," was the exceptionally insightful response I managed, before stumbling further into the hole I'd dug. "I'm sorry, I didn't realize—I mean, you didn't—"

"Strike you as gay?" The archness of her smile grew more prom-inent as she stared at me across the table.

I tried to look anywhere other than her inquisitive green eyes and finally settled with staring at her forearms, where a series of minimal-ist tattoos were scattered along the lean contour of her muscles.

I suppose I should have read the writing on the wall, but the one thing living in Hollywood had taught me was not to make assumptions. In my defense, half the dolled-up glamour girls I knew were gayer than Elton John's fanny pack. So despite her short crop of wild blonde hair and the striking angles of her androgynous features, I hadn't taken it as a sign one way or another.

At my non-reply, she continued. "Does that bother you?"

I practically choked on my spit in my rush to assure her it didn't. "No." I had to clear my throat. "Of course not."

"Good." And with that, she brushed the subject aside, and the conversation turned with the arrival of our dinner.

We talked for two more hours. Long after the sun had set and left the bay enveloped in a shimmering wash of shadows. I think we would have chatted all night if the cheerful Hawaiian hadn't threatened to charge Dillon rent if we stayed any longer. I learned her mother was English, her father was Welsh, and she had one sister. She'd been born in Wales and currently lived in London. But beyond the mention she hadn't turned on a TV or seen a movie in the last ten years—something that took the sting out of her lack of interest in my credits—I wasn't sure I could actually narrow down on any single subject we'd exhausted. I simply knew, on the drive home, that I couldn't remember the last time I'd laughed as much or enjoyed someone's company so effortlessly. She was the most original person I'd ever met, unapologetically certain of herself, but without the distasteful addendum of undue arrogance. Genuine. Witty. Amusingly competitive.

When we pulled into the resort's parking lot, I found myself disappointed at the closure of the evening. *Shake hands, call it a day, and go our way.* That's what she'd said on the phone. But for whatever reason, the thought left me with a ridiculous sense of melancholy. What had I expected to come at the conclusion of our meeting? That we'd exchange numbers, become Facebook friends, maybe she'd shoot me a text one day to say she'd finally seen one of my movies?

I stood on the loose gravel driveway and caught the Jeep keys she tossed over the hood.

Maybe I could ask her if she was on Instagram? Tell her I wanted to follow her career. That wouldn't be too creepy, right?

"Thanks for inviting me," I said, trying to find some of her same nonchalance as she strolled around the car, "I had a really great time."

"Makoa's cooking didn't kill you and you survived my first attempt at driving on the wrong side of the road," she winked to show she was teasing. "I'd call that a win."

The automatic headlights clicked off, sending a scattering of geckos into darkness.

I decided asking her about Instagram would be pointless. There was no way someone who hadn't turned on the TV in over a decade had anything to do with social media.

"If there's anything I can do for you—to make up for the other night —please just let me know. Your flight change fees, an admission of guilt to your sponsors so they know you're not at fault for your bike, anything at all—"

She put me out of my misery.

"There is, actually." She tilted her head with that cocksure confidence, pausing just long enough to weight the words with a slow smile. "Have dinner with me again. Tomorrow night."

# Scene 4

"You smell like someone pissed on a cinnamon stick."

Dillon toweled off as Kyle dropped his bag on the sand, reeking of Fireball whisky. He was forty minutes late for their recovery swim. By the look of his bloodshot eyes, he'd either made good on his quest to find someone to shag—or hadn't. It was difficult to tell.

"Shut your gob." Kyle tugged his swim cap in place, spraying on sunscreen. "Are you really leaving already?"

Dillon deliberately slowed the packing of her gear, not wanting him to realize she was in a hurry.

But she *was* in a hurry. She still had to stretch. Shower. Change. It was getting late, and she was supposed to meet Kameryn in little more than an hour.

Kyle just didn't need to know that. She knew the hell he'd raise if he ever found out about the night before—that she'd taken his mocking advice to heart and invited 'that girl' to dinner.

Not that it mattered. It was none of his business. He wasn't her keeper. She didn't need his permission. It wasn't like he could razz her for being on the rebound. She and Kelsey had been over a long time ago. If she wanted to pursue someone else, she didn't need Kyle's blessing. She just didn't want to hear him moan on about it.

Besides—it wasn't like that. It wasn't even a date. It was possible Kameryn wouldn't even show up. She knew she probably shouldn't get her hopes up.

But, if she was honest, it was too late for that. Her hopes had been up since they'd waved a casual goodnight in the resort parking lot. Before that, really. Maybe it started with the way Kameryn blushed when she caught her staring at her calf. Or the winsome way she laughed, growing flustered so easily. Or perhaps it had begun when she proved to take the mick as much as she'd been willing to give it. Or was it simply when Dillon discovered that there was so much more to her, hidden beneath her Hollywood beauty?

Whatever it was, Dillon liked her. She wanted to see her again. And without rhyme or reason, she hoped the feeling might be mutual.

She picked up her bag, starting off across the sand. "You were late," she said over her shoulder. "You'll have to finish without me."

"Hey, that's my line!" Kyle shot back, and then she heard his goggles snap into place, followed by the familiar sound of him splashing through the water.


Any concerns she had that Kameryn wouldn't show up turned out to be futile. Dillon arrived at the fountain—their agreed meeting spot—fifteen minutes early, only to find Kameryn already waiting.

She had her back to her, plucking the leaves off a Pohole fern, tossing the discarded petals to the stone walkway.

*Trainers*, Dillon noted, glancing at her feet. She'd dressed down—jeans and a t-shirt, a change from the sundress and sandals she'd worn the previous evening. It was perfect for what Dillon had planned.

Pushing on late afternoon—they'd agreed to an early dinner—the sun was still high, promising at least another couple hours of daylight.

"Do you like birds?"

Startled, Kameryn dropped the fern to the ground, spinning to face her.

"Hey!" She seemed uptight, full of nervous energy. "You came."

"Are you surprised?" Dillon cocked her head. "Trust me, if I ever say I'm going to be somewhere—I'm there."

Without waiting for a response, she set off down the two lane road, Kameryn falling into step beside her. She had a destination in mind, away from the overpopulated tourist attractions. A place where they could watch what the sky was promising to turn into an epic sunset.

"So, back to the birds," she resumed, as they passed through Hāna Beach Park. "Fan or no fan?"

"It depends." The rubber soles of Kameryn's shoes squeaked along the damp tarmac. "Is that what you had in mind for dinner?"

Dillon laughed. "The sanctuary might frown on it."

She was glad to see Kam smile, some of her previous tension dissipating. "Then are we talking Hitchcock or *Rio*?"

"I can't say I've seen the latter," Dillon admitted, skipping the turn-off to the beach and cutting through a cluster of rainbow eucalyptus trees, "but I can assure you it's not the former." She stopped at a trail head winding up the base of Ka'uiki Pu'u, the hill towering over the southeast side of Hana. "Up for a short hike?"

"I don't know," Kameryn ducked beneath a low lying branch, taking the lead. "Do you think you can keep up with me?"

Trailing half a dozen paces behind, Dillon glanced up in just enough time to see Kameryn catch the gnarled root of a lantana shrub, and face plant into a sourbush. She stifled a laugh, uncertain how the girl from Hollywood would respond.

They'd been struggling up the single track path for twenty minutes. The hike to Ka'uiki Head was short—she'd given no misrepresentation there—but the reason it wasn't found on any tourist pamphlets was because it was arduously steep, the majority of the climb covered in a low-hanging jungle understory.

Dillon's concerns were abated, however, as Kameryn hopped up, laughing as she wiped her muddy palms across her jeans.

"You know," she said, plucking a sourbush blossom from her hair, "it should be a crime for a flower to look so pretty and smell like turpentine."

The greater crime, Dillon considered, was that in less than thirty-six hours, Kam would be back in Los Angeles. But she kept the thought to herself.

"Mind your step," she warned instead, turning to offer her hand as they descended a particularly slippery section of trailhead, but before the last word was out of her mouth, she'd lost her footing, sliding on her arse through the slick red clay.

Behind her, the sound of Kameryn's laughter raised a bright crimson honeycreeper from the dense shrubbery.

"Fair to assume there's no dress code for dinner?" Kameryn hooked her elbow, undeterred by the mess of sticky soil, and tugged her upright. Whatever had remained of her previous edginess had vanished, lost along the challenge of the climb, seeping away like the sludge of silt glissading down the hillside.

Dillon couldn't help but take a second glance at her smile. She loved the way she took it all in stride. The way she could stand there, covered in mud, without a care in the world.

Kelsey would have hated this. For her, an impromptu hike up a muddy trail would have fallen just below the Ninth Circle of Dante's Inferno. It had always mystified Dillon that a woman who earned her living as a professional footballer—required to make spur-of-the-moment decisions, accept hard knocks, and spend her life covered in splattered mud and grass stains—could remain so rigid and particular off the pitch.

She shoved the thoughts of Kelsey aside. She knew she shouldn't be comparing her to this girl, anyhow.

Stopping to catch their breath, Dillon leaned against the winding trunk of a hala and pointed down over the peninsula.

"There," she said, indicating the massive mound of lava rock detached from the hill of Ka'uiki. "Pu'Uku Islet Bird Sanctuary." Hundreds of wedge-tailed shearwaters and white-tailed tropicbirds were weaving and diving between the crashing waves, preparing to burrow in for the evening. It wasn't much to look at—the islet itself was little more than a hunk of solidified volcanic matter—but the saffron glow of the setting sun cast a metallic sheen atop the silvery wings of the seabirds, their glittering backs reflecting the light where the clouds had turned the sky into something ethereal.

Dropping onto the lava rock, Dillon dangled her legs over the ledge, joined a second later by Kameryn. A light drizzle had begun to fall, stirring a breeze up from the ocean. They sat in silence, allowing the rainfall to wash the clay from their skin and clothing.

"How'd you find this place?" Kam asked after a few minutes, staring over the blanket of cobalt water. The rain had darkened her long brown hair, turning it almost black, a dramatic contrast to the medley of color all around them.

"I was told by one of the locals no one could swim out to this part of the island. That the Hawaiian god who created this hill made the current too strong." She tossed a porous stone into the breaking waves a hundred feet below. "So I accepted the challenge."

Kameryn half laughed, shifting her gaze to catch Dillon's eye, before looking back at the horizon. "Of course you defied the gods. It must be nice to have that kind of confidence."

"Trust me, I didn't always."

Her thoughts drifted to long mornings in Hamburg, Henrik forcing her to swim through tides she was certain would drown her.

*Again, Schätzchen. Swim it again.*

She shook the memory from her mind. It killed her that he still lived rent free inside her head, even after all these years.

To hell with him.

In a fluid swing, she gained her feet and looked down at Kameryn. She wasn't about to let her past ruin what had turned out to be the perfect afternoon.

"Sometimes you just have to be willing to close your eyes and dive head first into the unknown—see where the current takes you." She held out her hand, wavering on an arch smile. "What do you say, Kam-Kameryn?"

To her surprise, Kam remained unflustered by her boldness, offering instead a coquettish tilt of her head. She leaned back to look up at her. "Are we still talking about swimming?"

Outplayed at her own game, an uncommon flush crept up Dillon's neck as Kameryn took her hand.

Yeah, she was way past trying not to get her hopes up.

# Scene 5

I should have been anxious to fly home. In the section of my brain labeled *sensible*, I knew my focus should have been on nothing more than the bright lights of Tinseltown. I mean, four days earlier I'd landed the most coveted role in the film industry. I'd beat out thousands—*tens* of thousands—of twenty-something hopefuls. I'd spent more than half a year jumping through hoops for the studio, knowing it was likely all for nothing. Only, it hadn't been for nothing. My career was about to sky rocket into a dimension I found incomprehensible.

I shouldn't have had to keep reminding myself.

I should have been refreshing my emails every three minutes to see if Aaron sent anything new, or scrolling obsessively through the best scoop-worthy sites, searching for casting rumors. In sticking with time-honored tradition, I should have been riding a rollercoaster of erratic emotions—levitating through an endless cycle of boosting myself up, certain I would rise to the challenge, and then drowning in a wave of panic: What if I wasn't up to the task? What if I wasn't talented enough? Charismatic enough? What if my chemistry was off with my co-stars? Who *were* my co-stars? What if the production was a flop? And then resurfacing to remind myself I'd won the job off talent and merit alone. *They* wanted *me*. Because I was perfect for the role. I was going to ace it. But what if…?

And so on and so forth, until I drove myself insane.

To be fair, each time it did cross my mind, my stomach made a queasy somersault with the realization it was not a dream. This was actually happening.

But honestly, those moments were fleeting.

The truth was, the only thing really on my mind, was Dillon. This girl I hardly knew. Who I would probably never see again.

Trekking back from Ka'uiki Head, all I could think about was how many times our hands brushed as we descended the slippery terrain. I found myself caught up in trying to decide the color of her hair—was it flaxen or ash—did she highlight it, or had the platinum streaks come natural by way of the sun? I wondered if it bugged her the way the rain had caused her bangs to hang in her eyes. I searched for ways to make her laugh, feeling as if I'd won the lottery with every success. And too many times—as I struggled to keep up with her energetic stride—I caught myself wondering what exactly the tattoo was on her shoulder, teasing a preview beneath the material of her tank top.

But more than anything, I wondered what the hell it was I thought I was doing?

I wasn't a lesbian. I mean, at twenty-three years old, wouldn't I have known that by now? Or at least had a sneaking suspicion? Half a dozen boyfriends later, my obsession with Harry Styles, and, of course, there was always Carter—On-Again-Off-Again-Carter, as Dani had coined him.

I would have known.

Right?

Yet here I was, punch drunk, schoolgirl stupid, worrying she might be able to feel the pounding pulse in my wrist each time she offered me her hand to step over a cluster of roots or down a slick boulder.

And I didn't know what to do about it.

I didn't even know if she was into me. I felt like one of those plastic idiots from the Valley who assumed every gay girl within their proximity had a crush on them. It was possible Dillon was just flirtatious by nature.

But even keeping that knowledge close at hand, it certainly didn't cease my own captivation. More than once, I knew she'd caught my sidelong glances, and each time she did, I could feel the color rise to my cheeks—thank you, overactive autonomic nervous system—but it didn't stop me from stealing another look. Her chapped lips, the wryness of her smile, the unusual color behind her intelligent green eyes—viridian in the sunlight, the irises tinged with blue, but jade in shadow, completely evergreen. I was taken by the ambiguity of her beauty—her high cheekbones and strong jaw, made only more attractive by the fluidity of her movement, the athletic command she held over her body.

But there was more to it than me simply finding her physically appealing. It was the way she made me feel, the way her unpretentious disposition put me at ease. She pulled me out of the Hollywood edginess which had grown over me like a defensive, rampant weed.

For the first time in what felt like forever, when her eyes caught mine, I felt like she was really seeing *me*. Not whoever La La Land was designing me to be. Not even whoever *I* wanted me to be. Just me.

It was revitalizing.

Whatever game we were playing at, I liked it. Even if it was nothing. Even if, in little more than a day, I'd be home in Los Angeles and the name Dillon Sinclair would become a distant memory. For now, she was all that was on my mind.

The nightlife in Hana on a Monday evening was about what you'd expect of a sleepy island town. By the time we'd slipped and laughed and stumbled our way back to the main road, it had grown dark and the few local restaurants had closed.

I considered suggesting the resort steakhouse. The food was decent and the bartender made a mean mai tai—according to Dani—but we were drenched, covered head-to-toe in red mud, and I didn't want to risk going to shower and having Dillon decide to call it a night.

Instead, walking along the beachfront, we found a food truck that still had a light shining behind the pull-down door.

Dillon tapped on the shuttered back window while I waited on the curb. I listened to the rolling inflections of her charming accent, followed by a man's laughter. Ten minutes later, we were sitting cross-legged on top of a picnic table in Hana Bay Beach Park, eating Pineapple Kalua pork out of a takeout container.

"I googled you last night," I said out of the blue, and immediately wanted to stick my wooden chopstick through my eye. What the hell possessed me to admit that? "I mean, not like—I'm not a weirdo, I promise. I just—" *Jesus, Kam.* Get a grip. "I just didn't know much about triathlons, so..."

"Still double checking I don't make enough money to call a solicitor, huh?" The full Hunter's moon revealed her smile—which meant it also betrayed how embarrassed I'd become. Even though I knew she was teasing, I didn't want her to think I'd been snooping. Which, obviously, I had.

"I hardly needed Wikipedia to tell me you could afford that," I scoffed, trying to save myself, "the way you splurged on dinner tonight told me everything I needed to know." I stabbed a pineapple from the shared plastic container, attempting to play it cool. "What I didn't know, however, was that I was dining with sports royalty."

"Ha," the single syllable was self-deprecating, the wave of her hand brushing me off. "Triathletes are the black sheep of the sports world. Jacks of all trades, masters of none. Swimmers hate us, cyclists laugh at us, and runners just ignore us. Ask a dozen random people what a triathlon is and only one is bound to properly guess the answer. And even then, they've only heard about *Ironman*."

She was selling herself short. A quick Google search brought up a wealth of information on Dillon Sinclair.

Twenty-eight years old—a short-course competitor—which meant she swam 1.5k, biked 40k, and ran 10k.

It exhausted me just thinking about it.

She turned pro at seventeen, competed in her first Olympics in London at nineteen—setting a record as the youngest triathlete to represent Great Britain—and placed just off the podium. Four years later, she won bronze in Rio, and last year, brought home a silver from the Melbourne Olympic Games. Every article I'd scanned hailed her as one of the most decorated athletes in the history of the sport. It was clear she was an icon in her industry.

*Do you know who the fuck she is* made a little more sense now.

"You know," I shrugged, hoping for casual, "modesty doesn't really suit you."

I didn't even bother lying to myself that it was her career I'd been interested in. My intrigue had been focused on the "personal" tab of Wikipedia. Or more precisely, one specific topic.

She'd been linked to dating an English soccer player—Kelsey Evans.

Soccer was a sport with which I was well-versed. Having played through high school, I was an avid fan and loved to follow the success of our Women's National Team. I wasn't familiar with many of the players in Europe, but remembered Evans as a starter for England. A tall, blonde, gorgeous midfielder who'd been a key player for the Lionesses' silver medal finish in Melbourne, it was putting it mildly to say she was something of a big name.

According to Wikipedia, along with a cursory search of fan mentions, Dillon and Kelsey had called it quits two years ago in the middle of the last World Cup. The timing of the breakup had been heavily criticized by the English football fans, who'd been stunned by the couple's unexpected split after three years together—but I hadn't allowed myself to sneak down that rabbit hole. It felt too invasive.

Instead, I'd browsed through Kelsey Evans' Instagram, where she'd amassed a few million followers, and taken note via her TikTok cult that she was now dating a USWNT legend, Abby Sawyer.

But on Dillon, there was nothing. Since her breakup with Evans, her online presence had entirely disappeared. There were no dish-all podcasts. No social media accounts. No juicy mentions of her personal life or who she was now seeing. The only thing a search generated outside her relationship with Kelsey was related to triathlon.

"Alright, enough about me. What about you, Kam-Kameryn? Are you going to tell me about your life in Hollywood?"

We'd finished eating, and without a mundane task to keep me busy, I'd found myself growing restless. Unaware I'd even done it, I looked down to see I'd folded the paper takeout bag into a tiny crooked triangle.

The night before, I'd spent the whole evening hoping she'd ask me about my work—but now that she had, I was right back to square one —having no clue what to actually say.

"It's, um—I don't know, not as glamorous as one might expect." I considered what lay ahead: The long hours on set. The sleepless nights. The stress. The hurry up and wait. The public scrutiny. The extreme highs. The inevitable lows. And those were just the things I knew to worry about. I wasn't so naive to be unaware I hadn't even scratched the surface of the Pandora's box I was about to open.

My last film had been shot in the sweltering basement of a rundown apartment building in the middle of summer. I'd spent three weeks on the project and earned just enough to cover two months rent. The producer had been a nightmare. The director high on oxy. I'd walked in to find my other three cast members having a threesome on the mildewed couch featured in the majority of our scenes.

Yeah, glamorous wasn't the word for it.

If she asked me the same question this time next year, I might have a different opinion.

However, if I wanted to look on the bright side, there was at least one thing of which I was certain: Dillon hadn't seen any of my crappy movies. And I felt pretty confident, unlike me, she was no internet stalker. I doubted my name would pop up in her search history. She knew nothing about me, and the anonymity was refreshing.

"Half the time I think I should have stuck with my original plan and majored in Marine Biology." I didn't volunteer the petty reason I'd stubbornly slogged through five lackluster years in Hollywood was primarily due to being unwilling to concede to my parents'—my *mom's*, more specifically—belief that my life would have been more fulfilling outside of the entertainment industry. Code for: *you should have gotten a degree.*

"Even though studying the mating rituals of killer whales sounds interesting, I have to say, I can't see it having panned out in your favor."

I feigned offense. "Why? I may have made an excellent cetacean sex expert!"

She laughed. "Perhaps. But it would never have worked out for you."

"How so?"

She lifted one dark blonde eyebrow, as if it should have been obvious. "You're made for movies."

"You haven't even seen my work." It came out defensive and I regretted it. She'd been trying to compliment me. But I had grown jaded to the subject. I was so tired of being told by men three times my age "you're perfect for the screen." And then being forced to smile and nod as they discussed my 'look,' my body, the symmetry of my face, the unfortunate unchangeable reality that my eyes were brown, and then the inevitable circle back to the most important aspect: I was pretty enough, *hot* enough—God, how I hated that word—to overlook the minor things. Heels could make me taller. Makeup sexier. Scriptwriting funnier. *Don't worry, they would handle the rest.*

If Dillon was thrown by my affront, she gave no sign. "I don't need to. Anyone could see why you'd succeed." She drew her legs up, sitting crosslegged, and propped her elbows on her knees. "I have no doubt you captivate an audience."

And here it was.

"And why's that?" I waited for the disappointing cliché. Instead, she surprised me.

"Because you're unique. Because there's so much more to you than meets the eye. You're magnetic. Smart. Funny. Clever. Shall I go on?"

The answer was so genuine, I didn't know what to say. I wanted to find a glib response to offset how touched I was by the compliment, but I came up with nothing.

And then panic struck. She hadn't mentioned I was pretty. Did that mean she didn't find me attractive?

Once again, as if reading my mind, she cut me off from my ridiculous carousel of conflicting emotions.

"You're the complete package, Kam-Kameryn. Far more than just a pretty face. And while I realize I'm no expert in filmmaking, I imagine all that counts for something."

*Oh.*

I found I had to swallow, and became suddenly fascinated with my fingers that had turned from folding to shredding.

"Is that what you tell all the girls you invite to dinner?"

"Only the ones so desperate to get my attention they hit me with their car."

I couldn't help but laugh, and when I looked up she reached to set her hand on mine, stilling the nervous busy work of my fingers. It was impossible for her to have not felt the aerobics of my cardiac endeavors. My pulse felt like it was going to jump out of my skin—go on a walk of its own.

"Relax, Kam."

I closed my eyes. I loved the way my name sounded in the lilt of her voice. I tried to exhale.

*Relax.*

I hardly knew the meaning of the word.

When I opened my eyes, she was looking at me again in that way she had of making me feel like she was really seeing *me*.

I would have glanced away, jumped up, suggested a walk to stretch our legs, but she didn't give me the opportunity. She, too, could see, perhaps, that my nerves were about to get the better of me.

"May I kiss you?"

For the second time in a matter of minutes, I was speechless. I'd never been asked for a kiss before.

I'd kissed plenty of guys. I'd kissed Dani, even, in a drunken game of truth or dare. That had been unexciting, except, maybe, for our high school boyfriends.

I'd been instructed on *how* to kiss: from directors, screen partners, scriptwriters who'd written detailed notes on how they wanted the scene played.

But I'd never been *asked* before.

I must have managed a nod. I know I never found my voice. But I knew I wanted her to kiss me—I'd been thinking about it all evening. Thinking about it, but never expecting it to happen. I thought the chances of that were about as slim as getting the call from Aaron. But somehow, over the last ninety-six hours, I was batting two for two. Unusual for my odds.

Her lips were softer than I imagined they'd be, the smell of her skin intoxicating.

I remembered to close my eyes—thank God for small favors. I didn't need to be that freak sitting there with my eyes wide open, unblinking like a fish out of water.

Though in the end, I doubted I was much different than kissing a fish, really. I couldn't breathe. I couldn't move. I just sat there, frozen, a myriad of broken thoughts swirling through my head:

I was kissing a stranger.

Her mouth tasted like pineapple.

A girl.

Aaron wouldn't like this.

Fuck Aaron.

Her skin had the faint aroma of sunscreen and chlorine.

*A girl!*

Dani wouldn't like it either.

Fuck Dani. And Darlene. *Especially* Darlene.

Had the wind gotten stronger, or was it the blood rushing to my head?

I was kissing Kelsey Evan's ex-girlfriend.

Ex-*girlfriend*!

Well then, fuck Kelsey Evans, too.

Somewhere, the sharp chime of a bell rang—was it the church from across the street?

*Mighty fine timing you have, Jesus.*

Well, fu—okay, that was taking it too far.

It startled us both, and I bumped my chin against her lips as I lurched away. "Shit, I'm sorry," I apologized, even while darting a glance around, furtive, feeling like I'd been caught at something I shouldn't have been doing.

I realized the sound had come from my phone. It was my ringtone. I rifled it out of my pocket to shut it up. I thought it might be Aaron. Or even Dani, to tell me what mind-blowing island excursion they had gone on today. It was neither. In the irony of what was becoming my bizarre universe, it was Carter.

I sent it to voicemail. I hadn't talked to him in a couple of months. Of course, he would call right now. He always had impeccable timing. That's why he was On-Again-Off-Again-Carter.

Dillon smiled, amused at my sheepishness.

"Need to take that?"

"No." I answered too quickly. "I—he's just—no."

She stretched and rolled her shoulders as I shoved the phone back in my pocket, and then with the agility of a cat, she jumped off the table.

"Come on." She offered me her hand, and this time when I took it, she didn't let go. "I'll walk you to your door."

We strolled to the resort. It was the shortest and longest half-mile of my life. The streets were empty, the town quiet, but I couldn't help but wonder if anyone saw us—two girls—hand-in-hand—wandering back from the beach. I didn't know if the thought scared me, or thrilled me.

"What time on Wednesday do you fly home?" she asked. We were standing in front of my door. I wanted to invite her in. A drink. Coffee. Whatever. But it was that *whatever* that paused me. I didn't have the guts. I got the feeling she might decline, even if I had.

"Early morning." My heart sank, realizing how quickly that was approaching. I should have scheduled the late-night flight. Or better yet, changed it to Thursday. I didn't *have* to be home until Friday.

If she was going to be here…

"You?"

"Not until Thursday."

Between her black eye and close-lipped smile and the damp curtain of her hair hanging across her face, she was seriously attractive.

I leaned back against my door. "I'll see you tomorrow, then?"

Her smile grew broader. "I'll have to check my schedule."

By the Gods of Decency, I managed a nonchalant shrug. "Well, maybe you can pencil me in."

"Same time, same place?"

I nodded.

This time when she kissed me I didn't think of anything else. Well, except changing my flight from Wednesday to Thursday.

"Goodnight, Kam-Kameryn."

# Scene 6

Economy was the only class available when Dillon changed her Maui flight from Key West to London. She hadn't planned on flying home before the race in Florida, but her foul mood had made her long for the comfort of her flat and listening ear of her best friend. It was worth it, even if she would only be home for a week and it added eight thousand miles of travel.

At least she didn't have a bike to worry about, if she decided to seek a silver lining.

But she wasn't really amendable to a silver lining.

As her flight to Heathrow bounced along over the Atlantic Ocean, she folded herself deeper into the middle row seat and tried to tune out the teenagers on either side of her engaging in a ten-hour war, trying to snap each other with hairbands.

Not much longer and she'd be out of the land of luaus and mac salad —misty afternoon hikes and girls who were better actors than they let on.

She stared at the greasy blonde hair of the passenger in front of her. She wanted to sleep, but her thoughts kept returning to Hana.

Kam had canceled on her. Tuesday morning, Dillon returned from her swim to find a message waiting for her at the front desk. It was handwritten, a brief apology that an emergency had come up and she had to fly home, but thanked her for a wonderful time, and left her with a mobile number at the bottom of the note. *If you're ever in LA* was jotted in the margin.

And just like that, she was gone.

Dillon didn't know if the emergency had been real or if Kameryn had developed cold feet and decided to run home, but it didn't really matter. She wasn't upset with Kam—she was annoyed with herself for having taken it so hard. What had she expected to happen in the last twenty-four hours they were sharing the same sedate island—both of them thousands of miles from either of their lives? It wasn't as if they'd see each other again. It had been a fun couple of nights, and the actress had simply flown home a day earlier than planned. That was that. It was sheer irrationality to find herself so disappointed.

A sentiment underscored by her best friend, Sam—more affectionately known as Hunt—in their favorite Wapping pub Friday night in London.

"I think I need another pint to get this straight," said the Tyneside native, disappearing to the bar, and returning with a Newcastle Brown and club soda with lime. Settling into her seat, she shoved the seltzer toward Dillon.

"Alright." Her umber eyes narrowed, her upper lip glistening with foam from a long draught of her ale. "Let me see if I have this sorted —two nights before your race, a tourist ran you over on your bike—"

"She clipped my tire—"

"You hit her *hood*—"

"I scraped my arm—"

"You left half your hide in Hana—"

"It's inconsequential—"

"*And*," Sam continued, her Geordie accent thickening with the second round, "in response to her trying to turn you into a pavement pizza—"

"it was an *accident*—"

"—you rang her up and invited her to dinner?"

"Like I already told you, Kyle was being a tosser. I called her to apologize, and offered to buy her a pint."

"After she ran you over?"

"*After* Kyle was an arsehole. Jesus—"

Sam snapped up a fast finger, her dark eyes shining and energy wound nearly as tight as the coils of her short black hair. "Now let's fast forward. You take this girl to dinner—you catch a crush on her— and you ask her out again. This straight, young, wannabe-movie star —"

"I didn't say she was straight."

"You said she was surprised *you* were gay! Haddaway, man! Any queer girl on the planet could look at you and know you were into kissing fish half a mile away. Unless this one's plain micey, she's straight. Straight or stupid."

Dillon busied herself digging the lime out of her seltzer, wondering why she'd ever brought the subject up in the first place. Or flown to London at all. She could be sitting on a beach in Key West right now, swimming in the balmy Florida shoreline. Anything other than trudging through the rain of an English October, listening to Sam's voice of reason remind her of why she was such a plank.

"So," Sam resumed after draining her beer, "you go out the next night and drag her along on some romantic hike—"

"There was nothing romantic about it—"

"I know you better than that—now zip it, and let me finish my assessment; you see her making moon eyes at you, you bide your time, pour on your charm, and kiss her." She paused for nothing more than dramatic effect. "This straight girl. Who ran you over. From Hollywood. And you're surprised she buggered out the next morning?"

When it was put like that…

But no matter how right Sam might be, it would be a cat in hell's chance before she admitted it.

"You weren't there, mate. It wasn't as simple as that."

"No, of course it wasn't. You're bloody Dillon Sinclair. Nothing's ever simple."

Dillon downed her drink, fished a tenner from her pocket, and dropped it on the table. "Good talk, Hunt."

"Oh, come on, man." Sam caught her arm before she could stand. "I'm taking the piss out of you, is all. It's not like you to get up a height. This lass has really wound you up, eh?"

Between the thirty-six hours of travel, jet lag, and her lack of sleep, Dillon didn't have the energy to deny it.

"I don't know—she was different. I just…" she shrugged. "I really liked her, I guess."

Sam sprawled back in her high top stool, a trenchant smirk working its way to her lips. "I cannot lie. I love seeing you flustered. It happens so seldom—"

"Right—I'm done. I'll ring you when I'm back from Florida—"

"Oh, belt up and sit down, Sinc. You aren't so delicate as all that. You came barking up the wrong tree if it was sympathy you wanted. But you already knew that."

She did know that.

Sam Huntley had once been one of the greatest footballers to ever play the sport. A world-class striker, one of the most prolific goal scorers of the century. She'd been at the top of her game—in the prime of her career—when a lorry slammed into her on her motorbike at a traffic light. She'd broken nineteen bones, collapsed both lungs, been on life support for three weeks, and by the time it was all over had lost her right leg above the knee. The accident had robbed her of everything she'd ever known, including a tragic end to her career.

She was not the mate you came to for sympathy over trivial matters.

Like a girl who'd stood you up on a non-date in Hawaii.

Dillon begrudgingly kept her seat.

"Good." Sam steepled her fingers. "Now that we have that settled, what's her name?"

"You know damned well I'll never tell you. Besides," Dillon picked at a lime seed that had dried on the table, "I don't even know her last name."

"But she left you her mobile number, yeah?"

She had. A detail she now regretted telling Sam.

"Let's give her a bell—"

"No!"

"C'mon, marra—a text at the very least. Or, even better! Let me send her a selfie. Let's face it, you just may not have been her cup of tea—perhaps she'd prefer someone with a little more flavor than your white, skinny arse." She made a grab for Dillon's phone, but Dillon was faster.

"You've lost your edge, Hunt. Too slow." She slipped her phone in her back pocket.

"We'll see about that. Kyle knows her name, yeah? How long do you really think it will take me to track her down—tell her how deep under your skin you let her?"

Dillon looked up too quickly. "Not a word to Kyle. I'm serious."

Sam's wicked grin only grew. "He doesn't know anything about this?" She drilled her fingers against the peeling laminate of the table. "Oh, this gets richer and richer."

"I mean it, Sam."

"I can see that. You don't want him thinking you're as daft as I do?" Her eyes were glowing with her impending victory. They both knew she'd found her edge—and won. And as much as Dillon loved her longtime friend, she really wanted to get up and throttle her.

"Here's how this is going to go," Sam crossed her brawny arms. "You take out your mobile. You punch in her number. You shoot her a text. Doesn't matter what you say—it was nice to meet her, you made it back to London, you had a bloody grand time snogging and wish you'd taken it further—whatever you want. End of story. I leave you alone about the whole situation."

"And if I don't?"

"Oh, you know the deal. I tell Kyle. The two of us hound you relentlessly. We track down Mystery Reckless Motorist and broadcast your pining obsession. The whole shebang."

"Sometimes I hate you, Hunt."

Sam smiled, but this time the loftiness was gone. "No, you don't. You flew eight thousand miles just for this. To sit here and have me tell you exactly what you knew I was already going to tell you to do. Now quit being a proper doylem and text the girl."

# Scene 7

"It was good of you to stop in, Miss Kingsbury. We look forward to working with you next month."

The door clicked resolutely shut behind me.

It was a twenty-minute walk back to where I'd parked my car on Cahuenga. Which was nothing, compared to the eleven hours of flights, five hours of off-the-beaten path layovers, and two hours I'd spent in rush hour traffic to get from LAX to the studio. Never mind the forty-five minutes I'd sat in the waiting room before being summoned to the corner office.

All for a three-minute meeting.

*Less* than three minutes.

I'd walked in to find the director, L.R. Sims, perched on the mahogany arm of a plush leather chair. Across from him, sprawled at a u-shaped desk scattered with papers, sat a sparse-haired, boulder of a man, toying with the label on an unlit cigar. I'd never seen him in person, but I recognized him immediately, his face just as ruddy as it had been during his acceptance speech three years earlier when he'd taken home the Academy Award for Best Picture. He was *Sand Seekers* executive producer, Waylon MacArthur.

The watery blue eyes beneath his creased brow turned in my direction. He offered no greeting, instead analyzing me as I crossed the floor, and then turned to give L.R. a nod of approval.

"Very good." The assessment came out in a voice half-an-octave higher than anticipated from a man of his stature. "She'll be easy to sell."

I stood in the middle of the room as he took another head-to-toe sweep of my body, then fished out a matchbook from inside his snug blazer, returning his attention to lighting his cigar.

"As we've discussed, Miss Kingsbury offers a malleable canvas," L.R. filled the silence, shooting me an acknowledging chuck of his square chin, before sliding to his feet to pace the room.

I'd met the animated director on several occasions during my quest for the role. He'd been friendly. Personable. It had been easy to see why he was one of the most highly regarded directors in the industry. Lauded as a visionary, praised for his decisive nature and open-minded innovation, having the opportunity to work under his direction was one of the most exciting aspects of winning the part.

But today he was a different person. His entire focus had orbited MacArthur as they picked up in the middle of a conversation carried over from prior to my arrival.

*Yes, the right decision had been made to cast me in lieu of Pugh.*

Florence, I'd assumed.

*No, it was good I wasn't too tall—I wouldn't look imposing beside my co-stars.*

Whoever they were remained a mystery to me.

*Yes, I was pretty, but not* too *pretty to be off-putting to the female audience.*

What?

*No, my previous work was entirely unremarkable, which gave the audience an opportunity to build a relationship with a character instead of a name.* Um, great—thanks? I think?

All of this was said in front of me, about me, as if I wasn't even there.

None of it was a new discussion. Most of the talking points had been addressed with me by L.R. and the casting director at one time or another over the course of my numerous auditions. Nor, obviously, was it the first time it had been debated between L.R. and MacArthur, either.

But for some reason, their one-hundred-eighty seconds of chitchat had been so vital, I had to fly home on a red eye flight from Maui, making four ridiculous connections—Honolulu, Seattle, Phoenix, Oakland—to make it to a five PM meeting in Universal City on a Tuesday afternoon.

And that had been it. I was dismissed.

Sitting in bumper-to-bumper traffic on the 101 heading back toward my apartment in Hollywood, I wanted to call Aaron to ask him what the hell just happened. What the fire had been? Was it an experiment to test my commitment? Some kind of point being made that the studio could say *jump* and I'd only ask *how high*?

I imagined that was the core of the exercise. It was such a typical power play. A reminder that this was exactly what I'd signed up for. *Let us point out, little lady, how fortunate you are.* Thousands of other girls had auditioned for this role, and I was the lucky one to answer at their beck and call.

I asked Siri to call Aaron, and then told her to cancel. What was the point? This *was* what I'd signed up for. I didn't need him to tell me that.

Rolling all the windows down in my base model Honda Accord, I smacked a frustrated palm against the steering wheel, unintentionally producing a honk. The guy in a BMW X5 ahead of me responded with a one-finger salute and shout of *fuck off.*

*Welcome home.*

I was pissed at the traffic. Pissed at Aaron. Pissed at the big wigs holding the keys to my career. But more than anything, I was pissed at myself for not having a backbone. Had Chris Hemsworth—Adam Driver—Leonardo DiCaprio—ever made a twenty-hour travel expedition just to stand in the center of a room while two men openly discussed how they were handsome, but not *too* handsome, which was a benefit due to the fact that it wouldn't alienate their viewers? Or had it ever been mentioned how convenient it was their height wouldn't affect the fragile egos of their fellow headliners?

I doubted it.

But then it occurred to me that probably wasn't the case for Meryl. Charlize. Cate. Sandra. I'd no doubt they'd all been through this before. And probably much worse.

That realization sobered me, and as much as it brought with it a new kind of outrage, it also simmered me down. I'd get through this. Just like they had.

I hoped.

Waiting in the gridlock, I glanced at my console. Three texts. All from Dani. Photos I hadn't responded to of her latest activities on her honeymoon. Swimming with sea turtles and dolphins. A helicopter ride over the Moloka'i sea cliffs. A night snorkel with manta rays.

I'd get back to her tomorrow. She didn't even know I was home.

It wasn't her text I was looking for, anyhow.

I turned my eyes back to the road, resisting the urge to scoop up my phone. Even if I was putting along at two miles an hour, the last thing I needed to do was to hit someone.

*Again.*

Which brought my thoughts full circle.

Why hadn't I asked for her number the night before? How could I be sure she'd gotten the message? The night clerk had seemed entirely unimpressed with the urgency of my departure. She'd been on Island Time, annoyed at having to check me out at midnight. For all I knew, my note had ended up in the trash can, along with her copy of *Us Weekly* and stack of empty *Red Bull* cans. In which case, Dillon would think I'd ghosted her.

Or worse—what if she had gotten my message, and thought I was full of shit? I hadn't been able to say why I'd left. It's not like I could tell her I'd landed the role of Addison in the upcoming production of *Sand Seekers*. Not that she'd have found that impressive, but at least she'd probably heard of it. A person would have had to have been living under a rock to have escaped the pop culture phenomenon. It would be like not knowing *Harry Potter*. Even Dillon couldn't be that far removed from modern society.

Regardless, I hadn't been able to explain that I'd received a call from my agent two hours after she'd left me at my door. That he'd insisted I get on a midnight flight to Honolulu, where I'd begun my nightmare trek to Los Angeles in order to spend three minutes having my body analyzed by two of the most important men in Hollywood.

I gave in to my miscreant behavior and snatched up my cell phone. We hadn't rolled more than ten feet in the last fifteen minutes, what was the worst that could happen? It's not like there were any cyclists on the freeway.

Swiping open my iPhone browser, I punched in Dillon's name for probably the dozenth time, hoping some new lead on her contact information would miraculously appear. An email address. A P.O. Box. An agent or manager. Anything that would help me reach her. But there was nothing. No old addresses. No phone numbers. No ancient MySpace account. Just her automatic wiki page, her race results, and a freaky number of Kelsey Evans fans obsessing over their breakup.

Her name pinged on half a dozen websites for upcoming races, and I considered emailing one of the race directors to ask if they could pass along a message. Then I realized how absolutely pathetic that would look. What did I think I was going to say? "Hi! I met a girl in Hawaii and I can't get her off my mind, but I don't have her contact information, so could you please pass this note along?"

Yeah. *Smart, Kam.* I was advancing from *Stalker 101* to *Stalker 102* at an accelerated pace. If Aaron received an email like that about me, he'd probably forward it to the cops.

When I finally got to my apartment, I forced myself to toss my phone on my nightstand, dragged myself into a hot shower, and then collapsed into bed at eight PM. I'd been up for almost forty hours, and despite my brain's desire to continue its fruitless wanderings, my exhaustion won the battle, and I dropped into a deep, pineapple lips-enriched sleep.

On Friday afternoon I drove to Venice to grab sushi with my friend Sophie. She'd been in Bangkok for the past three months, shooting a documentary on The Women's Movement in Thai Political Reform. Despite loathing the thought of driving home through Culver City on a Friday night, I'd missed her, and couldn't wait to hear about the work she'd been doing in Asia.

We'd met during my first—and only—year at UCLA, bonding over our misery of boredom throughout *The Art and Technique of Filmmaking*. Both of us had been new to the city, uncertain in our freshly minted eighteen-year-old independence, and had formed a lasting friendship—one that had remarkably endured, despite me dropping out of school by the time spring had rolled into summer.

Sophie had gone on to graduate summa cum laude—no surprise, given her history as a high school valedictorian—while I'd waded my way through Hollywood, trial-by-fire. Regardless our varying methods of breaking into the industry, neither of us had ever seemed to have a leg-up over the other, and we'd cheerleaded one another through every project—flop or showpiece. Unlike Dani, nothing in my friendship with Sophie ever felt like a competition.

As we worked our way through a second tokkuri of hot sake, I began to feel exceptionally guilty sitting on my silent knowledge of *Sand Seekers*. We'd spent the evening chatting about her time in Thailand. The big-budget human rights documentary was sure to be a tremendous success, and was by far her most notable undertaking. However, as the salmon rolls disappeared and the sake grew colder, true to Sophie's nature, she'd massaged the conversation in my direction, eagerly building me up about a handful of roles she'd come across in the recent publication of *Backstage*. All of which she felt I'd nail if I chose to audition.

"Listen to this one!" Sophie was scrolling through her phone, her sensibly manicured French tips tapping through the casting website. "Lead. Female. Twenty-one to twenty-six. Brunette. Petite build—five-foot-three and under." She glanced up, as if deciding whether my extra inch would exclude me from consideration. I must have passed, because her attention returned to her screen. "Smart, bougie, baddie. The type of girl who is simply unattainable." She made a voila gesture. "You're perfect."

"*Baddie*?" I laughed. "I don't think so."

"Baddie as in *effortlessly stands out*, not baddie as in *reprobate*," Sophie chastised, ever-astonished at my lack of keeping up with the latest slang standards. Before she could launch into the next casting opportunity, a text notification buzzed through my watch. The number was strange—it had more digits than I was used to—and my face must have given me away when I realized it was an out-of-country area code.

"Everything okay?" Sophie's pristinely shaped eyebrows lifted, the ceramic cup paused midway to her lips.

I fished my phone out of my purse, swiping open my texts as a bundle of nerves settled in my stomach.

*I hope you made it home safely to handle your emergency. It was good to meet you. Best of luck in Hollywood. D.*

And that was it. Formal. Polite. Conclusive.

I don't know what I'd been hoping for, but it wasn't that. That text was something I would have sent to a stranger who'd returned my AAA card they'd found in the convenience store on Beverly. There was no friendliness. No playfulness. No sharing-kahlua-pork-out-of-a-takeout-container-while-covered-in-volcanic-mud familiarity.

And why should there have been? She clearly thought I'd skipped out on her.

After I'd practically been swooning over her all evening.

After letting her kiss me.

She probably thought I'd been playing games. That I'd led her on and then panicked and bolted.

*Shit.*

How did I fix this? And was there even a point in trying? It wasn't like I was going to see her again.

But I also didn't want her to think I was an asshole.

I looked up, searching for an answer, and found Sophie's sagacious gaze bearing down on me.

"I know that look," she said, her heart-shaped lips puckering into a sympathetic smile. "Boy trouble?"

Sophie wasn't like Dani. To Sophie I could simply say *it's nothing* or, even more directly, *I don't want to talk about it,* and she would respect my privacy and courteously move on to the next subject. Dani would have tackled me for my phone. She would have grown belligerent with my reluctance to discuss it. She would have accused me of being a bad friend for keeping secrets to which she was not privy.

Not Sophie.

Which is likely why I abruptly unloaded my entire Hawaiian escapade onto her unsuspecting shoulders.

I started with the call from Aaron—admitting only that I'd landed a fortuitous role for an upcoming project—and ended with my last night in Hana, reading aloud the text I'd just received.

I worried I may have been crazy to tell her anything. Not about the project—I hadn't said anything that would break the rules of my NDA, and even if I had, Sophie was the last person on earth who would ever breathe a word that risked getting me in trouble—but I honestly wasn't sure how she'd react to my chronicles about Dillon.

Over the course of our friendship, I'd learned both of Sophie's parents were devout to the school of Theravāda, the most orthodox of the three major philosophies of Buddhism. Sophie's own beliefs were more relaxed—something which her Phuket-born parents frequently gave her grief about—but I still wasn't sure how she'd respond to my sudden uncertain attraction to a woman.

A concern which I immediately kicked myself over, given my knowledge that Sophie was one of the most open-minded individuals I had ever known, and it was sheer stupidity to doubt the genuineness of her nature.

By the time I'd stopped talking, she'd cleared the debris of our meal to the side of the table, poured us both another round of sake, and folded her hands in her *thinking* pose, giving me her full consideration. She appeared neither shocked nor troubled by my revelation.

"Tell me this: what is the outcome you would like to achieve?"

I stared at the disintegrating case on my phone, lost for an answer. I hadn't really considered what I wanted. I'd focused only on the problem. I'd given no thought to a solution.

In her ever-composed manner, she continued. "For instance, if there were no impossibilities—what result would you hope to attain?" This was pure Sophie. Thoughtful. Enlightened. Always searching for balance to allow life to flow with peaceful ease. A solid reminder why, at twenty-three, she'd just returned from making a documentary that was a shoe-in to win the *L'Oeil d'or* at Cannes, and I'd just set my elbow in the soy sauce dish while trying to match her halcyon equilibrium.

*Fuck me.*

I tried to casually mop up the mess while she proceeded to prove to me I was making a mountain out of a mole hill.

"Are you just wanting to smooth things over? To ease your conscience and make certain no feelings were unintentionally injured? Or were you hoping to see her again—to consider pursuing this? What would be your ideal scenario?"

When put like that, it wasn't difficult to decide which result I wanted most. If any of the options were available...

*I'll take See-Her-Again for $500, Alex.*

"I'd pursue it." I couldn't believe I was admitting this. Dani would have flipped out. Hell, *I* was flipping out.

But Sophie was not.

"Then let's find a way to take the next step forward."

I hesitated. This had gotten really real, really quickly. "I—I don't know. Honestly, I've got a lot going on, and—"

"You know, in the five years I've known you, I've never seen you as nonplussed over Carter, or any of your revolving door dates, as you have been tonight. I think that speaks for itself."

"I'm not saying I'm gay, Sophe!" I didn't even know where the defensiveness came from. It wasn't something I'd been overly concerned about. I just felt like I suddenly didn't understand myself. And it was a little freaky to think, at twenty-three years old, I didn't know who I was. I glanced down at the +44 number still lit on my screen. "I just... I've never found myself attracted to... I don't know why..." I trailed off. When I looked back up, sheepishly catching her onyx gaze, she let out a small sigh, composing herself as if she were about to explain something tedious to a dense child.

"You do realize, Kam, there's a lot more on the palette than simple black and white—gay or straight—right? It's not always so much about the gender as it is about the person. Finding yourself attracted to one individual doesn't necessarily label you in any specific classification."

Embarrassed by the sensibility of the lecture, I sank a little lower in my seat. "Yeah," I muttered, realizing that made sense.

"Good." She reached for her sake. "Now that that's settled—you said she has a race in Key West coming up?"

# Scene 8

Given her substantial lead in the final leg of the race, Dillon could have walked the last fifty meters and still been first to cross the finish line. Her failure in Hana had given her no choice but to win. A second-place finish was out of the question.

Not because her sponsors put pressure on her. Not because her coach, Alistair, had found anything wrong with her Hawaiian finish. Not because she needed any points to hold her world ranking. None of that was true. Her sponsors were thrilled—year in and year out—with her performance. Alistair felt her showing in Hana had been on target, given the circumstances leading up to the race. Her ranking would hold its own even if she came in last the next three consecutive races. A probability less likely than her stumbling across Atlantis on her morning swim.

No, it was Dillon who applied pressure on Dillon.

She couldn't tolerate defeat. She couldn't cope with mediocrity. She was rarely pleased with a result, always wanting better. And so, when she crossed the finish line and looked at the timing board, her first thought wasn't that she'd beaten the course record—which she had—it was that she knew she could have done it thirty seconds faster. She'd lost at least ten seconds with a caught zipper on her wetsuit in the transition from the swim to the cycle, and if she'd pushed a little harder on the last mile of the run, she was certain she could have shaved her time down another quarter of a minute.

"Jesus Christ," Alecia Finch panted when she threw herself across the timer, dropping to the ground next to where Dillon sat stretching her cramping muscles. "Do you think you could keep to your own side of the pond and give the rest of us a break for a little while?" Sweat plastered her long blonde hair to the tops of her heaving shoulders. She'd come in second, running the course almost a minute behind Dillon. "You're making me look like an amateur."

Dillon laughed. She and Alecia had been leap-frogging one another in the world rankings for the past four years, ever since Alecia burst onto the scene as a twenty-one-year-old unknown.

She liked the American. Alecia was gritty. Ruthless. She had what it took to be a champion. Never once had Dillon seen her back down from a challenge. When they'd raced against each other in Melbourne the previous year—Dillon taking silver, Alecia earning bronze—she'd watched the younger competitor run the last thirty meters of the race with a torn Achilles tendon. She knew—with Lena Ammann, the Swiss athlete who had beat them both out of gold—retired, if there was anyone that was going to give her a run for her money in the Los Angeles Olympics, it was going to be Alecia.

And Dillon loved every competitive second of it.

It didn't hurt that the pair shared a flirtatious raillery since pretty much the day they'd met. Alecia was straight, married last year to a fellow Olympian—a dinghy sailor from New Zealand—but prior to that, had Dillon not been committed to Kelsey, she was relatively certain they'd have found a lot of more enjoyable ways to celebrate their triumphs on the podium.

"Well, I did think the sun might set by the time you finally got here," Dillon razzed, dragging her adrenaline-depleted body to her feet as two more competitors crossed the finish line.

"Aren't you original," Alecia rolled her eyes, accepting her outstretched hand. "I thought you English were supposed to be clever."

It was a playful jab. Alecia was well aware, despite Dillon's English mother, that she unreservedly considered herself Welsh.

The two of them navigated toward the aid station, draining a cup of water and toweling off their dripping hair as another cluster of athletes finished the race.

"You coming to the after party?" Alecia sucked the juice out of an orange slice.

On another day, Dillon would have amused herself with an inappropriate comment, pointing out Alecia's impressively wide mouth, but today her thoughts were elsewhere.

"Nope." She tossed her Dixie cup into the biodegradable rubbish bin. "Going to finish up here and then it's back to the hotel for me."

"You know everyone else thinks you're a stuck-up bitch, right?" Alecia said at her elbow as they worked their way toward the waiting media. "It wouldn't hurt to come hang out."

"And ruin my hard-earned image?" She was long aware she rubbed many of her fellow competitors the wrong way. She was cocky. Confident. Sure of herself. She imagined the thing they disliked the most about her was that she could walk her talk. But Alecia got her. They were opponents cut from the same cloth. The only difference was that Alecia was willing to turn up at the post-race events and put on a happy face.

"Just think, if you came, you could ruin Dana Myer's standing bet you won't show up."

"After all these years, I'd hate to disappoint her."

"Well, what about disappointing me?" Alecia side-eyed her, putting on a fake pout.

"Pretty sure I saw your husband in the crowd."

Alecia shrugged. "Always room for a third."

Dillon laughed. "Hard pass."

They'd reached the media exit and, as the race winner, she was being shuffled toward the tent.

"I guess you'll just have to entertain yourself," Alecia whispered, covering her provocative smile by taking another sip from her disposable cup.

"Who said I'd be alone?" she returned, leaving her with a wink.

An hour later, with the race over, the media appeased, the podium vacated, and doping control testing met, Dillon finally allowed her one-track mind to wander.

As fanatical as she was about her training, her sleep, her diet, she was equally dialed-in on her focus. It was her self-imposed rule that her mobile was turned off forty-eight hours prior to her start-time. She had never been one for TV or social media, and intentionally avoided anything that could lure her thoughts in any direction outside of her primary objective: *to win*.

But for the first time in as long as she could remember, she'd found herself struggling to maintain her concentration. Even Kelsey had never succeeded in steering her from her habits—though it hadn't been for lack of effort. It had been a consistent fight of theirs—her reclusiveness during race season—and one the extroverted footballer had never managed to convince Dillon to break.

Yet today, nearly the moment she stepped off the podium, she found herself shouldering her way through the surplus of athletes and audience, hurrying for the gear tent so she could find her phone.

She'd been tempted to commit a cardinal sin and turn it on yesterday—even if just for a few minutes—but her ingrained sense of discipline had slapped her back into focus. She didn't need to send a goodnight text. She didn't need to inquire if Kameryn had made it safely to Miami.

*Need…?* No. *Want?* Yes. But she refrained, anyhow.

It had started two weeks ago when Kameryn responded to the text she'd sent, forced by Sam's hand. There had been no reply for hours—Dillon hadn't honestly expected one—so when her phone chimed in the middle of the night, she'd been surprised.

Kameryn's response had been sincere—a lengthy apology explaining her agent's request she catch the first flight out of Maui, and how she had a project in the works she couldn't talk about yet, but one important enough she couldn't say no. She'd gone on to reiterate how much fun she'd had, how glad she was they'd met, and—if their paths crossed again—she hoped Dillon would give her another chance. *The next dinner's on me*, she'd closed the text, followed by an emoji of crossed fingers and *please* hands.

And then, twenty minutes later, she'd texted again.

*I'm so sorry, I just realized it's 11PM in Key West.* Along with an embarrassed face.

Dillon had responded:

*It's actually 4AM in London.* Followed by a wink.

And so their conversation had resumed.

Casually at first. The next day, Kameryn sent her a photo of the iconic Hollywood sign, along with the caption *proof I do know how to communicate at a reasonable hour.* Dillon responded with *Sorry, I nap from 2-4.* And then, despite how much she enjoyed the thought of Kameryn panicking, and the blush that so easily rose to her cheeks, a photo of the Thames. *Taking the piss out of you—I've just finished a run.*

Day by day, the texts had increased, the subjects growing more personal. Dillon, who'd never been tethered to her phone, found herself bringing it with her on her long cycles, and looking forward to Kameryn's texts goodnight. A few days before she left London to get acclimated in Florida, Kameryn had texted that she'd be in Miami the same weekend as her race in Key West. *If you have free time*, she'd suggested, *you should hit me up*. Dillon hadn't initially imagined it would work out—Key West and Miami weren't exactly a drive across town. But by the time she'd landed back on US soil, she'd already decided—whatever it took—she wanted to see Kam.

And so, dragging on track pants, and slinging her gear bag over her shoulder, she worked her way through a dozen *nice race* and *well dones!* and skirted through the recovery area while powering up her phone.

There were a handful of texts. Sam. Kyle. Her sister, Seren. She skipped them, scrolling until she found the only one she wanted.

*I know I'm texting you in the middle of your 48 hour cell phone jail, so you won't get this, but I'm sending you good luck tomorrow anyhow. I doubt you'll need it. I landed in Miami last night. Text me if you have time.*

Dillon walked the half mile to her hotel, browsing the flight schedule from Key West to Miami. There were puddle jumpers leaving every hour. Despite it going against her recovery protocol, she could fly in for dinner. Or for breakfast tomorrow morning.

By the time she'd showered, drank another liter of water, and forced down a protein shake, another consideration came to mind. It was quiet in Key West. Beautiful. Without the city vibes of Miami. Stepping onto her oceanfront balcony, she snapped a photo of the view. Her sponsors were paying a fortune for the room. It was a shame to see it go to waste.

She selected the photo and added a message:

*Key West is nicer than Miami. Just saying.*

Then hit *send* before she could change her mind.

# Scene 9

There weren't a significant number of things in life that terrified me. I had always been adventurous, even as a child. I didn't mind heights. I loved swimming in the ocean. Every spider I'd ever come across in my apartment I'd gently trapped and relocated outside.

There were, however, three things I was not fond of.

1. Planes with fewer than four engines.

2. Planes flying over water.

3. Planes flying in heavy wind.

Okay, fine. *Planes.* Planes flying. Planes as soon as they left the ground.

It wasn't one of those terrors so overwhelming I couldn't fly. I flew. A lot. And I knew my *a lot* was about to quintuple—or sextuple—or whatever mathematical multiplication meant my time in the air was soon to increase exponentially. But I didn't like it. And I admit, I'd grown accustomed to downing Dramamine like it was going out of style. Nor will I deny irresponsibly chasing it with a shot of vodka if the slightest hint of turbulence arose. Whatever it took to put me to sleep as the steel death rocket hurdled at breakneck speeds seven and a half miles above the clouds.

But still, I flew. Even in twin engines—the unfortunate majority of all commercial aircraft. Even in the wind. And, more often than not, even over large bodies of water.

However, when I stepped onto the tarmac to catch the last minute flight I'd booked to Key West, I skidded to a halt so hard the family of four in matching *I Heart Miami* t-shirts piled into the back of me. I don't know what in the Indiana-Jones-relic-archive was sitting in front of me, but the brightly painted prop plane was not part of my future.

This was where I drew the line.

I stumbled aside, allowing the other eleven people on my scheduled flight to go around me—they were welcome to test their death-defying fortune—and pulled out my phone.

I quickly scrolled *American Airlines. United. Delta.*

Nothing. Nothing until tomorrow mid-morning. *Shit*. I'd already told Dillon I was catching a flight this evening. After Hawaii, I couldn't imagine standing her up again.

But I also couldn't fathom stepping into a fuselage the size of Dani's Range Rover.

I looked up the ferry. Four hour trip—okay, not bad. I clicked *book now*.

*Double shit*. Next departure: tomorrow morning.

I considered running back up the steps to the terminal and renting a car, but realized my license was in the backpack I'd willingly handed over during check-in. Something about "space saving." I should have taken that as a hint.

"Miss?"

I looked up to find a man in a suit peering out the cabin door. The flight attendant. No, God help me, the co-pilot. The *co-pilot* was seating passengers on this Lego-sized rust-rocket.

"Care to join us?"

*In what, death?*

The windsock on the flagpole was beginning to flutter, the breeze fanning my burning cheeks.

*Stone me.*

I don't know what the hell was wrong with me, but my feet started moving against my will, forward, up the rickety six-step ladder, and into the cramped cabin. If part one of this trip hadn't already proven I'd lost my mind, there was no question now.

I sank into the last seat available and clipped my seatbelt—all the good that strip of nylon was going to do me—forcing myself to try and breathe. It would be okay. I would be okay. Everything would be okay. Thousands of these puddle jumper planes flew safely every single day.

Well, except for the ones that didn't.

Just ask John Denver. Patsy Cline. Jim Croce. James Horner.

It's okay. I wasn't famous. The gravitational pull of the earth only seemed to want the talented elite.

Right?

I looked over the head of the grinning silver-haired grandma sitting next to me, trying to see out the window.

"Exciting, isn't it?" She had a Midwestern accent. "It's like stepping back in time with Amelia Earhart."

*Lady*, I wanted to say to her, *don't you know they never found her body?*

Instead, I closed my eyes and wondered who would be cast as Addison Riley after they dragged my lifeless corpse from the sea.

After the longest thirty-one minutes of my life—which turned out not to be the *last* thirty-one minutes of my life, so at least there was that to be grateful for—I bolted out of the aerial sardine can on shaky legs. Subduing the urge to kiss the ground, I shouldered my way through the single glass door to the baggage claim area. Neither of the two carousels had yet to kick to life, so I took the opportunity to call Sophie.

"What the hell am I doing here?"

Sophie's laugh, always perfectly melodic, sounded on the other end of the line. "I take it you made it to Key West. It's beautiful, isn't it?"

I couldn't have said. My eyes had been squeezed shut the entire flight, trying to keep down the coffee I'd had on my way to the airport. Now, however, with the concern of imminent death no longer relevant, a whole new anxiety was settling in my stomach.

"She's going to think I'm a psycho. What if she asks what I'm doing in Miami?"

I could practically hear Sophie's eye roll from three thousand miles away. "Kam, we've gone over this. You're an actress."

"I don't want to lie."

"Don't think of it as lying—think of it more as exploring a part. Just massage the truth. Tell her you came to do some research. You don't have to say what for." She paused. "And you *did* come for research. Research on yourself."

"I don't know how I let you talk me into this." The creaking conveyor belt of the baggage carousel lurched in front of me and the first suitcase came tumbling down the luggage chute, followed by my backpack. "Okay," I sighed, swooping my arm through the strap. "I gotta go."

"Just breathe, Kam. You've got this."

I wasn't exactly sure what *this* was, but I definitely didn't have it.

I'd told Dillon I would take an Uber from the airport. After the stress of her race earlier in the morning, I didn't want her having to come and get me. But when I stepped out of the single terminal exit, I caught a glimpse of wayward blonde hair sticking out from beneath a flat-billed snapback, and found Dillon perched on one of the sidewalk benches, her attention turned halfheartedly toward a chattering young woman.

"Welsh, actually," she was saying as I drew closer.

"So, basically English."

"Well, Wales shares a border with England, but we are not English. The English come only from England. Welsh come from Wales."

"But you sound British." The woman had grown almost impertinent.

"I am British. But there's really no such thing as a single British accent."

I was within a few feet of them, but neither had noticed me yet.

"British?" I interrupted their conversation, feigning shock. "I thought you told me you were from the United Kingdom?"

Dillon looked up, amusement appearing with her crooked smile. I'd forgotten how incredibly green her eyes were.

"I'm actually from the Commonwealth," she winked, climbing to her feet. "Hello, Kam-Kameryn."

I was at once reminded what had possessed me to fly across the country, pretending to have business in a city I hated, with absolutely no guarantee I'd even get to see a girl I'd spent less than five hours with three weeks earlier on an island in the middle of the Pacific Ocean.

It had been worth the last thirty-one minutes of mind-numbing terror, if just to hear her say those two words.

"Hello, Dillon from Cymru." It was a word I'd learned while browsing a UK travel magazine on my flight from Los Angeles to Miami. The Welsh word for Wales. "Did I pronounce that right?" I asked, suddenly self-conscious.

"Perffaith."

I had no idea what that meant, but she was smiling, so I took it as a good sign.

Taking hold of the crook of my arm, she glanced down at the woman still sitting on the bench. "Safe travels, mate."

"Oh!" Loath to give up the conversation, the woman tried again. "Australian!"

But Dillon was done, and steered me toward the street, looping her arm through mine.

"You made it."

"On a wing and a prayer," I said, meaning it quite literally. I matched her stride—longer than mine, despite her not being much taller than me—and noticed each time our hips brushed as we walked side by side. "You didn't have to come meet me. I would have just caught an Uber."

"Don't be daft—you just flew a hundred and twenty miles to get here. Of course I was going to meet you."

*A hundred and twenty miles.* Thank God that was all she thought I'd done. I tried to play it cool. "Yeah, and you covered thirty-two miles in your race this morning. I'm sure the last thing you wanted to do was trek across town to the airport." I second-guessed my choice of shooting off my newly acquired knowledge of Olympic triathlon distances. I should have said thirty. Something less accurate. At least I hadn't said 31.99, to prove how crazy I was.

If she was alarmed about my sudden mathematical insight, she didn't show it.

"So what drew Hollywood's rising star all the way to Miami?"

I momentarily forgot about the conundrum of answering her question. The term *rising star* threw me. It was something Dani called me, but always with a sense of mockery. Like my entire existence was as a social climbing upstart who would never quite make it to the top.

Well, wouldn't she be surprised.

My focus snapped back to Dillon. She wasn't mocking me.

"Uh—research." My voice sounded tight and I wondered if she could see straight through me. For all of Sophie's pep talk about being an actress, at the moment I was on track to receive a big green splat on *Rotten Tomatoes* for my inability to sound anything other than robotic.

"A new role?"

I nodded. *Something like that.*

She didn't press me.

We caught a cab on Roosevelt Blvd. and headed downtown. I'd been anxious about seeing her again, worried I'd made an enormous mistake. I didn't know this girl. She didn't know me. I didn't even know what I was expecting—or what I even wanted. I just knew I hadn't wanted to leave it the way we did. And now, sitting beside her in the taxi, watching the sun sink closer to the horizon, I found her relaxed affability put me at ease all over again.

"You haven't told me about your race." I was glad to steer the conversation in a different direction.

She pulled her hat off, running her fingers through her hair. Sun-bleached. Salt-bleached. Chlorine-bleached. Whatever it was, I loved the color of it.

"Another day, another dollar."

"That good, huh?"

She shrugged. "Nah, any day racing is good. It just could have been better."

I wasn't sure what to say to that. I'd really hoped she'd win. Everything online had indicated she was a strong favorite amongst the field. There were a number of high-ranking athletes competing, but according to the articles I'd read, the fast, flat track had favored Dillon. The race, being offseason, hadn't been televised or streamed, and the results hadn't been posted by the time I boarded the bucket of bolts I'd flown in on.

"I'm sorry."

She brushed off my sympathy. "Only one I've got to blame is myself."

I would have teased that at least this time no crazy motorists had tried to turn her into a pancake, but I didn't want to prolong the subject if she wasn't happy with her results. I imagined her competitive drive didn't handle losses lightly.

When the cab let us out downtown, the sun had dropped low enough for its golden orb to brush the cerulean water, turning the surface of the ocean into a mosaic of topaz glass. I'd learned on the ride over that Dillon had a destination in mind, but seemed in no hurry to get there as we strolled along the waterfront, comfortable in our intermittent silence.

"So when do you head for Sydney?" I asked, our steps slowing as we crossed a pedestrian bridge in front of the cruise ship terminal. A sign indicated we were approaching Mallory Square, where a small army of people had gathered to watch the sunset. Over the top of the crowd, I could see street performers on stilts and high wires, and pyrotechnic hoops being raised in preparation for an evening oceanside show.

Dillon stopped in the middle of the bridge, appearing as unenthusiastic as I was to enter the fray. The glint of a smile touched her green eyes as she turned to face me. "You remembered that?"

I was confused. "Remembered what?"

"That my next race is in Australia."

"Oh." For once it wasn't my internet sleuthing that was at fault for my rampant mouth. She'd mentioned Sydney the first night we'd had dinner on the lanai at the hole-in-the-wall restaurant. Still, I could feel my color rising. It probably wasn't normal to remember schedule details about a person you'd barely met. "I…" I stopped talking. I didn't need to dig this hole any deeper.

Her smile broadened. "It's nice, Kam-Kameryn. That you remembered." She reached out, sliding her fingers between the strap of my backpack and bare skin of my arm, lifting it to sling over her shoulder. "The race is the first weekend of December, so I'll head over a week early to get acclimated to the change in weather."

"Oh, right—it'll be winter on that side of the globe," I announced brightly, my thoughts too focused on where her fingers had grazed my skin to stop my mouth from committing its blunder. As soon as the words came tumbling out, however, I was aware of my error. "*Summer*," I corrected emphatically, "I mean—because, well," I gestured around us, "obviously it's winter here. Or, will be, after it's not fall."

*Oh my God, Kam. Just stop talking.* Clearly she didn't need my sixth-grade geography lesson on hemispheres.

"I've generally found it to work that way—winter coming after fall," Dillon teased, slipping her arm through mine once more as she turned our steps toward the growing crowd.

A schooner sailed by, the deck packed with party-goers on a sunset cruise. They waved and shouted and raised plastic glasses in a toast to the mob on land, who responded with an enthusiastic cheer of their own. It was loud and chaotic with far too many people, and my silent relief soared when I realized Dillon was navigating us away from the square, and down a lesser-populated brick road.

"Alright," she said, stopping in front of a weathered two-story building with an old-fashioned ticket booth out front. Beside the door was a replica jaw of a megalodon, displaying the 276 teeth of the extinct shark, and above the blue and white canopy, a sign that read *AQUARIUM*. "You up for a little excursion?"

I glanced from her to the ticket booth, uncertain whether she had noticed the sign indicating they had closed for the evening.

"I think we might be too late."

"I have it on good authority they make exceptions for *Almost* Marine Biologists."

I tilted my head, raising an eyebrow. "Apparently I'm not the only one who remembers random bits of conversation."

Throwing her arm around my shoulders, she drew me toward the landing. "Trust me, I remember everything about that evening," she said, her lips close to my ear, before knocking on the door.

Every hair on my neck stood up at the whispered admission, but I wasn't granted time to dwell on it as a million-year-old man appeared at the threshold.

"You came!" His wrinkled face transformed into a boyish grin when he spied Dillon, and he threw the door wide open. "And you brought your friend! Come in, come in!"

We were ushered into the aquarium—small, by the standards of the world-class aquariums I had grown up with—but it was clean and the animals well cared for. I learned quickly we weren't there for casual browsing, but instead Dillon had volunteered us to help "tuck-in" the marine life, assisting the caretakers as they prepared the animals for bedtime. It was a program, Roger—our guide—explained, exclusively offered over the summer months, but when Dillon had stopped by earlier, she'd convinced him to make an exception.

"She can be very charming, this one," he wagged a knotted finger toward Dillon, winking at me with one of his diluted blue eyes. "And you're very pretty, so I can see why."

I laughed at his compliment, very aware of Dillon's eyes on me as we were walked through the nightly routine.

"Do you always go to this much effort for pre-dinner-entertainment?" I asked, half an hour later when we'd been left on our own to drop a dinner of clams into the tank of a Caribbean Reef octopus named Sid. "A drive along the most scenic road in Maui, a hike to the top of a hill created by a god, now—this," I twirled my finger to indicate the sea life around us.

Dillon shrugged, holding out the bucket for me to grab another clam. "Are you having fun?"

I couldn't begin to hide the ridiculousness of my goofy smile as I watched Sid's bright green arms swoop in on his sinking meal.

Her lips flickered at the corners of her mouth. "I'll take that as a yes."

For another hour, we schlepped croaker fish and snappers to nurse sharks, skimmed a cleaning net through a tank of Moray eels, and, to my utter delight, found ourselves entirely soaked after helping the aquarium veterinarian scrub the backs of Lola and Hector—the resident sea turtles.

"I didn't even know this was on my bucket list," I laughed, leaning my head close to Dillon's as Erika—the veterinarian—offered to take our photo. We were still on our knees, just finishing washing the algae from Lola's shell.

"I may have been wrong about you," Dillon said, after we'd thanked Roger and waved our goodbyes, heading out the door. "Marine biology might have suited you perfectly."

We stopped in front of the building adjacent to the aquarium, the hokey facade resembling a high school theatre backdrop advertising the *Key West Shipwreck Museum*. With the sun having set, the building was locked up tight, the surrounding area vacant after all the tourists had disappeared to the nightlife down by the ocean.

"I can't believe we just did that." I wrung out the hem of my tank top, salt water dripping onto my tennis shoes. "I can't believe you arranged that," I looked up, "for me."

She didn't say anything, just leaned against the figure of a peg-legged man who looked like he'd been stolen from the set of *Pirates of the Caribbean*. In the distance, the music pounded into the night, reverberating from the Mallory Square party.

I wanted to kiss her. I mean, I'd been thinking about it since I stepped off the plane. Okay, fine, since I stepped *on* the plane. Not the prop plane. The plane from Maui. Over two weeks ago. I'd been thinking about it while L.R. Sims assured Waylon MacArthur I was pretty, but not *too* pretty. And while Sophie and I devised a ludicrous plan for me to fly to Florida. And yet again while I tossed anchovies into the barracuda exhibit and watched as the enormous slender bodies swept up from the coral reef to snap up their supper.

I wanted to, and yet, I couldn't bring myself to do it.

It sounds absolutely stupid, but I didn't know how. Carter I would have simply stepped forward and kissed. The way I had when I'd pursued him my Freshman year in gym class. The way I'd kissed a dozen or more boys during all the times Carter and I had been "taking a break."

But for some reason, with Dillon, I couldn't do it. Maybe, because, out of all those boys, not one of them had made me feel like this. Like I was suspended, walking along the tightropes with the acrobats performing in the square. Like I was floating, weightless through the water, as buoyant as the moon jellyfish in the aquarium tank. Yet also as frozen, as incapable, as the inanimate pirate grinning down at us from the museum display.

Dani had once told me, when she first met Tom, he made her insides ache.

I'd chalked the sentiment up to a silly cliché. But now, standing there in the dark, paralyzed in place, I knew exactly what she'd meant.

But amidst the desire—the newfound longing I'd discovered—was also the underlying discomfort of uncertainty. That was something, I was sure, Dani had not had to face.

She could fall in love with Tom, marry Tom, spend her life with Tom, without a single eyebrow lifted. Well, other than Darlene Hallwell's gross initial fit when she'd discovered his father was Mexican. That aside—Tom was idyllic. Educated, handsome, hardworking. Sure to be worth ten figures before he turned thirty.

But, obviously, more than anything, Tom was, well—a man.

I'd spent the last two weeks analyzing my feelings. I'd reached what I felt was a solid acceptance of the fact that I'd developed a crush on a woman. I'd convinced myself it didn't bother me. Queer, after all, was practically the new normal. So why, suddenly, did I find myself so nervous? Why, in the fleeting moments she'd held my hand in the aquarium, had I worried if anyone else was watching?

That wasn't me. I'd never cared what anyone else thought.

I was being ridiculous.

I loved the way her hand fit in mine. The way it felt like it belonged there. I loved the way she made me feel. The way my heart galloped its anarchic sprint whenever I knew her eyes were on me.

Nothing Carter had ever done had made me feel like this, and not for lack of trying. He was sweet, he was considerate, without a single domineering bone in his body. He'd never pressured me. He wasn't clingy. I couldn't have found a guy who was more laid-back, or ridiculously good-looking. I had no excuse not to be head-over-heels in love with him.

Yet never, in the eight years of our erratic dating history, had I ever once wanted to reach out and touch him so badly my fingers were shaking.

So what if Dillon hadn't been in the script I originally envisioned?

There was always time for a last-minute rewrite.

I released an unsteady breath and, though I didn't find the courage to kiss her, I did manage to shove aside the tilt-a-whirl of my uncertainties enough to catch her hand as she stepped in the direction of the ongoing party.

"Should we sort dinner?" she asked, and through the shadows I could feel her gaze on me again as I laced our fingers together, falling into step beside her.

# Scene 10

Dillon's older sister, Seren, had razzed her once—long before Kelsey —that she had a bad habit of fancying straight girls. A practice, Seren insisted, bound to set her up for failure. Dillon had been unconcerned.

"Every girl is straight until they're not."

"Touché." Seren had been unable to argue. "Still, it'll nip you in the arse one day."

But over the years, it hadn't proven to be much of an issue. Until Kelsey, Dillon had kept a very blasé approach to her love life—one she'd adopted again once her relationship with the footballer had ended.

Her theory: you won some, you lost some. And for the most part, she won.

Kelsey was a prime example. She'd been supposedly "straight" when they met, after all. And for a time, she'd been the best thing that ever happened to Dillon. For three years, she'd been unable to imagine her life with someone else. They'd been a perfect fit—driven to succeed—fierce competitors—in love. But then the Lionesses won the Euros, and their success had favored them to bring home the World Cup, and Kelsey's already prominent career was suddenly shoved into famedom. Kelsey became England's darling. The face of football. A national hero. Her fan base—already impressive—quadrupled overnight. She was on chat shows and television adverts, her face plastered across the United Kingdom. Where previously she'd only been recognizable to the devout football fans, suddenly, everywhere they went, people knew her name—who she was—and, by the laws of social media, who Dillon was, also.

The relative anonymity Dillon had enjoyed in her own career, and in turn, her personal life, was abruptly abolished. She unexpectedly found herself in the limelight, on the receiving end of fan mail, hate mail, love letters. She and Kelsey became an unhealthy fixation for obsessive football fans, along with acting as a beacon for homophobic hate. Men and women from across the globe spewed their disgust on every social media post, with some of the more devoted creeps even going so far as to track down Seren—sending her odd friend requests and follows on her own athletic profile.

None of it had been Kelsey's fault. She'd been no different than Dillon—a rising star in her career. But football was an international pastime—*the beautiful game*—popular across the entire world. Triathlons were different. Triathletes were unknown.

Olympic medalist. World Champion. Dillon Who?

Exactly how Dillon liked it. *Had* liked it.

Suddenly, the pressure of their relationship became too much. The night England won their home turf quarterfinal, advancing to the semis, Dillon called it quits.

She'd broken Kelsey's heart.

It had been selfish. It had been unfair. It had drastically backfired on her quest for anonymity, drawing a tidal wave of hatred from Kelsey's fans—and, at the time, what had felt like the entirety of England. She'd been forced to delete her socials to escape the wrath of the football fanatics, and spent a couple of years lying low. The whole ordeal left Dillon with few friends, and an albatross of guilt that almost killed her.

But that was neither here nor there.

Point being—Kelsey *had* been straight. Until she wasn't. And now, after Dillon, the English footballer had dated half the women in the WSL.

Thus… straight until you weren't. That was Dillon's theory and it had yet to let her down.

So it didn't faze her that Kameryn had clearly never previously questioned her identity. Sometimes you met a person and just clicked. What was wrong with that? Maybe it worked out, maybe it didn't. But for now, Kameryn appeared to be on the same wave length. Which was cool, because Dillon really liked her.

After leaving the aquarium, they spent a few minutes wandering through the crowd in Mallory Square, before deciding to forgo the food truck lines and head over to the Historic Seaport District. Dillon wasn't a fan of tourism related nightlife, but Kameryn had never been to Key West, so a tiki bar on the white sand beach seemed an appropriate choice for dinner.

Seated at a wooden spool table, Dillon ignored her body's dissatisfied opposition to the deviation of her routine. Usually, after a race, she spent the remainder of the day in recovery. Stretching. Icing. Rehydrating. Refueling. Always thinking ahead, preparing for the next victory. She'd rarely leave her hotel, and habitually forced herself to an early sleep, even when her adrenaline was still soaring.

Sometimes, however, certain circumstances made rules worthy of breaking.

Kameryn Kingsbury was proving to be a sterling example of exactly that type of situation.

As the tables around them filled, the patrons growing boisterous, Dillon enjoyed watching Kam take in their surroundings. She quickly forgot about her aversion to crowds and distaste for loudmouthed frivolity, and instead found herself enchanted by the paradox Kam presented. Where she was shy and uncertain on one hand, Dillon found her bold and unreserved on the other, her charm built in a macédoine of certitude and fragility—an enigmatic puzzle she was determined to piece together.

She found she loved the way she laughed when their server—costumed as a cabana boy—gave her a flirtatious wink, sashaying his barely concealed hips in his skintight short shorts as he took their order. She appreciated the respectfulness of her nature—always leading with please and ending with thank you—and how she didn't bat an eye when Dillon asked for a seltzer and lime, instead of matching her order of a rum runner.

After the drinks arrived, Kam pulled the tiny paper parasol out of her pineapple, and stabbed it into the lime Dillon had discarded on the table.

"I bet it gets wild here over the holidays." Kam's voice was muffled by the live brass band blasting out upbeat Cuban love songs.

Dillon plucked up the tiny umbrella, twirling it between her thumb and forefinger. "I imagine it's not much different than an average day in Hollywood. Surely this type of scene is your status quo by now."

"Not really," Kam slid one of two cherries off the plastic cocktail sword into her drink, and offered the remaining one to Dillon. "I'm kind of boring."

"Somehow I doubt that." Dillon didn't like maraschino cherries, but took it anyhow.

"Then you might be sorely disappointed."

Tugging off the stem, Dillon tossed the cherry into her mouth. "Somehow I doubt that, also." She washed down the offending fruit with a sip of her seltzer. "You won't convince me that the girl who was voted in school to be Most Likely to Drop Her Phone in the Toilet has *nothing* interesting about her." She smiled behind her glass. "I'm not the only one with a page on wikipedia, Kam-Kameryn."

Kam's dark eyes widened, her drink paused midway to her mouth. "Tell me it doesn't really say that!"

Dillon laughed. "I assure you it does."

"Oh my God." Her cheeks glowing scarlet beneath the flame of the tiki torch glare, Kam wrestled her phone out of her still-damp jeans pocket. "Fucking Dani!"

"It did also mention something about being voted Most Likely to Lead a Protest."

"I swear I'm going to kill her!" Kam fussed with her phone, before giving in and tossing it on the table. "There's no service." She stewed another moment, and then laughed. "Wait—I can't believe you looked at my wiki page! I thought you never went on the internet?"

Dillon swirled the ice in her glass. "I had to make sure I wasn't meeting with an axe murderer."

"If I was going to kill you, don't you think it would have been easier to do it during the privacy of our hike on Ka'uiki? Or even better, just finishing the job I started on the Road to Hana?"

"That sounds like something someone would say who's given the thought some consideration."

Kam gave a noncommittal tilt of her head. "Maybe I'm a thrill seeker? Just looking for a steeper challenge?"

"Lucky coincidence for you, then, that you had work in Miami."

As soon as the words were out of Dillon's mouth, Kam's face shifted, losing all its playful bluster. She stared at the melting ice of her cocktail, before looking resolutely up at Dillon.

"I lied to you."

Uncertain what to say, or where this was going, Dillon waited.

"I—I don't even know how to say this." Her brief determination to hold her eye faltered, and once again she returned her stare to the table.

Sitting up a little straighter, Dillon fought down the uneasiness that crept up from the bottom of her stomach.

"I didn't have work in Miami. I didn't—I didn't have any reason to be here." Kam's voice trembled, as if she were on the verge of tears. "I just… after the way we left things in Hawaii, I didn't… I wanted to…"

she swallowed. "I wanted to see you again. And," she rushed on, before Dillon could say anything, "I know that makes me look like a psycho. You have to think I'm a freak. And I really understand if you want to skip out now. It's probably what I would do. But I—" again she wavered, before turning her gaze to Dillon once more, her humiliation evident. "I didn't want to lie to you. And I didn't know how to tell you the truth."

Dillon stared back at her for a long second, wrapping her head around everything she'd said. It wasn't what she'd been expecting—though she wasn't sure what she'd been expecting. Just—not that. And, as caught off guard as she was, it still came as a colossal relief.

Kameryn hadn't blinked, or taken a breath. "Please say something."

Dislodged from her surprise, Dillon couldn't help but laugh. "You flew all the way across the country not even knowing if we'd find time to meet up?"

The color of Kam's cheeks—never fully recovered from her embarrassment over the wikipedia page—grew more deeply flushed. "Yeah." Her shoulders sagged. "I know how that sounds…"

"Flattering? Bold? Sweet?" Dillon shrugged. "And, yeah, a little crazy, maybe. Especially coming from someone who tried to convince me a few minutes ago they were boring—but, what can I say?" she smiled. "I think that might be the nicest thing anyone's ever done for me."

Kam's expression tentatively brightened. "So, you're not—freaked out?"

"By the girl who flew across the country to see me? No. No glaring red flags there. Now, having a tendency to drop your mobile in the toilet, on the other hand…"

Kameryn managed a laugh. "Just so we're clear, I've never actually done that before."

"Flown across the country on a whim, or dropped your mobile in the toilet?"

"Flown across the country on a whim. I mean, actually, neither. The yearbook superlative was an inside joke. I just—I can be, um, clumsy when I'm nervous."

As if to accentuate this admission, she reached for her drink, catching the lip of the glass with her pinky finger, almost tipping it over.

"Jesus," she righted the cocktail. "I swear—"

"Sinclair?" A shadow crossed their table. "I thought that was you."

The annoyingly familiar voice cut a nasal path through the din of the surrounding tables. Dillon looked up to find Isaac Fortin, the husband of one of her long-time competitors—a Canadian woman named Claudia—staring down at her, his hands settled on his slender hips, smile smug as ever.

Dillon tolerated Claudia. She'd seen her name on the start list. She was a regular middle-of-the-pack finisher, dumb as a fence post, but bearable enough on her own. Her husband, however, was a different story.

"Hello, Isaac." Dillon's voice was flat, leaving no indication he was a welcome intrusion. If given the opportunity, he would talk—strictly about himself—until the bar closed. Or they died by virtue of his outrageous ego. Whichever came sooner.

The man was a long-course racer, always clapping himself on his back for competing at an amateur level in the notorious Ironman competitions. An age-group athlete who'd never raced a professional minute in his life.

At least Claudia was actually sponsored.

His attention swept across the table, landing on Kameryn.

"Well," he sniffed, arching one of his thin eyebrows that creased his forehead, the lines disappearing into his receding hairline, "fair guess to say you aren't with Kelsey anymore?" It wasn't really phrased as a question. Nor should it have been. The entire continent of Europe knew they'd split almost two years prior. He was merely being impertinent, sticking his too-large nose where it didn't belong.

"Nope."

"Shame. I imagine she's worth a mint by now, branded the way she is. Hello," he stuck out his hand toward Kameryn, "Isaac Fortin."

"Hi." Kameryn didn't offer her name.

"Ah, American." Again, it wasn't a question. "Broadening your horizons, eh, Sinclair?" His smile never touched his pale eyes. "Speaking of—good to see you were back in form today. Saw the results from Hana last week; what a pity. Rough terrain, that area. Be glad it was as short as it was. I've done Kona twice—brutal race. I imagine you'll keep more flat courses in your future—wouldn't want to see those rankings fall."

Dillon opened her mouth, uncertain what variation of *piss off* was going to fall from her lips, but before she could squeeze a word in, he'd already turned back to Kameryn.

"You race? I don't imagine, you don't look the type. I'm an *Ironman,* myself. Certainly, you've heard of it? It's about four times the distance Sinclair here does."

Kam trailed a finger along the rim of her cocktail glass. "You know, it's only recently I've learned about it."

The pompous prick perked up at what he undoubtedly imagined was the prime opportunity for enlightenment. He didn't appear to notice the flicker at the corners of Kameryn's mouth or the tilt of her head as she sat back, crossing her legs, her gaze veiled beneath dark lashes.

Dillon remained silent, curious to see where this was leading.

"It's a grueling sport—"

"So I've heard," said Kam, disallowing him time to launch into his monologue. "What I've found interesting is the diverse levels of competition. I think it is wonderful that the longer endurance races have opened the door for aging athletes to continue to compete, even once they are well past their prime." She offered Isaac a brilliant smile.

The stunned Canadian opened his mouth, then shut it, and opened it again. No words came out, however, as he stood there, resembling a fish gaping for air.

"Be sure to give Claudia my best," nodded Dillon, before leaning into the table, cutting him off with the angle of her shoulder.

For once in his pathetically mediocre life, he took the hint and walked away.

"Oh, what an asshole," said Kameryn, once the crowd had swallowed him in its fold. "I'm sorry if I was out of line—I just..." she shook her head. "What a total prick."

Dillon laughed, dragging her hat off to run a hand through her hair. "I don't even know what to think about you, Kameryn Kingsbury. You are full of the most marvelous surprises."

"You still certain you don't want to bolt? I won't hold it against you."

She was certain she'd never wanted to bolt less in her life.

Glancing around at the sea of bodies taking over the narrow strip of sand, the only thing she wanted to get away from was the jam-packed hum of the bar.

"I swear I don't mean this the way it's going to sound, but do you want to go back to my hotel?" She couldn't remember the last time she'd really cared whether a woman said yes or no. She blathered on. "I can make us dinner. I'm a decent cook."

Without hesitation, Kameryn got to her feet, digging a twenty out of her wallet. "It sounded more fun," she teased, dropping the bill on the table, "when it sounded the way you didn't mean it to sound."

Dillon sat for a second, trying to decide how one person could be so many things. Forward, reticent. Knock-out-pretty, self-effacing. And somehow, she imagined, she'd barely scratched the surface.

Pulling her hat back on her head, she stood. The one thing she knew —for the first time since Kelsey—she didn't want to screw this up.

"Cart before the horse, Kam-Kameryn," she smiled, glad when Kam took her hand, weaving their way toward the street. "It may be you who wants to bolt once you've tried my cooking."

# Scene 11

Dillon wasn't a decent cook.

She was a chef.

And not the run-of-the-mill, garden variety, slap-a-sauce-on-a-pasta-and-call-it-gourmet kind. I'm talking haute cuisine, premium ingredients, artistry on a plate. I didn't know anyone could whip up a pan-seared sea bass with a chive velouté sauce and roasted kohlrabi from the kitchenette of a hotel suite, but I supposed, if anyone could do it, Dillon was the perfect candidate. I doubted there was much she couldn't do, if she put her mind to it. She just seemed like that type of person. Driven. Focused. Talented.

When she brought out the meal to where I was sitting on her private lanai, I'd been in the process of demolishing the polish on my left thumbnail. Until I saw the flakes of paint scattered on my lap, I hadn't even been aware I'd resorted to the nervous habit.

It had been one thing while we were out, crammed amidst the crowds of vacationing beachgoers, to talk big, to gasconade, to flirt like it was the Name of the Game. Like I had any clue what the hell I was doing or how to proceed. But now that we were alone, departed from the downtown bar scene, I felt like an overstrung bow—my synapses wound too tight, with no space for the neurons in between.

I know Dillon must have noticed. One would have to be insentient to not feel the tension radiating from me. But it never changed her languid demeanor.

"It's not Gordon Ramsay," she said, settling into the wicker patio chair overlooking the private beach, "but it's better than pub grub."

I took a bite of the sea bass—tender on the inside, perfectly seared on the exterior—and temporarily forgot my threadbare nerves. "Wow." I glanced at her. It was probably the best fish I'd ever had.

She smiled. "See, I told you I was decent."

"I didn't peg you as a humblebragger."

The admonishment brought her lopsided smile. "Alright," she conceded. "My dad had a thing for the kitchen. He was an engineer, but his passion revolved around everything culinary. I guess a bit of it rubbed off on me."

"So I see."

We ate in silence—I think both of us were hungrier than we realized—and when we finished, she scooped up our plates, and returned a few minutes later with a pair of frosted bottles. I was a little surprised as she popped the metal caps—though she'd ordered a beer in Hana, I noticed she never actually drank it, and at the bar tonight she'd had a seltzer. My interest must have been apparent, because she raised her eyebrows in inquiry as she handed me the bottle.

"What?"

On the spot, I didn't have time to think of a better response. "For some reason, I didn't think you drank."

"I don't, typically. I like to be the best at everything I do. Drinking was no different. I got a little too good at it a while back, but found I race better without a hangover." She took a sip. "Still, sometimes it's worth it to make an exception. How else am I going to get you drunk enough to sleep with me?"

I'd barely set the bottle to my lips, realizing too late it was nothing more than a non-alcoholic ginger beer, but her jesting comment caught me off guard. I immediately swallowed the pungent drink down the wrong pipe, and was overcome by a racking cough as I cleared the fizzy water.

"I'm sorry," I managed, gasping as my choking drew to a minimum. I don't know if my ears actually turned red with embarrassment, or if it was only my imagination.

"Easy there. I'm just winding you up."

Tears continued to stream down my cheeks as I shook my head, mortified she felt the need to clarify. Of course I knew she was teasing.

"I'm sorry," I said again, "I don't know what's wrong with me."

And I didn't. I don't know why I was so incredibly nervous.

Dillon studied me, her thoughts unreadable, before discarding her ginger beer on the outdoor table. She crossed to sit in the adjacent chair, drawing her knees up to her chest.

"Kam-Kameryn," she said with a dramatic sigh, her chin resting on her hands. My only saving grace from utter humiliation was the lurking smile behind her placid expression.

I shifted, uncomfortable under her scrutiny.

"I would tell you to relax, but I feel it might be a bit like telling a drowning person to swim."

She dropped her bare feet to the floor and leaned forward, elbows on her knees, her face level with mine. "How's this—I'm going to tell you my plans for the evening. Then maybe, if you approve, we can get on with this night without you flinching every time I come within a few feet of you?"

I had no idea what that meant, but I must have nodded, because she continued.

"I'd like to sit here for a few minutes, enjoying the ridiculous poshness of this suite while my sponsor foots the bill. I plan to appreciate the view, the company, and the fact that I can sit out here in short sleeves while my friends at home are freezing the balls off a brass monkey.

"Then, I'd like to go inside. I intend to shower, change, stretch—my usual routine. After, I'll come back out and offer you the ensuite while I brew a tea—or coffee, if you'd rather. We'll chat. I want to know what daily life is like living in Hollywood. And learn more about your hidden rebellious streak that pinned you most likely to lead a protest. At that point, I'm going to take the couch, and you're going to take my room. You're going to toss and turn and fret all night, because, well—that seems to be who you are. And I'll sleep soundly, because I'm knackered. At seven AM, I'll go for a swim, come back, knock you up for breakfast, and we'll start our day again from there." She sat upright. "Would that be acceptable for an itinerary?"

For someone who excelled in soliloquies, my talents certainly let me down at the most inopportune times. With no cohesive thoughts forming, I tried to buy myself an extra moment to think. I needed something witty, something casual, to hide my embarrassment. *Embarrassment, relief, disappointment.* I hadn't realized you could experience all three conflicting emotions in such short succession. So, in an effort to delay, I opted to take another sip of my drink—but my motor skills appeared to have eloped with my ability to speak, and I somehow managed to miss my mouth, losing half the soda down the front of my tank.

"Oh, for the love of God." The only thing I could do was laugh. "Just shoot me now." I wiped away the ginger beer dripping off my chin.

Dillon's smile returned. "That's not part of the schedule, Kam-Kameryn."

The layer of ice I'd managed to materialize since we arrived at the hotel began to melt, and along with it, my tension.

Despite the ridiculousness of an agenda—leave it to me to require one—the evening played out as she said it would, and an hour later I reemerged from showering to find Dillon sitting on the living room floor, applying K-tape to her left knee.

"Kettle's on, if you want a cuppa." She didn't look up from her project.

I poured a tea, then wandered to the middle of the room. The comfort of the hot shower had helped restore my sense of humor.

"I know the blocking put me on the couch at this point in the scene, but does your directorial style allow for minor improvisation?"

"I'd say there was some space for self-expression—just so long as you don't get too carried away with your ad-libbing, Miss Kingsbury."

"I'll stick close to the script, I promise," I quipped, dropping to sit cross-legged beside her.

Of course, now that I knew she had no expectations of me, it was human nature, I suppose, to want what was no longer up for offer.

I watched her tape an intricate line of zigzags around her knee. It was a process I was familiar with after playing varsity soccer.

"Did you get hurt today?" I asked, watching as she laid the final strip beneath her patella.

"This? No." She straightened her leg, grimacing at the various snaps and crackles from the effort. "Just wear and tear from an old ACL repair. I usually can't feel it in the warmer weather. With Alecia on the field today, I probably pushed it a little harder than I had to."

"Is that who won? Alecia Finch?" Hers was a name I'd become familiar with during my accelerated crash course as I tried to brush up on my knowledge of triathlons. She was an American. One of Dillon's strongest competitors.

"Alecia?" her brow furrowed. "God, no. I couldn't let that happen. Not on a fast course. She'd have rubbed it in my face all next season. I beat her by over a minute."

"I thought you said… when I asked you earlier…?" I was confused and it must have shown, because she laughed.

"I won today. I just could have been faster."

"And I thought *I* was self-critical," I tsked.

"I guess we're our own worst critics, right?" She clapped her hands to her thighs, closing off the subject, which in turn drew my focus back to her legs, where I noticed a coin-sized tattoo just above her ankle. It was a soccer ball.

She saw it caught my attention.

Her smile turned cynical as she ran a finger over the line drawing. "They say nothing lasts forever—except bad tattoos you get with your ex."

I only half laughed, trying to decide if it would be indecorous to inquire about Kelsey. It wasn't like me to ask about exes. I'd never cared before. And in Kelsey Evans's case, I wasn't even sure what I wanted to know. But my curiosity was piqued, and I decided since she'd offered the segue, it was fair game.

"Ex as in Kelsey Evans?"

If Dillon was surprised, she didn't show it. "Wikipedia or Isaac Fortin?"

I admitted I'd seen their names linked previous to Isaac Fortin's snarky comment.

"Are you a football fan?"

"I like to follow the US Women's team. I played through high school."

"Winger?"

I rolled my eyes. "What gave that away? Let me guess: Wikipedia?"

She laughed, reaching over to tap my thigh. "Your quads and hamstrings say you're built for speed."

"Oh yeah?" I tried not to allow my thoughts to get carried away by the knowledge she'd clearly taken a detailed assessment of my body. But who was I kidding? My stomach turned a little celebratory somersault. I'd spent the better part of the year working out with a personal trainer in WeHo who could be classified as nothing less than a sadist. During my first audition for *Sand Seekers*, I'd been informed the role would be vigorously demanding, so I'd taken it upon myself to turn my willowy frame into something more substantial. An action that, for once, had indisputably paid off.

And not—given the way she'd glanced at me—just for the movie.

I cajoled my wandering train of thought back to the conversation. "Then why not a fullback?" I asked. The position was notorious for some of the fastest players on a soccer team.

"Because you're an actress."

She lost me. "Which means…?"

"Which means the odds are good you enjoy a certain amount of attention."

"With that theorem, why not a striker? They're always the stars on the field."

"Because I think there's an alternate side of you—an unassuming side—that would rather share the spotlight, preferring to distribute the pressure of performance." She swiped her bangs out of her eyes and dropped her head back against the cushion of the couch. "That screams winger to me."

"Well then." I held her gaze for a second, before resorting to fixating on a loose thread dangling from the hem of my shirt. I felt suddenly vulnerable beneath her analysis, uncertain how much deeper I wanted her to look. I tried to make light. "I'm assuming your wiki page forgot to mention you majored in psychology?"

She laughed, but it wasn't genuine. "My mam would've loved that."

Realizing I'd touched on something sensitive, I returned my focus to the tattoo on her ankle. "You're deflecting," I razzed. "All that psychobabble to avoid telling me about your matching soccer ball tattoos, huh?"

"Matching?" she laughed, sitting up to drag her leg beneath her, hiding the topic of discussion. "God no. That matchy-matchy girlfriend rubbish isn't for me." She seemed to consider leaving the explanation there, but after another beat, continued. "It was a bollocks challenge. Our entire relationship was like that—one long, endless competition. The Rio Olympics were coming up, and we were both breaking our backs trying to earn a spot in the games. So one night, daft as we were, we made a bet that whichever one of us made selection, the other would get the opposing tattoo." She flipped an indifferent hand. "When it all came down to it we both ended up representing Great Britain. So now I'm walking around with a football on my ankle and she has a swim/bike/run logo on her arse." She redirected her gaze to catch my eye, offering her wry smile. "I got off easier, if you ask me."

I tried to picture England's darling—blonde-haired, blue-eyed, cover girl Kelsey Evans—with the triathlon logo on her ass. It certainly made Dillon's soccer ball a lot more low key.

"And this one?" I asked, reaching to take her forearm in my hand, turning it over to run a finger across her wrist where the dragon for the Welsh flag was inked in red and green.

"You have used up your introductory credits on question Number One, Kam-Kameryn. Additional tokens will need to be earned." She withdrew her arm from my grasp, but instead of pulling away, slid it forward, bringing our palms together, our fingers intertwined.

I don't know why the gesture robbed me of my breath, emptying my brain of proper cognition. She'd held my hand before—I mean, we'd held hands half the night strolling the downtown district. But here were those axons again, misfiring in every direction.

"In fairness," I said, hoping to mask the hitch in my breath as I played into her teasing, "this coin-op came with no manual. I have no instructions on how to advance to the intermediate level of Dillon Sinclair."

"You'll want to pass the training level, to start. You cannot run before you can walk." My hand still in hers, she leaned back against the cool tile and closed her eyes, her face turned up to the ceiling. "Tell me something about you, Kameryn Kingsbury. Something I won't find on the internet."

I balked. Something about me? What was there to say even? I didn't want to bore her with details of my prosaic life.

I'd grown up in the outskirts of Palo Alto. I was the only one in my set of friends whose parents weren't filthy rich from their efforts in the tech industry. My mom was a horse trainer. My dad worked in the boating industry maintaining the yachts my friends' parents sailed on the weekends. Our home was on a small ten-acre horse farm surround-ed by suburban neighborhoods. I hadn't been certain I wanted to be an actress, but I'd not gotten the soccer scholarship I'd been hoping for at Stanford, so when UCLA accepted me into their film school, I hadn't turned it down. My parents hardly spoke to me—not since I'd dropped out of school—and though I'd had little notable work in the industry, not once in the five years I'd been on my own had I asked them for a single dime.

In a few months, I was going to be knee-deep in shooting the big-gest blockbuster of the decade, but as forward as I was looking to the paycheck, and creating something more memorable than a *Gillette* razor commercial, the thing I wanted more than anything was to make my parents proud—even if I tried not to admit it to myself. But my self-preservation tried to keep that hope on the back burner, because I also knew, no movie I ever made would trump that little slip of paper with UCLA's embossed seal.

What else couldn't I say? I loved the beach. My credit score was over eight hundred. I'd tried for years to be a vegetarian but repetitively failed due to my addiction to sushi. I hung out in a lot of circles, but consistently felt like I never fit in. My best friend was a spoiled brat who'd dated every chisel-jawed jock in Northern California before finding a man who was certain to keep her coffers overflowing. I spent months avoiding calls from my high school boyfriend, only to call him back when life got too lonely and I wanted his familiarity to fill that void. I hated my boring brown eyes. I had a tendency to cry when I was angry. My favorite color was salmon. And even though I was 120lbs, if the liquor was free, I could drink most of the guys I knew under the table.

And that was about it—my entire life story.

Aside from *Sand Seekers*, it was nothing interesting. Nothing like Olympic medals. Famous girlfriends. Hair the color of sunset beaches. Confidence radiating through every breath.

I couldn't tell her any of that.

So instead, I flopped down beside her, our shoulders touching, my hand still in hers. Her eyes were still closed, and I wondered, for a second, if she'd fallen asleep in my silence.

"I have a bad tattoo of my own," I finally said, watching her face out of my periphery. I saw her eyes twitch beneath their lids. She wasn't sleeping.

"Oh? And what's that?"

Propping myself onto an elbow, I looked down at her, absorbed in the stillness of her sunburnt face, the faint freckles highlighting her cheekbones, the unruliness of her still-damp hair. Without allowing myself to overthink it, I leaned down and kissed her lips—still faintly tasting of ginger beer.

"Maybe later on in the screenplay, you'll find out." I whispered against her mouth, and felt her smile, never opening her eyes, before I forced myself to my feet—*back on script, Kameryn*—and headed to call it a night.

# Scene 12

"Bloody scorcher!"

Kyle dropped into the folding chair, his long legs upsetting the beers littered across the table. "Whose brilliant idea was it to race in Sydney in December?"

There were a few murmurs of agreement from surrounding athletes, but Dillon—directly across from him—offered no acknowledgment. She knew the comment was intended for her. He was testing the waters, gauging her mood.

He took a long draught of his beer. "I'm positively melting!"

Dillon finally broke her silence. "Is that your excuse, then? The heat?"

Kyle met her glare. There was no possibility he hadn't known this was coming. His performance in the mixed relay had been farcical. Not only had he been bested by every other male competitor on the field, he'd somehow managed to come in twenty seconds slower than Dillon. A feat which—as a woman, up against the superior strength of a man—shouldn't even have been possible at this elite level.

There was no excuse. He'd cost Team GB the win.

"We were second, Sinc. By less than 15 seconds. It's not the end of the world."

"*Your* fifteen seconds."

Harry Boyles and Georgina Potter, the other two members of their team, remained silent. Both competitors were younger and knew better than to get in the middle of an argument between them.

"You were fine with second yesterday," Kyle challenged, referring to Dillon's results in the individual women's competition. Alecia Finch had arrived in Sydney intent on retaliation. After her loss in Key West, she'd laid out a textbook performance, and no matter how hard Dillon pushed, she'd been unable to catch her.

She considered telling him to fuck himself. He knew damn well she wasn't 'fine' with a silver podium finish. But what was the point? Kyle was Kyle, and no matter what she said, it wouldn't change the placings.

Seeking a truce, she reached across the table and dipped her finger in his beer, flicking foam in his direction. "Just stop whinging about the heat, will you?" She uncapped her water and brushed a trickle of sweat off her brow. It *was* hot. But she'd be damned before she complained about it.

"Incoming." Georgina gave a nearly imperceptible nod, just in time for the pinched voice of Isaac Fortin to ring over Dillon's shoulder.

"Tough luck today, eh?"

Dillon's grip tightened on her water bottle. It was bad enough to run into the vapid prick after a win in Florida. The last thing she wanted to do was listen to him gloat after their loss.

"Can't win them all, though, right?" The Canadian swept a glance around the table, before fixing his gaze on Kyle, seemingly oblivious to his unwelcome intrusion. "How are you holding up, Wood? Can't imagine how I'd feel, losing to a woman." His eyes flicked to Dillon. "Though, I suppose, in the case of Sinclair, I'm using the term loosely." He laughed, pretending to soften the jab with a wink. "She might just be the manliest member of your team."

Before Dillon could tell him to get stuffed, Harry was on his feet.

"How about you jog on, old man?" He crossed his heavily inked arms. Despite being the youngest member of their team, there was little doubt the twenty-year-old London boy could hold his own on the streets.

Isaac was unperturbed. "Cute, Sinclair—traded in your American fangirl for an English bulldog?" He brushed a flippant hand in Harry's direction. "Easy, pup. All in good fun. Don't get your shorts in a knot. See you all in Bermuda, eh?" Touching his brow in a mock salute, he walked away.

"God, I can't stand that bastard." Harry dropped back into his seat.

"Oh, cut him some slack," said Georgina, who'd been silent through the exchange. "It's not like he can go sit with his wife." She winked at Dillon. "She's probably still on the course."

Dillon would have laughed, but already she could feel Kyle's skeptical stare drilling into her, his attention long drifted from the meddling Canadian.

"Hold up a minute—American fangirl?"

*Fucking Isaac Fortin.* Of all the people she had to run into in Key West…

Dillon crushed the plastic bottle and screwed the cap back on. "No clue."

"Lies." Kyle drummed his fingers against his knee. "You're seeing someone—"

"I called it, didn't I?!" Jubilant, and returned to his boyish self, Harry pounded a fist on the table. "I told you both—she's been too bloody pleasant this whole trip. Texting. Smiling at her phone when she thinks no one's looking."

Georgina rolled her eyes. "Thank God someone on Tinder finally swiped right."

"Back to the *American* part." Kyle narrowed his eyes. "What was he talking about?"

For the last week they'd been in Sydney, Dillon knew he'd grown suspicious. Perking up at her phone calls. Trying to glance over her shoulder while she texted. Typical Kyle, unable to mind his own business.

"I ran into him in Key West while I was at dinner with a friend." She knew he'd never let her off that easy, but had to try.

"Who?"

"You're not her bloody keeper, Kyle, Jesus." Georgina rolled her eyes. "Tell him to piss off, Sinc."

"It's that girl from Hawaii, isn't it?" He barked a laugh. "You're unbelievable! Sam said you hooked up with her after——"

"—fucking Sam!" Of course she couldn't keep her mouth shut.

"Wait—the girl who hit you on your bike?" Now even Georgina wasn't on her side. "You ran into her in Florida?"

"She happened to be there on business. We got dinner. End of story."

"Bollocks." Kyle crossed his arms. "Let's hear the rest of it."

"There's nothing else to tell." And there wasn't, really. They'd had dinner. Well, *two* dinners. Two breakfasts. Lunches. Sunsets. Sunrises. Forty-eight of the best hours she could remember. They'd hardly shared a kiss between them, but it didn't even matter. By the time Kam left for Los Angeles, Dillon was wholly besotted.

"She's bloody why you're going to California, isn't she?" Kyle nearly tipped over his beer in his epiphany. "I couldn't understand it—

traveling over Christmas—when you're always so dead set on being home with Seren and your mum in Wales! But it's *her*, isn't it?"

"Kyle, simmer." Georgina swatted him, aware his outburst had brought the attention of other tables. "Sinc's a big girl—she can do as she pleases."

He ignored her. "You're the only human on the planet who could get hit by a car and end up on a date with the driver. I don't even get it."

"Photo, mate." Harry knocked his knuckles on the table. "Let's see the girl. Judge if she's worth it."

"I don't have one." It was a lie. Dillon had several. One from the aquarium. One the following morning after her swim, when Kam surprised her by wading out to join her in her street clothes. And one on the sidewalk outside the airport, where Kam had snagged her phone, pressed her cheek to Dillon's, and taken a selfie.

"Something to remember you by when you're famous one day?" Dillon had teased, secretly chuffed to have the picture.

Kameryn had shaken her head. "A souvenir in the hopes you won't forget me."

*Impossible.*

And a week later, Dillon had booked a charity race in Santa Monica over the Christmas holiday.

"She's an actress," Kyle was saying, scrolling through his phone. "We can find a photo. Sam said her last name was something like Kingsford…"

"Kyle, I swear—" Dillon looked to Georgina for help. "Georgie—"

The girl shook her head. "Sorry, Sinc. Mates judge dates. It's our duty."

With no help from Dillon, the trio managed to pull up a photo of one of Kameryn's headshots on IMDb. She looked a couple years younger, her hair a little shorter, but Kameryn all the same.

"Who the hell names their kid Kameryn E. Kingsbury? Makes her sound like she came from a line of long dead members of parliament." Kyle scrolled the page while the other two looked over his shoulder.

"I'll concede—she's hot." Harry shot Dillon a thumbs up, to which she returned the finger. He grinned. "I swear, in my next life, I'm going to be a lesbian. I don't know how you land the women you do, Sinc. Kelsey Evans. That one proper fit ting on the German team. *This* girl," he flicked a finger at Kyle's screen. "What the hell do you have, that I don't?"

"Charm," Georgina cut in, "manners, humor, good hygiene—"

"Whose side are you on? The two of you might as well bloody date —"

"Don't give them any ideas," Kyle sipped his beer. "He's got a point, though. It's not right, the girls you date—"

"To be clear: we aren't dating. I hardly know her."

"Right. Because you fly halfway across the globe for every lass that knocks you off your feet." He winked. "Pun intended."

"Look at this!" Harry's voice rose an octave in his excitement. "She was the voice of Relay in *Dragon Kingdom II*! My sister loves that movie."

Kyle wagged his eyebrows. "You struck gold, Sinc. Your Hollywood superstar was the voice of a polka-dotted dragon in a kid's cartoon. Big winner, there. Hope you're the one paying for dinner. I doubt those royalties will buy dessert."

"If you'd run a little faster this morning, I may have been able to afford it," Dillon shot back, but she couldn't hide her smile. Even Kyle's petty jealousy—or their second-place loss—couldn't put her in a bad mood.

# Scene 13

It was unlikely the sight of an eighty-one-year-old woman sitting in a plushly upholstered armchair would strike fear into the hearts of most people they encountered, but in my case, the moment I stepped over the threshold and laid eyes on the silver head of hair, I froze, immobilized with panic.

This wasn't just *any* eighty-one-year-old woman. This was Margaret Gilles. *Thee* Margaret Gilles. The author of *Sand Seekers*.

This was the woman who had stood toe-to-toe with the most powerful studio executives in Hollywood, for more than forty years, denying them the rights to turn her creation into a motion picture. The woman who penned a trilogy so epic, it had been translated into thirty-nine languages and sold more than 150 million copies worldwide, bypassing *Lord of the Rings*.

The woman who, five years ago when Spielberg had famously tried to woo her with the promise of "immortalization," had clapped back on the cover of *Vogue* with the quote "don't think you can dangle a rhinestone in front of a woman's face and tell her it's more valuable than the diamonds she already owns. I may be old, Mr. Spielberg, but I'm not an idiot." She'd gone on in the article to explain that eight-figure offers and guarantees of idolization were not something she was interested in. She had money. The fans had already canonized *Sand Seekers* and given her more than she ever dreamt of. *What would it take for her to sign on the dotted line, allowing her words to be put to screen,* the journalist had queried.

"Authenticity," had been her answer. "I want the story done justice."

It had been an admirable display of conviction, of belief in one's art, and holding true to one's own ideals.

And somehow, five years later, for reasons I couldn't begin to fathom, it had been Waylon MacArthur who convinced the stubborn Iowa author he was the man to tell her tale.

She'd accepted an offer from Universal for less than half of the other proposals on the table in order to maintain creative authority on the film.

But because of her famous principles and devout dedication to seeing her beloved characters done justice on the silver screen, it sent me into a tailspin when I walked into the table read and found the frail, hunchbacked, gray-haired woman sitting beside L.R. at the head of the room. She was smiling warmly, welcoming the actors who would turn her words and imagination into a living, breathing being.

I'd already been suffering from an intense wave of *what-if* self-doubts. What if I wasn't the right person for the project? What if I was too inexperienced, too boring, too… *me*? What if L.R. had made a huge mistake? What if today, at this first read-through, they realized I was nothing more than a fraud?

It was imposter syndrome at its finest.

It hadn't been until the complete script arrived three days earlier that I'd gone into full panic mode. I'd been wavering on uncertainty, but it was nothing like the surge of terror that struck me after finishing the screenplay, when I'd come to realize the magnitude of the role in which I would play.

I'd read the books. Four times I'd read the books. Beginning in junior high, when I discovered the series at the Scholastic Book Fair, and then again when I first heard about Universal's obtainment of the rights. And twice more over the months I'd been auditioning.

I'd felt I had a solid understanding of the character arc, the plot, the message. I was comfortable with what I thought Margaret Gilles wished to convey.

In short: I'd felt prepared.

Which should have been my first indicator that I had no idea what I was getting into.

In the novels, the six main characters were an ensemble piece, without any single one standing out above the rest. But when the entirety of the script was hand delivered to my apartment by a runner for the studio, sealed and marked confidential, I discovered the cast had been revised for the sake of filmmaking, and my own role amended. Previously, with only partial sides to go off of, it had been impossible to judge the complete weight of my part. But after a full read-through, I found the ensemble piece had been overhauled to highlight three main leads—the standout of which clearly belonged to me.

Suddenly, instead of sharing top-billing with half a dozen equals in a film projected to be the first to reach the billion dollar mark its opening weekend, I found my role, *Addison Riley*, leading the cast.

*I* was the central hero. *I* was the principle focus, supported by a star-studded list of names.

It was horrifying.

I could hardly make eye-contact with Margaret Gilles, even when she rose to bypass my outstretched hand—fingers shaking—and kissed me on the cheek.

"You are brilliance personified, my dear." Her midwestern accent held that gentle warble of a woman well past her prime. "L.R. was right—you're everything I envisioned Addy to be."

I stared at her, struck speechless. I was about to let this woman down. This woman who had held on to her principles in defense of her art. This master storyteller whose cherished words had transcended generations, captivating the minds of millions with the world she had built.

I managed a mumbled thank you—it was better than *boy, won't you be disappointed,* and took my seat.

I felt like the only nameless face in the room. If L.R. Sims wanted Addison Riley to be an unknown, he'd had the polar intention for the supporting cast. Aaron had called me a week prior—two headlining names had been leaked.

*Grady Dunn.*

*Elliott Fleming.*

Two of the hottest young actors working in the industry today.

Grady was a two-time Academy Award nominee, and had taken home the Oscar last year for his exquisite portrayal of Martin Luther King, Jr. in the film, *King*. A movie that had snagged every prestigious award the industry had to offer—including Best Picture. He was textbook handsome, and rumored to eat, sleep and breathe his characters from pre-to-post production, without a moment's break in between.

And Elliott Fleming was just… Elliott Fleming. He was the Leonardo of my generation. An actor whose versatility rivaled the likes of Timothée Chalamet, Christian Bale, Edward Norton. He'd headlined three features in the last twelve months alone. There was nothing he couldn't play. And from those who'd worked on set in his films, he was said to be charming, brilliant, sincere. Talented beyond comprehension.

Both men were established Hollywood elite.

They would play Noah and Oliver. Protagonist and antagonist. The love triangle of the story.

Grady. Elliott. And *me*.

And until I saw Margaret Gilles, they had been my paramount concern—the terror that I would seem like nothing more than a starstruck fan girl, out of her league.

But disappointing them took an immediate back seat to the overwhelming certainty I would let down the mastermind behind the epic saga—that I would fall horrifically short of her expectations of me.

By nothing short of a miracle, I stumbled my way through the first few scenes without breaking down in the tears that threatened my every breath. I was supposed to be strong. Forceful. Dogmatic, even. A girl who rises as a leader in a post-cataclysmic dystopian society in the midst of a nuclear winter. But I felt the furthest thing from it. I knew I was stiff, wooden, wrong in every way. I could feel L.R.'s stoney gaze focused on me. *I* knew he'd made a mistake. *He* knew he'd made a mistake. And from across the room, behind the plume of his bourbon-scented vape, Waylon MacArthur made no attempt to conceal his disgust unfolding with every line I uttered.

After MacArthur cleared his throat in unmistakable annoyance for what felt like the hundredth time, Margaret Gilles looked up from where she'd taken a seat beside me, her quick, dark eyes unaffected by age.

"Are you in need of a throat lozenge, Mr. MacArthur?" She didn't care that she was interrupting the scene. She hauled her bag onto the table—the stereotypical old lady purse with the contents rivaling an estate sale from the seventies—and rummaged through it noisily. What wasn't seen, however, was the hand she tucked under the table and pressed to my knee.

"I'm fine," Waylon barked, his chin sinking further into his chest as the vapor clung in a cloud above him. "Let's get on with it."

Over the commotion, Margaret gave me a reassuring squeeze. "Breathe, love. Just breathe."

I don't know why her simple gesture—her whisper of encouragement—touched me. Why her words soothed the disintegration of my thundering heart. Maybe it was seeing a woman—old, frail, seemingly weak—stand up to a man like MacArthur, challenge him as an equal, undaunted by his overbearing presence, his wealth, his esteem. Or maybe it was simply the gentle reassurance from a stranger that moved me in my time of need.

Whatever it was, it helped. We started again, and this time, I felt like I could find something of myself. Something of the resolute, competent person I knew I could be. I could finally focus on the words—the lines I'd read two dozen times. Maybe I could do this. Maybe this wasn't out of my reach.

When it was over, I knew I wasn't up to par, but I hadn't failed colossally. L.R. told me we'd talk soon to go over some notes he wanted me to focus on for the coming weeks.

It meant I wasn't fired. At least not yet. And Grady and Elliott and the rest of the cast were warm and welcoming.

Margaret Gilles hugged me, whispered in my ear that I was everything she ever envisioned for Addy, and slipped me her cell phone number on a gum wrapper, telling me to call her if I wanted to discuss anything. I assured her I would, and wished I'd known how to better thank her. For everything. Even Waylon MacArthur grumbled Merry Christmas as I passed him at the door on my way to the street.

I'd survived day one, even though all the way to my car I half expected L.R. or Waylon to rush out and fire me. But they didn't, and as I hit the 101 North, I wasn't sure whether to laugh or cry or scream.

There were twenty-one days until we started principal photography. But before that, I was scheduled for a handful of role discussions, combination rehearsals, costume fittings, and camera tests. Which meant I didn't have much time to get my head on straight, to figure it out, and prove I belonged in this industry.

However, despite my professional concerns and the attention they demanded, there was another thought that had been hammering on my door, waiting all night to be granted admission. I hadn't permitted my thoughts to wander during the table read—I wasn't so scattered as that —but now that it was over…

I flipped off the Christmas tunes humming through my radio and checked the time. It was shortly after eight. Dillon would have landed several hours ago—probably around the same time Waylon MacArthur was trying to figure out a way to justify cutting me from his cast. But Waylon was no longer forefront on my mind.

Dillon had flown to California… to stay for the holidays. She'd signed up for a charity race in Santa Monica, and while I wasn't entirely sure what that entailed, I knew it meant it wasn't rated and she wouldn't get paid. This trip was on her own dime, her own agenda. And it wasn't Santa Monica she'd come to see.

The thought was almost thrilling enough to wash away the vision of Waylon MacArthur glowering at me through his vapor haze.

I knew I wouldn't see her tonight. The race was first thing tomorrow morning. And if I'd learned one thing about Dillon Sinclair over the last two months, it was that *nothing* could disrupt her focus before a race day. Even an unrated one. She disappeared. Closed herself off. Ran her race. And then, picking up wherever she left off, reappeared as if she'd never missed a moment.

A habit I could probably benefit from in my own career. If I'd only had that kind of laser focus.

But here I was again—not ten minutes off the backlot, with my entire career in jeopardy—thinking about her. Daydreaming about her arrival. Wondering if it would be okay to text her? It wasn't that late, but I knew she was obsessive about her sleep.

Still, she'd only arrived a couple hours ago. She probably wasn't sleeping.

"Hey Siri, text Dillon." ApplePlay swirled to life, ready to do my bidding.

"Just finished with the read-through. Rough night, but survived by the skin of my teeth." The message immediately showed *read*, but there was no reply. I told myself not to take it personally—I already knew she'd be in her competitive mode. I'd see her tomorrow. Until then, well—I knew it was best to leave her be.

I pulled off on Melrose and inched my way through Hollywood. By the time I got to my apartment it was after nine PM.

I parked, grateful to find a spot two blocks over, since the shared driveway was full, and hurried for my front door. I'd lived there almost a year now—the neighborhood was decent—but I still didn't care to walk home by myself after dark. Even with two self-defense classes under my belt and can of pepper spray in my purse.

"Hey."

I startled, tripping over the short walkway step, almost falling on my face. I'd been searching for my keys and hadn't noticed the figure sitting on my stoop, or the bike leaning against my door frame.

"Holy shit." I stepped back, then laughed, unable to hide my smile. "What are you doing here?"

Her hair was matted to her head, her helmet hanging off the crook of her arm, her bare feet stretched out in front of her with her bike shoes still attached to her pedals.

"You said you had a rough evening. I thought I might swing by to wish you goodnight."

"Shouldn't you be sleeping?"

"Sleep is overrated."

This, I knew, for her was a lie. She slept ten hours a day, minimum. Without fail. Without regards to outside circumstances. It was part of her job. As important to her as training. Diet. Rest. Recovery.

Maybe I wasn't the only one neglecting my profession.

"Do you want to come in? Have a cup of coffee?" I panicked thinking about the mess on my kitchen sink. The post-it notes all over my dining room table. I'd planned to tidy things tomorrow morning, since Dillon had insisted I not come to watch her race. It was too trivial of a competition, she'd insisted. When I came to watch her—I'd loved that word, *when*—she wanted it to be something worthwhile. Something she could be proud of. I'd conceded.

"Can't." She stopped me before I got the key in the door, rising to her feet in that languid style of hers, like a cat waking from a nap. "Early morning."

"You really rode all the way here from PCH just to say goodnight? I thought you were supposed to rest before a race?"

"A pre-race ride didn't turn out so bad in Hana," she smiled. "I just wanted to see you, Kam-Kameryn." Leaning over, she kissed my cheek, then collected her bike, and disappeared down the poorly lit walkway.

# Scene 14

"Zero chance you'll ever kick it in."

"No?" Dillon looked over her shoulder at Kameryn, shifting the child-size soccer ball from hand to hand. She raised an eyebrow. "And what do I get if I win?"

Even in the neon glow of the Saturday night lights on the Santa Monica Pier, she could see the color touch Kam's cheeks. But tonight, instead of growing reticent, Kameryn remained committed to her flirtation, holding Dillon's insinuating gaze.

"It appears you'll have a choice between a pink dolphin or a blue leopard," she deadpanned, tilting her head toward the stuffed animals hanging on either side of the carnival game.

"Ah. High stakes, then," Dillon returned, dropping the ball to her feet. Her legs felt rubbery and unpredictable, weariness finally setting in from the race earlier in the day. Or, more likely, she knew, from jet lag and lack of sleep. The race had been irrelevant. A breeze of a swim along the shoreline, a flat cycle through the city, and a run down the famous oceanfront footpath with two hundred weekend warrior Southern Californians who'd turned out for the Christmas Charity fun.

*Tom Hanks was going to be there*, Kameryn had texted her the night before.

If he had been, Dillon never saw him. A disappointment, since she'd have enjoyed lapping him on the run.

But the race had given her the excuse to be in California over the holiday. It had given her an excuse to be standing on the overstated landmark pier, packed in amongst the sightseers and local teenagers, playing silly boardwalk games. It had given her the excuse to be there with Kameryn.

She sighted the target, drew back her foot, and tried to flick the ball through the largest hole at the cardboard goalkeeper's feet. It was poorly struck and sailed harmlessly off the fake net.

"All the good that soccer tattoo did you now," Kameryn whispered over her shoulder before reaching down to scoop up the ball and placing it on the plastic turf. Before Dillon could sling back a response, Kameryn neatly arched the ball through the smallest target in the furthest corner of the net.

"Winner winner!" The disinterested game attendant unenthusiastically rang a bell, waving his hand at the wall of stuffed animals. "Take your pick."

Kameryn smiled pointedly. "Did you hear that?" She grabbed a ridiculously large dolphin and pressed it into Dillon's arms. "I'll have you remember, I've won choice on prizes."

It wasn't often Dillon found herself flustered. Dalliance was her pastime sport, something in which she was well-versed. She knew how to play her cards and maintain the upper hand. It was seldom words or wit ever failed her. But tonight, Kameryn had her number. Dillon wasn't sure if it was because she was home, on her own turf, secure in her surroundings, or if she'd simply grown more comfortable in her skin—more comfortable with the idea of whatever this was. More comfortable with each other.

They'd talked almost daily since parting in Key West. About anything, everything, nothing. Dillon had worried, after the six weeks that had passed since they'd last seen each other, that an uncertainty may have arisen once again. But as soon as Kam showed up at the coffee bar where they'd agreed to meet earlier in the afternoon, she knew something had shifted. Something had evolved. There was none of the awkwardness she had expected. For the first time, nothing about them felt like strangers.

But in that absence of unfamiliarity, a different tension was beginning to surface—an awareness they both knew where this was heading, but with neither one willing to take the first step in that direction.

Kameryn had taken her free hand, drawing her away from the games toward an empty spot on the pier railing.

"I can't believe you swam in this this morning," she said, leaning over the side, staring at the gentle tide lapping against the pilings. "I can't even handle Dani's heated pool in the winter. Let alone the ocean."

"It's balmy, compared to the water off the Isle of Anglesey."

"Is that where you're from?"

"No, I was born in South Wales, in a village called The Mumbles, not far from Swansea. Anglesey is in the northernmost part of the country. My dad used to take me camping there every spring. It's where I learned to swim."

"Is he the one who got you into triathlons? Your dad?"

Dillon hesitated. It was such an innocent question. It deserved a simple answer—not the vortex of emotion it unintentionally summoned.

He'd taught her to swim, to bike, to run, hadn't he? So by default, the answer was yes, wasn't it?

It didn't matter that it was Henrik who'd crafted her—who'd molded her into what she was.

No, Henrik did not deserve the credit. He'd not been the one to spend hours treading water in the river, helping her perfect her stroke. Running behind her bike after removing her stabilizers, making sure she didn't fall. Doctoring every scraped knee and elbow after her runs down the trail.

All Henrik had done, day by day, year by year, was teach her to hate herself.

Shifting the oversized dolphin under her arm, she leaned her shoulder against Kam's.

"Yeah," she tried to curb her sigh, "he was."

Kameryn misunderstood the sorrow laced beneath her tone. "I feel guilty keeping you out this late. Isn't it past your bedtime?"

Dillon cleared her thoughts, inhaling the warm California evening, so different than the cold, rainy winters on the coast of Wales—where she would usually be celebrating the holidays with her mam and Seren.

"Well, technically it's almost morning back home. So at this rate, you're going to owe me breakfast soon."

"Oh yeah?" Still holding her hand, Kam stepped close enough that her hair—hanging loose around her shoulders—fluttered against Dillon's cheek in the breeze. "Is that what you expect from every girl who keeps you up all night long?"

"Only the ones I want to see again." Dillon knew she hadn't managed to hide the quiver in her voice, her breath falling shallow in response to the nearness of their bodies, standing as close together as they were. She darted her eyes away to the glittering reflection of the water, certain her pounding pulse was visible in her throat.

Kam smiled, clearly aware of the effect she had on her, and doubled down on her teasing as she leaned closer.

This was a girl Dillon could picture in the movies, a girl who made sense on the silver screen. There was no shyness, no uncertainty.

"And what do you think?" asked Kam. "Are you going to want to see me again?"

All at once, the current coursing between them made the sea air torrid. Dillon suddenly couldn't stand the people milling around them. The jaunty Christmas carols blaring through the buzzing speakers. The bright lights of the Ferris wheel. The laughter of rowdy teens enjoying the freedom of their weekend. She wanted shadows. Quiet. A cooling breeze.

"C'mon, Kam-Kameryn," she drew her off the rail, walking backward toward a set of wooden steps that led to the beach.

"Where are we going?"

"For a swim."

"No, absolutely not!" Kameryn laughed, defiant, but offered no resistance as Dillon lured her toward the sand.

Stepping off the staircase, she pulled her into the shadow of the pier, moving closer to the water, where the barnacled pilings grew mossy, the air turning damp, smelling of salt-soaked wood and drying seaweed.

"Okay, this is where I draw the line," Kam protested, still laughing as she drew up short just feet shy of the rippling tide. "I don't want to get my shoes wet."

"That's why we generally take them off for a swim," needled Dillon, kicking off her trainers and tossing the stuffed dolphin further up the sand.

"You know I'm not swimming with you," Kameryn said, even as she stepped out of her sandals. "I know you know that."

"Just your toes," Dillon coaxed, backing a few steps into the chilly water, stopping when it reached her calves. "Don't bottle out on me now."

"I'm not *bottling out*," Kam mocked her accent, taking a tentative step and gasping as a gentle comber broke against her shins. "Holy shit! It's freezing!"

Dillon laughed. It *was* cold. But she wasn't willing to admit it. "It's tepid, at worst."

"You're crazy. Has anyone ever told you that?" Kameryn stepped to her, catching her hands, preventing her from moving further away.

"Yeah, maybe once or twice." Dillon cocked her head. "Is that going to scare you off, Kam-Kameryn?"

"No." Kameryn brought her hands to her neck. "It's one of the things I like most about you." The response was more serious than Dillon had been expecting, the answer firm. It was as certain as the hands Kameryn slipped into her hair, pulling their faces together. As adamant as the mouth that covered hers.

Her thoughts, chaotic, spinning, diminished into a single collective channel as she became aware only of the warmth of their bodies pressed together, and the unfettered desire flaring through her, head to toe. She couldn't feel the water rising, soaking her to her thighs, or hear the muted strains of Mariah Carey belting out of the speakers fixed to whirling carnival rides.

She knew only that Kameryn's skin smelled faintly of jasmine, that her mouth tasted of peppermint from the tea she'd sipped as they'd strolled along the pier.

How long they stood there, knee-deep in the surf, she wasn't sure.

Long enough for her feet to go numb in the undulating tide. Long enough for the cold winter moon to work its way toward the middle of the starless sky.

When they finally drew apart, Kam's breath was shaky, despite her attempt to make light. "So, was that the swim you were hoping for?"

Dillon could feel a shiver flow through Kam's fingertips as she drew her back to dry land.

"Better than, I think." Her thoughts were momentarily derailed as her eyes swept across the dark shoreline. Wherever their shoes had been, the advancing surf had claimed them for the Gods of the Sea.

Kelsey would have gone mental. Kameryn only laughed as she realized the situation, kicking a clump of seaweed in her direction.

"It's going to be a long walk back to the car barefoot."

"Look on the bright side," Dillon scooped up the stuffed dolphin that had survived the rising tide, "we didn't lose your choice prize."

"Good thing. I'm expecting you to bring that all the way home with you, you know?"

"I'll buy it its own seat if I have to."

"First class?"

"Business, at least," said Dillon, tucking it under her arm as they started the trek across the sand toward the car park.

"So," Kam stopped to dig through her pockets in search of her keys as they approached her car. "Have you come to a conclusion?"

"About?"

"Whether you plan to see me again. Have I made the cut for breakfast?"

Coming up behind her, Dillon brushed aside her dew-damp hair and kissed the nape of her neck, drawing her lips slowly to rest against her ear. "What if I said the verdict was still out?"

"In that case," Kam huffed, feeding into her teasing, "I'd tell you—"

Her rebuke was cut off as she attempted to unlock the doors, inadvertently hitting the wrong button and setting off the car alarm. The sedan's headlights flashed and the horn and siren wailed, disturbing the peacefulness of the late-night atmosphere. "Shit!" She fumbled with the fob, punching at buttons until she silenced the car.

"You'd tell me what?" Dillon smiled against her temple. "To get stuffed? To go to hell?"

"Something like that." Kam leaned back against her.

"And what if I told you," Dillon whispered, breathing in the intoxication of the simple warmth of her body, the scent of her saltwater hair, "I was hoping for breakfast... lunch... dinner... midnight coffee... afternoon tea... whatever time you'll give me...?"

"Well, then," said Kam, carefully disentangling herself and reaching for her door handle, "I'd tell you I'd have to check my schedule. To see if I could pencil you in." She offered her a lofty smile before climbing into the driver's seat of her car.

"Don't break my heart, Kam-Kameryn. I make a pretty good omelette."

"I thought it was the girls who kept you up all night that owed you breakfast in the morning?"

"There's always an exception to the rules," Dillon laughed, bending down to kiss her before closing her door.

# Scene 15

My apartment seemed smaller, older, more cramped than it ever had before. I didn't know what I was thinking, inviting her here. Asking her to stay here.

Or, well, I knew what I was *thinking*. We both knew what I was thinking. What *we* were thinking. This wasn't a one-sided agenda.

But now I was having second thoughts.

Not about *that*.

I mean, it still occasionally flitted across my mind, the question of what the hell I thought I was doing—what exactly I had going on here? But for the most part, on that note, my worries were a distant matter. I'd cross that bridge when I actually managed to get there.

My primary concern currently revolved around this apartment, which I had previously loved.

It suddenly no longer felt up to par.

I imagined Dillon's flat was on the upscale end of London. From what I'd seen in the background during the few occasions we'd Face-Timed, her home was organized, modern, with high-beamed ceilings and a private balcony overlooking the River Thames. It wasn't the 1920s, copper-plumbed, five hundred-square-foot, Art Deco one-bedroom I lived in. The one I was presently loathing.

She'd booked a chic hotel a block off the beach in Venice. I could have stayed with her there. Last night, that had been my intention. After leaving the pier, it had been safe to say, neither one of us planned on sleeping alone.

But then, of course, true to Murphy's Law—which often seemed to be the guiding statute of my life—there had been no parking. I'd circled the block three times—almost as distracted by the narrow one-way streets as I was about her hand casually resting on my thigh—but it had come to no avail. There wasn't a single parallel space I could pull into, legal or illegal. I'd have gladly taken the risk of getting towed for squeezing into a *loading zone*, but it appeared I wasn't the first desperate driver willing to roll the dice on a Saturday night over the holiday weekend.

Heading into my fourth rotation of the surrounding blocks, it occurred to me I could invite her back to my place. But at the same time, it also dawned on me I'd neglected to finish washing my dishes, and it would have been nice to change my sheets, and there was a possibility all my clean towels were still wrinkled in my hamper.

So instead of making a rational decision, like realizing she probably wouldn't care if I had cups on the sink, I panicked in my growing agitation, and stopped double-parked in front of her hotel, throwing on my flashers.

"Well," I blurted, "tonight was fun. See you in the morning?"

Even in the moment, I knew I'd caught her off guard, but she was too considerate to question the change in our unspoken plans, no doubt assuming I'd lost my nerve.

"Uh, yeah," she'd given my knee a conciliatory squeeze, and then, before I could rectify my blunder, unfolded herself out of the car. "See ya tomorrow." Waving, she trotted barefoot to the double-glass doors, disappearing into the foyer.

I'd been so pissed at myself, I almost pulled out in front of an Escalade doing twenty over the speed limit.

By the time I crossed under the 405, I'd overanalyzed the situation so many ways, I couldn't drive another mile. I turned into a McDonald's parking lot and pulled out my phone, typing out a text and hitting send before I could second guess it.

*Is there any chance you'd want to stay with me the rest of the week? I could pick you up in the morning?*

*Sure* had been the immediate response. And then *I'm still looking forward to breakfast.*

I'd breathed a sigh of relief, pulled back onto the highway, and then panicked all the way home.

Where I was still panicking this morning.

As I scrubbed the crumbling grout from the backsplash behind my 1960s stovetop, I allowed my mind to wander.

*What would my morning have been like if I'd managed to find parking?*

Would I be asleep right now, in her bed, instead of whirling around my apartment on my third round of cleaning?

No. I knew myself better than that. There's no way I'd be asleep. We'd have… well, done whatever we'd have done, and then I would have laid awake all night, overthinking every aspect of my life in microscopic detail. I'd have internally freaked out a bit—I wasn't so naive to think I wouldn't have self-doubts about what I was doing—but then I would have circled back around to the undeniable acceptance that, for the first time in my life, whatever this was simply felt genuine.

Which would have led to my questioning, for the hundredth time, why I'd never seen it coming?

It wasn't like there were slide shows of *aha* moments flashing back through my childhood.

Me, catching a crush on the girl in pigtails who I'd sat next to in the third grade.

Me, realizing I'd developed an obsession with my fourth-period gym instructor my sophomore year in high school.

Me, suddenly registering the concept that all the boys I'd dated—Carter included—had just never felt quite… right?

None of that was true. I'd hated that girl in pigtails. Mrs. Williams, my PE teacher, had been a bitch—we'd called her Mrs. Blueberry—and as far as teachers I'd had the hots for, it had actually been Mr. Simon in homeroom with whom I'd had an ardent infatuation.

And when it came to the boys I'd dated? I liked most of them. I hadn't dated them because it was what was expected of me, or because I'd been pressured into wanting to fit in with 'normal' standards. I'd dated them because I wanted to. The same as it had been with Carter. Only him I'd actually loved—in my own way—off and on. He was thoughtful, smoking hot, and genuinely the kindest guy I knew.

Which led to the only *aha* moment that was true:

I'd loved Carter, but if I wanted to analyze it further, I hadn't been *in love* with Carter. I liked the sex, I usually liked his company, and when it was going well, I liked the *idea* of us. But it was only the idea. It wasn't the living, breathing reality. If it had been, we'd still be together. I wouldn't have dated half a dozen other guys in between. He wouldn't be On-Again-Off-Again-Carter. He wouldn't be my last resort whenever I got lonely.

Which meant I probably shouldn't have found any of this to be such a huge surprise. It was obvious I'd been searching for something—*someone*—different all along.

Insert—Dillon.

I didn't know where it was going. I knew where *this week* was going—I think we'd both made that pretty clear last night. But beyond that? Who knew? I don't think either of us cared. Which was just one more thing I liked about her. For as rigid as she was in her career, she appeared to have a pliant outlook on her personal life, taking things in stride.

My phone rang while I was balancing precariously on top of a pile of old textbooks I'd stacked on my dining room table, stretching to dust the blades of my noisy ceiling fan. Siri informed me it was Dani.

At 7:15 in the morning.

Which was not a good sign.

"Hey!" I called out to the speaker, carefully descending to the safety of the floor. "What's wrong?"

"You answered! Finally! Jesus, Kam. I've been trying to reach you for days."

She'd called yesterday afternoon. Once. No message.

"What's wrong?" I repeated, swooping up my phone, punching it off of speaker.

"Nothing's *wrong*," she sounded annoyed, "I just needed you to call me back."

"I'm sorry. I've got this thing going, and—"

"Yeah, yeah, your mystery commercial. I get it. Whatever. But listen—I need you to be here tonight."

It was Christmas Eve. We'd spent Christmas Eve together at her parents' house for as many years as I could remember.

The Annual Hallwell Gathering.

When I was a kid, my parents would go. So it would be the three of us Kingsburys—Darlene Hallwell's charity case—and the rest of Silicon Valley's Tech Elite.

"I can't." I'd told her this a week ago. I'd made it very clear.

*I was working.*

And no, so I'd lied, and wasn't working—but I sure as shit wasn't going to tell her about Dillon.

And for the record, I did actually feel bad. We'd never broken tradition. But I'd hoped, as a newlywed, she'd have her mind on other things. Maybe even begin her own tradition in her miniature mansion three miles down from her parents. Anything to let me off easy this year.

Apparently, it had been wishful thinking.

"You *have* to, Kam. Your parents are coming. I promised them you'd be here."

*What. The. Fuck.*

I was silent. The words racing to the tip of my tongue weren't things I could say. Not if I still wanted a best friend.

"Look, I know I'm kind of springing this on you last minute, but, honestly, Kam—it's less than a six-hour drive. It's not the end of the world. You can't tell me whatever project you're working on can't do without you for a few hours on Christmas Eve. Besides, your mom—"

"I'm not coming." I didn't give a shit what she had to say. *My mom.* My mom hadn't talked to me in over two years.

There was never a blowout, a specific event that ended our communication, but after my decision to quit UCLA in order to pursue my acting career, we'd just—fallen off. More and more, until eventually, we'd both stopped calling altogether. She nor my dad were ever happy with what I had to say. Every conversation turned back toward school, to their disappointment—how I'd let them down. Even when it wasn't said, it was always implied.

The morning I'd first heard about *Sand Seekers* holding open auditions, I'd wanted to call my mom. They were books we'd read together, a passion that we'd shared. She loved everything Margaret Gilles had ever written, often entertaining me at bedtime by quoting long passages from my favorite chapters by heart.

But I hadn't called. Nor would I call her when the news was released I'd actually landed the role. Somehow I doubted she'd care. Margaret Gilles held a master's degree, after all.

"You're seriously selfish, Kam." There was an edge to Dani's tone, a weapon I'd heard her reserve for others, but one she'd never used toward me. It pricked, slipping beneath my skin. "*You* closed them out. You can blame it on whatever you want, but it takes two to tango. Dinner's at eight. You know how to get here." And she hung up on me. For the first time in nineteen years.

Two hours later, I sat at my dining room table while Dillon heated water in my dented stainless steel kettle on the three-burner stovetop.

It wasn't the morning I'd anticipated, but at least it had convinced me to give up on my cleaning spree.

I'd picked her up, just as we had planned, but apparently Waylon MacArthur had validity in questioning my acting abilities because it took her less than thirty seconds to discern something was wrong. Despite promising myself not to dwell on Dani's phone call—she could take her unbalanced accusations and pound sand—I'd been unable to hide the hurt she'd stirred up revolving around the last five years of discord with my mom and dad. I don't know if it was because Dillon had respected my stated desire not to talk about it, or if it was the comforting hand she'd laid over the top of mine, or the weight of all of it combined, but we hadn't made it past Sepulveda before I burst into tears.

By the time we'd reached my apartment—thanks to the crawling drive through holiday traffic—I'd told Dillon about my parents, about UCLA, about Dani and her phone call, and Christmas Eve tradition at the Hallwells. Basically unloading the entirety of my pent-up frustrations in one long, run-on, red-eyed, blubbering mess.

Hot.

*Not.*

I'm sure a sobbing, emotional train wreck had been exactly what she'd had on her agenda for Christmas Eve morning.

But when I'd finished my lamenting—parked in front of my apartment—and offered to drive her back to her hotel, she'd laughed, pivoting in the passenger seat to stare at me.

"Don't be a clot, Kam-Kameryn," she said, reaching over to use the cuff of her sweatshirt to dry my dwindling tears. "I'll make us some tea." And then she'd let us into my apartment, complimented the hand-carved crown molding and black and white checkerboard tile, ignored the peeling paint, and sat me down at my own table, before making herself at home in my matchbox kitchen.

"You're not going to like what I have to say." She pushed a mug of tea in front of me and straddled the adjacent chair. "But I think you should go tonight—"

"No—"

"Hear me out before you make up your mind, alright?"

There was nothing I could argue about that.

She took a sip of her tea, cringing at the bitter-bagged brew, and then touched a finger to the Welsh dragon on her left wrist, exposed where her arm lay across my table. "You asked me about this one." She tapped the crisp design. "I got it for my dad—he died when I was nineteen."

"I'm sorry." I stared at the dragon, unsure what else to say.

"Yeah, me too, but it's beside the point." Folding her hands, she dropped her elbows onto the table. "I'd fallen out with him a few years earlier. He'd—," she paused, considering something before continuing, "he'd not seen eye-to-eye with a coach I'd had at the time. He felt I was pushing too hard—that I was *being* pushed too hard—to compete. To turn pro. And he'd worried I was losing my childhood in between. At the time, I didn't understand it. He'd always loved my sport, commending me on my dedication, encouraging me to follow my dreams. So it felt like a betrayal—him having hesitations. Proof, in my shortsighted mind, that he didn't believe in me." Her sculpted jaw worked side to side, her gaze turning distant into the cooling cup of tea. "In hindsight, his concerns had been well-founded, but I'd been so self-centered, I refused to believe he wanted the best for me. Instead, I cut him out. And, by default, my mam and sister, also. It was a decision I was encouraged to make. I was young and stupid—so focused on myself, I lost track of who to trust, and forgot the people who loved me."

She sighed, her thoughts heavy, before her eyes flicked back to the red outline of the dragon tattoo. I followed her gaze.

"When I made Team Great Britain, I'd just turned nineteen. The Olympics were two months away, and I was the youngest triathlete to qualify in history. It had been my lifelong obsession. A goal I'd shared with my dad since, well…" she shrugged, implying forever.

"I never even told him. We hadn't spoken in three years. My parents found out from the papers." Again, her jaw worked, the muscles of her neck tightening with tension. "He died two weeks before the Opening Ceremony. He'd been sick and I hadn't known." She brushed her thumb across the tattoo. "A lot happened over the next year—irrelevant to the moral of my story—but when I amended my relationship with my mam and sister, my sister—Seren—showed me a picture of this tattoo. My dad—a straight-laced, traditional, button-down kind of guy—had gotten it the day he learned I'd qualified. The only tattoo he ever had."

She laughed, but the sound was so full of hurt, it made my heart ache. I felt like I needed to look away, to give her space, but instead, she looked up and caught my eye. "Anyhow—it's not the same situation as yours, Kameryn. But if you'll consider a bit of unsolicited advice—go see your mam. Your dad. Make amends. You might be surprised. It's easy, while we're trying to prove ourselves—to *find* ourselves—to forget about the things that matter. Let them be disappointed in university. That's their right, as parents. They're allowed to have dreams for you, even if they don't align with your own. But don't hold it against them forever. Because most likely, what they want more than anything, is to see you happy. Even if they don't show it the way you'd like them to."

Raising her tea again, she touched the ceramic mug to her lips, and then knitted her brow in disgust. "I can't—you Americans simply have no taste buds." She rose and disappeared into my kitchen.

I stared at my checkered tile. She was right, it wasn't the same situation.

But I also understood what she was saying. If one of my parents were to die tomorrow, my heart would be shattered. As angry as I was at them, I loved them—I missed them. I longed for their Sunday morning phone calls. My mom's late-night texts. My dad's corny *You Might Be a Redneck If...* jokes from watching too much Jeff Foxworthy.

I wanted, so badly, to be able to call my mom when the cast was released for *Sand Seekers*. To send her a photo of me and Margaret Gilles. Maybe even invite her to the preview.

Maybe Dani hadn't been entirely wrong. It did take two to tango. It wouldn't kill me to give them a chance. I realized Dillon would probably give anything to spend a Christmas Eve with her dad again. No matter what humble pie was served.

Even if it meant spending it with the Hallwells.

She returned through the archway separating the living room from my kitchen and resumed her seat with a can of LaCroix from my fridge. "Hope you don't mind." She tipped the can in my direction.

"Would you go with me?"

Her eyes snapped up from where she'd been popping the tab. There was no hiding the fact that I'd surprised her. "To your mate's Christmas Eve?"

"To dinner. Even the Hallwells don't own Christmas Eve."

She laughed. "Don't you think they'd wonder what you're doing with me?"

I shrugged. "Bringing a friend to dinner?" Rising, I stepped in front of her, stealing the sparkling water and taking a sip. "They don't need to know what I *wanted* to be doing with you," I said, pressing the can back into her hands.

"No?" One blonde eyebrow lifted along with the corner of her mouth. "You've not exactly got a first-rate poker face." Smiling, she discarded the water onto the table and slid her hands to my hips, hooking her thumbs through my belt loops. "You think you're going to fool them, Kam-Kameryn?"

"I'm an actress! Of course I can," I tsked, entirely uncertain that was true.

But of two things I *was* certain. One, I wasn't driving to Northern California without her. And two, if we didn't leave immediately, my interest was going to be turned in another direction, and we wouldn't be leaving at all.

# Scene 16

Silicon Valley should have been named Saccharin Valley. That was Kam's warning as they pulled off the motorway and navigated through a series of densely wooded streets. Each brief clearing revealed a herculean estate grander than the last.

"Everything is fake here."

It seemed an odd observation from a woman who lived amidst the sparkling veneer of Hollywood, but Dillon didn't ask how one differed from the other. She was too busy trying to figure out how she'd let Kam talk her into joining her. Not because she was intimidated by her minted friends. Life as an elite athlete had given her plenty of experience navigating the circles of affluent culture. She was more concerned with how her presence was going to be received in regards to Kameryn.

From everything Kam told her about the Hallwells—about her best friend, Dani, in particular—the arrival of someone like Dillon in Kameryn's company wasn't going to be swept under the rug. She didn't want to be the cause of unnecessary adversity. Not when the evening was already destined to have Kam ill at ease.

But they were already there, pulling through the wrought iron gates and handing off the keys to a valet—hired, Kam assured her, only on the off chance Mark Zuckerburg finally accepted Mr. Hallwell's standing invitation—so there was no backing out now.

"How generous of you to decide to join us." Dani Hallwell wasted no time snarking her greeting the moment they passed through the entry archway built entirely of glass. The young woman was everything Dillon anticipated: Supercilious. Affected. Disdainful. Three things she'd found common amongst those whose wealth was vaster than their class.

Her blue eyes, disappearing behind lashes too long to be natural, flicked in Dillon's direction, sweeping her khaki trousers and white button-up blouse—the dressiest attire she'd had in her suitcase—and then immediately flipped back to Kam, the subtlety of one penciled-on eyebrow raising in question.

"Dani, this is my friend Dillon. She was in town for work over the holidays, so I invited her to join us."

"Hm." The sound was no more than a disapproving hum. "I'll see that my mother updates the seating chart." She didn't greet Dillon, or even bother to hide the look she shot Kameryn, promising a dozen other questions as soon as they were alone. "Your parents are in the game room." Her head tilted in Dillon's direction, but her pale gaze never met her eye. "Drinks are at the bar. Feel free to help yourself."

Kameryn hesitated when Dani tried to lead her away, but Dillon waved her on. "I'm good," she promised, and meant it. She was perfectly happy exploring the Hallwell residence on her own.

When the pair disappeared down the cathedral-vaulted foyer, Dillon spent a few minutes wandering the halls of the opulent home. It was gaudy, glittered in gold, and reeking of pretension. The other guests, packed in around the bar and kitchen, said nothing to her, but she could feel their eyes follow her as she left each room.

Finding her way to the second-story balcony, she stepped through the open French doors and settled in at the glass railing, looking out over the crystal blue infinity pool.

The home, despite falling in the middle of the suburbs, had been built on elevated ground, surrounded by mature oaks and buckeyes offering an elusion of privacy, veiling the proximity of the neighboring estates. It was an impressive spread, but nothing Dillon hadn't seen before. She'd become intimately familiar with the wealth behind "big tech" early in her career.

Leaning against the dew-gathered glass, she turned her gaze past the pool and terrace, to where the ground sloped down a grassy knoll. At the bottom of the hill sat several dozen rows of grapevines, their barren arms and gnarled trunks desolate in the grips of the winter chill.

She'd been at another Christmas party once, at a private home in Königswinter, south of Cologne. There, the grapevines had grown by the thousands, disappearing into a valley outlined by the Rhine. It had been her first holiday away from her parents, the first time she'd ever spent a Christmas outside of Wales.

Henrik had brought her there.

They'd made the four-hour drive from Reitbrook, a tiny quarter on the outskirts of Hamburg, where she'd been living at his newly established training center. A place that allowed her to swim in the Elbe in the mornings; run and cycle the narrow backroads of the farming community in the afternoons; be coaxed to his bed at night.

The drive had been picturesque, Western Germany rolling out like a panorama on a postcard.

The winery estate had belonged to Jonas Klein, the co-founder of *Innovixus*, a wearable data analytics company—the first sponsor she ever signed. The man had been married to Henrik's cousin and was his prime focus for obtaining a per annum endorsement for *sein hellster Stern*—his brightest star.

Six months earlier—exactly one week after her sixteenth birthday— she'd won the World Triathlon Junior Championships in Gamagori, Japan. The youngest athlete ever—male or female—to claim the world title. It had been enough to convince Jonas to shill out twenty thousand euros a year. A sum that had seemed staggering to Dillon at the time.

But she'd not really remembered much about Christmas in Königswinter, or her apprehension about meeting Jonas, the man who'd financially kicked off her career. Instead, she remembered the garden shed a stone's throw from the firepit where Jonas and his guests were toasting one another over Glühwein.

Henrik had steered her away from the view of the vineyards, pulling her through the small shed door. She'd felt unsteady, addled on wine, and high—on what, she wasn't even sure. Whatever Henrik had pressed into her palm earlier in the night. *Relax, mein kleiner Schatz,* he'd laughed at her uncertainty. *Have a little fun.*

It hadn't felt fun—the spinning in her head, the sweat dripping in her eyes. The swaying movement of the world around her.

The shed smelled of earth and pesticides, the walls lined with gardening tools to tend to the grapevines.

She hadn't needed to be sober to know what he was after.

And, like always, she gave in.

Twelve years later, she could still smell his breath, foul with alcohol. Feel the abrasiveness of the wooden door against her cheek.

It was the night she'd first realized she was in trouble. The night she should have gone home.

And still, she'd stayed.

How could she leave?

Henrik had made her a winner. At sixteen, she was already a world champion, wasn't she? It was everything he'd promised her. Her title.

Her ranking. A sponsorship worth more than all the prize money she'd ever earned.

*There's so much more to come, Schätzchen.*

And so, she'd stayed. Stayed while the money from *Innovixus* lined his pockets, paying nothing more for her than her entry fees. Stayed while he pushed her toward impossible expectations, rupturing her ACL in the first race of the following year's World Series. Stayed while she listened to him call the next girl *sein hellster Stern*—just one more of what turned out to be many 'brightest stars.' Stayed while he browbeat her, belittled her, and convinced her that without him, she was nothing.

Stayed until he'd cost her everything.

Shaking herself from the memories, she refocused on the Hallwell vineyard.

Tonight, of all nights, her mind had no right to take her places it didn't belong.

"Lobster roll?"

She turned, surprised to find she was no longer alone.

A young man leaned against the railing beside her. The cuffs of his dress shirt were rolled back, the top button at his collar undone. It wasn't, however, the pseudo-slum style of distressed dress she'd observed on Dani Hallwell's little brother and his mates. This boy wasn't wearing £1000 loafers or designer jeans with scuffs fashioned into his knees. His oxfords were well-worn. His trousers crisp, but the cut untailored. Something off the rack from a department store.

Observations courtesy of her sister, Seren's, fashion degree.

Whoever this boy was, he wasn't part of the "elite."

He held out a plate. There was a top-split bun overflowing with lobster meat beside a cup of melted butter.

"My eyes were bigger than my stomach. And as much as I'd enjoy tossing forty bucks worth of Hallwell seafood over the balcony to the birds, I don't think I can get away with it." He flashed dark eyes side to side, his lips curling into a conspiratory grin. "Cameras everywhere. I'd never hear the end of it."

He was handsome. Handsome in that way girls who liked tan, fit, five-o-clock-shadowed kind of boys would be driven wild.

"Not really my thing," she said, eyeing the secondhand sandwich.

"Haven't touched it, I swear."

Dillon laughed. "Thanks, but I'm good."

"You don't know what you're missing. The first two were—" he circled his thumb to his forefinger, touching his hand to his lips in a chef's kiss.

"Best make room for a third, then."

"Well, it was worth a try." He resumed his casual stance against the railing, plucking a strip of lobster off the sandwich and popping it into his mouth. "So, I take it you're not from around here?"

"I can't imagine what gave you that idea," Dillon rolled her eyes but didn't turn away. He didn't seem like a prick. Nothing like the other guests strolling around with their judgmental gazes and affected cavalier style.

"Well, if I commented on your very non-California accent, I'd feel incredibly cliché. So I'm going to go with…" he stepped back, taking a head-to-toe assessment, before nodding with conviction. "Your smell."

Dillon shot him a dubious glance. "I'm sorry?"

"Or, lack thereof."

"You've lost me."

"You don't smell like bullshit." He gesticulated around them. "Like the rest of this crowd."

"I see." She was careful to maintain her neutrality, not one to put her foot in her mouth on a whim. "Yet here we both are, at their invitation."

"Well, not exactly." He toyed with another piece of lobster. "I was a last-minute add-on—Darlene's going to pop an artery when she finds out—and you, it sounds like, were something of a *plus one* they weren't expecting." He cringed. "I'm sorry, that didn't come out like I meant it. What I'm trying to say is, on my way to raid the appetizer tables, I overheard Darlene ranting to Dani about her 'seating diagram'. Then when I came across you out here, it wasn't too hard to put two-and-two together and guess who she was referring to." His lips disappeared into a single line. "At the risk of digging this hole deeper, all I'm getting at is—I thought you might need a friend." He finally quit his rambling.

It should, she knew, have probably offended her, being told she was an unwelcome guest, knowing she was a topic of hole-and-corner discussion. But he was so appalled at his own lack of grace, it was hard to find herself indignant. Besides, it was exactly what she'd expected of arriving unannounced with Kameryn.

"And you felt a good consolation prize was a hand-me-down seafood sandwich?"

"No! Honestly, I—" he paused, realizing she was teasing, and offered her a broadening smile of pronounced relief. "I just know how it can feel here, sometimes. That's all."

Behind them a bell sounded from inside the house, ringing sharply through the double glass doors opening onto the balcony.

"The cocktail bell," he whispered with exaggerated mock propriety, glancing at his watch. "Seven PM on the dot. Summoned like a herd of cattle." He motioned toward the house. "Join me for a drink? It makes the night more tolerable."

"I should probably find my friend," said Dillon, following him through the door. She'd kept an eye through the glass, surveying the faces waltzing by, but Kam hadn't been amongst any of them. A good sign, she hoped, that perhaps her reconciliation with her parents had been successful. That, or she was about to find her crying in a bathroom.

"Oh, Mr. Hayes!" Darlene Hallwell's piercing voice accosted them as they passed through the unfriendly setting of the formal sitting room. Half a dozen men lounged around a flatscreen showing the reruns of an American football game, while other guests filtered in from adjacent hallways. "I was unaware you were joining us."

"As was I. Dani texted me last minute. Someone off the A-list invitees must not have shown," he matched her spurious smile. "Always gracious of you to host on Christmas Eve, Mrs. Hallwell."

"Hm." It was the same censured murmur as her daughter, from the same botoxed lips. Her gaze drifted over his shoulder to Dillon. "Leave it to Dani to take in all the wanderers. I don't know how she possibly expects me to squeeze in another setting at the table."

"If you loan me a tux, I could make myself useful with the serving staff, Mrs. Hallwell. Problem solved."

The woman ignored his jest, her attention diverting to where her daughter was approaching them from her most recent trip to the bar.

"Are there any other unexpected arrivals I should be made aware of, Daniella?" she asked, brushing past her daughter without waiting for a reply.

Dani paid her no mind.

"Carter!" she squealed, the sound cutting through the jazz instrumental of *God Rest Ye Merry Gentlemen*. "You came!" Her uneven steps and glassy eyes attested to the fact that the martini in her hand was not her first of the evening. "How good it is to see you!"

*Carter.* The name returned Dillon's attention to the young man beside her. Kam had mentioned a boyfriend from secondary school. One who still lived in her hometown. And by the simper on Dani's lips, there was no question the last-minute invitation hadn't been coincidental.

"I—hi," he gave her an awkward side hug, evidently taken back by the overt enthusiasm of the greeting. "Thanks for the invite."

"Totes," Dani trilled, still swaying. Vodka spilled over the rim of her glass as she tipped it toward Dillon. "I see you've already met Kameryn's friend Damian."

The mistake was so deliberate, Dillon almost let it go, not wishing to give the conniving twit the satisfaction of the correction. But the annoyance of being called by the wrong name all night trumped her desire to skip the little game.

"It's Dillon, actually—"

"Oh, right," Dani waved off the error as irrelevant. "I knew it was one of those—what do they call them—*gender-neutral* names?"

"Kind of like the name *Dani*?" Carter asked with zero attempt to disguise the dig. He winked at Dillon, who hid her smile, but it was unnecessary because Dani's attention was already whirred in another direction.

"Kameryn!" she sloshed her glass through the air, waving it like a beacon. "There you are! Look who's made a surprise appearance!"

Dillon turned to see Kam stop midstep, the smile fading from her face as she laid eyes on Carter.

"I was just making introductions. As I was saying—Carter, this is Dillon, one of Kameryn's work acquaintances—she didn't have anywhere else to be for the holidays, so she's joined us. And *Dillon*," she overannunciated the name, "this is Carter, Kameryn's boyfriend."

"He is *not* my boyfriend." Kam haltingly resumed her forward motion.

"Riiight," Dani singsonged, "whatever you're labeling it these days —we all know you're a thing." She shot a pseudo-confidential smirk at Dillon. "Sweethearts since high school, she just likes playing hard to get."

Kameryn's hands balled into fists at her side. "Dani. *Stop.*"

A roar went up from the men watching the TV, briefly diverting the tension in the room, and then the low murmur of the pundits returned.

"Hey, Kam." Carter's laugh was tentative as he turned his efforts toward peacekeeping. "Safe bet to say you didn't know I was coming?"

"No." Kameryn didn't smile.

"Well, I guess it wouldn't be a Hallwell Christmas without one of us playing the pigeon in Dani's games." The line of his smile turned hard as his gaze shifted to Dani. "We can certainly always count on you to be a meddling pain in the ass, can't we, *Daniella*?"

It was impossible not to appreciate the entire disregard he had for caring whether he got tossed out by the Hallwells. Though Dillon suspected he knew the action was unlikely. He had the sort of demeanor of someone accustomed to getting away with blatant effrontery.

"I have no idea what you're talking about." Dani turned up her chin, speaking down the barrel of her perfect nose. "I simply thought we might all spend the evening together, for old time's sake."

"Always you, Dani Hallwell—so full of thought and consideration," Carter mocked, before continuing. "Tell me, what are you ladies drinking?" The question was aimed toward Dillon, but his eyes were only on Kameryn. It was obvious he wanted to please her. "Is it still a Manhattan?"

Kam's hands slowly unballed from their fists, though Dillon could still feel the edginess radiating off her. "No. I mean—okay, I guess."

"Great." He glanced toward Dillon. "And what can I get you, my balcony buddy?"

Dillon held up a palm to decline. "I'm good."

"You sure?"

"It's *free*, if that's what you're worried about." Dani fished the olive out of her martini, sucking the pimento from the fruit.

Kam's mouth shot open, but Dillon pressed a halting hand to her forearm. The woman was a despicable bitch, but she wasn't worth a scene.

"Well, with that kind of generosity, how could I refuse? A water would be grand."

"One Manhattan, one water, coming up," said Carter. "In fact," he smiled, "Dillon, I'll make yours a double." He turned to Dani, who gave a shake of her nearly empty martini glass, but instead of acknowledging her unspoken request, shoved his plate of dissected sandwich into her unsuspecting hand. "Be a dear and toss that for me, will you, Dani Girl?" Without looking back, he sauntered toward the bar.

# Scene 17

I could have killed her.

I could have literally shoved her off the second-story balcony and watched her body splatter on the hand-carved Italian marble framing the saltwater pool.

Okay, maybe that was a step too far. I didn't want her to splatter. Just a dull, satisfying thud. Anything to knock the wind out of her conniving little sails.

I couldn't believe it, her audacity to call Carter. She didn't even like him. Ever since he'd turned down a lacrosse scholarship at Notre Dame to study plant biology at Berkeley, she'd insisted he'd lost his 'jock card.' He'd only ever been invited to Christmas Eve dinner as my date, which meant he'd been absent the last two years.

And the only reason he was here now was because she—the Queen of Provocation—wanted to cause trouble.

She'd taken one look at Dillon and not liked what she'd seen. She'd practically said as much to me as soon as we left her in the foyer.

"You know what people are going to say about you—seeing you with someone like her!"

*Someone like her.*

If we hadn't already stepped into the game room—if my mom hadn't already spotted me and been making her way across the imported Turkish carpet—I'd have turned around and walked straight back to my car.

"You think I give a shit what any of these people say about me?" I hissed. And then, like the coward I am, added, "she's my friend and nothing more."

My mom had reached us at that point and I'd forgotten about Dani and her bigoted bullshit, trying instead to navigate the rollercoaster of emotions drummed up after not seeing my parents in over two-and-a-half years.

I'd survived that crucible. We'd spent an hour—my mom, dad, and I—tentatively maneuvering the murky waters of a strained relationship, building a bridge with small talk and carefully chosen anecdotes of holidays past. It had only been a bandaid, but at least it had been a start.

By the time the bell had rung for Darlene's 'cocktail hour,' I'd been feeling pretty good about my decision to come. That was, until I'd excused myself from my parents to go find Dillon, and discovered exactly how guileful Dani had been in my absence.

*She just likes playing hard to get.* Fuck you, Dani!

It had been all I could do not to lunge at her and wrap my fingers around her skinny little throat.

"I hate her," I practically yelled after Dani had disappeared for another martini and I'd dragged Dillon with me into the furthest downstairs guest bathroom. "I can't believe she invited him!"

Dillon was unperturbed. "He's honestly quite a nice guy."

"He's always nice, but that's not the point!" I was mad she wasn't as mad as I was. "She only did this because—because—" I threw up my hands, almost knocking a vase of fresh-cut flowers off the sink. "Just —God! She can be such a bitch, I swear!" I emphasized my frustration by snatching a petal from one of the innocent orchids propped in the ceramic vase.

"Well, I won't refute you on that one."

I looked up to find her smiling at me in the mirror. She stepped closer until I could feel the heat of her body through the black mini-dress I'd decided to wear. One that stopped mid-thigh, and hung off my shoulders just right. One I'd chosen without anyone but her in mind.

"I take it she doesn't approve of the company you're keeping?" she continued, reaching around me to recenter the clasp of my necklace that had slipped to the hollow of my throat. It brought goosebumps to the nape of my neck, her slow, deliberate fingers, and I had to close my eyes when she pressed her lips to the tender skin just behind my ear. "I mean," she said, and I could hear that she was still smiling, "I guess you can't blame her."

"It's none of her damned business." I'd meant it to come out with conviction, but instead, the words had barely escaped my lips. They'd fallen breathily short as her free hand trailed a linear path down my side, the tips of her fingers stopping just below where the satin hem of my dress hugged my thigh.

I don't know how she did it, turning my thoughts away from everything but her. How the simplest of touches could make me forget Dani and her meddling. Darlene and her asinine seating chart. My parents and our inability to scratch anything below the surface. Carter and his wounded puppy dog look when he realized I wouldn't be going home with him tonight.

"Let's bail before dinner," I said, leaning back against her, wanting nothing more than for her hand to explore further. Caring nothing for the fact that we were locked inside a bathroom in the bowels of Hallwell Hell.

"No chance of that, Kam-Kameryn," her fingers traveled the wrong direction, back to the safety of my hip, her lips still smiling against my ear. "No way you're getting off that easy. You dragged us all the way up here. We're sitting through dinner, dessert, after-supper cocktails, whatever this tradition entails. You have to make nice. Smile. Sit wherever they seat you. Give your parents your full attention. Humor your high school boyfriend—because, really, I'll say again: he *is* a nice guy. Do whatever it is you normally do. And all the while knowing," her mouth traveled down the slope of my neck, her breath warm against my bare collarbone, "that after we leave here tonight, I'd really like to locate that hidden tattoo."

I didn't even know a heartbeat could hammer through a hipbone, but I was certain she could feel mine. It was a good thing, I guess, that the soundproofing in the Hallwells' thirty-million-dollar mansion was no more up to par than the cardboard-thin walls of my apartment. If I hadn't been able to hear the Christmas music and murmur of voices filtering through the ceiling vent from the floor above, I was positive I would have attempted to convince her that commencing a Where's Waldo exploration for my quarter-sized tattoo would have been far more gratifying than suffering through dinner with the Northern California edition of Keeping Up With the Kardashians. And despite her teasing showcase of impassivity, I had a feeling it wouldn't have taken much to change her mind. Which was entirely *not* what I needed to do in my best friend's bathroom with my parents sipping cocktails twenty feet above.

Resigned to return to the party, I turned to face her, leaning back against the marble counter as *Jingle Bell Rock* filtered in through the air duct in the wall.

"You think you'll get so lucky?" I asked glibly, tossing my hair over my shoulder, aware of the way her eyes lingered against my bare skin. I reached forward, tucking the bruised petal of the orchid into the front pocket of her slacks.

"I do." There wasn't even a smile of humility behind her shrug, and I was the one who ended up blushing, foiled at my own coy game. She reached up, toying one final moment with the emerald pendant that hung at my throat—the gift of my birthstone my parents had given me on my eighteenth birthday—and then drew the tip of her finger up my neck, past my chin, to rest at my bottom lip. "And what's more," she said, her green eyes glowing, "I think you're going to sit up there the rest of the night, unable to think about anything other than how I'm going to find it."

She leaned forward, having to tip her head up to conquer the height of my heels, and kissed the corner of my mouth. Then, with all the insouciance in the world, she turned, unlocked the bathroom door, and vanished into the hall.

Darlene, of course, won.

I'd wanted to sit next to Dillon. It was what would have been appropriate, given she was my guest and all. But between Dani and her mother, they were never going to let that happen.

Instead, I sat wedged between my parents, forcing myself to swallow down braised duck while doing my best not to stare at the far end of the table, where Dillon and Carter had been squeezed into a corner hardly large enough to accommodate a toddler. Neither seemed to mind. They laughed over things I couldn't hear, and I watched from the corner of my eye as Dillon surreptitiously pointed out which fork to use for the oysters, saving Carter from what would have been deemed an unforgivable faux pas in the Hallwell household. I wondered where she'd learned the proprieties of an extensive formal dinner setting, and I also wondered what it would feel like to graze my lips along the v-shaped sliver of skin above her top button.

I could feel Dani's inscrutable gaze on me every time I dared a glance toward that end of the table. She was willing me to misstep, willing me to show something I shouldn't.

Part of me wanted to pull out my phone and shoot her a text. *Whatever your suspicions are, triple them, and then maybe you'll be headed in the right direction.* But of course, I didn't. *Keep the peace,*

*Kameryn*, I told myself. Just get through dinner, tell my parents good-bye, and then—out that door, into the car, and from there, I'd just go with the flow wherever the night led us.

But no, Dillon hadn't been kidding about forcing me to stick to tradition.

When the meal ended and the majority of guests departed, leaving behind only the immediate family and friends, I tried to make a break for it.

"Well, this evening was lovely, as always, Mrs. Hallwell," I said as the remaining company worked their way from the dining room to the salon. *Thank you, of course, for having us* had been the words waiting at the tip of my tongue. But before I could utter them, Dani had poured herself to my side, balancing between my arm and a life-size sculpture of a muscled torso I thought might be an original Rodin.

"You aren't skipping out now, are you?" she demanded, teetering on her sky-high stilettos. I could see her husband, Tom, watching from a dozen feet away, gauging whether it was time to intervene.

*Do so at your own risk*, I thought, but without any true pity. He'd been the one stupid enough to marry her, after all.

"Yep—long drive home." I carefully extracted my arm from her grasp. If she was going to topple over, she could take the Rodin with her. I wasn't taking one for the team.

"We still have dessert! And what about *Two Truths and a Lie*?"

It was the party game they played every single year. It was the last thing I was hanging out for.

"Yeah, what about *Two Truths and a Lie*?" Dillon appeared, holding a bottle of *Pellegrino*. "We couldn't possibly miss that."

Dani was too drunk to discern the subtlety of her sarcasm.

"See, even your friend wants to stay." She stumbled, clutching the nub of a severed shoulder, her nails grating down the bronze chiseled six-pack.

Tom made his move, coming to the rescue of his damsel in distress, and I took the opportunity to snag Dillon's arm, drawing her away from the circus.

"What are you doing?" I hissed once we were tucked safely away in an alcove. "We'll be here all night!"

"Another hour hanging out with your folks won't kill you, Kam-Kameryn. Besides, I was promised dessert."

I jerked my head up too quickly, looking for her double entendre, and was rewarded with a smile that made my spine tingle.

"Get your mind out of the gutter, Miss Kingsbury. I was referring to the banana cream tart. Carter said the one served tonight is unparalleled."

"It's from *Tartine Bakery*—I promise, it's overrated. We can find something better on our own."

"Well, I guess I'll need to try the tart first to be the judge of that." She hiked a brow at me, before tipping her head toward the salon. "Shall we?"

"You're really going to make me stay here, aren't you?"

"I told you—you talked me up here, I'm entitled to the full experience. Not just the abridged evening."

"I think you just enjoy tormenting me," I said, reaching for her hand, but then thought better of it and settled for hooking my arm through hers. Everyone else had disappeared from the hall, but I wasn't going to risk it. "I'll have you know, Dillon Sinclair, I can give as good as I get."

"I'm counting on it," she whispered, before drawing me from the alcove to rejoin civilization. "Now tell me, what are your two truths and a lie?"

"I can't tell you before the game," I faked indignance. "That would be cheating."

"Then give me a preview of how to play—something different than whatever PC banality we'll have to suffer the rest of the evening."

I stopped a dozen steps from the open doorway where I could hear Darlene ordering her husband to open a bottle of Brut. Dani was arguing with Tom. My parents, I knew, would be sitting on the couch nearest the fireplace. Dani's little brother, Marcus, would be watching silent videos on his phone. And Carter would be on the loveseat beneath the painting of a fig Dani loved to boast had cost seven hundred thousand dollars. An odd flex, I always thought. For seven hundred Gs I wanted a lot more than abstract fruit on a wall.

"Fine, but you'll never guess correctly," I postured.

"We'll see."

I rolled my eyes at her cockiness, secretly loving it.

"I've had a one-night stand."

"Okay." She waited.

"I've never been to Wales."

Her lips twinged. "Okay."

"I've never slept with a woman."

Her smile widened. "Okay."

"Well? Now you're supposed to guess which one isn't true."

"A guess, by definition, indicates uncertainty."

"And are you so positive of being right?" I baited, already knowing she would be. I'd made the answers easy enough. She already knew I'd never been to the UK. And, well, the other two didn't take much deducing to determine which was which.

"A hundred percent." She fiddled with the tie of my dress, letting the black satin slide through her fingers. "The only question I have is whether you want to turn one of your truths into a lie?"

I could feel the pounding of my heart in my bones again. "I don't know—do you think there's a last-minute flight from San Jose International to Wales?" I leaned closer to her, lowering my voice. "We could convert both truths then."

I loved knowing how badly she wanted to kiss me. Knowing, for all of her bravado, how easy it was to put a crack in her veneer. Slowly, purposefully, I tugged the tie of my dress from her fingers, edging closer still. "And that way," I whispered, "it would also prevent you from turning my lie into a truth."

Her lopsided smile appeared as she worked out the implication. "No flight across the Atlantic necessary to safeguard that lie, Kam-Kameryn. I already canceled my hotel. You're stuck with me for at least a few days."

Before I had time to respond, Darlene's voice called out from the threshold.

"Are you planning on joining us, Kameryn, or shall I start charging you rent for my hallway?"

I took a staggering step away from Dillon and lunged toward the door.

*Smooth move there, moron.*

I may as well have shouted "no incriminating behavior here, Mrs. Hallwell. We're certainly not talking about punching a stamp on my lesbian card as soon as we escape your heteronormative compound."

Instead, I smiled brightly and asked if I could be of any help with the dessert tray.

The chitchat. The game. The champagne. It all felt endless.

I'd once again taken a seat by my parents—directly next to the fire, as anticipated—and mentally twiddled my thumbs as Uncle-This and Cousin-That took turns boring everyone with *I've never had liposuction* and *I attended Bill Gates birthday party*.

I pretended not to know Carter's lie claiming he'd never been to Carson City. I knew the clue had been aimed at me, trying to gauge where we stood. The weekend before we'd started our junior year of high school, the two of us had driven to the former gold mining town on a whim. It had been there, in a seedy motel room on a duvet covered in cigarette burns, that I'd lost my virginity.

I felt a little bad, making a point of choosing *I built a greenhouse for George Lucas* as his fiction, knowing full well the job had been a major sense of pride for him as one of his first commissions after graduating Berkeley. But I'd needed him to get the hint. I hadn't returned his calls in months, long before meeting Dillon, and no matter what happened with her, he and I were over. And not over like the other times. This time, we had to be finished. It wasn't good for either of us to keep stringing things along.

He took the blow on the chin, shooting me a two-can-play-at-this-game wag of his eyebrows, and returned fire by declaring "yeah, maybe on a week of Sundays," to my truth that I'd gotten straight As my senior year in high school.

*Well played.* I tipped my glass in our silent communication. I hated that behind his bluster I knew he'd been stung. It was all the more reason I wanted to murder Dani for inviting him and giving him the wrong impression.

"You're up, uh…"

My thoughts resurfaced to the present as Mr. Hallwell waved a stubby finger in Dillon's direction. I realized he didn't know her name. In truth, he probably had no idea where she'd come from. But he was fogged, having joined his daughter in the race to get loaded, and didn't seem to mind or care that a stranger was sitting in his living room.

"Alright," said Dillon, catching my eye from where she was lounging beside Carter. "Let's see. I speak four languages. I don't own my own apartment. I've won two Olympic medals."

"You understand it is *two* truths and one lie, yes?" verified Darlene from where she'd kicked off her Jimmy Choo heels and tucked her stockinged feet beneath her husband.

*Oh, for God's sake.*

I spun the stem of my glass between my fingers, grateful I'd stealthily swapped out my champagne for sparkling cider several rounds earlier. Usually, I'd be a bottle deep by now—turning down free Dom Pérignon wasn't something I was in a habit of—but tonight, I wanted to be sober. A good thing, probably, for both me and Mrs. I'm-a-Douche Hallwell.

"Uh, yes. Got it." Dillon smiled innocently. I knew she'd set them up. They'd refuse to believe someone like her was as accomplished as she was.

After a rapid-fire discussion in which I didn't take part, a consensus was reached and Darlene, taking over for her daughter—whose speech had become too slurred to be intelligible—assumed the role of spokesperson.

"Well, given you look very... *athletic*," she chose the word carefully, "I suppose the Olympics are a possibility."

The way she said *athletic* hadn't meant fit. It meant *gay*. I dug my fingernails into my palm, but Dillon didn't bat an eye.

"And I believe earlier you mentioned you lived in London. As my husband pointed out, it is one of the most expensive housing markets in the world outside of Asia. Owning property there is no small feat. So, I'm inclined to believe the most likely falsehood is your ability to speak four languages."

Dillon flicked her fingers in a *fair enough* gesture. "All good reasoning, but I'm sorry to disappoint. Aside from English, I speak Welsh, German, and French."

"*Damn it*! I knew it was the Olympics," said Tom, smacking his fist to his knee. As the newest member of the Hallwell clan, he took losing in front of his in-laws very seriously.

"Dillon's competed in three Olympics and is a two-time medalist," I said, unable to hold my tongue any longer.

This snapped Dani out of her torpor. "I thought you were in the film industry?" She swallowed the remainder of her champagne, staring straight at me. "In town for *work*?"

"Different line of work." Dillon drew Dani's attention back to her. "I'm a triathlete."

"But what do you do for a living?" asked Darlene. Of course the woman who'd gotten her stilettos stuck in the football field turf at our first high school home game couldn't comprehend life as a professional athlete.

"Well, I swim, bike, and run mostly."

"For a career? How impressive," she said flatly. "And a gold medalist as well?"

It wasn't a mistake. She'd caught on that I'd said *medalist* and not *gold medalist*. If you'd won gold, you said so. Everything else fell under the umbrella category.

Dillon remained unperturbed. "No golds. Just silver and bronze."

"Oh, how terribly frustrating." Darlene swirled the champagne at the bottom of her glass. "To come so close to winning and fall short."

"Fall short?" I uncrossed my legs so quickly I nearly upset my mother's spiked eggnog she'd been balancing in her lap.

For two decades I'd remained silent while being insidiously put down by nearly every member of the Hallwell family. I'd taken their underhanded barbs without a breath of defense for as long as I could recall. But tonight I'd had enough. I wasn't going to just sit there and listen to them put down Dillon.

Dillon, however, cut me off short, preventing my rush into battle.

"Extremely frustrating," she said, overriding my outburst while giving me a subtle shake of her head. She appeared unaffected by the woman's onslaught of insults, and I realized the last thing she needed was a knight in shining armor. Unlike me, she had nothing to prove to these people who weren't worth her effort.

"Fortunately, if all goes well, I'll have another chance."

"You have your sights set on Los Angeles, then?" my dad asked. As a true-blue sports aficionado, there wasn't a competition across the globe he wouldn't relish discussing. He was also, however, a pacifist who hated altercations. I'd felt him side-eyeing me, aware of my growing frustration, ready to dive in wherever he could to avoid any possibility of contention. *Kiss-up Kingsbury* he'd once told me they'd coined him in high school. I supposed the apple hadn't fallen far from the tree.

Settling back in my seat, I stewed over my missed opportunity to shove Darlene's crystal chalice up her cosmetically-constructed tight little ass, nursing my Martinelli's as the game dwindled to a conclusion. Small talk took over with the arrival of dessert, as two tuxedoed caterers distributed plates and offered the choice of sgroppino or Irish coffee.

"I understand you train hunters, Mrs. Kingsbury?"

Dillon had come to sit on the ottoman across from me, where she'd spent a few minutes chatting about the upcoming Olympics with my dad, before turning the conversation toward my mother.

My mom brightened and my heart sank.

We were never going to get out of here.

They chatted about horses as I gave in and snagged an Irish coffee. I learned Dillon's sister was an equestrian—an eventer who had served as an alternate on Great Britain's Olympic team—and Dillon had grown up riding as well.

"Two Olympians in the same family!" My dad was enthralled.

I could tell they liked her. And honestly, what wasn't there to like?

She leisurely chatted with them about the UK, about travel—my mother was fascinated by all the places she had been—and even held her own on my father's favorite topic: sailing. She listened patiently as he launched into his retirement dream of circumnavigating the world on a thirty-foot ketch. My mother, unsurprisingly, managed to direct the conversation toward education, where I discovered Dillon had graduated from Cardiff University, earning a degree in physiotherapy.

And there it was—the clincher. Hook, line, and sinker, my parents were officially enamored.

I wondered, absently, as my head lightened with whiskey, if they'd still be so enamored if they could see beneath the ottoman, where I'd slipped off my heel and snuck my toes up the hem of her slacks.

Probably not, I decided, entertaining myself as I teased the bare skin of her calf, watching her try to keep a straight face while my mother droned on about the difference in the cost of horse-keeping between the US and UK.

My parents weren't homophobic. Collectively, they were moderate in their views of politics, supported equality in both gender and sexual orientation, and I'd never heard a disparaging word about the queer community from either of them.

But the thing was, their daughter wasn't gay. It was perfectly acceptable for someone like Dillon. Someone else's daughter. Just not theirs. I knew my mom still clung to the hope that I would marry Carter. Since the day he'd shown up on my doorstep to pick me up for our sophomore homecoming—red rose for me in one hand, yellow rose for my mom in the other—I knew she'd been planning what pony she would buy for her grandchildren.

I doubted she'd have felt the same if my tenth-grade date had been named Candice instead of Carter.

"Jane!" Darlene swept over, interrupting my mother's conversation with Dillon. "I'm taking a head count for breakfast. You and John will be joining us, I'm certain?"

My mother looked at me. "You'll be staying the night, I hope? Breakfast tomorrow morning?"

I dropped my foot, fumbling around the carpet for my lost heel. "I'm sorry—I've got work, and Dillon—"

My mom's face fell. "Kam, it's Christmas—"

"Don't be ridiculous, Kameryn," Darlene interjected. "You always come for brunch. The menu tomorrow is exceptional. Finger sandwiches of hen's egg mayo with English cress. Cucumber with mint cream cheese. Suffolk ham with Bavarian mustard. Fortum's smoked salmon with tartare dressing. And of course scones," she nodded toward Dillon, as if she should find that appealing. "Cornish lobster with brandy egg cream. Isle of Mull cheddar and sun-dried pepper with rosemary butter. Terrine de Campagne. Wild Mushroom Truffle Eclair. Flourless molten lava cake, lemon and raspberry tarts."

It took me a moment to realize she'd finished speaking. I'd tuned out at *don't be ridiculous, Kameryn. You always come for brunch.*

The answer was a resounding no.

No way in hell. Over my dead body. Not on your tintype. Nixie. On the Day of Saint Never—however she needed to hear it, we were absolutely *not* coming to brunch.

"I'm sorry," I repeated, this time more firmly. "We can't."

"Can't?" Dani sauntered over, looking dangerously pale. "Or don't want to?"

The room grew uncomfortably silent.

I don't know why twenty years of friendship seemed to suddenly hang on those four lingering words. And more, I don't even know why I cared.

Tonight I had seen Dani in a different light, revealed in colors I'd never scrutinized before. I felt like I could finally see all the ways she'd trespassed against our friendship, all her snarking remarks and subtle digs, the constant way she put me down.

But even still, even with all of it in technicolor, I struggled to kick it to the curb. She'd been my best friend—or rather, *I'd* been *her* best friend—for twenty years. I didn't know how to just let that go. I didn't know how to cut that cord.

"Of course I want to," I stumbled, the words sticking in my throat as my tongue grew very dry. "It's just…" I wanted to look at Dillon, to beg her help, but I didn't dare. Not with Dani staring at me the way she was. "I mean, I guess. Yeah. We can come for a little while."

"Wonderful!" Darlene filled the ensuing silence and my mom patted my knee.

"I'm glad you'll stay, darling. Do you have a hotel for the night? You know you're both welcome to stay with us."

"That's very kind of you, Mrs. Kingsbury," said Dillon quickly, rising to her feet, "but I'm afraid I have to drag Kameryn with me up to the bay. I have a little business there. But we'll be back in time for breakfast." She smiled at Darlene. "Thank you for the invite, Mrs. Hallwell."

I stood, sinking my foot into my wayward heel, kissed my parents' cheeks, thanked the Hallwells for their hospitality, and muttered *goodnight* to Dani. All the while hating myself for caving in.

*Good old Kiss-Up Kingsbury.*

# Scene 18

"I promise, as soon as we pull out of here, I'm going to text her and cancel," Kam said as the valet disappeared to bring up her car. "I don't know why I didn't just say no!"

"How could you say no to Terrine de Campagne?"

"Oh, my God." Kam groaned from behind the hands she flung over her face. "I'm so sorry!"

"Why?"

"*Why?*" Kam dropped her hands. "Where should I even start? *Them!*" She tilted her head toward the house. "That entire family. Carter. My parents giving you the third degree. That stupid game. All of it. The whole night!"

There was something wildly endearing about the way her words all ran together when she was frustrated. About her unintentional dramatic flare.

"I don't know what you're talking about. I had a wonderful time."

Kam shot her a pointed glare. "You're being a smartass."

"Me?" Dillon donned her best expression of disbelief. "Never. I'm simply looking forward to hen's egg mayo and English cress in the morning."

"Oh, shut up!" Swatting at her with her purse, Kam laughed as Dillon easily caught her wrist, pulling her half a step closer.

"Careful, or I'll have to kiss you here with Mrs. Hallwell looking on." She flicked her eyes over Kam's shoulder to the second-story window, where a lone silhouette stood watching through the dew-streaked glass.

"I wish you would. It would feel like a win to send her rushing to her medicine cabinet to pound a fist full of valium."

The worn tires on Kam's Honda squealed across the damp brick of the driveway as the valet hopped out of the car. Dillon swiped up the keys, handing the boy a tenner, and opened the passenger door for Kam. "Up for a drive to the city?"

"Got some pressing 'business' to handle?" Kam needled as Dillon jogged around to the driver's side and slid behind the wheel.

"In fact, I do." She fumbled for the ignition and adjusted the rearview mirror. "I want to check out the bay. I'd like to see the distance between Alcatraz and the mainland."

Kam laughed. "And here I thought you actually had an ulterior motive for not wanting to stay with my parents." She kicked her feet out of her heels and propped them up on the dash. "I should have known you were just thinking about a swim!"

It was partially true. She *was* thinking about a swim. An unrated race that had nothing to do with the World Triathlon Championship Series. One that fell a week between Leeds and Montreal, the two most important competitions of the year. She didn't know if her coach, Alistair, would go for it. Two races in one month was one too many—three was absurd. Especially when one of them didn't count for anything. A little prize money. A striped black and white jersey that read *I Escaped from Alcatraz*. Bragging rights to say you swam, cycled, and ran in one of the most iconic cities in the world.

But—and it was the *but* that mattered—it got her back to California. Got her back to Kam.

She just couldn't admit any of that.

How pathetic would she look if Kam knew she was already contemplating plans to see her six months in advance when they hadn't even made it through a single night together?

It wasn't like her. Not one girl she'd dated since Kelsey had made her wonder where they'd stand the following week—let alone half a year later. Hookups. Weekend rendezvous. An occasional fortnight fling. None of them had meant much.

Yet here she was, arse-over-tits-stupid, trying to figure out how she could convince her sponsors that the Northern California race would benefit her season.

God, she had it bad.

Any other year, she would have been home in Wales, where it was already Christmas morning. She'd have been the first one up, brewing tea for her mam, grinding coffee for Seren, making a full Welsh breakfast. They'd exchange gifts. Her mam and Seren would chat over sparkling mead while she tried to recreate her father's recipe for laverbread in the kitchen. They'd all paste on a smile, stumbling through the holiday, pretending there wasn't a giant black hole in their lives that never got any smaller.

She hadn't missed a Christmas with them since her dad passed away. She hadn't dared. It was what she owed to them—her time, her presence, her willingness to share in the silent hurt that came with every holiday. It was her penance for all the heartache she had caused, the sorrow they'd endured brought on by her own making.

Never had they blamed her. Not once in all the years had her mam or Seren cast a single word of fault in her direction. They hadn't had to. She'd cloaked herself in guilt, carrying it like a millstone from which she could never escape.

Which, perhaps was why, when she'd mentioned Kam to her sister, she'd woken up the next morning to an email from her mother about the race in Santa Monica.

*I think you should go to this.*

Dillon had emailed back. *Can't. It's over the holidays.*

Her mam had replied: *You should do what feels right.* And immediately after, the following P.S.: *Seren says you really like this girl. Please go, for all our sakes.* Her stoic English mother had closed it with a winking face.

Five thousand miles later, her mam, as usual, had been right.

"I don't know what else you'd expect me to be thinking about," Dillon razzed Kam as she threw the car into drive. "That swim is one of the most famous water crossings in the world."

"Well, if it's caught that much of your attention, perhaps you'd like to drop me off at my parents' place so you can give it a go tonight? I wouldn't want to be a distraction."

"Ohh," Dillon cast her a sideways smile, "salty." They'd rolled to a stop at the end of the drive, the headlights fanning the iron gates as they slowly swung open. "I like this side of you, Kam-Kameryn."

"Yeah?" Kam pulled her bare feet from the dash, twisting in her seat to face her. "Tell me," she leaned as close as the seatbelt would allow before reaching a finger to trace a line from Dillon's ear, across her neck, and down to the top button of her blouse. "Do you like this side of me enough to table your one-track mind for the rest of the evening?"

Despite her eyes never leaving the road, Dillon nearly clipped the Hallwells' mailbox.

"Trust me, it's not that one-track," she said, veering back to the center of the tree-lined street rolling out through the darkness. "It's got plenty of latitude for wandering."

"I see," Kam smiled smugly as she abruptly withdrew her roaming fingertips and flopped back in her seat. "Then I guess I'll stick around." She flipped on the radio and closed her eyes. "Turn right on Marsh Rd. North on 101. Forty-five-minute drive and we'll dead end right into Aquatic Cove, which is where the swim ends. The race isn't until June, so you've got a little time to work it into your schedule."

Surprised, Dillon glanced over to see the corners of Kam's lips flicker in the light of the display panel.

"You think I'm considering doing that summer race, do you?" she asked, glad Kameryn's eyes were still shut so she couldn't see her idiotic smile.

Apparently she wasn't the only one looking toward the future.

"I don't know what happened! There are usually hundreds of them here." Kam's voice was muffled from behind the upturned collar where she had bundled herself into Dillon's jacket.

They'd found parking in one of the structures along the waterfront, and without much discussion between them, Kam had led the way down to the sea lion platform at the end of the tourist pier. It was after midnight, the streets were vacant, and the city was covered in a fine mist that turned the festive lights of the holiday into a starburst of color.

Dillon doubted marine life observation was a pressing subject on either of their minds, but she'd humored Kam all the same.

"I'm beginning to think you just like to lure me onto dark piers in the middle of the night to keep me up past my bedtime."

The docks below them were empty, with only a trio of the slumbering sea mammals hauled-out on the algae-covered jetty. Beyond the breakwater, Alcatraz flashed its silent warning as the mountainous silhouette of a cargo ship glided across the still surface of the bay.

"Hey, I'm not the one to be blamed for your lost sleep tonight." Kam hooked her index fingers in the pockets of Dillon's trousers, drawing her off the railing. "You turned down a perfectly good offer to stay with my parents where you could have caught all the Zs you wanted."

"It would have been a little awkward, don't you think, when I declined the guest sofa?"

Kam laughed but didn't immediately respond. In the dim glow of the pier lighting, it was difficult to make out her expression, to guess where her thoughts had drawn her. She'd grown nervous, Dillon knew, despite her bold banter, and had been stalling since they'd reached the city.

"I, um—I just wanted to say—before we—well, before I forget. I wanted to thank you."

"Thank me?" It wasn't what Dillon had been expecting. "What for?"

"All of it. Everything. For flying here when I know you could be home with your family. For convincing me to go to that stupid party. For reminding me how much I missed my parents. For coming with me. For laughing off the Hallwells and not allowing them to get under your skin. For—I don't even know—for making me feel like—like it's okay to just be me." She retreated behind an embarrassed laugh. "God, I'll stop now. I'm rambling."

Dillon didn't say anything. Her thoughts were split in two directions —one route hanging on the way Kam chewed her lower lip when she got nervous—the second path drifting over her shoulder to the black expanse of nothingness between where they stood and Alcatraz Island.

*Three races in one month.*

*No problem.*

"Why are you smiling at me like that?"

"Because I'm onto you, Kam-Kameryn," Dillon teased, pushing aside thoughts of June for the moment. "I see what you're about. You think flattery is going to talk me out of Isle of Mull cheddar in the morning." She reached up, tugging down the zipper below Kam's chin. "I'm sorry, but it's not going to work. You're not getting out of Christmas brunch."

Laughing at the turn in conversation, Kameryn slid her hands deeper into Dillon's pockets, drawing herself closer, until there was no space between them. "Then I'll take that as a challenge," she said, the warmth of her lips falling just shy of Dillon's. "I think it's time to convince you there are far better ways we could spend our Christmas morning."

# Scene 19

I fumbled with the door handle, the locking mechanism flashing red. No matter how many times I crammed the keycard into the slot, my brain turned the task of opening the hotel door into the Pythagorean Equation.

"It's not working!"

Dillon reached around me, easing the card from my shaking hand, and calmly turned it over, slipping it back into the keycard reader where the light immediately turned green.

*Smooth, Kam. Note to self: things work better when you line up the arrows.*

We'd booked a room at the first hotel we came to off the Embarcadero. Dillon had suggested going back for the car, uncertain if the structure permitted overnight parking, but I'd pulled her off the sidewalk, straight into the lobby.

I'd worry about the car in the morning.

The hotel was above my pay grade. A boy with metallic blue hair combed into a fauxhawk had lazily sprawled behind the front desk, listing off amenities: Top floor. Waterfront view. Balcony. Breakfast included. Complimentary high-speed wifi.

*Yeah, fine, whatever. Get on with it.*

One bed or two?

*One.*

I hadn't even had the presence of mind to be embarrassed. The limited space in my brain had been reserved for the taste of Dillon's mouth, the way she'd just kissed me down at the docks, and the knowledge that we were really doing this. Without looking at the room rate, I slid my credit card across the desk—thank you, *Amex*, for your liberal definition of my credit limit—and proceeded to trip over the *welcome* mat in my rush to the elevator.

But now that we were here, behind closed doors, my precipitancy had abruptly ended.

I wasn't sure what to do.

I don't know why I felt there should have been a manual. *How To Sleep With A Woman When You're A Woman—a First Timer's Guide To Success*. Had Ellen penned a handbook? Chappell Roan a song? Maybe Megan Rapinoe had posted a podcast?

I felt like such an idiot. Sex was sex, right? I hadn't needed instructions for Carter. Ryan. Diego. Matt. That one guy from Theatre 101B —whatever his name had been. And whoever the last one was I couldn't place at the moment. I don't know why I allowed myself to feel like this was different. Was it just the mental barrier—the drummed-in propensity to regard it as taboo?

I crammed the thought away. That was bullshit. The only thing that should have been tabooed were the obnoxious blue and pink robes hanging on the closet door, labeled *Captain* and *The Missus*.

Still, I stood there, frozen to the floorboards of the entryway as she relieved me of her jacket, flipped on the bathroom light, and drew the sheer curtain across the waterfront balcony window. When she returned, I tried to convince my arms to do anything other than hang useless at my sides, but they didn't get the memo.

"I, uh—I don't know what to do."

Her smile turned amused and I wanted to cover my head with the empty ice bucket from the counter.

*Well done, Kam*: *Master of the obvious*.

"It's alright. I happen to be something of an expert."

I laughed, swung back to some sense of composure by her unfailing bold-faced certainty, and applauded myself for not flinching when she reached to unclasp my opal earrings.

"Of course you are."

"Do you doubt me?" she asked, turning back from where she'd dropped the gemstones onto the entry table.

I wanted a clever repartee, but her hands had drifted to my waist, her fingers lingering at the tie of my wrap dress.

"Is this okay, Kam?"

Her playful insolence was gone, her hands stilled, waiting for permission. She meant it, I realized. She wasn't pressuring me. She wasn't pushing toward the endgame. I could have told her no and there wasn't a single particle of me that believed she would have made me feel small or met my hesitation with resentment.

I won't lie—her search for consent was an incredible turn on.

"Yes," I think I articulated. I couldn't hear my voice over the ocean of blood crashing through my arteries. Whatever I managed, she must have received the message, because her lips turned again with her arch smile as she worked loose the satin tie, allowing the wrap to fall open.

"You know," she whispered, sliding her hands to my hips, forcing my audible inhalation, "I recently heard somewhere you liked playing hard to get—so I wholeheartedly appreciate the convenience of tonight's choice of attire."

"Fucking Dani," I tried to laugh, but my body had gone into survival mode, its only focus on not imploding.

She leaned to kiss my neck, her hands sliding higher, her fingers grazing every ridge and channel of my ribcage. I closed my eyes, tilting my head back, absorbing the sensation of her palms against my breasts, her thumbs teasing my nipples to attention. The plunging neckline of my cocktail dress hadn't allowed for a bra, and despite being aware that Dani's brother and his friends had spent the entire night staring at my cleavage, I was now glad to be sans one less complication.

I felt, as her mouth traveled along my collarbone, her hands moving to slip the dress off my shoulders, that I needed to respond in turn. That I should reciprocate her actions. But at the same time, I was struggling to even breathe, and she seemed to read my mind, aware I was already beginning to panic I wasn't doing this correctly.

"Kam," she gently captured the hand I'd raised to struggle with her buttons. "Just wait. For now, let me."

She was offering the license just to experience it. The allowance to not know what to do and let it be okay.

And, to clarify—there were things I wanted to do. Things I'd been thinking about doing since she'd kissed me on a picnic table while eating take-out in front of Hana Bay. Things I *would* do, I didn't doubt. But for the moment, I was relieved to let her lead.

It was entirely erotic, the unabashed way she stepped back to look at me. Knowing the ways she wanted me. I should have felt self-conscious, standing there in nothing but my heels and underwear—an impractically lacy pair I'd spent a puerile amount of time selecting earlier in the morning, for exactly this purpose—but there was something about her that didn't allow me to feel uneasy at all.

"You're really beautiful, Kameryn," she said, finding my gaze again as she stepped forward to entwine her hands in mine, drawing me backward toward the bed.

I didn't say anything. I couldn't. Not as she bent, sliding the lace material down my hips, trailing her knuckles along the bare skin of my legs as she knelt to slip off my heels. The grazing touch sent my heart on an expedition, drubbing a hole through my chest. I had to reach back to steady myself against the pillow-top mattress, wondering what the statistics were of dying from anticipation? I was only twenty-three. If I was found dead in the morning, no one would believe my obituary when it read *died peacefully in her sleep*.

Slowly, leisurely, she rose, kissing the curve of my calf, the tender skin at the crook of my knee, the inside of my thigh. Impatience gnawed at me, and before her lips had grazed their slow path up the plane of my stomach, I'd laced my fingers through her hair, pulling her upright, anxious to find her mouth.

I loved the way she kissed me. I loved the fullness of her lips, unlike any boy I'd ever kissed, the brush of her eyelashes, the inebriating smell of salt and sea that belonged to her and only her. I think I surprised her with my fervency, with the urgency of my need, because when at last she drew away, I wasn't the only one fighting for breath.

"*Amynedd piau hi*, Kam-Kameryn," she laughed, the musical rhythm of the unfamiliar words filling the silence in between my heartbeats. "Patience in all things."

I doubted, somehow, that she was prone to follow the same advice, given the competitiveness of her nature, but whatever retort I sought to return was stifled as she pressed me back against the quilted comforter, and moved to kneel above me.

My mind was turned to other things.

Things like her fingertips—the way they teased, giving and retreating with their unhurried, deliberate exploration. Or her mouth that followed suit, retracing every inch of skin with the same prolonged reiteration.

My body ached. Ached in ways I didn't know it could, vulnerable with wanting.

I gave in to closing my eyes, my fingers grappling for purchase on the varnished wooden planks of the headboard, allowing myself to fall into the intensity of every heightened sensation.

Nothing in my life had ever been like this. As out of control. As intolerable as it was intoxicating.

I felt torn apart—and then pieced back together again.

It felt like an eternity before I recovered sentience, though I imagine in reality it was probably only a few seconds. I could feel her hovering above me, the brush of her untucked blouse against my naked belly. When I opened my eyes, she was smiling.

"You alright, Kam-Kameryn?"

Was I alright? Did alright mean something different in Wales than it did in the land of Uncle Sam? Was it the plain old "a-okay" but nothing outstanding? Because if that was the case—no, I wasn't *alright*.

I was top-shelf, Versace-clutch, Michelin 5-star restaurant living. I was Dodgers-won-the-World Series and Kings-took-home-the-Stanley-Cup winning.

In other words: I was pretty sure I'd just transcended my body.

So, yeah, I guess I was alright. But, maybe even a little better.

"Is it still the twenty-first century?" I asked, slipping an arm around her neck and drawing her to me.

I hated that she was still dressed. I hated that there was fabric between us. But I wasn't quite ready to move yet and just wanted to revel in the weight of her against me.

"Hate to break it to you," she smiled, "but you're still stuck in an era without robot butlers."

I laughed, bringing my hand up to trace her jaw. "No BB8s or R2D2s? How disappointing."

Her smile turned wry. "I'm not going to pretend like I know what that means, but I will say—you didn't seem terribly disappointed."

God. I don't think such a simple look should have turned my entire body into liquid. Into lava. Into whatever it was I was feeling. I knew my flush gave me away, broadcasting my sharp U-turn from the space-age future, back to the present.

Still, I tried to play it off like she hadn't just hand-delivered—mouth-delivered—*whatever*—the best orgasm of the decade... century... millennia... and I'm only stopping there because I don't know what word represents the length of time that comes after. Epoch? Eon?

"What if I said the verdict was still out?" I teased, handing back her taunt from the night before, unwilling to feed the monster of her ego—

though, if I'm honest, she deserved her own ticker-tape parade. Because, the way she made me feel… I hadn't even known that was possible.

"Is that so?" She was still braced on her elbows, my hand casually toying with the short hair at the back of her neck. "Are you requiring further physical evidence to make a final ruling? Because I assure you," her smile broadened, "I can provide more in-depth testimony for your consideration."

She started to push herself upright, but I caught her arm, pulling her down beside me. I'd started to resurface from my post-climax bliss, and there was no way I was letting her move forward without my active participation.

"Excuse me, but I believe it's my turn for cross-examination."

I loved her laugh. I loved the retort that never reached the tip of her tongue when I bent to kiss her throat. I loved the way her breath hitched as my hands found their way under the hem of her shirt, her shudder when my palms reached her skin. I loved the way she tried to keep up her blasé demeanor as I clumsily undressed her, and the way her shallow breathing sold her out. I loved her patience with my tentative explorations, discovering every line and plane, curve and angle. The way she had to close her eyes. The way her fingers pressed into my hips, dragging me closer, closing the space between us. I loved knowing just how much of an effect I had on her by the quickening cadence of her pulse pounding in her chest.

And more than anything, I loved this world she had shown me—this piece of myself I hadn't even known was missing. This feeling of being found. This feeling of being completed.

# Scene 20

"And this one?" Kam ran her finger along Dillon's forearm. "What does it mean?"

Dillon didn't respond right away.

Kam's cheek was pressed flat against her shoulder, her hair curtaining her breasts, the tip of her index finger mapping out the scattered tattoos across Dillon's body. It was late—Dillon wasn't certain of the time—but the Cimmerian darkness promised the impending arrival of sunrise.

If she was responsible, she would drag herself to the shower, go out for a run, something—anything—to make up for the lost day of training. But then again, if she was responsible, she'd probably be home in Wales, and have not spent the small hours of the morning putting on a show and tell of how to properly tip the velvet.

*Piss it*. Responsibility could wait a day.

But at the moment, Dillon wasn't relishing this conversation.

Kam was asking about her tattoos. An innocent, curious investigation. Her fingers currently lingered over the short phrase running down her right forearm, handwritten in German.

*Gewinn oder stirb beim Versuch.*

Suppressing a sigh, Dillon translated. "Win or die trying." She hated that even when she spoke the words aloud, it was Henrik's voice in her head.

Kam remained quiet, waiting.

Dillon knew she wanted more from her. She wanted a story, a comment, some elaboration, the same as she had done when Dillon teased her about the line drawing of a penguin she had found on her hip—a memento from Kam's first trip to Vegas.

But these weren't something Dillon wanted to talk about. Not here, at least, lying naked beside Kam in the king-size bed. Not on a night like this. She didn't want to scare her away. Because where Kam saw ink and art, Dillon saw only reminders of all the mistakes she'd made.

So instead, she tried to appease her with crusts of the truth.

"I had a coach—the one I told you about—who was a firm believer of winning at all costs." She made a fist, watching the letters twist with the muscles of her forearm. "The phrase was something he never wanted me to forget."

Kam shifted the weight of her head against her chest. "How old were you?" She ran her thumb over the sun-faded cursive.

"I don't know," Dillon lied. "Seventeen, eighteen."

*Fifteen and a half.*

She remembered everything about that day. It had been the first week she'd moved to Henrik's training center in Germany. Her first morning swimming in the Elbe. The current had been stronger than she was used to in Swansea, the swim longer. She'd been tired. Cold. Nervous about being so far away from her parents.

At the end of the swim, when she'd begun to lag, Henrik called her to the bank, where he stood with his stopwatch. He asked her if she could swim it again—faster.

Her German at that point had been limited, but he'd refused to speak to her in English as soon as they were out of Wales.

*Nein*, she shook her head.

It had been the first and only time she'd made the mistake of saying no.

He signaled her to get out of the water. He made her run sixteen miles from Reitbrook to Hamburg—to a tattoo studio in the middle of the city, where he'd had the saying inked on her forearm. On the way home, he told her if she ever quit on him again, he'd have the word *Drückeberger*—quitter, coward—tattooed across her forehead.

She believed him.

And she'd stared at that unwanted tattoo, a hundred times a day, ever since.

But it served its purpose. It was those hated words that had driven her back into the race after she'd crashed her bike in Rio. It hadn't mattered that she'd fractured her clavicle, or embedded her hipbone with gravel.

*Win—or die trying.*

That simple phrase had pushed her across the finish line to claim her first Olympic medal. It had been the doctrine she was taught to live by —one permanently etched upon her skin.

"Is that where you learned to speak German? Your coach?"

Dillon gave a curt affirmative. She didn't want to talk about Henrik.

She wanted to focus on the warmth of Kam's body draped lazily across hers. To get lost in thoughts of her clumsy hands and uncertain mouth. She wanted to drift to sleep replaying the way Kam had been willing to laugh at herself. The way she hadn't shut up with her apologies—*I swear, next time I can do this better*—making Dillon laugh in return, caring nothing about *better* and everything about *next time*. Because it meant Kam wanted there to be a next time. She'd not just been here to satisfy her curiosity. And Dillon knew, despite all the reasons this was unlikely to work, she wanted a next time, too.

But Kam's attention had already drifted—along with her fingertips—to the next tattoo.

The words *REMEMBER WHO YOU ARE* printed in block font just above her left knee. Below it, the letters *DFS*.

This one, at least, she could elaborate on more easily.

"After my first Olympics—after my dad had passed away—I had a rough competition year. I lost badly at a few big races and started to question whether I belonged in the sport. I'm not built for it. I'm too short for swimming. Carry too much muscle to run. Too broad-shouldered for cycling. I came home from the Commonwealth Games and told my friend, Sam, I thought I might be done. She thrashed me for wallowing in self-pity. Told me to grow up and remember who the fuck I was. Swore we wouldn't be mates anymore if I didn't compete the following month at the world final in Leeds.

"Long story short, I showed up, and on the last stretch to the finish, got myself into a foot race with the woman who'd won gold in London the previous year. Sounds silly, but it was Sam's words—*remember who the fuck you are*—that gave me the edge I needed to best her.

"We went out drinking that night on my prize money and by the time we'd stumbled back to her flat in the morning, I had a new tattoo." Dillon offered a subdued smile. "Can't say I really remember getting it—but I'm glad I had enough sense to go with the PC version. Not sure my mam would have approved of the uncensored edition."

Kam laughed. "You were so drunk you put it upside down?"

"Nah. It faces me so I can see it when I cycle."

"Ah." Kam lifted her head to give it a second look, before flopping back beside her. "And *DFS*? Your initials?"

"Nope. My middle name starts with B."

It took a moment before Dillon could feel her smile against her chest. "Of course, I should have known. Dillon *Fucking* Sinclair."

"For better or for worse," Dillon conceded wryly.

The room grew still. Kam's head had gotten heavier, the whisper of her inhalations slower, the pre-dawn hours finally luring her questions to rest. Dillon stared at the ceiling, idly combing her fingers through the silken strands of long dark hair. The clock on the nightstand hummed in the silence, but Dillon didn't turn to read its digital face. She knew the hour well. The hour when the night was darkest. When daybreak seemed eternities away.

Her thoughts drifted across the Atlantic. It was afternoon in her mam's two-story brick home facing the sea. She knew she should call —wish them happy Christmas.

Tell them she missed them.

But there was a part of her that didn't want to interrupt their day. The part that knew a certain peace came with her absence.

Kam stirred, the cadence of her breath shifting to wakefulness, drawing Dillon's thoughts away from Swansea Bay. Lazily she stretched and rolled onto her side, tucking her head into the crook of Dillon's neck.

"For better," she murmured, echoing Dillon's earlier words, settling onto the shared pillow. "Definitely for better."

Then she was asleep again, and drawn into the warmth of her body, Dillon shortly followed suit.

# Scene 21

There was not one scintilla of an iota of an atom in me that wanted to go to brunch.

I lay beneath the plush comforter and bemoaned every ounce of Dillon's rationale persuading me not to call and cancel.

"Traffic's going to be miserable," I mumbled through the quilted down.

"No one drives on holidays."

I humphed. "I have nothing to wear."

"You have a perfectly good cashmere jumper in the car." She tugged the comforter down past my head. "I saw you pack it."

I snatched a pillow and covered my face. "They won't even know we're missing."

"*Please*. There's going to be a place card with your name on it."

I couldn't help but laugh. She wasn't even wrong. *Miss Kameryn Kingsbury,* it would read, with a curlicued serif at the end of each gold-plated letter.

She took a seat at the edge of the bed and I peeked out from beneath my place of hiding. "I have a script I'm supposed to be memorizing for an upcoming project."

"You're a fast learner. You can get to work when you get home."

I didn't *want* to get to work when I got home. I wanted to pull the curtains in my bedroom and spend the remainder of every millisecond Dillon was here naked in my bed.

"Who said I was a fast learner?" I huffed again. "For all you know, I might be entirely inept."

"You seemed to get the hang of things pretty quickly last night."

God, I loved her sinful smile. The way her hair—still damp from a shower—hung in front of her eyes. The phenomenal masterpiece that were her cheekbones. Her sculpted jaw and graceful neck.

I aimed for casual, even as my brain careened straight to a short film of highlights from the past six hours. "I had a decent instructor."

Judging by the warmth radiating off my face, my attempt to play it cool had epically failed. Was there a color darker than crimson? No one ever said *oh, she flushed a charming garnet*, or *she blushed a pretty merlot*.

"Decent?" She dropped beside me on an elbow, prying the pillow from my face. Her smile told me all I needed to know about the state of my cheeks. "Run-of-the-mill night for you, huh?"

"Oh, it was tolerable. I'd definitely rate it a passable experience."

"Passable?"

I don't know what was more agonizing—the wickedness of her slow smile, or the unhurried, deliberate way she drew aside the cover of the comforter. I was still in that in-between state, knowing she'd already thoroughly examined every inch of my body, and yet still fighting back modesty in the cold light of morning.

"Are we talking two-and-a-half stars? C average?"

"Oh, I'd say at least three stars—" I shrieked and laughed as she suddenly lunged for my wrists, capturing them in her strong hands. "Okay, okay, three and a half!" I put up a mock struggle as she pinned my arms above my head, lowering her weight atop my body. It was no longer only my cheeks that were on fire.

"You should know by now, I'm not keen on doing anything medi-ocre. The only option is to try again...."

I was so pathetic. I couldn't even pretend like this wasn't exactly what I wanted.

But on the other hand, I also knew—despite my protests of not wanting to go—that we were running the risk of arriving late to the Hallwells.

God forbid.

She ran her lips across my temple, down my cheek, along the side of my neck.

I should realistically have been rushing to the parking garage, trying to get there before they towed my car.

Her mouth dropped lower, taking a detour to explore the curves of my breasts.

Yeah, what car? If they'd already towed it, there was no need to hurry. We could catch a late bus to Palo Alto.

She trailed down past my navel.

You know, I could just move to New York—I wouldn't need a car there. Besides, it was two thousand miles closer to London.

She released her hold on my hands—we both knew I wasn't going anywhere—and turned them toward a more rewarding occupation.

But my bag was in the car. My clothes. My toothbrush. My makeup. I couldn't show up to the Hallwells in the same dress I'd worn the night before, my hair twisted into a fucked-and-forgot-my-brush bun.

*Shut up, Kam.*

I squeezed my eyes closed, my fingers tangling themselves in her wave of wet hair.

Who cared what I wore to the stupid brunch? I'd stop and buy an *I Heart SF* t-shirt in the lobby. Fuck it. Maybe I'd get one of those *Tacos and Titties* rainbow tanks I'd seen them selling on the street corners.

*Merry Christmas, Mrs. I-Guarantee-You've-Never-Had-Five-Star-Sex-Like-This Hallwell.*

An hour and a half later, I stood on the polished calacatta marble of the Hallwells front entry, listening to the symphony of their trumpeting doorbell. My reflection greeted me in the spotless glass as we waited for admittance into the Fifth Terrace of Purgatory.

I looked like shit. I'd yanked on my wrinkled cardigan as we pulled onto the freeway and dabbed on a layer of makeup in the rearview mirror. My eyeliner looked as if it had been applied by a first-year cosmetology student who'd suddenly developed a tremor. And to top it all off, I knew I smelled like sex.

"Stop fretting," Dillon hissed over the peal of chimes as I combed my fingers through my hair for the hundredth time. "You look fine!"

Dani opened the door. "Jesus, what happened?" She left no opening for me to feign misunderstanding. "Did you sleep in your car?"

"I—wow, thanks." The best defense was a good offense, right? "Merry Christmas to you, too."

She was unfazed. "You look awful."

"I was up late." I pulled Dillon past her into the hall. "Some of us still have to work to pay rent—as wild as that may sound to you."

If I had caught Dillon's eye—if she had laughed, or given me any kind of knowing smile—it would have been game over. Fortunately, I didn't look in her direction and felt I sold myself quite well. "We have to leave right after brunch. I have an early morning in the studio."

*Yeah, no.* My only pressing plans revolved around bolting from this hell, hopping on Highway 1, weaving our way down the coast, and stopping in one of the little waterfront towns for the night. Waking up to sex and seagulls.

Darlene appeared at the end of the foyer, announcing it was time for pomegranate mimosas and smoky mezcal-fig sours, and for the moment, I was off the hook. We were herded into the dining room, where I found my parents and the rest of the Hallwell clan, family and friends, already at the table. As it did every year, all topics of conversation turned toward the outrageous Christmas presents they had gifted one another. Mr. Hallwell's gift to himself—a 1961 vintage Aston Martin. Darlene showed off her Botswana diamond earrings, larger than the niçoise olives in her appetizer salad. Dani, evidently disgruntled with her gift from Tom, slung a Hermès Birkin Cargo bag onto the table. "I *do* like it," she snapped over the rim of her mimosa, shooting a glare at her husband. "I just would have preferred the Hermès Himalayan."

The conversation drifted.

To my right, my mom was intensely engaged in chat with Darlene's aunt, Helena, who had once been a prominent equestrian. Across from me, Dani's husband, Tom, was crowing to Mr. Hallwell about an investment he'd made that had tripled over the last seventy-two hours. And to my left, Dillon was politely nodding at Allyson, Darlene's sister, who was rambling on about how strange it was to call a cookie a biscuit, when a biscuit was clearly not a cookie.

And me?

I was staring at my plate of caciocavallo cheese and pancetta pecan puffs, my thoughts lingering around the fiery feathers of the phoenix tattoo I'd finally gotten to fully appreciate on Dillon's back. I loved the intricacy of the design. The woven colors of the flame. The way the wings touched the tops of her shoulders.

"Just a reminder that we all burn sometimes," had been her answer as to why she'd decided on the mythical bird. "It's who we are when we drag ourselves out of the ashes that counts."

"Holy shit!"

The blurted exclamation from Dani's little brother, Marcus, drew me out of my daydreaming, back to the land of thirty-year-old scotch and spoiled brats dissatisfied with twenty thousand dollar handbags. There was something about the sharpness in his tone, the excitement behind it, that made me look up. I felt an uneasiness begin to tingle at the bottom of my spine when I found him staring straight at me.

"You've got a serious Doppelgänger, Kam!"

Marcus and I seldom spoke. Mainly because he'd developed an obsessive crush on me when he'd hit puberty, and when he was younger, if I said anything to him, the encounter would send him running from the room. *Probably looking for a sock*, Dani'd always teased.

His eyes were wide above his acne-crusted cheeks. "I mean, like, no fuckin' lie—this chick looks exactly like you!"

"*Marcus*," Darlene warned, but her son ignored her rebuke. His attention was flashing between me and his iPad, propped against his whiskey sour.

"Wow." His best friend Nate leaned over to get a better look at his screen. "I'd do her."

"Yeah, yeah, totally." Marcus's whole body nodded the affirmative as he reached out to continue scrolling. And then he stopped. "*Wait. This is a joke.*" He looked up at me again.

The tingle in my spine turned into a full-fledged quiver, raising every hair at the back of my neck with its uncomfortable icy chill. He looked down. Up again. Nate's gaze followed suit, the pair resembling a couple of young cockerels, clearly confused.

The guests around the table had gone silent, all staring at Marcus, waiting for him to elaborate. It was only Dillon's eyes I could feel on me, her fork paused from where she'd been idly pushing around a bite of brie crostini.

*Shit.*

*Shit shit shit.* I hadn't been ready for this.

"This has to be a joke." Marcus continued to scroll.

Annoyed, Dani stood from two seats down and leaned over, snatching her brother's iPad. "What are you going on about, Mar—" she stopped short, pausing to read. "I don't—" her brow knitted, her face contorting in disbelief. She scrolled a few seconds longer, then darted her eyes to me. "Is this real?"

There was no point in playing dumb, they were going to find out eventually. It had just come sooner than I'd expected. If I hadn't left my phone in my purse hanging on the hall tree, I imagine I would have seen a heads-up from Aaron and the studio.

"Yep." It felt surreal, saying that. Having it out in the open. For months I'd been caught in limbo, stranded between exhilaration and disbelief that this was really happening. Every morning, part of me anticipated waking to an email, a *Dear Kam, we're sorry, but…* not allowing myself to truly commit to the excitement. But today—with whatever was on that screen—this was it. It was my turn to be someone. To take up space. To be more than just a seat filler.

Dani could kick rocks with her Birkin bag.

"I don't believe this." She tossed the iPad like a frisbee back to Marcus. "If this was true you would have said something."

"I couldn't. The studio wouldn't allow it."

Slamming herself into her seat, she upset a bowl of grapes that scattered across the table. "You said you were working on a project, Kam. A *project*. That—" she thumbed to where her brother had resumed an obsessive perusal of his iPad, "—is not a *project*."

"I signed an NDA, Dani. I wasn't allowed to say anything until the casting announcement was released."

Her sharp features warped into anger. It was exactly what I should have expected from her, but still it surprised me.

"Did *she* know?" She chucked her chin toward Dillon, her blue eyes smoldering.

"What? No one knew."

"Then why isn't she surprised?"

"No one knew *anything*," I snapped, my own resentment rising. I swore to God, if Dani referred to Dillon as *she* again—as if she wasn't sitting right in front of her—I was going to take her plate of tête de veau and cram it down her Giorgio Armani sweater. "Couldn't you just be happy for me?"

"Sweetheart," my mom was concerned, "what's going on?"

"Your daughter's apparently been holding out on a little secret," Dani seethed.

"It's fine, Mom." How was it I suddenly felt like I needed to defend myself? This was supposed to be *my* moment. This was the best thing that had ever happened to me. "I got a role in the upcoming *Sand Seekers* trilogy."

"The Margaret Gilles novels?" My mom's eyebrows nearly met her hairline. "Honey!"

"A role?!" Marcus reemerged from his scrolling, still brimming with incredulity. "A *role*?! You're fucking playing *Addison Riley*!"

"Marcus—!" Darlene slapped her palm against the table, sending a spray of pomegranate mimosa onto the damask linen. "Your *mouth*—"

"This is like un-fucking-believable!" Nate joined in, staring at me as if I'd sprouted a tit in the middle of my forehead. "Your sister's friend is *starring* in the dopest film of our lifetime!" His unduly large Adam's apple flopped up and down. "You're going to be like—famous." He seemed to shock himself by speaking directly to me and abruptly diverted his attention to his cheese-smeared fingernails.

"I don't understand." Darlene glanced between me and her son. "You got a part in a movie?"

"*Mom*! It's *Sand Seekers*, come on!" Marcus pounded his fist on the table. "*Sand Seekers*! It's like—like," he flung his napkin in frustration, "like *Star Wars*, but, with like blood and sex and—"

"Hot women!" Nate chimed in.

"Yeah!"

For a gross second, I thought they were going to fist bump.

Dani looked up from where she was scrolling on her own phone. "I can't believe you're going to be in a movie with Elliott Fleming." Some of her bitterness dissipated as her interest elevated. "You're going to kiss Grady Dunn!"

"The actor from *King*?" asked Darlene. Code for: you're going to kiss a Black man and you're okay with this? She'd nearly burned the world down when she found out her daughter was going to be a Cortés.

"He's *hot*, Mom," Dani snapped, but I ignored both of them, tuning out the increasing volume of chatter across the table. My only focus shifted to Dillon, who sat staring at the gilded pinecone centerpiece, saying nothing.

"Hey," I brushed the toe of my ballet flat against her ankle. "Sorry, I would have told you. I just—I couldn't say anything until—"

"Don't be twp!" She looked up, returning from wherever her thoughts had taken her. "You have no reason to apologize." Despite her attempt to brighten her tone, her words fell flat. "*Sand Seekers*. That's quite something."

"It's going to be big." I tried to find some of the enthusiasm I knew I should be feeling. It was just—there was something behind her smile that worried me. I'd expected her to be delighted. It was exciting news. "I wanted to tell you, really," I pled my case again.

"No, no, it's not that. It's—it's great, honestly." The pallor of her face said it was anything but great. "I'm glad for you, Kameryn."

*Kameryn*. Not Kam-Kameryn. Not even Kam.

"This is so sick!" Marcus was still ranting. "Like the whole world's going to know your name!"

"It's just a movie, Marcus," Darlene was attempting to curb her son's enthusiasm.

Over the din of the table, my dad was trying to ask me a question. Something about contracts—Had I had an attorney look at mine? Young women could be taken advantage of in Hollywood, did I know?

I wanted to tell them all to shut the hell up. To give me a moment to think. Something had happened. Right in front of me, I could see Dillon closing down.

"Will you excuse me?" Dillon stood abruptly, her chair scraping across the marble. She didn't look at me. She didn't look at anyone. "I..." No one else paid her any attention. "I just need a minute." Without waiting for a response, she fled through the towering arch leading into the hall.

I felt like an invisible door had just been slammed. Like I'd been sucker punched, the wind knocked from my gut. My name was being called from every angle, but the only opinion I really cared about had just walked out the door.

This wasn't how this was supposed to go at all.

# Scene 22

"It's absolutely cracking, is what it is! Bloody brill!"

Sam dropped the barbell onto the mat, wiping sweat off her brow.

Dillon stepped around her. "It is absolutely *not* bloody brill." She sank onto a weight bench. "Spot me, yeah?"

"So where'd you leave it?" Sam's obnoxious grin greeted her over the bar catch.

She'd been positively giddy, as Dillon expected, over the news of Kam's upcoming role. Sam was the only reason Dillon even knew what *Sand Seekers* was. The dystopian saga was practically a religion to the footballer. Dillon had always rolled her eyes when Sam got a chin-nod or thumbs-up from fellow fanatics when they spotted the tattooed mural on her calf depicting the apocalyptic tale.

Which was entirely why she'd dreaded this conversation all the way across the Atlantic ocean, admitting that—*yes*, it was *that* Kameryn Kingsbury—*yes*, the one who'd just been announced as the star in Sam's long-awaited film.

But now, she knew, the dialogue was about to take a sharp u-turn.

*Where had she left it?*

She hadn't.

She'd walked away and left everything unresolved.

The shock of the announcement had stunned her. And then the growing realization of the magnitude of the news had sent her on a downward spiral.

She didn't dispute that she'd not handled it well.

After the brunch, they'd driven the six hours back to Los Angeles with hardly a word between them. Dillon had been searching for something to say, some way to explain, but every time she thought she'd found a segue, Kam was interrupted by another phone call. One after another, after another. Her agent. The studio. A publicist. Her friends. On and on.

It was a flashback to three years earlier when Kelsey had scored the winning goal in the UEFA Women's EURO final.

Only this was worse. So much worse. And it had only just begun.

She'd tried to find a way to tell her she was happy for her. To show her the support she deserved. But Dillon knew everything she said fell short. She wasn't good at pretending. And she knew Kameryn hadn't understood. This was her lifelong dream being realized, after all. This was everything she'd worked for—everything she'd planned. There was no question the role would fling open the doors to what would become a phenomenal career.

And Dillon *was* happy for her. She wanted Kam to find success. To have her dreams come true. She just… she'd made a mistake.

She should have left well enough alone. She should have dusted herself off on the road in Hana and never looked back. A year from now, she would have glanced at an advert on The Tube—she would have nudged Sam, *Hey, that's the twit who hit me in Hawaii.* And Sam would have blown her gasket that *Reckless Driver Girl* was starring in her favorite film. It would have been simple. It would have been humorous. And it would have been the end.

It wasn't as easy, now.

"I told her I'd call her. I needed to come home to think."

"Haddaway, man! You've got to be bloody fucking shitting me right now!" Sam jerked the bar from Dillon's hands and slammed it on the rack. "You just got on a plane and left?"

"Yes." Dillon sat up, staring at the mirror on the wall.

"You flew out there to see her. You shagged her. You spent Christmas with her family. And then you flipped out on what was probably the best news of her life and just *jumped on a plane and left*?!" Sam flung herself onto a stack of barbell plates, clicking the blade of her prosthetic heel against the metal. "You really are every bit the tosser Kelsey says you are—"

"Go easy, mate," Dillon warned, but Sam brushed her off.

"No, man—you're an all-out twat. Did it ever cross your pea-sized brain how she might perceive that?"

"Of course it bloody did, Hunt! Don't act like I don't know how fucked up this all is!"

"It's got a familiar tune, doesn't it?" All of Sam's excitement had vanished, replaced with a lethal tone. This was none of her playful prodding. Her jesting efforts to get a rise. She was as angry as Dillon had ever seen her. "It's almost like you've sung this song before."

Dillon drew a shaky breath through her nose, then deliberately counted the length of her exhale, trying to relax the muscles that had tightened through her core. She didn't want to say something—do something—she would regret.

"Save it, Sam. I don't want to hear it." Kelsey had been Sam's teammate for years. They'd come up through the youth national team together. But after they split, Sam had stuck firmly by Dillon's side. Until now.

"You didn't want to hear it the last time you fucked someone over who didn't deserve it, either, did you?" Sam leveled, unwilling to back down. "Never is a proper convenient time to be told you are a selfish wanker—"

"*Sam.*" Dillon stood. "The movie thing's got you wound."

"The only thing that's got me wound is the fact that one of the people I love best in the world is a thoughtless bastard—"

"You don't even know this girl—"

"But I know *you*, Sinc! And I know a pattern when I see one. Fear's got the better of you, marra. You're so worried about all the things that could go wrong, you won't let anything go right. Instead, you just run away and slam the door. I'm starting to think you really are a coward—"

"You're blowing this out of proportion—"

"Am I?" Sam shoved herself off the stack of weights. "Then tell me where I'm wrong!"

"For one thing, I didn't *run off*. I told her I'd call—and I will. I just needed time to think."

"About what? It's all very obvious, Sinc! You caught feelings for her. There's no denying it. You flew all the way to the States—"

"I wouldn't have, had I known—"

"Had you known what? You already knew she was an actress. What did you expect?"

"I don't know! Not *that*!"

"So it was all okay as long as she was some D-list nobody, right? Kind of like how it was fine when Kelsey was just a no-name second-half sub, yeah? Everything's good as long as no one else finds success in their career."

"You damn well know it isn't that!"

"I don't know, man," Sam gave a cursory shrug, "seems like you don't mind the limelight when it's you standing on that podium. Maybe you just don't want someone standing beside you?"

"I swear to God, Sam—because you're my mate, I'm going to pretend you didn't say that. But if you ever—"

"If I ever *what*?" Sam swooped up her towel with the blade of her leg, snatching it into her hand. "Call you out again for being an apathetic fuck? I'm sick of watching you throw away your chances. You think your life's so hard? You got the whole bloody world lying at your feet, and all you ever do is piss it away." She tried to grab her water bottle, but in her fury, struggled with her balance, and tipped it over, where it rolled out of reach. Without thinking, Dillon bent to gather it, but before she could, Sam punted it away. "Go on, then, Sinc. Shove your head in the sand and keep on running. But when you've chased off everyone else, don't come looking to me for sympathy."

Dillon said nothing as the click of Sam's uneven gait disappeared into the dressing room. For a horrible second, she felt like she might cry. But the sensation was fleeting. She hadn't cried in nine long years. She certainly wasn't going to start today. Instead, the only thing she really wanted to do was put her fist through the face staring back at her in the sweat-streaked mirror.

# Scene 23

I thanked the Uber driver, took one last glance at my reflection in the untinted window of his Nissan Sentra, and hopped out of the car. The sidewalk was packed. A line of people wrapped around the building on the southeast corner of Sunset and Vine, but I'd been instructed to head straight to the front door.

"What do I say?" I'd asked Elliott.

"Nothing. They'll know."

Approaching the black and white awning, I expected to find myself sent to the back of the line, but instead, before I even said my name, the bouncer waved me through the door. A woman—wearing leopard-print pants so snug they looked as if they'd been painted on—was waiting for me.

"This way, Miss Kingsbury. Mr. Dunn has not arrived yet. Mr. Fleming is at his preferred table on the rooftop." She ushered me into an elevator and swiped a keycard, beaming us to the top floor.

Elliott Fleming had called me a few hours earlier. When I'd realized who was on the other end of the line, a portion of my soul had departed my body.

Meet him and Grady Dunn at *Bartholomew's*, he'd said. Something about it being a rite of passage.

After hanging up, I panicked. I'd flown around my apartment tearing through my entire closet, changing at least a dozen times. I stood glaring at my face in my dollhouse-size bathroom mirror, wondering what miracle concealer would cover the bags beneath my eyes.

I looked like hell. Dillon's abrupt departure had left me in a slump. On the days I hadn't had to meet L.R. for role discussions, or sit through hours of being taped and measured for costume fittings, I'd spent my time sitting on my couch eating peanut butter out of a jar, staring at the notes from my rehearsals.

To further celebrate my pity party, I'd canceled both the Brazilian blowout and manicure I was desperately in need of. A decision I regretted while spending an hour dragging a flat iron through my uncooperative wavy hair.

*Bartholomew's* wasn't just an exclusive club. It was *thee* exclusive club—the hottest joint in Hollywood.

As the elevator door slid open, Leopard-Print-Pants pointed me toward the furthest corner of the open-top terrace. The dim lighting revealed Elliott's unmistakable profile, accentuated by the backdrop of the Hollywood hills. He was tipped back in his chair with his feet kicked up on the marbled ivory table, spitting pistachio shells onto the glass tile floor.

"Ah." He shot me a mock salute as I approached, brushing aside an empty tumbler with the toe of his Balenciaga sneaker. "You made it."

There was still a part of me expecting to blink and find out none of this was really happening. That I wasn't standing under the stars on the string-lit patio of a members-only nightclub, meeting Hollywood's golden boy to talk about our film. That at some point, I was going to wake up back in Hawaii on the morning of Dani's wedding and find out this was all just a cruel, elaborate dream.

"Thank you for the invite."

He flicked another shell to the ground. "With pleasure."

Sitting up, he flung his feet off the table and gave me a none-too-subtle once-over. I could feel his eyes slide over the fitted cut of my dress—a favorite of mine, not too priggish, but one that required imagination all the same. It had seemed an appropriate choice for the company and locale.

"Don't take this the wrong way, Kameryn—but I know a great stylist. She'll be perfect to help you freshen up that wardrobe."

*And strike me dead.*

The pinprick to my ego sent me plummeting to the ground.

Don't take it the wrong way? What other way was there to take it?

But before my burning humiliation could permit me to defy the scientific laws denying the existence of spontaneous human combustion, he gestured toward the seat across from him and bid me to sit down.

"Now," he leaned forward, tapping the rim of his crystal tumbler, "on a more important note: name your poison."

I was still reeling from the wardrobe comment. I couldn't begin to connect the dots in my head fast enough to come up with an intelligent answer. Did I say something fruity? Something classy? The way he was smiling at me, the question felt like a test. I'd been expecting to find the same friendly, supportive guy who'd encouraged me through my disaster of a table read. The fellow actor who had assured me my nerves were only natural, and not to worry, we were all in this together. The man sitting in front of me wasn't that guy at all.

"Or perhaps," he continued in my silence, "you'd prefer me to guess what kind of girl you are?" He made no attempt to hide the implication behind his wordplay. There was a shine in his eye that promised he was enjoying my discomfort, aware of my glance toward the empty seat, wondering how soon Grady would arrive. "Let's see." He set his elbows on the table. "You're too cautious for tequila—you'd find it too garish. But you're not bold enough for whisky. Rum would be too sweet, and gin too… boring?" He spun his tumbler between thumb and forefinger, his smile growing smug. "The hem of that dress says more than wine, and you're too skinny for beer. So—vodka. Versatile, readily available, and packs a punch when you least expect it."

I hated that he was right. Vodka was my go-to. Mainly because it was cheap—and yes, it had the fewest calories. And also because tequila and I had broken up after Dani's 21st birthday party. But I didn't appreciate his analysis.

"Wrong," I said, hoping to regain some of the dignity I'd lost after the dig at my attire. "Vodka might do the trick when you want a cosmopolitan, but personally, I prefer whisky."

I knew from his smile he could see right through me.

"You know," he leaned forward, "we're supposed to be honest with each other. Having a drink together is the second best way to build real chemistry." He lowered his voice. "And I'm sure you already know the best way."

And there it was. The quintessential douchebag. Nothing I'd expected from him based on the raving interview I'd read in *Rolling Stone* from Saoirse Ronan, who had boasted about her experience working with him. She'd called him sensitive. Praised his thoughtfulness. I believe the word *enlightened* had been used a time or two.

Apparently, his gallantry was limited to those sharing his same pay grade. I was not Saoirse Ronan and we both knew it. It was obvious he was aware he could push the envelope. What was I going to do? Go rushing to MacArthur?

"So what do you prefer, Kameryn? A drink? A shared drive home?" He flashed me his famous Hollywood smile. "Both?"

It disgusted me that I knew myself well enough to know a few months ago I might have considered taking him up on the offer. Not because he was coercing me. Despite his inappropriate insinuation, I didn't feel like there would be consequences if I turned him down. He may have been a slimeball, but he didn't give off a threatening vibe. Instead, I would have considered it simply because he was Elliott Fleming. I doubted many girls told him no.

Fortunately—or unfortunately, depending on how I wanted to look at it—I wasn't about to degrade myself to two one-night stands in less than a week. I was still incredibly hung up over Dillon. She'd left with no explanation beyond 'I need a little time to think,' and promised me she'd call within the week. Well, tomorrow was day six and I'd reached the conclusion she was ghosting me.

At least Elliott had more ethics than to pretend it would be anything more than a fuck.

"Is this little bastard already giving you a hard time?"

Elliott leisurely sat back as we both looked up to find Grady Dunn striding toward the table. He was dressed as sharply as he had been at the read-through and greeted me with the same succinct, courteous manner. "Hello, Miss Kingsbury—whatever he's said to you, ignore him. He's honestly just an insecure attention seeker."

I didn't risk a laugh, but I did offer him a smile, relieved to have his company.

Elliott did laugh, however. "Says the grown man who brings his pets with him everywhere he goes." He thrust his chin in the direction of two men in suits waiting a dozen feet away. Grady's bodyguards.

The day after the casting announcement, I read on *TMZ* that Grady had already received death threats from outraged fans.

In the books, there was no mention of race. Ethnicity was irrelevant to the storyline. But unshockingly, there were a gross number of readers who were furious the role of Noah had been cast as a Black man. They'd assumed a male protagonist written by a little old Caucasian lady from Iowa in the early eighties would be white. But Margaret Gilles herself had made it publicly clear she could imagine no actor better suited for the role. Grady was the apogean hero. Handsome. Athletic. Dashing. He exuded charisma. Everything the part demanded.

"The day you wake up to be a Black man in America, call me and we'll chat. Until then, shut your mouth."

"Don't get your panties in a twist, Dunn. We haven't even had a drink yet. Which reminds me," he raised two fingers in the air, motioning for a server I hadn't even realized was waiting for his signal, "I've just learned our lovely friend here is a whisky girl. Watch and learn, Kameryn. I'm about to introduce you to the life you've just stumbled into."

The waiter was instantly at the edge of the table. "Another of the usual, Mr. Fleming?"

"Not today. The evening calls for whisky, I think. Glenfiddich 30."

"My apologies, Mr. Fleming, the thirty is not a bottle we shelve. We do, however, have a very nice twelve."

"*Porter's* carries it."

The waiter hesitated. "I'm sorry?"

"*Porter's*. On Argyle." Elliott waited, expectant.

"I—" the man, twice Elliott's age, worried the cuffs of his dress shirt. "Yes, of course, Mr. Fleming. I will send a runner."

"Excellent." Elliott smiled out of the side of his mouth. "And our friend here, Miss Kingsbury, is a single malt connoisseur. She'll have a Bruichladdich X4. They carry it at *Bombay* on Ivar."

The waiter glanced my direction, but Elliott tapped a finger to the table, drawing his attention back to him. "That'll be all."

The man walked away to do as he was told.

Elliott grinned. "And that, my dear, is the gift you've just been given."

"And what gift is that?" Grady demanded, unsmiling. "The license to be an asshole?"

"Come down off your high horse, old boy. Both those shops are less than a block away. Do you really want to deny this is the world we live in?"

"You mean the world where my wife can't even get the mail in her pajamas without fear of dozens of photos being posted online? Commenting on her choice of dress, the sag of her breasts after feeding our child, the audacity she has for asking them to leave her alone. *That* world?"

Elliott blew an exaggerative sigh. "You can't have your cake and eat it too, Dunn. You know this life is full of perks and tonight is nothing more than our normal." He looked at me. "You just learn to take it all in stride. Here's a bit of advice, kid: smile for the cameras. Make the press feel welcome. They can be your worst nightmare or your best friend. Keep them on your side and you're golden. Piss them off, and, well," he side-eyed Grady, "they'll be hashtagging your saggy titties."

I expected Grady to be outraged. I *wanted* him to be outraged. But instead, he just ignored him, turning his focus to me.

"Here's the truth, Miss Kingsbury. Very soon you're going to wake up and you're not going to recognize the planet you are standing on. Your life is going to seem ethereal. You are going to find it hard to breathe. Hard to think. Hard to simply *be*. I'm not trying to scare you, but don't listen to this idiot pretend all of it is glitz and glamour. What you need to know is—we've all been through it. We're all *going* through it. And usually, it gets better—or at least we grow more accustomed to the atmosphere—and life moves on.

"You'll do okay. Just focus on the work and what you want to bring to the table. We all get caught up in the bright lights and madness of this new universe, but try not to let it change you. Keep the people who matter to you close, and let the rest slide away. And when things get too overwhelming—"

"Get blackout drunk," Elliott laughed, cutting him off as he slapped his palms on the edge of the table.

Grady rolled his eyes, but as the minutes passed, the two fell into a more amicable existence, the conversation drifting to the upcoming shooting schedule, and the inconvenience of the offbeat location filming destinations.

I tried to stay focused, but despite my star-studded company, my thoughts were anxious to wander. I wanted to check my phone. There was an off chance Dillon could still call. An off chance this was all just a gigantic misunderstanding.

"And here's the man of the hour!" Elliott stood suddenly, offering the returning waiter a slow, patronizing clap, and pulled a wad of bills out of his wallet. "Well done, my friend. Well done." He tucked the cash into the man's breast pocket and swept up the two bottles. "Keep the change, okay?" As the waiter departed, Elliott filled our glasses, shoving them across the table. "To the newest member of our miserable little band." He raised his glass to me. "Drink up, Kingsbury."

I could smell the heat of the whisky before I'd even picked up my tumbler. I wasn't concerned about holding my own when it came to hard liquor—I'd mastered that art in high school—but I wasn't a fan of sipping it neat and always preferred a mixer. It kept me from doing stupid things. But I wasn't about to ask for juice or soda.

Setting the glass to my lips, I downed a deep swig, and—*holy fucking slam me in the face with a mallet!* There was no avoiding the racking, gagging, sputtering cough that hit me as the brutal inferno of heat burned the lining off my esophagus. Whatever poisoned concoction I'd just inhaled certainly wasn't the typical run-of-the-mill whisky.

"Easy there, m'girl." Through my streaming eyes, I could see Elliott's cocky grin across the table. "I'd pegged you for someone who could swallow."

"You are the epitome of a tool, Fleming," Grady snapped, setting a hand on my shoulder. He waved the waiter over for a carafe of water.

"What?" Elliott feigned indignance. "We're all friends here. I mean hell, I'm going to see Kameryn naked in a couple of weeks—it's the least I can do to learn how she likes to take her liquor."

I'd been blessedly too overwhelmed since learning I got the part to find time to worry about individual aspects of the filming. The nudity scenes—something I had never done—had been only a source of low-key apprehension. Now, however, with his disparaging comments and innuendos, that subdued apprehension had turned into full-fledged anxiety. I couldn't imagine playing those scenes with *him*. He was so much more of an asshole than I ever imagined possible.

"See, she's all good," he gave my arm a playful slug. "Aren't you, Kameryn? That's quadruple-distilled 184-proof single malt. Strongest whisky in the world. You could power a sports car off it." He pried the glass from my white-knuckled hand and downed the remaining finger. Sweat broke out on his upper lip and he had to clear his throat, but otherwise managed to pull off the gesture with indifference. "Easy-breezy, no?" He poured another. "Your turn."

"You do not have to drink that—" Grady started, but I swept up the glass and downed the measure.

*Fuck Elliott Fleming.*

This time I managed not to choke, even as the equilibrium of the rooftop swirled around me.

"Atta girl. What a pro. I knew you could take it."

"You're taking this too far, Fleming!" Grady launched to his feet, his own drink untouched on the table. "I will not tolerate this!"

"Did I miss an *or else*?" Elliott's eyes shined with malice. There was nothing about him that resembled the charismatic boy in the posters filling the cinema halls, or the smiling headshot currently plastered across the entertainment news announcing his role in *Sand Seekers*. All he looked like was a thorn in my side I was going to have to bear for the indefinite future.

Once again, he refilled the glass and pushed it toward me. He was leaning close enough that his aftershave was beginning to make me sick to my stomach.

"Do you know, Kameryn, that this is my third film with MacArthur? He and I have done some incredible things together." He moved the glass into my hand. "You might not realize it, but I spent weeks watching film tests with L.R. as we combed the globe looking for a suitable actress for the role of Addison. Were you given that same opportunity, Grady?" He held up a dismissive palm. "Save your breath, I already know the answer." His steely gaze returned to me. "You don't need a knight in shining armor, do you, Kameryn?"

I may have responded with a shake of my head, but I couldn't be certain. I was already seeing double. I knew behind his veiled threats he wasn't bluffing. He had history with MacArthur. He had clout. He'd put his own money into the project. Grady may have been the more decorated artist, but Elliott was the draw. All three of us knew it. But I was the only one in jeopardy of losing my job. I realized suddenly this was why he'd asked me here. He had a point to make. On this production, he was king. He wanted to make sure I knew it. Grady, too.

I picked up the whisky. This time it didn't burn going down. Beside me I could feel Grady's rage, but he didn't say anything.

I couldn't remember if I'd eaten this morning. It may have been last night. My stomach felt like it was disintegrating from the inside out.

"What a champ you are, Kingsbury! Way to put it down!"

Standing, I steadied myself with the table as Grady leapt to take my arm. I suddenly didn't care if I lost my job. I had to get home. I was going to puke. "I—I have to go."

"Oh, c'mon, Kameryn, we're just getting started—"

"Fuck off, Elliott!" Grady hissed over my shoulder as I staggered across the glass tile. Their voices sounded far away, despite Grady still holding my arm. "I'm going to take you home."

"No, no, thank you…" I'd made it to the elevator, my fingers desperately searching for the down button. "I can Uber." I was vaguely aware he'd waved off his security as he guided me through the sliding doors.

"You really shouldn't—"

"I promise, I'm fine!" My voice broke and I was sure I was going to cry. "Please, just..."

Just what? What could he do?

"Let me have your phone." Without waiting for permission, he reached into my purse. "Type in your passcode."

We were on the ground floor by the time I could put the four digits in the right order. I handed my phone back to him and he ordered my Uber.

There were bursts of light and raised voices. It took me a moment to realize they were camera flashes from the waiting paparazzi. Grady pulled me away from the front door, sheltering me through a crowded room into a darkened hall, until he'd shouldered his way through an unmarked exit leading to a quiet back alley.

"I'm sorry," I choked, leaning against the brick wall. "I don't think I ate earlier, and, the whisky—I think it just went to my head..."

It wasn't what I was sorry for. I was sorry for being a pathetic, wilting, spineless coward. A jellyfish who didn't have an ounce of courage to stand up for herself when it really mattered. Grady had tried to stand up for me, and I'd just pushed him aside.

"It's going to be okay, Kameryn." He gave my arm a squeeze. I was grateful he didn't ask me if I wanted him to talk to L.R. or try to approach MacArthur. It would have done no good and just made the humiliation all the more acute.

When my Uber arrived, Grady opened the door and poured me into the back seat. "Gallon of water and something greasy. I'll see you at the studio. You have my number if you want to talk." He closed the door.

On the short drive down Melrose, I stared out the window. I don't know how it was possible, but my thoughts were back on Dillon.

Tomorrow was New Year's Eve. I wanted to text her, but refused to give in.

What a clown I'd been.

Tonight. Last week. All the days in between.

I pressed my cheek against the cool glass, praying I wouldn't barf. That was all I needed in the headlines. *Kameryn Kingsbury Might Swallow, But She Can't Keep It Down.*

It would be the perfect start to the New Year.

# Scene 24

The athletic bay mare flew around the course, clearing fences as if powered by invisible wings. Triple bar, joker, Liverpool, an oxer as wide as it was tall. Both horse and rider made it look effortless, handling each jump with ease.

Dillon sat on the top rail of the arena, counting strides between combinations, marveling at Seren's ability to communicate with her mare through signals she could never see.

It was a dance. A duet. A pas de deux of perfect harmony.

She loved watching her sister ride. Loved the sheer grace of her form, the beauty of her style, the composure she radiated whenever she was in the saddle.

It seemed impossible they were related. Seren was everything their English mother was: graceful, tall, slender, with raven black hair and mahogany brown eyes. Studious and serious. Growing up, she had been the ballerina, the fashion aficionado, the girl who'd turned the head of every boy in secondary school.

Dillon had taken after their Welsh father.

Lacking in height, broad-shouldered, blonde-haired and green-eyed, with skin that burned at just the hint of sunshine. She'd been born with their dad's laid-back, jesting nature, and had built with him an ardent bond through their keen love of sport and competition. Where she lacked Seren's willowy lissomness, Dillon excelled at all things requiring strength and endurance.

They were two divergent seeds born of the same pod.

What they did share, however, was their parents' driving ambition. Both had inherited the desire for a challenge. It had been no surprise that the two competitive children had grown into adults with Olympic aspirations. A dream that had been realized for Dillon almost a decade sooner than her older sister—but one she always knew Seren would eventually achieve.

It had been one of the proudest moments of Dillon's life when, the year before in Melbourne, Seren was named as an alternate to Great Britain's equestrian eventing team.

Those Summer Games had been a personal disappointment for Dillon—not only because of her second-place finish, but because her sister had never been called to ride. It had to kill Seren, she knew, to have gone all that way and worked that hard and never be given the chance to compete.

The mare Seren qualified with, a Dutch Warmblood named Epic Forces—lovingly called Épée—was the most talented horse she'd ever ridden. The owners had given her carte blanche to develop her as she saw fit. And watching them work this morning, Dillon had no doubt the pair would be headed to Los Angeles with a guaranteed spot on the Olympic Eventing squad for Team GB.

"Two golds for Team Sinclair in our future," she grinned as Seren spotted her on the railing and brought Épée down to a walk.

"You and your gold medal obsession," Seren laughed, her breath disappearing into the cloud of steam rising from the bay mare's neck. "I'll just be happy to make the team."

"Bollocks." Dillon hopped off the fence, falling into stride beside the long-legged mare. "I know you want that hardware."

Seren drew Épée to a stop. "Hack out with me? She could use a long cool-off."

Dillon rarely rode anymore, but when Seren asked her to, she never turned her down. She loved any stolen minutes she could spend with her sister. So seldom did the two of them have time together alone.

Quickly bridling one of the old school horses, she swung up bareback and joined Épée and Seren on a leisurely excursion along the cross-country course running through the rolling hills surrounding the farm. It was the day before New Year's Eve, and the training center was quiet, leaving the two young women with the grounds to themselves.

"So what's up, Dilly?" They'd wandered down to the rippling creek and picked their way along the bank, avoiding the dripping tree branches that warmed with the rising sun. "I know you've not turned up in Swansea to ask me for a cuppa and watch me work."

*Dilly.* No one else called her that. No one else could get away with it. Dillon would throw hands before she allowed it. But somehow, coming from Seren, she'd always loved it.

Seren gave Épée her head to pick her way across a slippery patch of mud, with Dillon following closely behind. It had been a couple years since she'd ridden. When they were children, she'd tag along with Seren to the farm every Saturday. She'd help her tack up her horses and often end the afternoon with the two of them hacking out.

Then, she started training with Henrik. He convinced her if she wanted to make it as a professional, there was no time for extraneous pastimes. No time for school. And eventually, no time for family.

So the Saturday mornings at the barn had come to an end.

"Do you think I'm apathetic?"

She hadn't really intended to ask the question, but it had been gnawing at her for the past couple days. Ever since Sam accused her of having no feelings.

"What?" Seren almost laughed as she drew Épée to a halt, turning to look back at her. "*You?*"

Dillon hiked a shoulder, trying to pull off indifferent, but Seren saw straight through her.

"Dillon." She sounded exactly like their mother when she said it. It was her *listen to me, how can you be so daft* tone. They were both stopped now, the horses taking advantage of their distraction to snag a few mouthfuls of tall ryegrass. "Who put that idea into your head? The new girl—?"

"*No.*" Dillon was quickly defensive. "Forget I asked—"

"Whoever told you that is a pillock. I don't know if there's a person who could be *less* apathetic than you. And I'm not just saying that because you're my sister." She swung a leg over her mare's wither so she could turn and face her. "You feel *everything*, Dillon. You always have. Sometimes too much."

Dillon disliked the unfamiliar prick she could feel at the back of her eyes. The catch in her throat. She wasn't sure if it was because she'd feared the answer, or if it was because Seren so vehemently had her back—as steadfastly as she always had, ever since they were children. Even when Dillon least deserved it.

Sliding off the grey gelding, she dropped into the wet undergrowth, Seren following suit. They pulled the bridles off the horses and set them loose to graze. Above them, the sun had cleared the treetops and brought a warmth to the breeze.

Heedless of the damp grass, Dillon flopped onto her back, staring at the overcast sky. Seren joined her, shoulder-to-shoulder.

"Talk to me, Dilly," said Seren.

And then she waited. Waited like she always did.

Waited until Dillon told her everything.

From Santa Monica to San Francisco. *Sand Seekers* to Sam.

Seren listened patiently, never cutting in, and when Dillon had finished, she remained quiet, taking time to think.

"Sam has some fair points," she said at length, though her tone was devoid of judgment. "You have developed a pattern of running away, but not for the reasons she believes."

Dillon said nothing, watching as a blue tit flitted along the branches above them, its yellow belly glittering with dewdrops.

Rolling on her side, Seren propped herself onto an elbow to look at her sister through the curtain of meadow grass.

"You're different than most people, Dillon, but I don't think you realize it. Very few people have your kind of ambition. Your intense focus and tenacity. And because of that, I think you're drawn to women with the same qualities. You—intentional or not—choose extraordinary because *you* are extraordinary. It's only natural to be attracted to someone with a like mind—with like dreams."

"It's not the ambition that worries me."

"Of course not. It's what you're most attracted to. But it's what pushes these women to success. It's the reason they stand out in their careers. *Hufen yn codi*, right?"

One of their dad's favorite sayings: *Cream rises.*

It was always strange to hear Seren speak Welsh. She spoke so little of the language. It had never been of interest to her.

"So what are you getting at? I need to change my type?"

Seren laughed. "You couldn't change that if you wanted to. And for the record," she nudged her shin with the toe of her riding boot, "I never want you to change anything about you. You're exactly who you should be."

"Whoever that is," Dillon muttered, still gazing at the sky.

Seren was quiet a moment, contemplative, before continuing. "I know you're afraid what happened after Dad is going to happen again. You were really young and vulnerable, and the press exploited that—"

"It has nothing to do with that—!"

"It has *everything* to do with that and we both know it. It's why you panicked with the attention you were getting while you were with Kelsey, and it's why you're back home now." Rolling into a sitting position, she plucked the blossom off a creeping thistle and rolled it between her fingers. "It doesn't mean it's going to be like that again, Dillon. The year after Dad died was a tsunami of events that led to the perfect storm. You were already getting so much media because of the Olympics, and then, what Henrik said after Dad—"

"I don't want to talk about it, Seren!"

"We *are* going to talk about it! We've never talked about it, but we're going to talk about it now!"

Dillon turned her face away. Never had Seren pushed on her. Never had she forced her to address all the years of unspoken hurts lying dormant between them. But there was no escaping this conversation short of getting up and walking away.

The soft fingertips of Seren's lambskin gloves gently touched her cheek, turning her head back toward her. "I know you still tell everyone he died because he was sick. And I get it. I don't like to think about it either. But I also know, because of what you went through after he killed himself, that you're afraid it's—"

"What would you know of it, Seren?!" Dillon shoved her hand aside, leaping to her feet. She wanted to run. To be anywhere but here. "You aren't the reason he's dead! No one ever pointed the finger at you!"

Seren was up half a beat behind her, grabbing a hold of the collar of her jacket, staring down at her with the same furious intensity.

"The *only* reason Dad is dead is because *Dad* made a horrible decision to take his life. *No one* else made that decision for him, Dillon. *No one*. Not you. Not me. Not Mam. Not even that bastard, Henrik. That was Dad and Dad alone. And don't you ever fucking forget it!"

Dillon tried to pull away, but couldn't shake Seren's grip. It was the first time she'd ever heard her sister swear. The first time she'd ever raised her voice to her.

"That's easy for you to say." Dillon gave one last weak attempt to break free of her grasp, but it was already too late. She could hear the tears trembling in her voice. Feel them streaming down her cheeks. And there was nothing she could do about it. There was no place she could run this time to make them go away. No time to beat. No record to break. No medal to chase. And when Seren reached forward to take her in her arms, she wanted to cling to her, to let her sister burden the weight of her despair, but all she could do was stand there, her arms hanging at her sides, and cry.

Seren held her anyhow. Held her as her body wracked with the unfamiliar release. Held her through her choking sobs until, at last, she could finally breathe.

Sensing the ebbing wave of her emotion, Seren took a half step back, releasing her from her hold.

"You have to let it go, Dillon. You run and run and run, and keep everyone at arm's length. I know you're terrified of who you were when you were nineteen. I know the guilt eats at you. But we can't change the past. I'm tired of living in it. I'm tired of watching you live in it." She brushed the back of an impatient hand across her own eyes. "There's so much of Dad in you. There are so many things I loved about him I get to see in you every day. But you're *not* him. So don't let his decisions shape you. You're your own worst enemy. Henrik is gone. Dad is dead. It's time for you to let it go. It's time for you to figure out how to love yourself." She reached out, brushing the hair from Dillon's eyes. "Please."

Dillon looked away, out over the meadow, down the rolling hills to the sea. The tide had gone out in the bay, leaving a thousand shells sparkling in the rays of sun that had broken through the clouds. Above them, a goldfinch burst into a melodious tune, startling the horses, who raised their heads to hear the song.

"I wouldn't even know where to start." She tugged a black berry off a wild privet, flicking the poisoned fruit into the brush.

"I think you do." Seren smiled. "Not that I'm overly fond of Hollywood."

Dillon took a long, shaky breath, before looking at her sister. "You better learn to be," she said, allowing herself to find her own half smile. "In a few years, you and Épée are going to be intimately familiar with Los Angeles."

"Leave it to you to always have your mind too far in the future," Seren chastised. "For just one minute, will you think about today?"

Dillon ran her palm over the sweep of ryegrass, thinking about how abruptly she'd left California. How unfair she'd been to Kam.

"What if she doesn't want to hear from me?"

"Don't be twp, little sister," Seren poked her with the nub of her spur as she bent to collect their bridles.

Dillon knew she'd chosen the word deliberately. Another of their dad's favorites—the Welsh word for daft. She wanted it to be okay to talk about him. To remember him. Without all the hurt.

"I promise you, she's waiting by the phone." Seren slung the leather crownpiece into Dillon's hand. "Any girl would."

# Scene 25

I'd always spent New Year's Eve with Dani. Either in Los Angeles or Palo Alto, or her family's summer retreat in Tahoe.

If we were at the lake, we'd talk our way onto a cute guy's boat, ringing in the New Year watching fireworks from the water. Up north, we'd take a midnight swim in her parent's infinity pool while Marcus and his friends passed a joint around the hot tub. In LA, it was always the club scene in Beverly Hills with knee-high boots and miniskirts, the only recollection of the night restored by half a dozen wristbands.

Whatever we did, we were guaranteed to be drunk, Dani would be high, and the next morning I'd regrettably be nursing a hangover. Since we'd been old enough to drive, the tradition had continued like clockwork.

This year, however, Dani didn't ask me to come, and I didn't offer. We hadn't spoken since Christmas. I'm sure she thought she was punishing me, but honestly, the silence had been a respite. I just didn't have the energy to coddle her bruised ego.

I'd been invited to a party at the studio but opted not to go. After the night out with Elliott and Grady, I'd woken feeling like I'd been trampled by a herd of rhinos. No matter how many Advil I chased with Gatorade, or how long I stood in the trickle of water from my 1920s showerhead, there was nothing that was going to revive me enough to drag myself into Universal City to face a second consecutive night with Elliott Fleming.

"You *have* to go!" Sophie had pitched a fit when I called her and told her about the night at *Bartholomew's*. "You can't let him get away with this! You have to show him you're not afraid of him!"

I'd held the phone away from my ear and shielded my eyes from the cheerful sunlight audaciously filtering through my kitchen window. There was no way in hell I was leaving the creature comforts of my apartment, let alone pulling on a bra or heels any time over the next ninety-six hours. Not until midweek, when I was due back in the studio.

After a futile list of reasons why I shouldn't turn down an invitation to one of the most exclusive New Year's Eve parties in the industry, she launched into her next bullet point: I needed to file a sexual harassment complaint against Elliott.

"Report him for what?" I asked, chugging another Gatorade, revolted by my own cottonmouth. "Snubbing my wardrobe? Making lewd comments while egging me on to knock back 92% whisky? Reminding me I'm no one in this industry?"

"Yes!"

"*Sophe.*" I chucked the empty bottle toward my trash can, where it banked off the wall and skidded into my living room with just enough force to knock over my guitar. My head still hammering, I dragged myself across the checkered tile of my kitchen to right the old Fender, my oversensitive ears reviling against my foiled attempt to shoot for three. "You know we're talking about Elliott Fleming, right? The guy's listed as an executive producer on the film, for God's sake. Which one of us do you think will be sent packing if I show up crying that he didn't like my outfit?"

"He suggested you sleep with him!"

"Not in so many words."

"I can't believe you're defending him!"

"I'm not!" I wholly regretted relaying to her the details of the evening. I didn't know how to explain that despite him being a pig, I didn't feel threatened by him. It wasn't like he'd gone full Harvey Weinstein on me and requested a blowjob in his trailer. He didn't strike me as that type. But I should have known that Sophie—who had more guts in her little fingernail than I had in my entire abdominal cavity— would want his head on a spike.

"Then don't just let him get away with being an asshole!"

I wanted to ask her what industry she'd been working in these last five years? Eighty percent of these people were assholes. The other twenty just did a better job of putting on a cover. And yes, the Gloria Steinem devotee in me knew she was right, and I shouldn't let him get away with it.

But I was going to.

I wanted this job, and I knew exactly what a complaint about the insinuation of a shared ride home was going to get me—a *trivia* note on IMDb: Kameryn Kingsbury was the original actress cast as Addison

Riley before a scheduling conflict with the studio didn't allow her to proceed. She is now known mostly for her bit part in *Mean Girls III*.

"I'll think about it," I assured her before we hung up. And I did think about it—the full seven steps from my dining room table to my living room couch, where I promptly filed it away in the category of *things just not going to happen.* In less than two weeks I was scheduled to be on a flight to the southwestern coast of Greenland, where we would begin principal photography.

I wanted to be on that plane.

I spent the remainder of the day poring over the script for the two-hundredth time in between googling the conversion of -15°C into Fahrenheit. I could appreciate L.R.'s dedication to utilizing as little chroma keying as possible—I'd never met a single actor who enjoyed working on green screen—but I was also a little nervous about frostbite. Weeks on end in sub-freezing temperatures definitely had me browsing Amazon for the highest-rated thermal underwear.

By the time evening rolled around, the city sounded like a warzone outside my apartment. I'd drawn my curtains and flipped on the radio, trying to drown out the gunshots and fireworks blasting in tandem with the wail of sirens, but there was no escaping the chaos reverberating through the usually quiet streets of my neighborhood. I gave up on my backstory analysis and opened a new browser on my Macbook. I was halfway through a twelve-step article on *How to Get Someone Off Your Mind* when my phone rang.

It was a private number.

"Hello?"

"Duuude!" There was a hushed whisper followed by a peal of laughter from a handful of high-pitched male voices. "She picked up! What do I say?"

I hung up. My number was unpublished, but over the last few days, I'd received at least a dozen of these phone calls. Mostly teenagers, I imagined, based on the imbecility of their stuttered dialogue every time I answered. I needed to change my number—it had been leaked somewhere—but I couldn't bring myself to do it yet.

Tomorrow, Monday—New Year's Day—it would be a week. If she hadn't called by Tuesday, I'd give in and change it.

The blast of an air horn on the sidewalk outside my window made me jump, sending my iPhone clattering to the hardwood floor.

*Son of a bitch.*

I snatched it up, examining it for damage.

On second thought, maybe I'd just go ahead and change it. First, maybe I'd shoot her a text message of my own, telling her what I really thought—and then cut off the line before she could respond.

Because, well—fuck her. Fuck her for all her charm and her windswept hair and her bullshit about not turning lies into truths. Fuck her for making me think she wanted something more than just a casual screw. She could have been upfront. I wouldn't have turned her down. But at least then I wouldn't be sitting here googling how to forget someone I barely knew.

Yeah, forget Tuesday. First thing in the morning I was calling Verizon and requesting a new unlisted number. A fresh start to the New Year. A cleansing of the old me.

As was fitting of the drama of my Hollywood lifestyle, my phone rang in my lap before I could return my attention to my computer screen. There was no doubt Momus—the god of Satire and Mockery— had been peering down through the LA haze, biding his time to make a fool out of me.

*Rolling. Speed. Action.*

It was Dillon's face lighting up my caller ID. Oh, the pathetic, well-timed irony.

*Chill pill, Kam.*

I counted five beats, certain not to answer on the first ring. The last thing I wanted was for her to think I'd been sitting around waiting for her call all week.

I didn't, however, go with my initial plan to pretend I didn't know who she was. *I'm sorry, who? Oh—yeah, sorry, it's been quite a week. Yeah, yeah—Dillon—of course. How are you?*

Instead, I promptly blurted out, "Wow! Just over three hours to spare. Nice."

Perfect. So much for playing it cool.

"I'm sorry, Kam."

I at least had the benefit of knowing I had stung her. Her voice was quiet and sounded like she was stuck in an echo chamber. The Tube, I realized. It was four in the morning in London. She'd be on her way to Kensington Gardens for an early run.

On our drive up north, we'd chatted about our holiday rituals. She told me she loved to ring in the New Year with a 10k through her favorite park. I doubted she remembered what I'd told her. I liked to sleep in before starting my day with two cups of coffee—not mentioning a third was usually needed to combat my hangover—and then sit in bed and read a book cover-to-cover before making a trip to the local AMC to watch my first film of the year.

This year, I'd planned to spend it a little differently—swapping out reading for other extracurricular activities—but obviously that had been before Dillon disappeared to the UK.

"Okay." I returned my attention to the phone call. *So what* was what I wanted to say. Instead, I went with a surefire classic. The polite rebuff. "What can I do for you?"

She cleared her throat. It was the first time I'd heard her nervous. It gave me back a shred of dignity, boosting my resolve.

"I was hoping we could talk."

I worked at a splinter on the edge of my table, tearing bits of wood off shard by shard. "So, talk."

Again, the conversation was stilted by her unfamiliar hesitation. "I —would rather—well, not like this. I thought maybe we could speak in person, if—"

I wasn't going to let the fact that I loved the lilt of her accent, the low, full tone of her voice, trick me into letting her lead me on. What was her plan? Hop on another twelve-hour flight back to California? Show up on my doorstep to wish me goodnight? Make out with me beneath the Santa Monica Pier? Maybe we could drive up PCH for another one-night stand in the heart of Fog City?

Nah, that was so last week.

"Yeah, sorry. I'm leaving for Greenland to shoot a film. I don't know if you heard, but I'm in this new movie. It's got my schedule pretty tight for the next few months." I hated the bitterness in my voice. But she deserved it. I wasn't the one who'd cut and run. Still, I couldn't help adding, "I'll be in Scotland after that. I know London's not exactly around the corner, but, if you happen to be on the same land mass at the same time, and want to meet for a cup of coffee, you know how to reach me."

I didn't want to shut her out completely. Honestly, I didn't want to shut her out at all. But my feelings were hurt and I didn't want her to think I'd let her off scot-free. I was tired of being walked over.

*New Year, New Me.* My new mantra.

As if any of that motivational shit worked anyhow.

"What part of Scotland?" she asked.

"Aberdeen."

"Ah. It's beautiful up there. You should drive to Stonehaven if you get the chance. See the ruins of Dunnottar." In other words, she wasn't coming. "When do you leave for Greenland?"

"In two weeks. Why, is there a particular glacier you think I should see? Any other tourist tips?"

Shit. *Shit*. I'd taken it a step too far. This was a girl I actually *did* want to see again, regardless my injured ego. But my mouth was on a one-track effort to sabotage the likeliness of that ever happening.

"No," she sighed. "I haven't been there." In the background there was an announcement from the conductor. I needed to say something before she got off at her stop.

"Look, Dillon," my voice had lost its edge, the wind quickly spilling from my sails. "Last week—I—I just—I don't know. It wasn't what I expected. I really like you, to be honest. I'd be lying if I said I wasn't hoping our paths will cross again."

"I'd like that, too." She sounded sincere. But then again, she'd sounded sincere all along. I waited.

*Please, please, please say something else.*

She didn't. There was just a long pause of silence.

"Well," I finally said, "Happy New Year, then."

"Happy New Year, Kam." And that was it. She hung up.

I returned to my script as another gunshot went off.

An hour passed before I realized I'd reread the same page at least two dozen times.

I flipped the script onto my coffee table and shoved myself to my feet. It wasn't even nine yet. The ball hadn't even dropped in Times Square, but all I wanted to do was go to bed and wake up next year. Or maybe the following century. One where I hadn't screwed up everything.

Discovering my bathroom drain was clogged, I was brushing my teeth in the kitchen sink when I was interrupted by a knock at the door.

Sophie'd talked about stopping by after leaving the Night Market in Silver Lake, but I can't lie—an unwarranted flicker of hope begged for it to be Dillon, teleported five thousand miles across the sea, showing up on my porch to make things right.

Of course, that wasn't the case.

I cracked the door to find two men, dressed in disheveled three-piece suits, standing on my stoop.

"Can I help you?"

The taller of the two tilted his head to look through the crack. "Kameryn Kingsbury?"

I should have said no, but I wasn't thinking fast enough. "Yes?"

"Right on!" He slapped the other man on his back and pulled a branch out of his pocket. Mistletoe, it finally registered to me as he held it above his head. "How about a kiss for the New Year?" He stuffed his dress shoe through the gap, forcing the door open another foot, reeking of alcohol.

"What?" I braced my shoulder against the door, beginning to panic.

The second man had pulled out his phone, recording a video. "Smile for the camera, baby," he laughed as his buddy tried to lean in to kiss me.

"Get the fuck out of here!" It took two slams of the door—the first on his foot, and the second against his fingers in the doorjamb—before I could successfully close it. I wasn't certain what was loudest: his shout of agony, his friend's laughter, or the trapeze work of my heart. My hands were shaking too badly to fit the security chain in the tarnished slot, so I settled for the top bolt, and then leaned back against the peeling paint to try and catch my breath.

I needed to call my agent, Aaron. Or the cops. Someone.

But then what? Those guys were long gone. It wasn't like there were any charges I could press.

I stood frozen for I wasn't sure how long. Long enough for my heartbeat to slow down, but not so long that my fingers quit shaking. I thought about what Grady said the night before—about waking on another planet and finding it hard to breathe. And I knew this was just a teaser trailer. I hadn't even caught a glimpse of the feature presentation.

Across the room the clock on my mantel chimed once, informing me it was nine-thirty. I'd been there for more than half an hour. Wiggling my toes, I tried to return some feeling to my bare feet. I realized I was going to be featured in some jackass's TikTok wearing my high school gym shorts and a white tank top without a bra. Running my thumb across my lips, I confirmed my fear that I still had dried toothpaste at the corners of my mouth.

I would have been better off making headlines by puking in the Uber.

Outside, steps sounded on my walkway again. Outrage tore through me at the invasion of privacy. Abandoning all sensibility, I spun to unbolt the lock and hurled open the door, losing my grip on the handle and smashing it into the wall. I didn't care. My landlord could send me the bill for damage in prison. I was going to murder these bastards.

"I swear to God, if you take one more step, I'm going to—!"

I stopped dead, my hands planted firmly on the doorjamb, and stared into Dillon's stunned face.

"I—oh my God, I'm sorry," I stammered. I couldn't think straight. "There were some boys—I thought…" I looked down, spotting the dropped mistletoe, and gave a *see* gesture, trying to prove I wasn't crazy.

"Boys, huh?" She bent and picked up the sprig.

My mouth slowly rediscovered English was my first—and only—language.

"What are you doing here?"

"Well, it appears I'm a little too late on the idea of stopping by with mistletoe." She smiled, but I could tell she was nervous. "I am still holding out hope, however, that you might be up for a chat in person?"

# Scene 26

Dillon flinched as a vacuum toppled onto the living room floor from the overstuffed entryway closet. She watched Kam shove the Dyson back onto the shelf, cursing under her breath. It was clear she was embarrassed by the casual disorder of her apartment. She'd made a brisk sweep of her couch and dining room table, gathering discarded articles of clothing and a half-eaten bowl of cereal, dropping the latter on the kitchen counter and the clothes onto the closet floor.

"I wasn't—I mean, I don't usually—I'm not an untidy person. I just hadn't..." She forced the closet door shut with her shoulder. "I wasn't expecting company."

"I'm sorry, Kam," Dillon kept to the safety of the threshold, "I should have asked you if it was all right if I came over."

Kam had already moved on to her coffee table, where she was stacking what looked to be a scattered screenplay. Her entire body was radiating with tension. "Will you close the door?" She busied herself slipping the pages into a manilla envelope, not looking at Dillon. "I've had… there's been… just close it, please."

Dillon pulled it shut and flipped the oxidized lock. Based on Kam's outburst on the doorstep, she imagined she wasn't the first to show up uninvited. She knew that look. She'd watched Kelsey suffer the same anxiety.

Turning to toss the envelope onto her table, Kam bumped a classical guitar resting against the wall, tipping it over, where it emitted an angry chord. "God damn it!" For a second Dillon thought she was going to boot the offending instrument, but with a groan of exasperation, she changed her mind and sank onto the arm of her couch instead.

"Why are you here, Dillon?"

She had spent the past twelve hours going over the question, ever since stepping onto the last-minute flight from Heathrow.

*Just be honest*, Seren advised her. *Just tell her the truth.*

"May I?" she motioned at a dining room chair. It felt too presumptuous to sit beside Kam on the two-seater couch.

"Might as well, you're already here."

If she had to guess, Kam was clinging to her bitterness as a form of self-preservation. Her body language didn't match her tone. Beneath her anger, she looked like she was going to cry.

"I can come back tomorrow, Kam, if you'd rather. Or not at all. I promise I came here with no expectations."

"Oh no?" Kam crossed her arms, defensive. "Didn't just swing by for a midnight booty call before hopping another flight back home?"

Leaning against the edge of the table, Dillon released a slow exhale. She deserved Kam's resentment, but it didn't make it easier to face.

"I know I handled things poorly. It was unfair for me to leave the way I did."

"Unfair?" Kam's laugh was derisive. "You said less than a dozen words to me on a six-hour drive home. You got out of my car, grabbed your stuff, and told me 'I'm sorry, I'll call you this week. I have to go.' And *left*." She tapped the envelope with her script in it against her calf, before tossing it back to the coffee table. "I think the worst part is, I don't even know why I cared so much. We spent a fun night together —so what? You don't owe me an explanation—"

"I *do* owe you an explanation, and I hope you'll hear me out."

She took Kam's silence as permission to proceed.

Lacing her hands behind her head, she stared up at the ceiling. "I panicked when your movie was announced. I know I should have been happy for you—it's amazing, *you're* amazing—but I..." She trailed off. She wasn't certain where to start. The hardest part, she decided. Just once more, she could do this. And then Seren was right—it was time to let it go.

"I told you my dad passed away when I was nineteen. That he'd been sick. What I didn't say is that he died by suicide... because of me."

Her mouth felt chalky. It didn't matter what Seren said. They all knew the truth.

None of them more so than Dillon.

She continued. "When I was fourteen, I began training with a man named Henrik. Up to that point, my dad had been coaching me, but he'd heard a rumor that Henrik Fischer—a two-time Olympic gold medalist—was beginning to accept students for his new training program. We met with him. Henrik didn't have a facility yet, but said

—since he was currently living in London, and I was still in school—
he could come to Swansea and coach me on the weekends.

"It cost my parents a fortune, but my dad was elated. Henrik was
world-class. I immediately hated him—he was very strict and very
demanding—but my dad was so certain he was the answer to achiev-
ing my dreams, I stuck it out. I didn't want to fail my dad or the faith
he had in me. And there was no denying the results.

"Within the first six months, I was placing higher on the podium,
breaking all my personal bests. But the more success I had, the more
dependent I became on Henrik. I no longer felt I could compete
without his guidance. I grew terrified of disappointing him. Terrified
he would quit coaching me. I was certain the only way I'd ever become a world champion—the only way I'd ever make the Olympic
team—was with his help. So I did anything to please him." Dillon
shifted against the edge of the table, dropping her gaze from the
ceiling, but instead of looking at Kam, refocused on the ticking clock
on the mantel. "Which, um," she swallowed, forcing herself to continue, "meant that by the time he wanted more from me—I didn't know
how to say no."

She risked a glance at Kam, making certain she'd understood, and
then quickly continued. "Bear with me, I promise, there's a reason I'm
telling you this, and I will come full circle to your question."

Outside, a shadow moved across the drawn window blinds as a
group of laughing revelers passed along the sidewalk.

"Eventually, Henrik announced his retirement as a competitor and
turned his full focus to coaching. He'd taken on several students at the
time, and was opening a training center in his hometown of Hamburg.
The only way I could stay in his program was if I moved to Germany.

"My mam didn't like it. She'd begun to feel I was under too much
pressure. She wanted me to finish school, insisting there were other
coaches—and if none of them were good enough, Henrik's training
center would still be there when I turned eighteen.

"I freaked out. I *had* to stay in training. So I enlisted my dad's help
to convince her. I'd just won the super sprint at Sunderland, which
qualified me to compete at the junior world championships in six
months when I turned sixteen. I knew I couldn't do it without Henrik. I
begged my dad and he helped persuade her. Neither he nor my mam,
of course, realized at the time just how much trouble I'd gotten myself
in…"

Dillon paused as the red and blue lights of a cop car filtered through the blinds, sirens blaring off into the distance.

"It was finally my sister who became suspicious. For months after I'd moved to Germany, she and my dad made the fourteen-hour train ride every weekend to see me. But eventually, Henrik monopolized my time, and made their visits impossible. I'm sure he knew Seren was on to him. And when she finally called me out, I didn't do a very good job of lying. She immediately went to our parents. And things…" Dillon pressed her lips together, "fell apart quickly.

"They immediately demanded I come home, confronting Henrik and threatening to press charges. But I'd just turned sixteen. A week earlier I'd won the championship in Japan. There was nothing that was going to convince me to leave him. I, of course, denied it all—as did Henrik. My mam's a solicitor—she knew they were fighting a losing battle. The age of consent in the UK is sixteen. Fourteen in Germany. I'd already sat for my GCSEs and was of a legal age to leave school. There was nothing they could do."

Dillon grew quiet, her thoughts drifting to the last time she'd seen her dad—the last conversation they'd ever had.

He turned up in Hamburg in the middle of the night, pounding on Henrik's door. Outraged at the disturbance and fearful of the potential for scandal, Henrik told her she had to choose between them. If her father showed up again, he was going to cut her from his program.

She led her dad away from the house, down to the river. It was the first time she'd ever seen him unshaven. The first time she'd smelled whisky through his pores.

"I'm struggling to understand, Dillon!" he'd yelled on the bank of the Elbe, his composure collapsing. "This isn't what you want! I know you're not in love with—with…" he gestured toward the house, "with that man!" His anger turned to pleading. "This isn't who you are!"

*Love?* The word blindsided her. Did he really think love had anything to do with it?

"You have no idea who I am," she spat, her mind stuck on Henrik's threat to drop her as a student.

How did her father not realize there was nothing she wouldn't do to keep him as her coach? Whatever the cost, she was willing to pay the price. She'd already paid it, and she'd continue to pay it—whatever it took to win.

"You're my daughter! And I know this person he's turned you into —this person isn't you! That man's a monster—"

"Don't pretend like you're not the one who pushed me to train with him!" Her voice was hoarse with tears as she flung away the hand he reached to set on her shoulder, aware of Henrik watching from the window of his second-story bedroom.

"Dillon!" The despair in his voice crippled her. "I didn't know!"

She kept her eyes on the river, on the freezing water she swam in every morning. Tomorrow, Henrik would make her life miserable. *Swim to the light tower*, he'd tell her. *Again. Again.*

But she couldn't leave him. In her sixteen-year-old mind, she was certain she couldn't do this without him. And her dad's midnight intrusion was going to ruin everything.

"You're just afraid I'll achieve more with him than I ever did with you," she snapped, whirling to shove past him. It was the cruelest thing she could think to say. The only thing she could think of to make him leave. "Stay away from me. I don't ever want to see you again."

And it was the last thing she ever said to him.

The minute hand on the vintage clock ticked forward and Dillon realized she'd been silent too long. Kam had slid from the arm of the couch to settle on the cushions, waiting for her to go on.

"To make a long story short, I cut off my family and stayed in Hamburg for three more years. For a while, my father wrote to me, but I never answered. I was afraid Henrik would find out. Then, when I made the Olympic team, he wrote to me again—telling me how proud he was, asking if he could meet me at the finish line. I told Henrik. Some idiotic part of me thought I could gain his approval. I *wanted* to see my dad, but I knew I couldn't do it without Henrik's blessing. I don't know why I ever thought things would change. Henrik told me to write back to him—to reiterate that I didn't want him in my life. And so I did."

Dillon forced herself to go on. "A week later, my dad hung himself in his study. On his desk they found my letter. He didn't leave a note. Seren called me that evening. I quit Henrik and finally went home."

Pulling out the dining room chair, she finally sat, looking over at Kam. "As I mentioned before, I still competed that summer. I didn't know what else to do. My dad was dead. I no longer had a coach. My entire life was upside down. All I had was that race. Somehow, I felt like I owed it to my dad to run. My mam and Seren supported my decision. I'd gotten a lot of press because of my age and the qualification, but we'd managed to keep my dad's death quiet. It wasn't something I felt like I could deal with publicly at the time.

"So of course, a few days before my start, Henrik posted a notice on his training page, claiming it was his decision to part ways with me as an athlete. He stated that while he sympathized with my family for our heartache after my father's suicide, he felt it best to end our partnership due to my 'blurred conception of understanding between professional and personal boundaries.' He went on to say that he wished me well in my future endeavors, and hoped I would take some time off to get the mental health help I needed."

Dillon laughed, the sound strangled in her throat. "I didn't even know about the post at the time. I was already in the seclusion of the Athletes' Village and had kept myself sheltered from everything circulating online. It wasn't until after the race, when a reporter in the media tent extended her condolences about the loss of my dad, that I knew his death had been made public."

Taking another breath, Dillon continued. "I was actually relieved, despite the hurtfulness of his comments. I was just glad it was over. He'd gotten the last punch, I'd managed to finish my race, and I just wanted to go home and hide until it all blew over. But the hopes of that ended quickly. A few days after the Closing Ceremonies, a sports reporter asked Henrik if he regretted his decision to part professional ways with me after I'd put out such a solid performance in my Olympic debut. Surely, she said, I was a loss as his star student. Henrik didn't miss a beat. He said," Dillon paused, still able to hear his voice verbatim. "He said: *If I had to deal with Dillon Sinclair for one more minute, I'd have killed myself, also*. And for the second time in as many months, my life crumbled. The soundbite went viral—well beyond the sports community. Most people were outraged by his comment, but it didn't stop the dialogue, or the fingers pointed in my direction. I was criticized for competing so shortly after my dad's death. I was called a narcissist. A head case. I was accused of being a *Lolita*. I felt like I was living in a glass house. I was already overwhelmed with guilt. Overwhelmed with grief. Overwhelmed with what I'd put my family through. I didn't handle it well, being in the center of the media scrutiny—my life being dissected online by total strangers. I..." Again, she hesitated. It felt impossible to explain how her life felt like it was over at just nineteen years old. "It was a rough couple of years after he died. Seren, and my best mate, Sam, got me through it. And by the time Rio rolled around, things were better. I'd rebuilt a relationship with my mam and sister. I'd established myself under a new coach and won my first professional World Triathlon Championship as an adult. For the first time in my life, I was head-over-heels in love, happy in a stable partnership. Everything finally seemed to be coming together.

"And then Kelsey and her team won the Euros. She'd always been a national team favorite, but suddenly she was a star—a household name throughout the country. People became interested in everything about her—on *and* off the pitch. And therefore, started taking interest in me. They created fan accounts, YouTube compilations, wrote fan fiction—publishing it all on the football forums with the tag #eclair. I was suddenly, very reluctantly, back in the spotlight—worse than ever before. And it scared me. I didn't want to go through that again. By the time England blazed into the World Cup semifinals, I couldn't take it anymore. I called it off in the middle of her tournament. I hurt her—very unfairly."

Releasing a long exhale, she looked away from Kameryn. "I'm only telling you all this because I didn't know any other way to explain my reaction to your casting. I'm not making an excuse. I should have found a way to talk to you without leaving. And I know it doesn't make things right—but it was worth it to me to fly here to apologize to you in person—even if you decide you'd rather not see me again."

Kameryn was quiet. After a moment she stood and went to her window, peeking through the blinds. It was almost eleven. Cars were driving by blasting music and in the distance there were muffled explosions of fireworks.

"And if I do want to see you again?" Kam turned.

"I'd like that," Dillon said simply.

"What happens if it gets as bad as it was with you and Kelsey?"

"This could be much worse than it ever was with Kelsey. I already know that."

Kam leaned against the wall. "Then why come back?"

Dillon finally felt the glimmer of a smile. "Because I really like you, Kam-Kameryn. And I'd like to earn a second chance."

# Scene 27

When I started the year three hundred and sixty-five days earlier, I hadn't expected to end it having sex on my dining room table.

At least not stone-cold sober.

Nor with a billion-dollar movie script serving as an impromptu pillow.

And definitely not with a woman.

But then again, I always had been a fan of third-act plot twists.

The year before, I'd been crammed into a club on Sunset, regretting my fourth martini, trying to avoid the wandering hands of a boy who soon found himself sorely disappointed. I'd woken the next morning on the glazed porcelain floor of Dani's ensuite bathroom, grateful for the impeccable cleaning habits of The Beverly Hills Hotel housekeepers.

Needless to say, in comparing the two nights, this year was 10/10 recommended. All the stars given.

I'm not actually sure when the clock struck midnight. It was sometime after she'd finally kissed me, but definitely before we'd abandoned the inconvenience of the old thrift shop table and stumbled the five steps through my nano kitchen into my bedroom. No doubt the entire city had erupted with bottle rockets and M80s, shaking my single-pane windows in their deteriorating framework, but at the time, the numerical change of the Gregorian calendar had been the least of my considerations. An honest to God Armageddon could have been going on outside and I wouldn't have noticed.

Now, however, with Dillon asleep beside me, I'd become aware of every creak and hum and rustle. I could hear the swing of my antique clock's pendulum. The murmur of my old fridge motor. The cycle of my upstairs neighbor's toilet. And, above it all, I listened, over the rhythmic beating of my heart, to the comforting whisper of Dillon's tranquil inhalations.

I enjoyed watching her sleep. The coral glow from my Himalayan salt lamp cast just enough light to bring her features into focus. It was the first time I'd ever gotten to look at her—to really study her—without feeling self-conscious.

I loved the strong lines of her face and subtle scattering of freckles dusting her high cheekbones. The way her defined jaw contrasted the suppleness of her lips. In the shadows, with the comforter kicked down to her knees, I could appreciate her extreme fitness. Her lithesomeness and strength. And yet also, in the curves and contours of her body, the femininity she retained.

I couldn't shake my thoughts from what she'd told me. About her dad. About her youth. About Henrik. I was infuriated for the child who'd been so horrifyingly manipulated. And my heart broke for the woman who had yet to learn to forgive herself. I had so many questions, so many things I wanted to say, but I'd kept them to myself. It hadn't felt like the time. She'd offered me a piece of her I didn't imagine she gave to many people, and the last thing I wanted was for her to regret it.

So I'd steered the night in a different direction—down a lighter path that allowed us both to escape to more pleasurable endeavors.

My thoughts were in the middle of revisiting some of those exact endeavors (who knew you could actually leave fingernail indentations on the softwood pine of a dining room table?) when my cell phone vibrated. It was Dani.

*Not today, Satan.*

I snatched it off the nightstand and immediately turned it off. The only person I'd wanted to hear from was lying right beside me.

Scooting closer to Dillon, I pressed my face to the nape of her neck, reveling in the warmth of her body. I couldn't remember the last time I slept beside someone and looked forward to waking with them in the morning.

When I opened my eyes again, my limbs stretching out across the full-size mattress in search of her, I discovered she wasn't there.

Based on the angle of light permeating my sheer window coverings, it was early morning.

I swung my legs over the side of the bed, tugged on a tank top, and padded barefoot into my living room. It was empty. Her backpack was lying open on the couch, her hat and jacket stacked beside it. I didn't doubt, if I peeked inside, I'd find her running shoes missing.

Apparently, there was no keeping her from her New Year's tradition.

Fifteen minutes later, when I cranked off the water and stepped out of my shower, I heard my front door open.

I quickly dried off and wrapped myself in a towel, slipping out of the steaming bathroom to find her sorting through my fridge.

"Hey," she looked up when she heard me.

God, I loved her smile. The way her dimples creased her cheeks.

From what I could see over the top of the fridge door, I also loved the way her shirt was clinging to her body, her face flushed and skin glistening. The after effects of a run.

I leaned against the counter. "Beware. I think the milk is expired."

She held up a new carton and I noticed there was a grocery bag on the floor. "Not anymore." Finishing stashing the items, she turned for the sink. "You were supposed to still be in bed. Sleep in. Two cups of coffee. Read a book cover-to-cover. Go to a movie. Isn't that what you told me?"

I stared at her, realizing there were two 7-Eleven cups on the counter. "You remembered that?"

"Of course I remembered," she chastised, "I listen to everything you tell me." Reaching into a second bag, she pulled out a weekly. "I'm afraid reading materials were slim pickings on a holiday—but I did pick up a magazine." She tossed the publication next to the sink. "There was a cute girl on the cover."

It was *Variety*. And there was Elliott, Grady—and me.

"God." I shook my head. I still hadn't wrapped my mind around all the publicity I was getting. "I wish they'd find a different headshot. I look so... boring."

"I promise, Kameryn Kingsbury," she pressed the coffee into my hands, "these reporters are going to find you anything but boring."

"Yeah?" I set the paper cup to my lips. "And how would you describe me?"

Ok, fine—I was fishing for compliments. So sue me. I'm an actress. Sometimes I need someone to feed my vanity.

She smiled, more than willing to take the bait. "Where would I start?" Stepping back, she gave me a sweeping survey. "Let's see. I could write a thesis on all the ways it should be deemed cruel and unusual punishment to be forced to stand here looking at you in nothing more than a towel. Torture to the highest degree. However—to describe you, I think I'd start with the color of your hair."

I rolled my eyes. "Stick with the towel. I hate the color of my hair. Boring brown. Mousy brown. Unremarkable brown."

"Winter chestnuts brown. Evergreens in autumn brown. Stradivarius brown."

I forced a sip of scalding coffee to hide my swallow. I'd not been expecting that from her.

"I don't think I've ever had someone compare me to a violin before," I teased in my attempt to keep it light.

"I'm surprised," she returned, "strung as tight as you are."

I laughed. "*Hey!* I resemble that remark."

Whatever response she had was interrupted by a knock at my door. *Shit.*

"Kam?" a voice called through my mailslot.

I breathed a sigh of relief, trying to ease my automatic hackles. It was just Sophie.

"A friend," I held a finger to my lips, motioning for Dillon to give me a second.

"Hey!" I cracked the door.

"Oh, hey." Sophie stood expectant on my doorstep. "I tried to call you, but your phone went straight to voicemail."

"Sorry, I think it's dead."

"I'm on my way to the Fairfax Farmers Market. Want to go?"

"Oh, uh, thanks—not today." I shifted my hold on the towel. "I've got a lot of work."

I could see her eyes sweep past my security chain, over my shoulder, to where Dillon's backpack was still on the couch. "Oh. *Oh.*" She took a step back, embarrassed, but then issued me a secret smile. "Is it…?" she lipped silently.

I knew what she was asking. I nodded the affirmative.

"Okay," she projected loudly, turning on her best stage voice, "have a good morning. I wouldn't want to keep you from your responsibilities." She laughed. "You get right to that. Call me later?"

"Mhm."

"Toodles, then." And she was gone.

I relocked the door. "Thank God."

"Expecting more boys with mistletoe?" Dillon asked. She'd pulled out a chair at my dining room table, where she was now sipping from her 7-Eleven cup.

"Worse—I thought it might be someone from work."

"Well, in that case, it would have been into the closet or under the bed—we certainly wouldn't want the powers-that-be finding their newly-hired Goody Two-Shoes keeping the wrong company."

My eyes snapped to her. "You're wrong if you think that's how I feel." I searched her face, trying to decipher her comment. It wasn't something we'd talked about. We'd yet to fully acknowledge an *us*, let alone how we wanted to proceed. But the simple fact that she'd flown from the UK to California twice in less than ten days was a pretty good indicator she wanted to pursue this as much as I did. So I skipped to the latter. "If we decide to keep this quiet, I'm fine with that. But it's important to me that you know I'm not afraid to own it in the open, either. That doesn't scare me."

I knew it was easy to say that now, standing in the privacy of my apartment, without the entire world prying into the details of my personal life. But I did mean it. If we were going to do this, I was willing to do this. Openly. Unashamedly. However she wanted. My biggest concern was that we did whatever was best for her, but I wasn't certain how to phrase that.

"I'd expect nothing less from the girl voted most likely to lead a protest," she smiled, but the humor behind the words was forced. I knew the subject made her uncomfortable, and I regretted bringing it up. After what happened with Kelsey…

I crossed the floor, stopping in front of her to run a hand through her damp hair. "For now, however, the less I have to share you with the world, the better. If that works for you?"

Her entire body slackened in unmistakable relief.

She gave me her half smile, bringing a hand to my knee. "Does that mean I'm getting out of a trip to the cinema?"

"No chance," I said, the rebuke falling short as she slowly slid her palm toward the hem of the towel.

God, it was ridiculous, the effect she had on me. I'd never known it was possible to want someone the way I wanted her. To find myself so unraveled by a touch—a glance—a smile.

She slid her hand higher. "I don't know. I bet I could convince you."

I let the towel fall, moving to straddle her.

"I'm very sweaty," she warned, even as she drew me closer, her lips traveling across my neck, her hands pressing into the small of my back. I was intoxicated by the windswept scent of her. The heat radiating from her body. The hint of mint tea on her breath.

She tried to shift, wanting to take over, but I pinned her against the back of the chair, unwilling to let her.

I'd discovered she liked to be in control. It was clearly what she was used to.

But I wasn't one to play by all the rules. Sometimes I liked to push the envelope.

Tangling one hand into her short wave of hair, I slipped the other between us, working loose the drawstring of her running shorts. I smiled as she attempted to measure her breathing, as her body tensed beneath me.

Never taking my eyes off hers, I teased her, slowly, unyieldingly, my mouth moving to the hollow of her throat as she strained against me. I teased her until her hands were on my hips, her nails digging into my skin. Until her breathing was ragged. Until she was forced to throw her head back, her eyes closed, the sound of her breath ceasing completely. I teased her until at last, writhing, she found my mouth with hers, her cry muted as she stilled beneath me.

"Okay, fine," she whispered into the crook of my neck, once I could feel her heartbeat resume its even cadence. "You win. I'll go with you to the movies."

I laughed. "Double feature?"

"You're pushing your luck."

"We could sit in the back row?"

She reached up, dragging my lower lip down with her thumb. "You know how to drive a hard bargain, Kam-Kameryn."

And so began the eleven short days we had together.

Despite my insistence at keeping to tradition, I was the one who decided we should skip the movies, and for the first three days, we didn't leave the apartment. Eventually, however, both stir-craziness and bare cupboards drove us from our libidinous haze, and we were forced to venture into civil society.

I felt like I was entering a whole new world.

We hiked to the Hollywood sign, walking hand-in-hand along the Sky Rim trail, taking photos cheek-to-cheek on the deck of the Observatory. We bundled in jackets and beanies and I dragged Dillon on one of those stupid double-decker buses that take a tour of the stars' homes, circling back through Rodeo Drive and past the Chinese Theatre.

The days rolled by, turning into a week that came and went too quickly. Dillon helped me run lines from my script, brought me coffee in bed, and we laughed until we choked on wasabi sitting on the checkered floor of my kitchen eating sushi.

When we went out, I felt like a truant teenager, sneaking around beneath the football bleachers.

We played footsie at dinner under the table, made out in the elevator at the Beverly Center, and had sex in my car in the AMC underground parking structure, missing all but the closing credits of the movie. "Zero-for-two in your attempts to convert me into a film buff, Kam-Kameryn," she'd razzed as we stood in line at Pink's Hot Dogs.

She bought a bike at a downtown cyclery and left early one morning, only to call me at noon, asking if I'd come have lunch with her in Santa Barbara. One hundred and three miles away.

I changed my phone number, got a P.O. Box to help keep my home address private, and after a frenzied emptying of every drawer in my apartment, found my passport in my freezer.

She was supposed to leave for London the Friday night before my Monday morning departure to Greenland, but Friday came and went and I begged her to stay until Sunday.

Saturday I'd been invited to a party in Malibu, but again I declined —a habit Sophie said I better learn to break. But I didn't care. I wanted to spend every last second with Dillon. I knew the next time I returned to LA, my life would look very different. Aaron was insisting I think about a new apartment, somewhere safer, where I could maintain anonymity. Sneak peeks and teaser trailers would begin to hit the public not long after I returned from Scotland, and I knew I would never have this freedom again. Already, these last eleven days, I knew I'd just been lucky. There'd been no more knocks at my door, and my new number remained unlisted.

But it was coming, waiting to blitz down on me like Mjölnir from the sky, and once it happened, there'd be no retreating back to Asgard.

So the parties and premieres and people could wait. For now, I just wanted Dillon.

We lay in bed that night—I'd made her watch *Thor: Ragnarok*, and yes, she agreed Cate Blanchett was hot in Hela's iridescent skin-tight leather armor—and I lamented every passing minute that brought me closer to Greenland.

"I don't even want to go."

"Bollocks." She stroked my hair as I lay against her chest, watching the TV turn black on automatic shutoff. "This is going to be the most incredible experience of your life. By the time you get to Scotland, you'll have forgotten all about me."

"Now that's *bollocks*," I mocked her, turning my head to catch her eye, wondering just how long it might really be before I saw her again. "Are you sure you can't come see me in Aberdeen?"

"You know I would if I could." She ran a fingertip along the channels of my ribcage, trailing off into a senseless design at my hip. "But the Championship Series will be underway. I'll be in Yokohama when you're in Scotland."

Yes, I knew. And after that Leeds. Montreal. Málaga. Cagliari. Abu Dhabi. And no telling what might get thrown in in between. It could be November before I saw her again. But by then, we'd be well into post-production. I'd be in the middle of the required promotional phase—interviews, talk shows, red carpet appearances. Pretty much whatever the studio wanted.

The dawning acceptance of our reality left me feeling hollow, with a sinking feeling spreading through my chest.

She must have felt my rising misery, because she wrapped her arms around me, holding me tightly against her.

"We'll find each other. I promise."

"And what if you forget me?"

I could feel her smile against my temple before suddenly rolling to pin me beneath her, brushing her mouth across the ticklish skin of my stomach. "I'm going to show you right now what happens when you play *What If.*"

But later, in the middle of the night, it was she who woke me, her lips pressed to my ear, and promised it would be a blazing day on Cairn Gorm Mountain before she ever could forget me.

# Scene 28

*Three seconds.*

That was the difference in $6000 of prize money and seventy-five fewer points toward the championship. A runner-up result leading to hours wasted of second-guessing every choice made on the course.

Dillon had lost Bermuda to the French track and field sensation-turned-triathlete, Elyna Laurent. Just twenty-two years old.

But it was worse than that. Elyna wasn't just a rising talent in the sport.

She was Henrik's student.

His new *hellster Stern.* One that, based on her performance that morning, might actually prove to be his brightest star. Perhaps even a frontrunner for Los Angeles.

No athlete of Henrik's had come within fifteen placings of Dillon since she left him. Going into the race, no one expected Laurent to beat the established veteran. Most especially Dillon herself. But she'd surprised everyone with a sit-and-kick strategy, holding the middle of the pack until throwing it in high gear over the last half kilometer of the run. And, caught in an unexpected footrace, Dillon hadn't been able to hold the lead.

*Three bloody seconds.*

"We, uh, skipping the piss-up, then?" Kyle's gear bag bumped against his hip as he matched Dillon's stride, taking the stairs two-by-two to the entry of their hotel.

"You should go." Mad at the world, she shouldered through the revolving door in her rush to get to her room. "Harry and Georgina will be there."

"Come on, Sinc. Shower and ride back with me. You ran a solid race."

"Not solid enough."

He trotted to catch up with her. "You can't beat yourself up over—"

Dillon spun in the foyer. "He knew, Kyle! He knew he could bait me to chase her if she sprinted the hill and I'd run out of gas on the carpet. He fucking *knew*."

"Yeah. He did." Kyle nodded, dropping his placation. It was a thing she loved about him. He knew when to quit with the bullshit. "There's no question that bastard knows you. He's just been waiting to have a competitor strong enough to put his knowledge to the test. He knew you wouldn't be able to deny your ego the effort to maintain the lead. But—" he held up a finger as she opened her mouth to tell him to piss off about her ego. "The thing is, Sinc, you, more than anyone, know you can't let him get inside your head. One race—that's all today was. First of the series. You learned a lesson and not the way you like to learn them. But you're not the only one who cocked up." The cleft in his chin deepened as he smiled. "Today they made two fatal errors: One—they showed their cards in the first round, and two—they forgot who the fuck they're dealing with." He thumped her chest with a knuckle. "You're still Dillon Sinclair."

What if that didn't mean anything anymore, she wanted to ask, but kept quiet. It wasn't so much that she'd been beaten that bothered her —it was that she'd been outplayed. By *him*.

But Kyle was right. One race. One mistake. She wouldn't let it happen again.

After showering, she met Kyle back in the hall, agreeing to let him drag her to the after party. They were in Bermuda, after all. No reason to sit in her hotel room and forgo the perfect weather. It was better than stewing over the loss.

On the way to the lobby, the lift dinged on the third floor. As the door opened, Dillon immediately regretted skipping the stairs. There was Elyna Laurent's expressionless face. And behind her, of course, was Henrik.

It had been nine years since she'd come that close to him. They'd seen each other—at races, at the Olympics, at various events. Most often with Dillon on the podium and Henrik in the crowd. But not once since she'd left Hamburg had she allowed him to come within arm's reach.

"What a pleasant surprise." His lips twisted into a smirk, his lean cheeks camouflaged by his five o'clock shadow. At forty-five, he was still handsome—more so, even, than when she had met him. There was no doubt an endless line of women who'd find his roguishness appealing, willing to throw themselves into his bed. But by the way Elyna's entire body tensed as he placed a hand at the small of her back, it was clear he'd still not developed a taste for women his own age.

"Hallo, *Schätzchen*." They stepped inside.

Dillon said nothing.

"You ran like a weakling today," he continued in German as the doors took an eternity to close. "It was embarrassing to watch."

Dillon forced a long inhalation through her nose, unwilling to look at him. Elyna stared at the floor. There was nothing of the indomitable power and presence the Parisienne girl had displayed on the race course. She looked cowed next to Henrik, like she wanted to disappear. Dillon knew the feeling well.

"She is a force, is she not?" His eyes swept Elyna, speaking of her as if she weren't even there. "Built for speed. The lungs of a thoroughbred and ethics of a plow horse. She is going to demolish you in Japan, you won't even make top ten. She hasn't even hit her prime and is already challenging your records."

Dillon knew she should just get off the lift and walk away. He was only trying to slip under her skin, to find a way to provoke her. But her pride wouldn't allow it.

"She's a little old for your taste, isn't she?"

Henrik smiled. "Jealous, *Schätzchen*?" He leaned against the mirrored wall. "You needn't be. You may be in the twilight of your career, but I'd still take you for a ride—"

"Fuck you!"

"What a lady. I'm sure your papa would be so proud—"

She lunged toward him, intent on wiping the smug smile off the bastard's face, but Kyle was quick to restrain her.

"Don't, Sinc!" He may not have understood a word of German, but it took little imagination to know what had transpired between them. "The wanker's not bloody worth it!"

The lift settled on the ground floor as the doors slid open to reveal the main lobby. Half a dozen competitors milled about in boardshorts and flip-flops, their attention casually shifting toward the commotion. Elyna quickly slipped into the crowd.

Watching her go, Henrik leaned over, his breath warm against Dillon's cheek. "See you in Yokohama, *Drückeberger*." And then he was gone, disappearing behind Elyna.

"Sinc…" Kyle released her. "Just let it go."

"I don't need you to manage me," she snapped, knowing her anger was aimed in the wrong direction. "I can handle myself!"

"And allow you to earn a suspension over a cunt like him? He wasn't worth it. Now let's go."

Dillon slapped the button for the fifth floor. "You go. I'm going to call it a night."

"C'mon, Sinc—"

A couple in Bermuda shorts and sunglasses approached the lift, waiting for Kyle to clear the door. He hesitated, shooting her a disapproving shake of his head. "Fine. Let him get your goat. It's exactly what he was after. Go hide upstairs and hand him his second win of the night."

"Sod off," Dillon muttered, but he'd already walked away.

Back in her room, she yanked the blinds shut, closing out the panoramic view of Hamilton Harbour. She wasn't in the mood for the turquoise waters or the beauty stretching across the bay.

She stood in the low light of the living room, staring at the silver medal she'd flung onto the coffee table.

Bermuda was her race. Unlike Yokohama, or Málaga, or even Montreal, where it was always a scrap to the podium, Bermuda was *hers*. She'd won it more times than any other athlete in the history of the sport. She owned the course record. She was the unquestionable favorite to win. It had never even crossed her mind that she'd fall short.

Henrik had played her perfectly.

But—and it was the *but* she had to force herself to focus on—Kyle was right. They'd shown their cards too soon. Elyna was a sprint finisher. Dillon knew now she couldn't match her closing speed, so she would simply have to adjust her strategy. Surge early and vary her pace. Make her chase her. Make it hurt.

It was this last part that mattered most. Elyna may be younger. She may physically be at an advantage with her height and physique. But there was one thing Dillon knew she didn't have. She didn't have her drive—or her capacity for pain. The entire success of Dillon's career had stemmed from her willingness to do more, to push harder, to commit herself to do the things others wouldn't. Even when they hurt. *Especially* when they hurt.

Striding across the room, she snatched up the silver medal, and dumped it in the rubbish bin.

*Fuck Henrik Fischer.*

She sank onto the couch, rubbing absently at her left knee. It had begun to grind halfway through the cycle, but she hadn't paid it much attention. She'd worry about it at the end of the season. Or after Los Angeles. Some other time.

Exhausted, she closed her eyes. Tomorrow she'd fly to London, where she'd spend two weeks before heading to Japan. Then it was back to Leeds. And after that, she wouldn't see home for a while.

When she opened her eyes again, the sunlight streaking through the edges of the blackout curtain had softened, the color warming to the golden hue of late afternoon. Her watch said it was four PM. Five PM in Nuuk. With the long daylight hours, Kam would probably still be working.

She rocked her stiff body forward, dragging her duffel onto the couch, and dug out her phone. She'd meant to text her earlier, before things had gone sideways.

As the mobile powered to life, she sat back and stared at the photo on her lock screen. It was a selfie Kam had sent her a few weeks earlier, standing on the ledge of a glacier overlooking the sea. She was bundled in a parka, her nose red and lips cracked from the cold, still somehow managing to look runway pretty.

*The infamous ice sheet* Kam had captioned the text, followed by a winking face. She told Dillon she'd had to spend two days filming 'practically nude' on the ice-covered coastline, beneath the northern lights. Dillon had sent back a photo of her in a hot tub after an early morning training session, to which Kam had responded with an emoji of flipping the bird.

It had been two months since they parted in Hollywood, but they'd managed to talk almost every day. Dillon looked forward to Kam's texts in the morning, and had made it a habit to call her—if even just for a few minutes—before she went to bed at night.

It hadn't been like that with Kelsey. When they were in the middle of their respective seasons, they could go days—weeks, even—without speaking. It had frustrated Kelsey, Dillon's inclination to grow reclusive, but it was simply how it had always been.

This, with Kam, was different from the start.

*I miss you.* Dillon typed out a text and hit send.

Her phone immediately rang.

"I thought you might still be on set," she answered, watching a palmetto bug scurry up the wall.

"I hate this place." Kam sounded like she was in a tunnel. "It finally stopped snowing, and instead rained all day. We couldn't get anything done."

Dillon tried to repress her disappointment. Kam's filming in the Arctic had been close to a wrap, on track to finish two weeks early—a windfall which would have allowed them to meet in Aberdeen for at least a day before she left for Japan. But a late spring storm had hit the southwest coast of Greenland, halting the production, and now they were behind schedule, dashing the hopes of a rendezvous in Scotland.

"Well, if you look on the bright side, you're going to love Scotland's weather compared to what you've been through these last two months."

"I'd have loved it more if I'd gotten to see you in it."

Dillon couldn't help but smile.

Kameryn continued. "Tell me about the race."

"I lost."

"I followed the feed on Twitter. Coming in second isn't *losing*."

"It's losing to the winner."

"And beating forty-seven other women in the process."

"It still isn't a win."

"Oh, please." She could practically hear Kam's eye roll. "Even if you'd won you wouldn't be happy with the result."

Dillon half laughed, and turned the subject back to filming. She didn't want to talk about the race.

They chatted for over an hour as the sliver of light from the curtain narrowed its stretch across the floor. Usually, their conversations were brief, interrupted by timezones and conflicting schedules, but tonight Dillon lingered, loath to say goodbye.

Kam seemed to understand.

"Is everything okay?"

Dillon suppressed a sigh. "I'm just tired." She swung her legs over the side of the couch, stretching. "That's probably not something I should be saying after the first race of the season."

Kam quieted. "I saw that he was that girl's coach today."

Dillon pressed a finger into the sore spot on her knee. "Yep." She blew out a long breath. "But whatever. Today they just got lucky."

Standing, she went to the window and drew back the curtain to look out over Pitt's Bay. "So—tell me something you're not allowed to tell me."

Kam laughed. So much of what she did was kept under wraps. She'd explained how the entire production had been managed as carefully as a special ops mission, complete with fake scripts, multiple takes, and last-minute rewrites to entire scenes. The producers were taking no chance with leaks.

"You just want to know if I had to film any more scenes without my clothes on."

"Obviously." Dillon smiled. "I'll accept photos as proof."

"Wouldn't you like to get so lucky," Kam returned, but despite the playfulness, she couldn't hide her wistful sigh. "I really do miss you, you know? I wish I could have been there for you today."

"I wish Aberdeen had worked out."

"Me, too." A brief silence ensued. "You promise you haven't forgotten me yet?"

"It's still freezing on Cairn Gorm, last I checked."

"You should have promised on the Greenland Ice Sheet. Then I wouldn't have had to ask you twice."

"I like when you ask me."

Another beat passed as Dillon watched the beachgoers scattered across the white sand, their silhouettes bathed in the orange glow of the setting sun. She turned back to the emptiness of her room. "Will you text me tomorrow when you're finished filming?"

"You'll be traveling."

"I like to get your messages when I land."

"Okay. If I survive another night in subfreezing temperatures."

"You'll survive. You're Addison Riley, after all."

"I don't know—it's Margaret Gilles. Her heroes tend to die in the end."

"Not in the books I read."

"Ha," Kam scoffed. "You've never even read *Sand Seekers*."

"I hadn't," Dillon admitted, "until…" she paused. What? Until she started to fall in love with a girl halfway across the world? She couldn't say that. "Until I heard a hot tip the actress playing the lead was just my type."

"Frost bitten toes and all?"

Dillon laughed. "Ten digits not required."

"I'll text you."
"Send me a photo."
"Oh yeah?" Kam singsonged.
"Yeah. Make it a good one."
"I'll expect recompense."
"You know I always pay my debts."

# Scene 29

Elliott slammed me into the moss-covered stone so hard it made my teeth rattle.

"I knew you'd put up a good fight," he hissed against my ear, his breath reeking of something sour. I clawed at him, digging my nails into the forearm he'd shoved against my neck, desperate to escape the pressure of his body. I found everything about him repugnant. His laugh. His lips. The way he so easily overpowered me. No matter what way I twisted, I couldn't escape his hands tearing at my clothing. He pressed me harder into the wall. "Stop pretending you don't like it."

Beginning to panic, I tried to tell him to fuck himself, but he cut off my protest as he crushed his mouth against mine. It enraged me. The sudden, unwelcome intrusion—the bitter taste of his tongue, his cold fingers forcing their way beneath the winter layers of fabric. Finding strength I didn't know I had, I managed to shake loose an arm, and without thinking, hauled back and struck him. Hard.

"Cut!"

*Oh. My. God.*

Struggling to recover my breath, I stumbled back a step, horrified. That hadn't been in the script. But then, none of it had. Elliott and L.R. had decided it would be best to leave the scene improvised. Something, I discovered, Aaron hadn't protected me from in my contract.

"What do you mean there's no intimacy coordinator?" Sophie had ranted when I called her a few days earlier after landing in Scotland. "This all should have been stipulated in your nudity rider."

The provisions written into my intimacy scenes covered a lot of things. Angles—as in, nipples or no nipples. I'd insisted on the latter. It was one thing for the movie to open with an ultrawide shot of a stark naked Addison Riley stumbling through the snow of a nuclear winter, but it was another entirely to have the whole world become acquainted with the color of my areolae. Aaron had spelled out the length of time my unclad body could be shown in a continuous shot—four seconds—

and even specified the types of modesty garments to be provided. Who knew a Hibue could make Grady Dunn look like a Barbie doll?

When signing the contract, I'd felt like we covered all the bases. But that was before discovering Elliott Fleming was a complete asshole.

In Greenland, my more sensitive scenes had gone off without a hitch. I'd been nervous—the most skin I'd ever shown on camera was my calf in the *Gillette* commercial—but between the crew and Grady, I'd felt very protected. But then, part of that reason was because Elliott hadn't been there.

We'd shot all of his scenes in Nuuk in the first ten days. His schedule was the priority—that had been made abundantly clear—and before the second week was out, he'd boarded his private plane and jetted off to Africa, where he was starring in an adventure film.

His departure had come as an immense relief to me. I'd have rather shot a hundred simulated sex scenes with Grady in the arctic blast of winter than filmed a single frame with Elliott in the comforts of a studio.

I loathed everything about him. Shooting with him these last three days had only reenforced the validity of my hatred.

Our present scene together wasn't a love scene—it was an assault. One I was grateful L.R. had kept in tune with the book. The novels were adult-themed, but they hadn't been explicit. But it was no surprise the script had placed more on-screen emphasis on the tumultuous love triangle. I got it, sex and violence sold—this was Hollywood, after all.

Swords and dragons may have lured viewers to *Game of Thrones*, but it was the titty shots and gory fight scenes that kept them returning for more.

So, I was relieved when I read the script and found they'd left the majority of Oliver's assault off-screen, implied the way Margaret Gilles had written it. But I still hadn't realized just how violating it would feel to film the lead-up to the insinuation.

A fact indicated by the trickle of blood dripping from Elliott Fleming's lower lip.

*Holy shit.* I was about to get fired.

"I'm—" I started, with no real sense of what I was going to say, but was saved by L.R., who had burst to my side, his face barely visible beneath the cinched hood of his rain jacket.

"Brilliant!" He pounded my shoulder with a gloved hand. "We're going to roll with that. Beautiful, Kameryn." He looked to where Elliott was dabbing blood off his chin. "You going to live?"

Elliott worked his jaw, his eyes fixed on me. "Glad my contract included dental insurance."

L.R. was unperturbed, calling for makeup. "Get him cleaned up, will you?" he clapped his hands. "Last looks! Let's go, people! Moving on!"

"You know," Elliott whispered as we set up for the continuation of the scene, "you even hit like a pussy."

I dug my dirty fingernails into my palm. I may have gotten away with it once, but I doubted I'd get away with slugging him a second time. I was just grateful L.R. was satisfied with the take. We'd filmed it at least a dozen times.

For the next two hours, I crawled through the mud-covered grass of the dilapidated castle courtyard, feeling the weight of Elliott's boot pressing me into the saturated ground. It was the last shot scheduled on the call sheet, the end to the nightmare of this scene, and there'd been more than one time where I'd wondered who was crying—me or Addison Riley?

"Cut! Let's call that a wrap!" L.R. finally hollered through the north Scotland drizzle, drawing cheers of *Thank God, I'm freezing*, and *Who's up for a pint?* from various crew members.

I pushed myself upright, making sure the drenched tatters of my threadbare shirt were still covering what they were supposed to, and was surprised by Elliott's outstretched hand. I ignored it, forcing my shaky legs beneath me, not wanting to linger on my knees too long for fear of whatever comment he would fling at me.

"Solid work."

I thanked the costume standby for the warm jacket handed to me and scrubbed fifteen-hundred-year-old soil from my face, ignoring Elliott. Not once had he offered me so much as a word of encouragement. I wasn't about to let him compliment me now.

The time for that had passed.

Three months ago I would have sold my soul to gain his approval. It had been without question that he and Grady were two of the most talented actors I'd ever witnessed work. When paired with one another, what they created was simply genius. And I knew, when we filmed our scenes together, some of that magic rubbed off on me.

But I was past the point of hoping to impress Elliott. We'd wrapped up our major scenes together, and other than some minimal studio shoots and whatever pickups would be needed, our work together on this film was finished.

The crew had it right. It was time for a pint.

"Excuse me," I brushed by him, beginning my trudge up the steep switchbacks toward civilization.

An hour later, showered and dressed in what practically felt like summer clothes compared to what I'd been wearing in Greenland, I stepped out of my trailer to find Elliott waiting for me.

It had finally stopped raining, the midafternoon sun highlighting the cliffs overlooking the ruins of Dunnottar Castle.

"Am I needed for something?" I asked, trying to appear unbothered, but missed the first step of my trailer ladder and almost landed on my face.

"Careful," he caught my arm as I stumbled to find my feet. "It would be a drag to break something now."

"Wouldn't you just love that?" I snatched my arm away. "Maybe you could convince L.R. to find someone to replace me?"

Circumventing him, I headed for the path that wound along the cliffside down to the town of Stonehaven, where we were staying for the week. It was a beautiful walk, and I decided, after spending the day being dragged through the mud by my hair, and slammed up against fourteenth-century castle walls, I could use the time to unwind and stretch my aching limbs.

"Can I give you a ride, Kam?"

I didn't look back. "Nope."

My heart sank when I heard steps jogging up behind me.

"Can I walk you to town, then?"

I stopped. We were fifteen feet from the edge of the cliff. Maybe he'd trip. It was at minimum a three-hundred-foot drop. Most of his scenes were shot. Anything we had to reshoot could be handled with CGI.

I sighed. "What do you want, Elliott?"

"To be friends."

He probably could have seen my tonsils the way my mouth hung open. I couldn't even convince the muscles of my jaw to close it. "Are you drunk?" I finally managed. I almost hoped it was the case. He couldn't possibly be so disillusioned to think, after what he'd put me through, we could somehow now be buddies. I mean, three hours ago, he'd driven his knee into the small of my back and whispered 'imagine how fun this would be in real life,' out of range of the microphones.

I had the urge to spit in his face, the way he'd ad-libbed doing the same to me earlier in the morning.

"No," he said. "I'd just like to put this all behind us."

"Behind us?" I could feel my heartbeat accelerating. *"Behind us? Just one word from you and—"* I snapped my fingers "—bam, everything's A-okay, just like that?" I laughed, almost delirious, taking a step forward.

He didn't need to trip off the cliff. A good push would do it.

"Do you have any idea how you've made me feel? What you've put me through? Do you know, every actress on the planet thinks I'm the luckiest girl alive, because what could possibly be better than landing the role of the most beloved heroine in the twenty-first century? And then—to have the *privilege* to star with the great Elliott Fleming! What could possibly be better than *that*?"

I hadn't realized I was shouting. I took a glance around. There were still crew members mulling around the castle down below. I lowered my voice. "Do you know what a single kind word from you could have done for me?"

He nodded, unsmiling. "Yes. Gotten you fired."

I snapped my eyes back from where I'd looked out over the bay. "What?"

"You were out of your league, Kameryn. Not with talent—you're very talented, that was never a question—but you wouldn't have made it. It was obvious after the first few minutes of the read-through."

"And you thought somehow it would help me if you turned into an absolute bastard?" I asked, incredulous.

A part of me knew I was toeing the line—this was still Elliott Fleming, still the headlining actor, still the man who had dangled my job above me like a carrot on a string, threatening to cut the cord at any time. But the other part of me could hear all the horrible, degrading things he'd whispered, the ways he made me feel inferior, the person responsible for all the nights I promised myself I'd quit the next morning.

"Do you know how much I've hated every minute working with you?" I continued when he didn't immediately respond.

"Then it worked, didn't it?"

"What?"

"You hate me, don't you?"

I laughed. "You're unreal."

"Listen Kameryn, you were so nervous and so overwhelmed. I knew you needed something else to think about, to help you stay grounded—even if it meant turning your anxiety into rage directed at me. I didn't want to see you fail."

"Ah, got it. The old *I only hit you 'cause I love you* theory, huh?"

"It wasn't exactly a cakewalk for me, either!" It was the first time he broke the even keel of his tone. "But I knew MacArthur would shred your contract the first week if something didn't change—and change quickly. So when I talked to Grady—"

"—to Grady! Grady knew?"

*God damn it.* I could feel the tears threatening.

"Yes." His hazel eyes held mine without blinking. "And L.R., too."

I whipped my gaze away, returning it to the water. I couldn't believe this. I couldn't believe him. "I must have been the laughing stock of the whole crew."

"No one else knew, Kameryn. I swear it. And none of us were laughing at you."

"You really want me to believe that?" I heard my voice crack. I swore to everything that was holy I was going to fling *myself* off that cliff if I cried.

He took a step closer, daring to set a hand on my elbow. "We've made a good film, Kam. You're an incredibly talented artist. You just needed a little help."

The first fat tear slid down my cheek, disappearing into the collar of my coat. I didn't budge. I'd apparently lied to all that was holy. The water in Stonehaven Bay was way too cold for a plunge, anyway.

"I get it if you won't forgive me. Like I said, believe it or not, it wasn't exactly an enjoyable experience for me, either."

I slowly extracted my arm from his hold, taking several steps away. I didn't doubt he was genuine. Even he wasn't so great an actor to pull off a performance like this. And if he was, well… an Oscar awaited him.

"I'd like to walk back alone," I said, not looking his direction. I didn't know how to feel. Or what else to say.

"Okay." He stood back, respecting the distance I'd put between us. "If you want to grab a drink sometime—I owe you something that isn't practically jet fuel." A smile crept into his voice. "Or, if you decide you'd rather take another swing at me, I'll give you another shot for free." Out of the corner of my eye, I saw him touch his lower lip. "I lied earlier—you've got a hell of a left hook, Kingsbury."

I almost laughed, but I wasn't quite there yet.

Two hours later, I sat at Downie Point, looking out over Strathlethan Bay. I'd spent the walk scrutinizing every last interaction I'd had with Elliott—from the first time I met him at the read-through, where he'd been charming and sincere, to our night out at *Bartholemew's*, where everything had changed—coming full circle to his proclamation on the cliffside. I decided he was telling the truth—and was probably right. I'd have been canned the first week of filming if left to my own devices.

It didn't make me feel what he'd done was justified, but I did understand it. He hadn't just been looking out for me—he'd helped himself, in turn. He cared about this film. I'd never seen him feature in anything less than sublime. He needed me to be his equal. And, despite the misery he'd inflicted on me, he may have saved my career in the meantime.

I wasn't sure I wanted to be his friend. I didn't really know who he was. But, at least I hadn't pushed him off the cliffside.

So that was a start.

As the sun disappeared behind the rolling hills, the ocean turning to ink a hundred feet below me, I pulled out my phone, checking the time.

It was almost eight PM, which meant it was already early morning in Yokohama.

I was surprised I hadn't heard from Dillon. She'd have raced almost twenty-four hours earlier. I'd sent her a text that I knew she was going to crush it, and then turned off my phone to keep my head in the game, aware that today's shooting schedule was going to be taxing. But I'd expected to have a message from her by now, and it worried me that I didn't. If she came in second again…

Opening *Twitter*, I lingered, listening to the herring gulls settling in along the shoreline.

She'd been intensely focused these last four weeks, training harder than I imagined was good for her. But it wasn't my place to ask. She knew what she needed to do, and she knew her body. And I knew this race had a lot more riding on it than points and prize money.

She hadn't said much, but knowing the French girl was Henrik's student had to be eating her alive. I'd never been one to wish ill on a stranger, but I admit, I secretly hoped the woman had woken with an extreme case of Montezuma's revenge.

Resigned to look, I pulled up the account for World Triathlon. I clicked on the video of the podium celebration for the professional women, certain it would be Dillon in the middle.

It wasn't.

Again, it was Elyna Laurent. But this time, it wasn't Dillon standing to her right. Or even her left.

A herring screamed in the distance and a glacial chill worse than anything I'd experienced in Greenland slid up my spine. I minimized the video and pulled up the race results. Fifty-five competitors in the Elite Women's start. I scrolled. Second from the bottom I found her name. Dillon Sinclair. Time: DNF.

*Did Not Finish.*

# Scene 30

Dillon watched as raindrops pooled on the screen of her mobile, distorting the endless stream of notifications. She considered chucking the device off her eleventh-floor balcony and watching it plunge, dashed to bits against the pavement.

But that wouldn't solve the furious note pinned to her door from Sam.

Or the dozen text messages from Kameryn.

Or the frantic voicemails from her mother.

Nor would it erase the four words, written in Seren's impeccable handwriting, printed in lipstick across her washbasin mirror.

*CALL. ME. DAMN. YOU.*

Underlined. Angry. Scared.

She'd fucked up, and she knew it.

She left the mobile on the railing, where it continued to buzz as she stared across South Bank to the Thames, where the London Eye brightened the skyline with its hazy purple glow.

Where did she even start?

Sam?

No. She could wait. It wasn't her she owed the first apology to. She'd have to get in line.

She finally swiped up the device and dragged it across her hip to dry the screen. She couldn't put it off anymore.

"Dillon?"

Her call was answered on the first ring.

The amount of fear, and fury, and frustration emanating from those two syllables forced her throat to constrict. She swallowed.

"Hey, Seren." There was a long silence. "I got your note."

"You're home, then."

Another beat passed. Dillon closed her eyes. "I'm really sorry."

"*Don't.* Please." Her sister sounded tired, her voice losing its edge of resentment, only to be replaced with disappointment—the washing away of grief. "You know what I thought."

It wasn't a question.

"I didn't mean to make you worry."

Seren's laugh was brittle. "I thought we were past this, Dillon?"

"I—just had to get away. I wasn't thinking clearly."

"Or at all, apparently. For seven days!" There, the fury began to return. Fury, Dillon could handle. Disappointment, she could not.

Not from Seren.

"Look, I'm sorry. I screwed up. I just wanted to hide for a little while. To have some time to wrap my head around things—"

"—a fucking text, Dillon! A bloody fucking text would have sufficed. 'Hey! I'm going to turn off my phone and disappear for a week. Don't worry about me. I'm not dead.' You don't think you owed us that at the very least?"

"Like I said, I wasn't thinking! I just needed—I needed some space."

She could hear Seren suck in a breath on the other end of the line—holding it as she deliberated whether or not to unleash how she really felt. Dillon braced herself, but finally Seren exhaled, curbing whatever tongue-lashing she'd prepared. They both knew how this conversation went. It wasn't the first time. It had just been a long time.

Dillon didn't know how to explain the mistakes she made. The way her panic took control. She didn't know how to tell Seren that three days had passed before she even realized she'd not told anyone where she was going. And that it had taken her three more days to find the courage to come home—to face the music she knew she was due.

To everyone else, she knew Yokohama was just a race. The second in a series of seven. A DNF wasn't the end of the world. With five more races, she was still in the running for the world title.

But it wasn't concern over the championship Dillon had found crippling.

She'd *needed* the win in Japan. She'd needed it more than any win in her career.

*You won't even make top ten*, Henrik had told her.

*You ran like a weakling.*

*It was embarrassing to watch.*

*Drückeberger*, he'd called her.

She'd *had* to beat Elyna. To prove Henrik wrong. And she'd known she could do it. All she had to do was outmaneuver her, and set an unrecoverable distance between them once they started the run.

And she'd done just that.

But it had been unusually hot in Yokohama, and Dillon had come out too strong. She ignored her body's warning signs as she powered through the swim and cycle, and then pushed even harder on the run.

A hundred meters from the finish line, however, Dillon's body had had enough.

She collapsed on the course.

She didn't remember much, but she knew she'd been crawling on her hands and knees when Elyna Laurent had run past.

"You were almost two minutes ahead of her," Kyle said when he visited her in the emergency room that afternoon. "Three hundred more feet and you'd have set a new course record."

After he'd gone, Dillon signed herself out of the hospital, left a note at the hotel asking Kyle to handle her gear, and jumped on a plane to Heathrow. But by the time she landed, she'd decided she wasn't ready to go home.

"Where'd you go?" Seren asked, after a long silence.

"Holyhead."

Seren didn't respond. Dillon didn't expect her to. Holyhead was where their dad used to take her camping every spring, just off the Isle of Anglesey. It had been a place that was just theirs. Her sanctuary.

"It's not fair, you know." Seren finally said. "What you put us through."

"I know." Dillon stared at the glistening pavement a hundred feet below. The rain had tapered to a drizzle. She cleared her throat. "You'll tell mam I'm sorry?"

"You'll have to tell her yourself. You might want to wait a day or two for her to simmer down." Seren sighed. "I met Kameryn Kingsbury."

"You called her?" Dillon didn't know why she was surprised. Seren would have called every person she could think of. Just like last time.

"No. I didn't know how to reach her."

"She called you?" Dillon slumped onto the wet balcony chair.

*God, she'd made a royal mess of things.*

"No." Seren paused. "She drove to Swansea and found me at the barn."

"What?!"

"You're a real arsehole when you want to be, Dillon—"

"—she came to Wales?"

"Did you ever consider how you'd make her feel? At least mam and I—Sam, even—we've been through it before. But—"

"What did you tell her?"

"Exactly what I was praying for! That you were probably fine. That you'd resurface in a couple of days. That sometimes you just needed a little time."

Dillon closed her eyes. "What did she say?"

"You need to call her, Dillon. You need to apologize. She's a really nice girl. She doesn't deserve this any more than me or mam."

A breeze had picked up, bringing gooseflesh to Dillon's arms as she sat, unmoving in her drenched clothes.

How could she begin to apologize? Kameryn would want an explanation. One Dillon didn't know how to give. She couldn't even explain her actions to herself.

"I know. I will."

"I mean it, Dillon. And call mam. Just not tonight. I'll let her know I talked to you."

Dillon could tell she was about to hang up.

"Seren?"

Her sister was silent, but hung on, listening.

"Do you think I should throw in the towel?"

It was quiet so long Dillon thought she may have been mistaken, and Seren had already ended the call. But eventually she heard her take a deep breath, before blowing out a long, slow exhale. "I don't know which is more dangerous: you giving up on your dreams, or trying to see them through."

It was Dillon's turn to be silent. She couldn't answer what she didn't know.

"I love you, Dillon. Don't you ever forget that." And then Seren hung up the phone.

# Scene 31

I burrowed deeper into the hood of my sweatshirt, avoiding eye contact with the man across the aisle who kept glancing my direction. In my vanity, I worried he might have recognized me from the plethora of *Sand Seekers* promo photos circulating the internet, which had been released a few days earlier when we'd wrapped up shooting in Scotland. But as I shifted to angle my body away from him, I realized, in my rush down the broken escalator to catch the late-night train to London, I'd spilled half my mocha onto my beige leggings.

It wasn't a great look. Between the coffee stain, the dark circles under my eyes, my hair falling out of its messy bun, and the midnight train ride, it didn't take much to guess what he thought of me. I half expected him to drop a few coins into my empty coffee cup as he disembarked one stop before Paddington Station.

As the train started moving again, the dark world gliding by outside the foggy windows, I began to wonder if I'd lost my mind.

Everyone from the film production was already home in Los Angeles, taking advantage of the ten-day hiatus before we were due back in the studio. And here I was, traipsing through London in the middle of the night.

Which was nothing, compared to three days earlier, when I'd rented a car in Aberdeen, and, despite having never driven on the wrong side of the road—and I say *wrong* side, because every time I got to a right-hand turn, I assure you, it *felt* wrong—made the trip from the northern coast of Scotland to the furthest point of South Wales. *That*, no doubt, was the beginning of my decline into insanity.

But in fairness, it had been quite a week.

Initially, after watching a reel of Dillon collapse on the course in Yokohama, I'd assumed I hadn't heard from her because she was still being treated in the hospital. I'd considered jumping on a flight to Japan. But then I came across a post from *British Triathlon* stating that, despite suffering heat exhaustion and postural hypotension,

Dillon had been released from medical the evening of the race. And still, her phone went straight to voicemail.

Two more days went by and I began to think she iced me out. It just didn't make sense. We'd spoken daily for months. After all the delays with my shooting in Greenland, it had even worked out for us to rearrange our schedules, planning a few days together in London after she got home from Japan.

But there was no other explanation.

When filming wrapped up in Scotland, I knew I should go home. I had no reason to stay. Still, I'd found myself unable to board a plane. Not without some closure. Not without knowing for sure.

So I hunted down every article I could find on Seren Sinclair, until I found the name of her training barn in Wales—*Golden Crest Farms*. And then, like the fool I was beginning to feel I was, drove five-hundred sixty miles to Swansea, to pay an unexpected visit to a woman who I wasn't even certain knew I existed.

"You must be Kameryn," was the first thing she said, however, when she brought her horse down to a walk and approached where I'd stood watching on the rail.

From the photos I'd seen online, I knew Seren looked nothing like her sister.

Tall, willowy, dark-featured, with a gorgeous olive complexion that radiated a life spent outdoors on the back of a horse.

It was surprising, then, to find so much of her reminded me of Dillon.

As she sat with her reins resting on a chestnut gelding's withers, it was obvious she shared the same tranquil stillness, the same quiet confidence I was so attracted to in her sister. A little more serious, a little more somber, but reminiscent of Dillon all the same.

I'd prepared a dozen ways to explain who I was, and why I was there, but they turned out to be unnecessary.

"I imagine you're here about my sister."

Just like Dillon, Seren seemed inclined to skip the pleasantries, cutting straight to the heart of the conversation.

"I—yes. I haven't been able to reach her."

"No," she said simply. "Nor have I." Swinging down from the saddle, she waved for a waiting groom. "I understand you ride. If you want to hack out with me, we'll talk about Dillon."

Fifteen minutes later, in a pair of borrowed field boots and a Troxel that smelled like sweat, I followed Seren on a quiet lesson horse out a rear gate and down a wooded trail. When we came to the bottom of the hill, into a valley of chest-high grass, Seren slowed her young mount, allowing us to ride side-by-side.

"My sister is a destructive perfectionist," she said without preamble as we ducked under the hanging branches of an enormous hornbeam. "She's always been a chaser of unattainable goals. And when she isn't winning—and sometimes even when she is—her mind leads her to believe she isn't good enough." She paused, helping her horse across a ditch cut from the rain. "I'd like to blame it on Henrik," she said shortly, not asking me if I knew who he was.

It was clear she knew exactly what I knew—and what I didn't. It was obvious few secrets were kept between the two Sinclairs.

"But even though it may have been exacerbated by him, it's something I've had to come to accept is just part of who she is." She soothed the hot young warmblood as a branch brushed across his flank, and a ridiculous part of me couldn't help but think how much my mother would love her quiet seat and gentle hands.

I turned my attention away from her horsemanship. "Where is she?"

Seren hiked a narrow shoulder. "I don't know."

"Has she done this before?"

"Yes." She didn't hesitate to answer. "But not in many years."

*When*? I wanted to ask, but didn't feel it was overtly relevant. Instead, I went with my more pressing concern. "Should we be worried?"

The gelding fussed with his snaffle, wanting to snack on the tops of the meadow grass, and Seren spent longer than was necessary schooling him, taking her time to respond.

"I'm not sure," she said at last, and the candor in her tone made my heart quicken. "But honestly," she turned to look at me, rallying half a smile that did nothing to successfully hide her own distress, "she's probably fine. She'll resurface in a day or two and our mam will give her a right telling-off."

We let the conversation drift. Seren asked me about my mom and her career with horses, and I asked her about her quest toward the Olympic Games. I realized, by the nonchalance of her answer, that representing Great Britain was not the end goal for her, but simply part of her journey as an equestrian. Unlike her sister, she didn't seem to view life in singular achievements, but instead enjoyed all the small successes along the way.

It was something I could understand. It was the same way I felt when she asked me about *Sand Seekers*, and what I looked forward to most in starring in what was sure to be a blockbuster film. She seemed to believe me when I said I just really wanted to do the story justice—that would be the pinnacle achievement for me.

By the time we dismounted, the globe of the sun had disappeared beneath the horizon. The horses were sent off with a groom as I unclipped the helmet and wiped sweat and hair from the borrowed boots, before Seren walked me to my car in the gravel driveway.

"When my sister turns up—" *when*, I noted she said, still trying to ease my concern, "I know it's unfair to ask this of you, but go easy on her, if you can. I truly don't believe she realizes what she puts everyone through."

"I just want her to be ok." The statement didn't remotely express how desperately I wanted to see her sister. How much she meant to me. But, I imagined driving the entire length of the UK probably spoke for itself.

"Trust me, you'll be angry later." She tapped the calf of her boot with a riding crop she'd carried with her in her back pocket, and waved goodbye as the sign for *Golden Crest Farms* disappeared in my rearview mirror.

And as I stepped out of Paddington Station and failed to hail the third cab that sped past me in the pouring rain, I realized Seren hadn't been wrong.

I *was* angry. And growing angrier by the minute.

Dillon had called me an hour and a half earlier. I'd been sitting in my hotel room near Heathrow, where I'd stayed the last two nights after driving to Wales, and had been in the process of booking a flight leaving for LAX in the morning. With little more than a week before I was due back in Los Angeles, I'd resigned myself to going home. I knew I couldn't wait around in the UK forever.

She hadn't said much on the phone.

I asked her if she was okay.

*Yes.*

She asked me where I was.

*Reading.*

She asked me if I'd be willing to see her in the morning before I left for LA.

*Okay.*

I told her to text me her address.

And we hung up.

My text tone chimed a moment later, and after a few minutes of staring at the flight itineraries on my computer screen, I snapped my laptop shut, pulled on my *UCLA* hoodie, stuffed my feet into a pair of Uggs, and walked out of the shoebox-sized room.

I'd turned in the rental car after leaving Swansea—I couldn't handle another roundabout—so I walked a block to *Reading Station* and grabbed a coffee at Pret a Manger, almost missing the last late-night train to Paddington.

And there I now stood, drenched by the downpour, cussing at the passing cabs, and regretting my decision to not wait until morning.

Yeah, angry didn't quite cover it.

By the time I got to South Bank, and had shouldered my way into the lobby of Dillon's apartment building, I'd decided I was going to slap her. A decision that sounded more and more promising as I slipped past the sleeping concierge and discovered I needed a keycard for the elevator, so instead found myself panting up eleven flights of stairs.

It turned out I was all bluster.

The moment she opened the door, I forgot all about my anger.

She looked different than I had last seen her, more than four months earlier.

I know it was the middle of the night, and I had surprised her, arriving unannounced, but still, she was less put together than I'd expected. Her hair was longer, hanging shaggy below her ears, and her cheeks were gaunt, her t-shirt loose on her body—a testament that she'd lost more weight than she could afford to lose. I was taken aback by the dark circles under her eyes, heavily contrasted by the paleness of her face.

But still, when she smiled at me after losing the look of startlement at the unexpected intrusion, she had the same mild composure, the same equable good nature I'd learned to love so much.

"You're a little early," she said, and the next thing I knew, I'd flung myself into her arms.

I could be angry later. I wouldn't let her off the hook that easy. But for the moment, the unburdening relief of seeing her there, in flesh and blood, alive and well, was all I could focus on. It had unlodged the seed of fear that had taken root, spreading the idea that I might never see her again. And with its uprooting came a flood of tears I could no longer contain.

"Hey," she soothed when she realized I was crying. The force of my embrace had pushed us several steps into her hall, and with my eyes still squeezed shut, I could feel her reach to close her door. "Come here, Kam-Kameryn." She pressed her lips to my temple, wrapping me in her arms.

"I thought you were gone," I choked into her neck as she stroked my rain-slogged hair.

"Shhh," her lips brushed my wet cheeks, traveling to my mouth. "I'm right here."

I let her kiss me. I let her turn my thoughts from all my questions—from all my anxieties and fears. Later, I would ask her the things I wanted to know. But for the moment, all I wanted was to forget every-thing for a while. To feel whole again, the way she'd made me feel in LA. And to find a way to make her feel the same.

Angry voices filtered through the closed door.

One, I realized, in my blinking wakefulness, was Dillon's. The other I did not know.

It was morning. The day was bright, the skyline of London visible through the bedroom window. In my midnight arrival, I hadn't really familiarized myself with Dillon's apartment. Bedroom. Bathroom. That's pretty much as far as I'd gotten.

I would have liked to have had a moment to examine my surround-ings. To take in the simplicity that was just Dillon. The navy blue comforter that matched the open curtains. The streamline furniture sparsely stationed against the walls: bed, dresser, single bedside table. There was a framed photo—Dillon and Seren as young teenagers, piggyback and laughing—and a smaller print tucked into the corner of the frame—a man, young and handsome, holding a toddler with white blonde hair. It was Dillon's father, no doubt, and I would have liked to look closer, but the voices had grown louder, and the altercation more intense.

"You're a bloody selfish cunt, Sinc! Don't you dare tell me to tone it down!" came the unfamiliar voice, thick with what I'd recently come to recognize as a Northern English accent. "You think it's fair, marra, to disappear—leave us all thinking you're belly up, floating around with the driftwood off some Japanese beach—and then just turn up and carry on? I had to hear it from Seren that you'd resurfaced—"

"Sam," Dillon's tone was softer, more placating, "I was going to call you today. Now just hear me for a moment—"

"Don't you try to put the lid on me, man!"

Unable to find my leggings—I might have left them in the hall—I rummaged through Dillon's dresser, finding a pair of shorts and t-shirt to pull on.

"Seven bloody days, Sinc! I even called Kelsey, for fuck's sake!"

Whatever pacifying attempt Dillon made backfired.

"You think you can shush me? If you didn't want me radgie on your doorstep, you should have thought about that before—"

"Simmer, mate—"

There was some kind of scuffle, and a muffled thud, before I heard Dillon curse.

"Damn you, Hunt!"

Barefoot, my hair still haloed in a rat's nest, I rushed out the bedroom to find Dillon pinned against her entryway wall. The woman, not much taller than me, but twice my weight in muscle, had her forearm jammed against Dillon's chest, and her other arm drawn back, promising another blow.

"Swing again at me, man—let's have a bloody go!"

I don't know what I was thinking. Dillon probably could have held her own—though in the woman's fury, the stranger definitely seemed to have the upper hand. But in the split second I had to make a decision, I lunged forward, grabbing the woman by her waist, and knocked her legs out from under her with a forceful sweep of my foot, tumbling us both to the ground.

Five years in LA and two self-defense classes later, it turned out to be my stunt training for *Sand Seekers* that actually served as a practical application.

"What the—" outraged, the woman bellowed beneath me, but I pressed her firmer into the hardwood floor.

"Hey!" I'd managed to get a grip on her tightly spiraled hair. "Chill out!"

"Kam…" Dillon dropped to her knees beside me. "It's all right—honest, let her go."

Nothing seemed quite *all right* about the way I was certain this thrashing, livid woman was going to get up and pummel the crap out of me, but I did as Dillon bade, and stepped off her, quickly backing away.

"You fucking wanker!" To my surprise, as the woman scrambled to her feet, she didn't come after me, but instead bent over, fussing with her knee.

It took a moment to realize that she was realigning a prosthetic. I'd just blindside-dropped a woman to the ground, dislodging her bionic leg.

"I—I'm so…" I stopped. I mean, what? She'd had Dillon in a wall pin. What was I supposed to do?

Her slew of curses ceased abruptly as she turned dark eyes to me, her face shifting from fury into a delighted grin. "Oh my God." She stood up straighter. "Dog shot by Addison Riley herself!"

"Sam—" Dillon tried to cut in.

"*You*, not a word," the woman flicked a finger in Dillon's direction, "I'm still of a mind to drill you into the floor." But her tone was lifted, the lividity gone. She smiled at me. "You're a lot cheekier than you look in photos. Stronger, too," she laughed. "Gotta admit, fit as you are, you'd look even more lush coming out of my bedroom with a hickey on your neck, wearing my shirt backward." She motioned to the tag sticking up from the reversed collar.

I'm sure I blushed crimson, because of course, pulling off nonchalance was not part of my readily available repertoire, and brought a hand to my neck.

"No, no, other side," she winked, and then wagged her full brows at me. "Oh, never mind, both sides, maybe."

"*Sam*," Dillon scolded, but again the woman—who was beginning to seem familiar—showed her her palm.

"Silence, Sinc." She looked back to me. "Sam Huntley." She stuck out her hand.

The name immediately jogged my memory. I knew her at once. I'd seen her face plastered all over the TV for years. One of England's greatest soccer players. Her accolades were endless. And then, later, I remembered her being in the news—no longer for soccer, but because a terrible motorcycle accident had ended her career.

I shook her hand.

On so many occasions Dillon had referenced her best friend, Sam. Of course it would be Sam Huntley—because, after all, she was Dillon Sinclair.

"Hi—Kameryn," I managed. "Kingsbury."

"Could have fooled me for Tonya Harding." Again, she winked. "Won't lie—I'd half believed Sinc made up the whole thing. Didn't for a minute imagine you'd settle for an ugly mug like hers. I promise you, lass—you could do so much better."

Before I could answer, she turned her attention to Dillon. "Don't think you're in the clear—I'm not done with you. But I'll leave you to it for now. Nothing worse than acting a spare tire." Taking a step to the front door, she looked back at me one last time. "You ought to come to my bash on Saturday. I promise, I could find you someone to leave with a whole lot dishier than ol' Sinc, here." She gave her friend a pointed glare. "See you then, marra." And shut the door.

# Scene 32

"How can you live here, with this view, and have never been on it?"

Dillon followed Kameryn's gaze to the London Eye, just a few hundred meters from where she sat at the railing of her balcony. She tipped her head back, resting it against Kam's chest, who had come to stand behind her.

It was the third morning they'd woken in London together, and the day was unusually bright, the sky clearing across the city. The slowly revolving observation wheel gleamed against the sunlight, its reflection bouncing off the slow pull of the river. Dillon closed her eyes, enjoying the sensation of the idle fingers Kam ran through her hair.

"I don't know. It's like the people who live in New York City who've never been to the Statue of Liberty."

"I bet most of them have, they just don't admit it."

"Nonsense. You live in LA. Have you ever been to the Capitol Records Building?"

"Yes."

"Madame Tussauds Wax Museum?"

"Yes."

"Hollywood Walk of Fame?"

"Yes."

"Griffith Park Observatory?"

Kameryn laughed. "With *you*."

"The Farmers Market at the Grove?"

"Also with you."

"Universal Studios?"

Kam tugged a shaggy lock of her too-long hair. "Now you're just messing with me."

"Never." Dillon smiled, wishing she could bottle the moment, to find a way to permanently absorb the happiness, this feeling of contentment. Kam bent to kiss her. "How about the pilings beneath the Santa Monica Pier?" Dillon asked against her lips.

"Once or twice."

"Twice?" She pivoted in the chair to face her, tilting her head in mock indignation. "With whom?"

"Wouldn't you like to know?" Kam slid to sit on her lap.

"Tosh." Dillon poked her in the ribs. "What about the Petersen Automotive Museum?"

"The what?"

"*See*! You've proven my point. Just because you live near a tourism landmark doesn't mean you have to partake."

"Whatever that is is *not* a landmark."

"Absolutely is! It's on Miracle Mile!"

"And when did you become an expert on LA's tourist hot spots?"

"Wouldn't you like to know?" Dillon ribbed, toying with the hem of another shirt Kam had borrowed from her—her luggage still sitting in a hotel in Reading they kept swearing they'd go pick up.

"I want to go on it."

Dillon slid her hands beneath the shirt. "On what?"

"*Dillon*," Kam scolded, though she didn't pull away. "The London Eye."

"There's a pretty good view of the skyline from here." She slipped her hands higher, forcing Kam's breath to shorten in response to her roaming fingers.

"I know what you're trying to do. It's not going to work."

"Care to bet?" Dillon kissed the exposed skin above her collar, feeling Kam lean her weight into her as the morning dew dried atop the glass banister.

It did work.

For about an hour.

And then, showered and dressed, Dillon let Kam drag her out the door, always knowing it had been a losing battle.

"C'mon," Kam chided at Dillon's reluctant steps. "It's going to be fun." She tugged her through the foyer, sneaking a kiss onto her neck as Dillon held open the door. "We could always have a continuation of our morning from the top of London."

"Maybe if you're into voyeurism." Dillon linked her arm through hers. "You realize they pack like two dozen people into every capsule."

Hitting the pavement, they started the short walk through Jubilee Gardens. The day had grown warm and the park attracted a plethora of foot traffic, with couples and children sprawled on the grass beneath the shadow of the glorified Ferris wheel.

"Don't be such a killjoy. Their website says they offer a private pod. And if they won't take a same day reservation, I'll buy however many tickets it takes to turn it into an exclusive ride."

"Is that how it works, Miss Hollywood Big Shot?" Dillon tucked her hand into Kam's back pocket. She'd found her a pair of Seren's jeans left behind from one of her sister's weekend visits, and a hoodie with *British Triathlon* screenprinted across it—one Kameryn already warned her she was taking home to Los Angeles.

With a beanie and sunglasses, she looked like every other wandering tourist.

"I had a big payday. It's only fair I get to blow a little of it some-where—what better way than to buy the right to kiss my girlfriend looking down over Buckingham Palace?"

*Girlfriend.*

She could feel Kam's side eye, feel her waiting for a response. With all the confines that surrounded them, it wasn't something they'd put a label on. But she loved the easy way she said it, the offer to continue to build on the groundwork they had laid.

"Well, I mean, if you're going to blow it somewhere…" Dillon drew her a little closer as they walked, their hips pressed together. "I just hope you know, you'll never need to buy a kiss from me."

"I do know." Kam laced their fingers together, and they strolled down The Queen's Walk hand in hand.

As they reached the ticket window, however, Dillon considered stepping aside—distancing the dynamic between them.

But changed her mind.

Soon, they wouldn't have this. This freedom to be out together, with no heads turned their way. The ability to blend into crowds and do as they pleased. Kam's face would be everywhere, and their worlds would never be the same. So for now, she kept her hand in Kam's as they wound through the queue. No one noticed. No one cared. Not even the disinterested ticket seller, who hardly raised an eyebrow as Kam forked over nearly a thousand pounds to reserve thirty minutes of privacy.

"No refunds. Enjoy the ride," came the man's monotone drawl as he shoved the ticket through the window with the credit card receipt.

An hour later, Dillon sat on a bench in the center of what felt like a revolving fishbowl as it slowly made its way toward the sky. Kam stood at the outer edge of the capsule, with her forehead pressed to the glass.

"The view is gorgeous! Won't you come see?"

"I can see from here." She swallowed down the discomfort of the lump that rose in her throat the higher the pod climbed.

Kam turned to look at her, and in her dawning realization, an amused smile touched the corner of her lips. "Dillon." She crossed to the bench. "Why didn't you say you were afraid of heights?"

"I'm not afraid," she was at once defensive, "I just…"

"You're practically green." Kam laughed, tussling her hair, before flopping down beside her, and laughed again as Dillon flinched at the mild sway of the floating capsule. "I'd never have asked you to come on it if I'd known!"

"I know. It's why I didn't say anything."

The smile Kam gave her made the slowly disappearing ground more bearable, even as Big Ben turned into little more than a mantel clock.

*Four more days.* That's all they had left before Kam flew back to Los Angeles. And every hour seemed to fly by faster than the one before.

She knew Kam's schedule was packed. She knew, even once Kam wrapped up filming next week in the studio, there would be endless obligations she had to uphold. But still, she couldn't help but ask the question that had been gnawing at her. The one she'd been holding out hope for.

"If I race Leeds—" the *if* tasted stale on her tongue, but hung there, unpleasant all the same, "—would you come watch me?"

Kam's smile slipped, her expression shifting to surprise.

"I thought you didn't like anyone to watch you compete?"

"I…" She didn't, usually. Sam. Seren. That was about it. And only because neither of them took no for an answer. But the pressure of racing, after Bermuda, after Yokohama… It had begun to feel insurmountable. She'd found it almost impossible to drag herself onto her bike trainer each night, after Kam had fallen asleep, or down to the private pool in her building, or off for a sunrise run. But, if Kam was there, somewhere on the other side of the finish line, she thought, maybe, she could find her fire again. "It's different with you. I know it's asking a lot—for you to fly back here so soon—"

"—of course I'll come! I'd love to come!"

The bitter taste of *if* began to fade.

"Yeah?" Dillon smiled.

"Yeah."

"I'll win it for you, if you come."

This time, Kam didn't return her smile.

"I don't need you to win it for me, Dillon. I just need you to not disappear on me again."

It was no longer the dizzying height of the pod that made it feel stuffy. Dillon swallowed, her gaze drifting to the skyline.

"Dillon." Kam took her hand, squeezing it, drawing her attention back to her. "There's something I want to ask you, and I need you to answer honestly."

She'd known this conversation was coming. She'd known Kam had been sitting on it, waiting for the opportunity. And she knew she owed it to her.

"Alright."

"Should I have been worried? About you?"

She didn't need her to clarify what she meant.

"No." The answer was too simple, but still, it was the truth. "I just needed some time to clear my head."

Kam digested this. "And have you ever… In the past, I mean…"

"I thought about it." Dillon cut her off, saving her the discomfort of asking. "Once. Shortly after my dad died." She worked her jaw, again glancing away from Kam's searching gaze. "I was—it was a rough time for me—with everything that happened. But I got through it."

Thoughtful, Kam slipped her hand into Dillon's. "Please don't scare me again." She stared at their entwined fingers. "If you need time—if you need space—that's all you have to say. You don't even have to tell me where you're going. I just want to know you're safe."

The observation wheel continued to revolve, their pod cresting the highest point of the circle, but Dillon didn't notice. She'd forgotten any fear of falling. There were other things in life far more frightening to face—like being asked to make promises she wasn't certain she could keep.

"Okay," she said at last, as the wheel began to descend over South Bank. "I can do that."

"You give me your word? You won't just disappear?"

"Yes." She meant it. Never once had she taken a promise lightly.

Kam's hand relaxed. Behind them, Buckingham Palace slipped out of sight, but neither of them cared. The view had been forgotten completely.

Sighing, Kam leaned forward, resting her forehead against hers.

"You should know—I think I'm in love with you, Dillon Sinclair," she whispered, before pushing herself to her feet, giving Dillon no chance to respond as the pod settled onto the offloading track and the door slid open.

# Scene 33

The thump of a pounding bass vibrated the lamppost on the sidewalk before we'd even reached the pub door.

Dillon shot me a look beneath a raised eyebrow. "You sure you're up for this? It's going to be a melee of British athletes—guaranteed to be chopsy and hanging."

This last phrase brought me to a pause. "Chopsy and hanging?"

"Fighting and drunk," she translated.

"Oh." I laughed. "Yeah—*Fight Club* I can handle. *Texas Chainsaw Massacre* would be a different story."

It was Sam Huntley's thirtieth birthday party. *A wee do*, Sam had described it, when she'd texted Dillon to reiterate the invitation was extended to me. There would be nothing *wee* about it, Dillon had warned. But she'd also mentioned my attendance would likely make Sam's year—once again reinforcing my belief that I'd gone to sleep Kameryn Kingsbury and woken up in a parallel universe living someone else's life. Because in what reality did I exist where I was being invited to the birthday of one of the most famous athletes of the twenty-first century?

There was no way I was going to turn that down.

Well, unless Dillon had wanted me to. I hadn't been sure how she would feel being linked with me in public. We'd already agreed—in that easy way people set terms before things really matter—to keep our relationship private. I'd allowed her to cite my career as the primary reason. And it was true, while we may have been living in one of the most progressive eras in history, behind the scenes, Hollywood was still an unfriendly place for anyone who strayed from the so-called "normal."

But I think we both knew the decision was made for her sake more than anything. And I was all right with that. It was no one's business but our own.

"Would it be better if we went separately?" I'd asked as she sat on the edge of her tub, watching me apply my makeup. "On the off chance someone recognizes me?"

"Nonsense." She stood, stepping up behind me as I blended my foundation. "No laws against me bringing a mate along to a party." Slipping the strap of my dress aside, she kissed the top of my arm. "But you'd be daft to think you might go unnoticed. Even if Sam wasn't positively giddy over your upcoming film, there's no chance you could walk into any room and not turn the heads of everyone around you."

"I think you might be biased."

"Rubbish. I just have impeccable taste." She rested her chin on my shoulder. "You know, it took me a while to see it—the relation between the girl I fell in love with on a Pacific island and the woman in the headshots preparing to make her Hollywood premiere. But I can see it now."

I turned my attention away from where I'd begun to apply my mascara, catching her gaze in the mirror.

The previous morning, I'd told her I loved her while we were on the London Eye, and to hear her admit she felt the same came as an immense relief.

"And which one do you prefer?" I asked, my mascara brush still paused midair.

She shrugged. "I'm a fan of both."

"But if you had to choose," I goaded.

"Fine—this one," she said, her eyes gesturing down the snug cut of the cocktail dress she'd helped me shop for earlier in the morning, then back to my made-up face. "*And* the other one," she continued, "the one drenched to the skin, covered in mud, slipping down Ka'uiki Head, who let me kiss her in the rain." She leaned closer to my ear. "Along with all the other women you are, who I've yet to meet. I'll love them all the same."

"Keep it up," I'd had to tease, finding it suddenly hard to breathe, "and when we get home tonight, you just might get lucky."

"I'm already lucky," she'd winked and kissed my cheek, before disappearing to change for the party.

The pub was packed. I'd expected a few dozen people who looked like Sam had a few mornings prior—sporty, casual, laid-back. But the dimly lit dining room and covered terrace were teeming with bodies clad in sleek silks and vibrant vicuña, most of which looked as if they'd tripped off a fashion runway and landed unexpectedly around the high-top tables.

I was grateful Hollywood had taught me that a little black dress never went out of style. It wasn't the nearly see-through number half the women were wearing, but it wasn't something I'd wear to Easter service with the Hallwells, either.

"Hello, Sinc!" an exceptionally slender man clapped Dillon on the back in passing as we worked our way through the crowded main hall. He offered her a high-wattage smile. "Good to see you, as always!"

He looked familiar, but it took me a second to realize why.

"Was that really Mo Farah?" I whispered as we continued to work our way toward the bar.

"*Sir* Mo Farah," Dillon confirmed.

I didn't know if I was more stunned that I'd just brushed shoulders with arguably the greatest long-distance runner of all time, or that he'd greeted Dillon by name, and she was completely unfazed.

People continued to greet her as she navigated the tables, searching for Sam. I recognized a few of them—Andy Murray, the Scottish tennis sensation, Rory McIlroy, the former world number one Irish golfer, Jess Fishlock, the Welsh football legend.

Most were *hiyas* and *alrights* in passing, and the few that detained her attention for more than a word or two, she introduced me to as "my friend Kameryn."

In response, I maintained a respectable distance between us—close enough that we didn't look awkward, but far enough apart to lose the *they're-clearly-fucking* undertone.

We found Sam on the terrace. She was tipping back a shot with a tall redhead, her dark skin glimmering beneath the light of the swinging glowsticks dangling from the framework of the outdoor bar.

"Well, behold! Look who's graced us with her presence!" She immediately discarded the shot glass and loped to intercede us. "Cracking duds, marra," her eyes swept Dillon's black t-shirt and distressed jeans. "Nice to see you go out of your way."

"I'm here, am I right? Not everyone has to look like they've been spit out a unicorn's arse."

Sam waved two fingers her direction—the English equivalent of the bird—before her gaze flicked to me. Her face was hidden in shadow beneath the brim of her checkered yellow fedora, but her smile flashed as brightly as her chartreuse pinstriped suit. She cocked a hip, tapping the glossed cement with one of her neon orange bowling shoes.

"Well aren't you a vision, my bonny lass?" She gathered my hand in hers, pressing it to her lips. "You're stunning, Miss K. I'd say you knock me off my feet, however…"

"A touch of déjà vu?"

Her Cheshire smile grew. "Radiant *and* cheeky. A woman after my own heart."

The fiery-haired woman beside her ah-hemmed.

"After you, of course, pet." Sam slid her arm around the taller woman's waist. "Imogen, meet Kameryn Kingsbury. Miss Kingsbury, my date, Imogen Howard."

"Goalkeeper for the Lionesses," I smiled, pleased to put together where I'd heard the name before. I recognized her from England's last World Cup roster.

"The one and only." Her smile was frigid, never touching her emerald eyes.

*Oh.*

I was taken aback by her unmistakable hostility. Well, in that case—*one of two and only*, I thought to myself, considering I was pretty certain she served as the *second*-string keeper for her national team.

The venom of her gaze turned toward Dillon. "You've got some nerve, Sinclair—showing up here."

"Hey now," Sam warned, "you know Sinc's my best mate—and tonight we're all friends." She chucked her chin toward the bottle of scotch I was carrying. A last-minute birthday gift I'd picked up on the way to the train station. "Canny good taste, Miss Kingsbury."

I handed her the bottle, my mind still working around the obvious discord between Imogen and Dillon. "Happy Birthday."

Reviewing the label, she turned toward the bartender. "Uncork us, will you, man? That's a mint single malt, alright."

A short pour later, we were presented with four tumblers of scotch on the rocks. Dillon quietly passed hers to Sam and asked for a water, which wasn't missed beneath Imogen's watchful glare.

"Rich of you, giving up the bottle now, Sinclair—"

"You mishear me, Imi?" Sam snapped, tipping back her glass before swiping up Dillon's. "It's my bloody birthday—and I'll be damned if we don't all get along."

The goalkeeper scowled but was wise enough to keep silent as the bartender returned with Dillon's water.

"Say," he paused, his gaze falling on me as he passed Dillon her glass. "I know you."

*Oh, goodie.*

*Know* and *recognize* were such vastly different words.

I forced myself to smile. "Sorry, I don't think—"

"I saw your photo in *Daily Mail*." He dropped his elbows on the bar top. "Yeah, I'm certain of it—you're that American girl in *Sand Seekers*. Whole article about how you just finished shooting up in Aberdeen." Standing upright, he gave me a sweeping once-over. "Those photos made you look so much taller."

*Um, thanks?*

I started to pick up my drink but he fished out his phone, leaning the upper half of his body across the bar.

"Can I get a photo? My old lady's never going to believe this!"

"Um, sure."

He draped his perspiring arm around me, forcing our heads together. "Ace!" His phone flashed.

I resisted the urge to wipe at my cheek with the back of my hand.

"Gawkers look like stalkers," Sam cut in when he continued to stare. "The drink, man." She pointed to my glass, drawing him back to his job.

"Oh, yeah, yeah." He slid it toward me. "On the house."

"It's my bloody bottle, knob," Sam leaned over and snagged the remainder of the scotch, clinking her glass to mine. "Drink up, marras!"

We toasted to Sam and she returned the salute for me and my up-coming film, confessing that she'd been in love with Addison Riley since she first learned how to read.

"Not long ago, then, huh?" Dillon teased, earning a flick to the forehead.

I loved the easy friendship between them. The way they communicated through an unspoken language, with looks and gestures built from years of attention to detail. It was obvious how much respect they had for each other, even as it was demonstrated through banter and horse play. It was something, I'd grown certain, Dani and I would never share.

Lost in these thoughts as I sipped my whisky, I was startled by Imogen, who let out an ear-piercing squeal. She'd grown sullenly silent since her rebuke from Sam, but now her whole body brightened as she lunged across the terrace floor.

A moment later, she returned arm-in-arm with a strikingly attractive blonde whose plunging neckline on her silver-sequined mini-dress left little to the imagination. As the woman glided over on the towering stilettos of her knee high leather boots, she offered a brilliant smile toward Sam, which faltered immediately when her gaze fell on Dillon. Imogen tugged at her elbow, continuing to drag her along.

I didn't have to guess who she was. All of Europe knew who she was. Even if her face hadn't appeared on everything from train station posters to Gatorade commercials, it would still be impossible not to recognize the cobalt blue eyes and poster girl figure of England's pride and joy.

It was no wonder Kelsey Evans had turned Dillon's head. Hell, she'd have made Mother Teresa do a double take if she'd been strolling down the convent halls.

I mean, really—*those legs…*

Without further hesitation, she extracted herself from Imogen's grip, kissed Sam's cheek, cast a quick glance at me, and then turned to face Dillon head on.

"Hello, Sinc. It's been a spell."

*Sinc.* Everyone called her that. I'd heard it from at least a dozen mouths tonight alone. But somehow, from her, it struck me differently. It made me realize there was this whole part of her world I didn't share. I would never call her Sinc. It was like a club I couldn't join. A clique to which I'd never belong.

"Kelsey."

"Time for another round!" Imogen blurted, turning for the bar.

A beat of silence passed before Kelsey took a step forward, offering Dillon a side-arm hug—a clear peace offering amidst the awkward atmosphere.

"You look good." She turned on a smile, one I'd seen in her roster headshots, a boilerplate gesture I knew well. Every actor on the planet had one. Not too forced, not too broad. "I was sorry to hear about Yokohama." She seemed genuine. Nice, even.

Dillon's shrug of indifference was not convincing. "No matter. Can't win them all."

"Won't ever stop you from trying though, will it?" Her smile softened, growing authentic, before she turned to me. "Hi, I don't think we've met? I'm Kelsey."

"Kameryn." I shook her hand.

"American?" She seemed surprised, but there was none of the hostility as had been with Imogen. "Footballer?"

"Oh," I laughed, nervous, "no."

"Kam's an actress," Sam supplemented, sounding like a little kid with a secret they just had to share. "That's okay to say, right, Kam? That's not taboo?"

I laughed. "Only for my parents, who are a little less enthused."

"What brings you to London?" Kelsey asked. There was no hidden dig or covert agenda. It made me feel guilty, despite having no reason to. She was just nothing of what I'd imagined. There was no resemblance to the cocky, self-assured, occasionally belligerent player I'd watched on TV. Here, she was nothing more than a regular girl—no different than me—navigating the awkwardness of an uncomfortable breakup.

It didn't matter that she was dating someone new—that she was in love with someone else. It didn't change the reality that she still clearly cared about the person who'd made up her past.

I knew the feeling, and though the jealous side of me had geared itself up to hate her when Dillon mentioned it was likely our paths would cross tonight, I found I didn't feel that way at all.

"I was filming up in Aberdeen…"

"Lass is being modest! Not just any film shoot. Kam's starring in *Sand Seekers!*"

Kelsey's blue eyes widened. "*Sand Seekers*—as in the books?" She glanced from me to Sam. "Wow. I mean—isn't that huge?"

Imogen poked her nose back into the conversation, returning with two drinks in hand. "What's huge?" She passed a glass to Kelsey.

"*Sand Seekers!*" Sam hadn't lost her kid-in-the-candy-shop grin.

"Oh, God, not this again," the goalkeeper rolled her eyes. "I swear that bloody movie is all we're going to hear about all night."

"Wey aye, man!"

"And how do you two know each other?" Kelsey asked, the question aimed at me and Sam. Before Sam could answer, Imogen felt the need to interject.

"She's here with Sinclair." The statement was spat with such annoyance she may as well have rolled her eyes.

"Oh." Kelsey's canned smile returned. "Of course. I didn't realize…"

Behind us, through the double doors leading into the tavern, the smooth beat of *Murder On the Dancefloor* kicked on.

"I love this song!" Imogen clapped her hands, grabbing Kelsey's arm. "Come dance with me! Let's get this party started!"

With half-hearted resistance, Kelsey allowed herself to be dragged off as Sam was swept away by another group of friends.

"Sorry about Imogen," Dillon whispered, drawing her face close to mine to be heard over the music. "She's can be a real rotter—"

"—she's just protecting her friend," I cut her off, my fingers wanting to find hers, but remaining obediently by my side. I didn't have to look to know Kelsey's eyes were still on us, stealing glances through the door. "I won't fault her there."

Obscured amongst the crowd of people snaking their way toward the bar, she let her fingertips graze mine. "You know, we don't have to stay too long…"

"It's your best friend's birthday," I scolded.

"Yeah, and? She's got a couple hundred people who want her attention tonight—I just want yours."

"Worried I'm going to take Sam up on her offer to find me someone *dishier* to leave with?" I teased.

Dillon lifted a bold brow. "Not a chance."

I laughed. "Has anyone ever told you you have a bit of an ego, Dillon Sinclair?" I slid my thumb to her palm, trailing it to brush the soft skin of her wrist.

"Did you see the woman I arrived with?" she whispered, closing her fingers around my hand. "How could I not let that go to my head?"

"Please." I rolled my eyes. "Flattery will get you nowhere."

"On the contrary—I think it will get me exactly where I want to be."

Still pinned between two groups of jostling, oblivious partygoers, she snuck a hand onto my hip. "If we go now, we can make the next train to Waterloo."

I'd have been willing to meet her in homeroom closet after study hall with the direction her hand was traveling, but sweet vengeance got the better of me. "If I recall correctly," I said, drumming up a coy smile, "you once made me sit through an entire seven course meal, a game of *Two Truths*, after dinner drinks, *and* dessert, all while you chatted up my ex-boyfriend, before allowing us to leave." I made to step past her, pausing only to whisper in her ear, "payback's a bitch," before I straightened and said brightly, "now, go have some fun with your friends!" and strolled to the bar.

An entire *Spice Girls* soundtrack later, I stood nursing a watered-down gintini, watching Dillon clown around with Sam on the dance floor. Sam was blitzed, and Dillon couldn't dance, but neither seemed to care. It felt good to see Dillon having so much fun. To see her laughing. To see her happy.

"You should go and dance with her."

I hadn't noticed Kelsey come up beside me, where I'd found a quiet space at the end of the indoor bar.

Startled, I struggled through an uncomfortable laugh. "Oh, I'm not —it's, um—we're not like that."

*Like that.* For real, Kam? What was this, second grade?

"Ah." Kelsey leaned against the bar top. "Does she know that?"

"Come again?"

"Does she know you two aren't—" she paused with her glass at her lips, "—*like that*?"

*Ah, yes.* Here we were. The jealous ex and the next. Just the thing I would have preferred to avoid. I opened my mouth to protest, but she cut me off.

"Look—I know you're sleeping with her. I could read it all over her face the moment I walked through the door. There's no point debating it."

"Oh-kay," I drew out. She was so blunt, I didn't know what else to say. "Sorry," I added, after a beat of silence, even though the only thing I was sorry about was being unable to find a polite way to excuse myself from this conversation.

"Don't be. I'm relieved." She tipped back her drink, her pink manicured nails a unique dichotomy to the healing turf rash running down her forearm.

Surprise must have shown on my face. It wasn't what I'd expected her to say.

"Don't get me wrong—she cut me pretty deep. It took a long time to get over her, and the way she left things." A streak of condensation dripped off her glass. She dabbed at it carelessly. "But I'm really happy now—I, uh," glancing around, she lowered her voice, "I actually just got engaged. We've kept it quiet. I wasn't…" her gaze drifted across the bar to where Dillon was patiently steering an extremely inebriated Sam off the dance floor. "I wasn't sure how she'd take the news." She looked back at me. "So it was good, seeing her with you tonight. It's obvious you're more to her than just a weekend fling."

I looked away, feeling guilty about having misread the jealous-girlfriend thing. I was also a little concerned with how easily she'd seen through me.

"So much for keeping that on the down low," I tried to joke, but didn't quite succeed.

Kelsey smiled. "I doubt anyone else was paying that close attention. I just—I've seen her with enough women over the last couple of years to know—and tonight she just seemed different. It's been a long time since she's looked so happy." She let out a short breath. "Sorry, I guess I just—I still really want the best for her. When Sam called me last week…" she tapped her nails against the bottom of her glass. "I know it's no longer my place, but I still worry about her sometimes. I used to think she was indomitable. That nothing could bring her down. But she's too hard on herself, you know? Sometimes I think she needs someone to remind her life isn't just about the finish line."

It was an interesting outlook, I thought, from someone I imagined was as competitive as Kelsey Evans. But then again, I knew it was possible to be competitive without turning it into an obsession. Dillon, no question, bordered on the latter.

But we all had our things, didn't we? Our highs and lows. Our ups and downs.

"Anyhow," Kelsey's laugh was nervous, a sound that came as a contradiction from the perfection of her flawless lips, "now that I've made things super weird…" She shifted the conversation, asking me about *Sand Seekers*, and talking about playing in the WSL. She offered to get me tickets to a Chelsea match and I congratulated her on her engagement—Abby Sawyer was a legend on the US team.

I'd have to come and meet her, Kelsey insisted. One day when I was in town.

We chatted for a while longer, through one gintini too many, and by the time I left the tavern, it was me Dillon was inelegantly pouring into a cab.

"It's what you get, Kam-Kameryn," she needled as she guided me through the apartment door, "trying to win a drinking match with an English footballer."

There was something in her tone that sobered me momentarily. "Are you mad she was friendly to me?"

"No," she tossed her keys onto the dresser. "I expected nothing less. Kelsey's a good person." Even in my liquor-induced daze, I was aware of an uncommon tightness in her movements as she stopped to draw the curtains. After a brief silence, she turned to catch my eye. "So in this friendly chat, did you learn anything new about me?"

"It wasn't like that, Dillon. She was nice. She seems to really care about you."

"Worry about me, you mean."

"No." I paused. "Okay, yes, that too. I think she's just worried you put too much pressure on yourself."

"Well, whatever she said, take it with a pinch of salt—no matter what she thinks, Kelsey Evans isn't exactly the know-all authority on me."

I watched her dexterous hands struggle with the straps on my shoes. "Dillon." She didn't look up. "You do know there's more to life than winning, right?"

She tugged the buckle loose. "Another life message you learned from your new best friend?"

I let it go. I was drunk. She was irritable. The conversation was going nowhere. By the time she'd gone to shower, I'd passed out.

When I woke in the morning, my head celebrating the coming of dawn like a toddler who'd gotten hold of a bass drum, there was a note on her pillow.

*Gone on a long run. Back this afternoon. Leeds, T-minus 23 days.* Then, at the bottom, hastily scrawled as an afterthought, *xoxo*.

Apparently, she'd forgotten we were supposed to have breakfast with Sam.

"Well look you at that! You win, and it's still my stunning mug that makes the headlines!"

Sam flashed her mobile around the table, displaying the photo *British Triathlon* had posted on their Instagram. It was from the morning prior, when Sam had leapt the spectator fence and flung herself into Dillon's arms as she crossed the Leeds finish line.

*One GOAT to Another* the caption read.

"They got the goat part right," Kyle quipped, thumbing through the laminated appetizer menu. "You both look like you belong in a barnyard."

He let out a yelp as Sam gouged him with a strike of her toe. "Can it, ya gadgie!"

"Yeah," joined Georgina, "it's a bold statement coming from someone who put in the time of a tortoise!"

"Look—not all of us can pull off a *Sinclair Special*. Some of us are only human." He made a face at Dillon, who only rolled her eyes.

Yesterday, she'd set a new course record, smashing the previous one —also set by her—by more than a minute. The race commentator on BBC had referred to her ability to break her own leading times as a *Sinclair Special*, earning her a lot of ribbing from her teammates.

Under different circumstances, she would have allowed herself a pat on the back for running an exceptional race. One that had been flawless in its execution. Her swim had been strong, her bike had been stellar, and she'd entered the run with a lead no other athlete on the field could conquer.

But she hadn't beat Elyna.

Halfway through the swim, the Frenchwoman had pulled up with a shoulder injury and scratched as a contender. Dillon hadn't known it until after she crossed the finish line, and at that point, the win failed to matter. She didn't care that she'd broken another record. That she'd won, once again, in front of her fellow countrymen, on UK soil. It wasn't even a consolation that Kam had made it there to watch her.

She hadn't done what she needed to do—to prove to herself, to prove to Henrik, that she was still the stronger competitor.

But she'd done her best to put on a happy face, knowing no one else would understand her disappointment.

"All right—I'll take first shout," Harry said, sliding his bean-pole frame to his feet as he stretched off the stiffness of the weekend. "Who needs liquid courage?"

It was Sunday night, the day after the race, and the six of them had come down on the train from Leeds to London. Sam had dragged the small party to her favorite seedy nightclub, where Dillon had found herself entirely unenthused to discover it was Eighties' Night karaoke.

"You may want to make it a double," Sam tuned her voice to a stage whisper when Kam ordered a whiskey sour. "I know it's impossible to believe, but Sinc actually sings worse than she dances."

"I happen to love her shower singing," Kam pertly defended, grazing her toe against Dillon's calf underneath the table. Dillon would have preferred skipping the evening out and spending it alone with Kam instead. They'd hardly gotten to see one another since Kam flew in three days earlier, and already, it was their last night together. Tomorrow, Dillon would fly to Canada with her teammates to begin acclimating for the race in Montreal, and Kam would head back to Los Angeles. It would be months before they saw each other again.

Sam curled a lip. "They say love is blind. Apparently, it's deaf, also."

The Geordie turned a quick smirk to Dillon, awaiting some riposte, but Dillon's attention had detoured. Behind Sam, a flatscreen on the wall was showing highlights of Manchester City vs. Chelsea. On the silent footage, Kelsey was blasting across the pitch, drilling a ball through City defense, putting Chelsea up 2-1 in late minutes. Dillon had forgotten, almost, the joy with which Kelsey played. The happiness the game brought her. It made her wonder—not for the first time —if she still loved her sport the way Kelsey embraced football.

Did she still crave that first blast of cold water on pre-dawn swims in the winter? Did she still love the burn in her legs or the nearly hallucinatory collapse that came toward the end of a run, when her body was propelled on nothing more than stubborn will and a refusal to surrender? A sport that had her sleeping in a hotel bed two hundred fifty nights a year, disallowing her from putting down roots as insignificant as a houseplant.

Or, when she left in the morning for Montreal, was it someone else's dream she was chasing?

"Bloody Chelsea on their way to another title," Sam huffed, glancing over her shoulder to see what had caught Dillon's interest. The match highlights ended and a news story flicked on about an American Senator who'd been found guilty of arms trafficking. She turned her attention back to the table.

"Do you sing, Kam?" Kyle was asking.

Kam gave a noncommittal shrug. "A little."

His pale eyes brightened. He'd spent the last two days regaling Georgina and Harry about the events of Hana, and how if he hadn't been a complete tosser, Dillon never would have given Kam a bell.

He could keep that claim to fame, Dillon had assured him.

"Right, then!" Kyle thumped Kam on the shoulder, grinning from ear to ear. "Up you are, let's have a song!"

Taking a quick inventory of the nightclub and its rough and rowdy crowd, Kam smiled her decline. "I think I'll pass tonight."

"What about tit-for-tat?" he pleaded, half-risen from his chair. "I sing one, you sing one?"

"Only if you sing *Girls Just Wanna Have Fun*."

"Oh, lord," Georgina moaned, "you've just challenged the wrong bloke. His favorite is *Man, I Feel Like a Woman*."

"At least that one fits him," Harry teased, all of them protesting as Kyle sauntered toward the stage, where the mic hung invitingly open.

Dillon leaned across the table as Kyle falsettoed his way through verse after miserable verse of Cyndi Lauper. "You know you don't really have to sing. They're just taking the piss out of you."

But as the music faded and the audience cheered Kyle's swishing departure from the stage, Kam shot Dillon a covert smile. "Oh, one song won't hurt, I suppose." She took a final sip of her whiskey and offered Kyle a high five as she passed him on her way to the mic.

"What's your name, love?" the DJ asked, eyeing her approach through black-rimmed eyeshadow as he carefully smoothed a misplaced hair back into his lime green mohawk.

"Kam."

"And what'll it be tonight, Kam?"

Standing in the center of the raised platform, Kam detached the mic from its stand, looking out over the crowded room as calm and collected as Dillon had ever seen her. She didn't seem to mind the lights, or the focus of the empty stage, or the dozens of eyes turned in her direction.

"Well, given that it's Eighties' Night, how about *I Wanna Dance With Somebody?*"

"Here here," cheered a ruddy-faced, bearded lad leaning against one of the high-top tables. "I'll dance with you!" He blew a shrill catcall. Kam ignored him completely. Her hip was cocked, her stance relaxed, one hand tucked into her jean pocket. It was clear being in the limelight didn't bother her at all.

It was a side of her Dillon had never seen. One more piece of a puzzle bringing her into focus.

"Out of your league, ya wanker," Sam shot off to the heckler as the DJ cued up the song, the opening lyrics appearing on the monitor. The audience, still keyed up from Kyle's hamming performance, had their full attention facing front. It didn't hurt, Dillon imagined, that Kam—despite her casual attire—simply looked like a movie star. That she looked like she belonged up there.

"I love a woman brave enough to take on some Whitney," the DJ hummed, settling back in his chair as the snappy percussion beat slid into the familiar synthetic intro. Kam's eyes skimmed across the crowd until she found Dillon, offering her a subtle wink and a smile, and then her attention was turned to nothing more than the song, with its soaring verses and chorus.

"A little?" Sam hissed as Kam effortlessly tackled the pop anthem, her voice rising above the music with a velvety warmth and fullness. "She calls that a *little?*"

"Shhh," Dillon shushed her, unable to peel her eyes from Kameryn. She was—there was no other way to put it—remarkable. All signs of the sometimes shy, often self-deprecating girl who, not so many months earlier, had allowed the entire Hallwell family to walk all over her were vanished.

This was the woman who had caught the attention of some of the most powerful kingpins in Hollywood. The woman who had beaten out literally tens of thousands of others to earn one of the most coveted roles in movie history. This was a person Dillon had yet to meet—and as much as it thrilled her, it was also a little unnerving.

As Kam sailed through the bridge, onto the final chorus, and into the outro, the boisterous patrons cheered and whistled their approval, chuffed by the unexpected brilliance of the performance.

Settling the mic back in its stand, Kam flashed an almost reticent smile to the DJ, who looked out over the crowd and said "well, who wants to embarrass themselves and follow up *that* showstopper?"

Kyle stood as Kam returned to their table, her face flushed with exertion.

"I'd say my hat was off to you, but you're a hustler, Kam Kingsbury!" He grinned. "Are you certain it was movies you were made for?"

"Oh, don't you bother sitting now, pet," Sam was immediately on her feet, interceding Kam's retirement to her chair. "You can't think we're going to let you pull a fast one on us, and then get off so easy!"

A moment later, Sam had dragged Kameryn back to the stage with her, where the Geordie intertwined her brassy voice with the dynamic clarity of Kam's as they belted through a duet of *(I've Had) The Time of My Life*. Immediately following, Harry, who—unbeknownst to his teammates—could also sing, convinced Kam to branch out of the Eighties and join him for *Señorita*, and then, as a final song of the night, *Rewrite the Stars*, from *The Greatest Showman*.

"Well, if he doesn't post a decent time for Montreal, at least he has something to fall back on," Georgina teased, watching their youngest teammate eat up the limelight, basking in his newfound stardom.

"Aren't you a little jealous, Sinc?" Kyle ribbed, chucking his chin at the stage where the duo harmonized the longing of lovers kept apart. "Your shower singing can't compete with that!"

Dillon shrugged, unworried. "I know who she's going home with tonight."

"Yeah, and if she keeps making moon eyes at you the way she does, so will everybody else," Sam teased, and then, seeing Dillon's stiffening expression, leaned over. "Don't get your dander up, I'm just ruffling your feathers."

But when Kam, politely refusing any additional songs, bypassed her chair and settled into the empty one beside Dillon, Dillon gently drew away from the shoulder Kam pressed against her.

She felt bad, aware of the silent apology Kam cast in her direction. Kam shouldn't have to apologize for sitting beside her, for showing her affection. But Dillon couldn't help but brace herself, feeling her self-preservation kicking in for what she knew was coming.

The first *Sand Seekers'* movie trailers were releasing at the end of the month. Kam was scheduled for a press tour with her co-stars beginning the week she got home to Los Angeles. Things were changing, fast. The next time they saw each other, Kam—whether she liked it or not—would be living the life of a different person.

"You were brilliant." Dillon smiled, trying to soften her withdrawal. "You know Harry's not going to shut up about this all the way to Montreal?"

Across the table Kyle laughed. "Montreal? He's going to be crowing about this until he's gray and old!"

"Something you have experience with already," Harry ragged Kyle.

"You okay if we call it an early night?" Kam whispered when Georgina rose to take orders for another round. "I'd love to spend what little time we have left alone."

Goodbyes said, Kam was stopped by the DJ at the door.

"If I'd known you were going to smash the Whitney tribute, I'd have recorded it for our video of the week!" He handed her a card. "I got your duet up, though—on my Insta, if you want to give me a follow. If you come back next week, I'll be sure to get you and your mates drinks on the house."

"Oh." Kam stared at the card. "I—thank you, but I'm afraid I'll be out of town."

"Well, when you're back in again, you know where to come!" He aimed a finger gun at her, clucking his tongue. "Don't forget to give me a follow!"

As soon as they were settled on the train to *Waterloo Station*, Kam pulled out her phone.

"Oh, thank God," she breathed a sigh of relief. "He's only got 159 followers. That video's going to get buried."

"You could make it 160," Dillon teased, and this time, when Kameryn rested her head against her shoulder, she didn't pull away.

"Do you know how much I'm going to miss you?" Kam asked, her eyes closed.

Dillon slipped her arm around her. "Double it, and you'll know how much I'm going to miss you."

"You don't get to win everything," Kam stuck her thumb into Dillon's ribs, not bothering to open her eyes. "I have this one on lock. I'm going to miss you more."

"I could try to come see you?" Dillon said, after a moment. "After Málaga?"

Kam settled more heavily against her. "Don't give me false hope."
She sighed. "Let's just stick to our plan."

It was the smart thing to do, Dillon knew. Five months wasn't
forever. Kam was going to be weighed down with promotional obligations prior to the premieres, and Dillon had to focus on her season.

Come the holidays, they would have time to spend with each other.
Time to see what life looked like from there. To move forward, building a future on a landscape neither was certain how to navigate—but
one, they promised, they'd figure out together.

# Scene 35

It was a miserable hour of the morning.

The sun hadn't yet risen and my room was washed in darkness, save for the muted ring of fluorescent light emitting from where my cell lay face down on my nightstand. I grappled for it, managing to dislodge a glass of water, an uncapped bottle of ibuprofen, and my reading glasses onto the floor.

It wasn't Dillon. Or, at least it wasn't her ringtone. But I scrambled to answer anyhow, unwilling to miss the possibility she was trying to call.

"Hello?"

"Do you have a boyfriend?"

I stabbed *end call*, flopping back to my pillow, disgusted.

*Oh, joy.* My new number must have been leaked. *Again.* Before I could return the phone to the table, it was ringing once more, but this time, as I swiped to hang up, I noticed the name on the caller ID.

*Shit.* I hit redial.

"Elliott?" I said, when I heard the line pick up.

"Let's try this again: do you have a boyfriend?"

I dug the heel of my palm into my right eye, trying to contain the splitting ache to one corner of my brain.

Last night had been the official wrap party for *Sand Seekers*, put on by one of the studio execs at his estate in Holmby Hills. I'd meant to stick to champagne. But how could I tell L.R. Sims no when he uncorked a Barrique de Ponciano Porfidio and handed me a shot? Certainly, I couldn't turn it down while Waylon MacArthur stood at my elbow, offering a chaser of limes.

The rest of the night was a blur. Venetian tile and crystal chandeliers, hundred thousand dollar Mulberry silk loveseats. A waterfall that spouted up in the middle of the dining room. Had I played pickleball barefoot on a private tennis court with Grady Dunn, or had that only been part of my disjointed dreams? I wasn't sure.

Of one thing I was certain, however: I needed to clear up any misunderstandings.

"Look, Elliott—I really appreciate the ride home last night. I got a little carried away. But if I somehow gave you the wrong impression, I'm—"

"—trust me," he interrupted with a derisive laugh, "you're not my type."

"I—okay." I blinked, uncertain how I could manage to find myself insulted when I hadn't started this in the first place. "So, you're calling me at the crack of dawn because…?"

"I just came from—" he stopped. "Dawn?" He was thrown off. "Kam—it's eight PM."

It couldn't be. We hadn't even left the party until after midnight. Unless—I glanced at my lock screen. *8:03.* Ho-ly shit! I'd slept all day!

"Listen, Kam. I'd say this was none of my business, but it kind of is."

"What, your choice in women?" I tried to joke.

"No." He wasn't laughing. "*Your* choice in women, actually."

Now I wasn't laughing, either. I went silent. My heart was so still I may as well have been interred in Cleopatra's tomb. I knew I should probably rush to a defense, but I was so stunned, I said nothing at all.

"Now that I have your attention," he continued, "I just came from the studio. I was in a meeting with MacArthur when he got a call."

I rolled to the edge of my bed, reaching down to gather two of the dropped pills of ibuprofen that had slowly been dissolving in the spilled water, and popped them in my mouth. Then I flopped back on my squeaking box spring mattress, and listened, without comment, as Elliott explained that a peon English reporter for *The Sun* had called Waylon MacArthur. The man had run across the video of me and Harry singing *Rewrite the Stars*.

This in itself wasn't a surprise. A few days after it had been uploaded to the DJ's Instagram, the video had been discovered by a *Sand Seekers* fan, who had shared it on TikTok. Overnight, it had gone viral —and by viral, I mean, within forty-eight hours, it had racked up over ten million views.

I'd panicked, initially, but the studio had been thrilled. *Free publicity. Free hype.*

The stupid cell phone-recorded sing-along had brought me more direct attention than the release of the teaser trailer that had come out the week before. I'd since been asked about it on talk shows and radio interviews during our press tour. The *Today Show* had extended an offer for me to sing the song live with Zac Efron, which I'd politely declined. Fans had flocked to my social media accounts, where I'd gained—literally—millions of followers overnight.

It was good for business, Aaron chastised me when I'd first called him in tears.

On a lighter note, it had been good for Harry, too, Dillon told me the evening I'd gotten home from filming *Good Day LA*. He'd never had so many *swipe rights* in his life. *British Triathlon* had even benefitted from the exposure, shining new interest on the sport.

But most important to me, Dillon had laughed it off. There was nothing in the video to link me to her. Blurred in the background were a few glimpses of her and Sam at the table, but theirs were just two faces amongst dozens of others. It was hardly surprising for Sam to be at one of her regular haunts with her best friend.

Only, this reporter had apparently covered Sam's birthday party, too. He'd remembered seeing me with Dillon. According to Elliott, he even had a photo that showed us standing together in the background. It had inspired the newshound to do some digging. When he saw Dillon at the nightclub, he'd drawn his conclusion, deciding the coincidences were enough that he could get away with running an opinion piece on the topic.

"Now, it's obvious," Elliott was saying, "that the guy has nothing. He was just looking for an easy payout. He'd banked on the hope that the studio would be willing to fork over some petty cash to bury the story. Even if there is no solid evidence, these kinds of articles always lead to rumors..."

Again, I was sure I should be defending myself—denying whatever it was Elliott was getting at—but I didn't have it in me. I didn't care about a tabloid speculating my relationship with Dillon—but Dillon would care, and that was all that mattered.

"What did MacArthur say?" My mouth was dry. One of the ibuprofen felt like it was lodged in my throat.

"He told the guy to fuck himself. That no one would believe it—you were too hot to be a lesbian. He said he wasn't willing to touch the topic with a ten-foot pole."

"So he didn't… care?" I asked carefully, trying to sort the situation out.

"Oh, don't be ignorant, Kameryn—of course he cares. He cares a *lot* if his prized romantic lead actress suddenly pops up as a full-blown lady lover! He just knows he can't get involved. If word got out he spent studio funds on hush money to squash a story like this, it'd be a one-way ticket to labeling him a homophobe." Elliott paused. "And he *is* a homophobe, Kam. Make no mistake."

I swallowed, unable to find the outrage I knew I should be feeling. "So why are you calling me?" The pill rattled around, forcing me to cough. I wanted to tell Elliott that he could be the one to fuck himself. That I wasn't ashamed of who I was. That he and MacArthur could ride their bigoted locomotive on the fast bus to hell.

But I was scared, actually.

Not about what it could do to my career—that came secondary. I was scared of what Dillon would do. How it would make her feel.

"I asked MacArthur for the guy's number. I've already been in contact with him. One of us is going to pay him off, Kam—be it you or me."

"You *what*—!" Now I *was* angry. Not because it wasn't the sensible thing to do. It was. Not for the reasons Elliott thought—because I *did* need this to go away—but because Elliott had taken the liberty of making the decision for me. "She's a *friend*, Elliott! How dare you—"

"I'm not your enemy, Kam." He didn't rise to my anger, remaining completely even-keeled. The same way he had on the cliffs above Stonehaven. It was infuriating. "Honestly, I don't give a shit what you do in your personal life. But that's beside the point. If this story runs, it will change things for you. I'm not talking about our film—the franchise is too big, the fanbase too loyal, to be thrown off by these kinds of things. That's why MacArthur won't step in. It won't affect his bottom line. Hell, it might even help things. But for you, on a personal level… Kam, this industry is brutal. On the surface, it may be all love-is-love kumbaya, but I promise you, it's not. Rumors start floating around about your deviating love life, and I guarantee you, the big, starring roles dry up."

*Deviating love life.* I thought I was going to throw up.

I couldn't tell him I didn't care about the starring roles. I just didn't want my girlfriend to leave me.

"What am I supposed to do?" I whispered.

"First, we're going to get this guy twenty grand—"

"*Twenty gra*—!" I started, appalled.

"—he wanted fifty, but it's not worth it. *The Sun* wouldn't even give him a quarter of that, not when it's nothing more than speculation." Elliott went on as if this were just daily business. "I've already got my lawyer drawing up a contract. This guy breathes a single word after payment, and he's finished."

"Elliott, I don't just have twenty grand to…" It was ridiculous to be embarrassed. But the way he talked about the money, it was like he was discussing chump change. He and Grady had been paid more than ten times what they'd offered me for the first film.

"I'll handle it, Kam. I'll get him paid off, the story goes away, the picture disappears, and then," he paused, and the weight of the pause was enough to distract me from arguing that I couldn't possibly allow him to spend twenty thousand dollars on my behalf.

I waited.

"And then, Kam," he resigned to continue, "we have to find you a boyfriend."

*Oh, yeah, no.* This was where this madness ended. I'd heard of the beards of Hollywood. I wasn't about to allow myself to give in to that deception.

"No way. Out of the question—"

"Get a grip, Kam! You don't have to fuck him! But you need someone to stand in!"

To stand in… like my life was in need of a stunt double. Like this was a lighting test or blocking rehearsal.

"Don't you have a friend—someone you trust," he asked, "who'd be willing to go to functions with you? Someone you can take on holidays, plaster their face on your socials? If you don't, I know some guys—"

"No!" I ended that offer abruptly. I may have needed his twenty Gs, but I didn't need him to find me a pseudo-boyfriend. "I… I know someone." I coughed again, the pill burning a slow progression down my esophagus. "I… I'll call him."

"Good."

"Why are you helping me?" I asked, filling the silence.

It was his turn to clear his throat. To dally on the other end of the line. "You have a huge career ahead of you, Kam," he finally said, as uncomfortable as I had ever heard him. "You're more than… you deserve more than playing the quirky best friend. The class clown. The serial killer next door." He tried to laugh. "It's bullshit, that that's what it comes down to. But it's the truth. Take it from someone who knows. We're worth more than that—people like us—but this industry's not there yet." He exhaled. "Look—I have to go, I have some calls to make. Just hold up your end of the deal and this will all go away." Again, he forced a laugh. "Oh, and make sure he's cute, okay? No one's going to believe a girl like you has hooked up with an ugly dude."

And with that, the line was dead.

I stared at the blinking amber charging light on my computer across the room.

*People like us.* Had he really just said that?

Had he meant...? I shook the rabbit-hole train of thought from my mind. There were other things I needed to handle first.

Like calling Dillon.

But I didn't want to scare her. Not until it was handled. Then I could explain it all.

*FUCK*! I wanted to scream. I had the urge to leap from my bed and tear the curtains off my windows for no other reason than to be destructive. To take out my fury on something that couldn't talk back.

Instead, I pulled myself together and scrolled through my phone. I hovered over the first name that popped up under the letter *C*. Was this really the right thing to do? If I was just more careful... If we were just more discreet...

But I'd thought we had been careful. I'd thought we were discreet. And the thing that mattered to me above all else was protecting Dillon. She couldn't go through this again.

I punched the number. Two rings later, a familiar voice came on the line.

"Hey, stranger! Long time no talk."

I swallowed, already hating myself. "Hey, Carter."

# Scene 36

"Kameryn, the world has been waiting on the edge of its seat for the release of *Sand Seekers*. I think we'd be hard-pressed to find a single corner of the globe not talking about this movie. How does it feel, knowing the first premiere is less than a week away?"

Dillon tuned out the anchor's chattering commentary, instead watching Kam's easy confidence and relaxed posture, her legs crossed and smile genuine as she continued to field questions about the upcoming film. She looked very different sitting there on the set of *Good Morning America* than she had months earlier, during the first press appearances Dillon had watched from lonely hotel rooms. No longer did Kam fidget in front of the camera, or force a laugh to hide her unease.

At this point, she'd certainly had enough practice. This morning's interview marked the twenty-first TV appearance she'd made in the last two weeks alone. Seventeen cities across three countries, with more than a dozen stops scheduled over the next four days. All paving the way to the Hollywood premiere.

"I'm so sick of smiling," Kam lamented to Dillon when she'd called her the night before.

One wouldn't know it, looking at her now. She laughed and joked with the talk show host, answering questions in turn.

*What was one word she'd use to describe filming in Greenland?*
Frostbite.

*How did it feel to portray a character who had been an inspiration in literature to millions, knowing her face would forever be connected to the role?*
An honor—and a daily panic.

*Had she seen herself in the eighteen-story-high ad in Times Square outside the studio?*
Well, yes. It had been hard to miss.

The anchor shared in her embarrassed laugh.

The interview went on and Dillon's mind wandered as she stared at Kam's image on her mobile. She tried to decipher all the ways she looked different since they'd last seen one another five months earlier. Her hair was shorter. Her makeup heavier. Her eyelashes fuller than they'd been before.

There were moments when Dillon hardly recognized her, when she seemed like a stranger on the screen. And then would come flashes of the Kam she knew. The person hidden beneath the glamorous persona of the rising movie star. She could find her in the way her heel caught on the hem of her dress when she went to uncross her legs. The smile she hid behind each time the host asked her a question she found mundane. The graciousness beneath her aplomb. The humility in her habit of deflecting individual praise to that of the production as a whole.

"This is your first major film, am I right, Kameryn?" the anchor asked, straightening her horn-rimmed glasses. She didn't wait for a response. "Can you tell me—what has been the most difficult part of taking on this role?"

Kam didn't hesitate. "Being away from the people I love."

Dillon flipped the volume off as the anchor asked Kam about her boyfriend—how he felt about *Sand Seekers* and if he'd be accompanying her to the premieres. Dillon didn't care about the answers. She knew Kam had been talking to her.

Two days before her race in Montreal, Kam called her in tears. She'd told her about Elliott's phone call—about the reporter from *The Sun* who had threatened to run the piece linking Kam's name with hers.

A small part of her had wanted to tell Kam to let the bastard run it, allowing the chips to fall where they may. But she couldn't deny the unfettering relief she'd felt when Kam told her she'd already called Carter, coming clean with him about everything, and asking if he'd be willing to play a different part.

"It's only temporary," she told Dillon, her voice still tight from crying. "A few well-timed photos. Maybe a public appearance or two. I promise, it's not real."

*Real* hadn't been any part of Dillon's concern. She never questioned Kam's heart. She simply hated her own cowardice—that because of her, she'd now forced all three of them to live a lie in order to preserve the comfort of her privacy.

"He doesn't mind," Kam assured her when she asked how Carter felt. "He told me to thank you—because if you'd not come along, he'd never have believed the old *'it's not you, it's me,'* was true."

And so the wanker of a reporter had been paid off, Dillon's name had slipped back to oblivion, Hollywood's newest star was caught on camera holding hands with a boy who turned out to be her high school sweetheart, and life had slogged on as Dillon knew it.

Race after race, flight after flight, day after day of blisters, cramps, stiff muscles, aching joints, and the daily grind of training that never ended. As Kam jet-set across the globe with the cast of *Sand Seekers*, chained to their promotional tour, Dillon had closed out her season with another championship win.

It was her fourth world title, double the number of any other woman in triathlon history. She'd wanted it to come with some sense of gratification—to bring her the feeling of accomplishment she'd been lacking.

But the win had left her empty. The week before the race in Montreal, rumor had spread that Elyna Laurent had undergone rotator cuff surgery. The injury in Leeds had forced her to withdraw from the rest of the season.

So a win in Montreal, a second in Málaga, a fourth-place finish in Cagliari—despite a rolled ankle on the final lap of the run—had all meant nothing. Even her massive ninety second lead to win the final in Abu Dhabi, clinching the world title, hadn't felt rewarding.

For the first time in her career, the series had completely drained her. Even without pitting herself against the youth of Elyna Laurent, it had taken everything she had to finish the year.

"Why are you still racing, Dillon?" Seren asked when she stopped by her flat the evening Dillon returned from the Middle East. Her sister had unboxed the gaudy World Championship trophy Dillon had dropped in her hall, and placed it on the shelf alongside the others.

"Same reason you ride. It's what we do."

Whatever Seren had wanted to say, she chose not to. Instead, she took a moment to study the wall of medals in Dillon's living room, before turning back to face her. "Will a gold in Los Angeles be enough?"

"How could I know? I've never won one."

"Dillon, I'm serious—"

"If mam's got you here on another *what are you going to do with the rest of your life* quest, just stop while you're ahead," Dillon had snapped, booting a pair of running trainers across the room. "I don't ask her when she's going to quit the courtroom. I don't ask you when you'll retire Épée. So you can both just climb off my back, will you? I've got enough of a load without carrying around dead weight."

But long after her sister had gone, Dillon stewed on the unfinished conversation.

Time was ticking. She'd turned twenty-nine in Canada. Her body felt like it was twice its age. The Summer Games were a year and a half away.

If she won—no, *when* she won—what was next? Kyle had suggested she turn her sights to the longer endurance races. Or throw her hat in the women's cycling ring. There was longevity there, he pointed out. Or, she could take up coaching. Help bring up the next great British athlete.

But it wasn't the same.

"What are you banging on about?" Sam had asked when Dillon turned up at her door after a late-night run. "It's not a decision you have to make right now. Train for tomorrow—focus on today." And so Dillon had taken her friend's advice and set the worries aside.

The buzzing of her mobile woke her. She'd dozed off on her sofa.

Kam's face lit up her screen.

"So, Christmas!" Kam blurted as soon as she answered.

"Weren't you just in the middle of an interview?" Dillon glanced at the time. She'd been asleep less than fifteen minutes.

"Just walking out the door. We've got a flight to Chicago. Anyhow—Christmas? Where do you want to spend it?"

Dillon hadn't gotten that far. Her only focus had been on knowing she would see Kam the day after her London premiere. Exactly a week away. The holiday hadn't yet made it to her radar.

"Wherever you are."

"I was wondering," Kam was momentarily muffled by the sound of horns and shouting voices, along with the threatening command of a man warning someone to stand back, followed by the slamming of a door. "Sorry," Kam was breathless, "there was a crowd in front of *ABC*. We just got to the car. Anyhow, I was wondering—is a sweater warm enough for Wales in winter, or would I need to pack my Greenland parka?"

"Wales?" Dillon was surprised. "What about the Hallwells?"

"I understand if that's your first choice," Kam quipped, "but I was thinking perhaps we could go somewhere that didn't involve steak tartare."

Dillon closed her eyes. For one hundred eighty-three days she'd been counting down the hours until they'd be together again. She'd never known she could miss someone so badly. Need someone so much.

"Do you like roast potatoes and parsnips?"

"Let's see," Kam hummed, "you mean more than Darlene's cuisses de grenouille? I could probably survive."

"What about making taffy?"

"I'm a first-class taste tester. I wouldn't want to put anyone to shame with my epic cooking skills."

"We couldn't have that," Dillon smiled, well aware Kam's kitchen prowess involved ordering take-out. "It's cold and wet and cloudy."

"Not to brag, but I survived Greenland."

"Fair enough. Then last question: how do you feel about going door-to-door in a song rhyming war wearing a horse skull on your head?"

"I—wait, what?"

Dillon laughed. "Come on, it's a Welsh tradition!" She didn't tell her the wassailing folk custom had mostly died out in the twentieth century. Better to let her stew on that image for a while.

"I..." Kam hesitated. "Sure, why not? I'm game."

"Are you really wanting to come to Wales?" Dillon was serious again. "You know you don't have to—I'll go wherever you are. Even if it's with the Hallwells."

"I want you to bring me home with you for Christmas. Do you think your mom would be okay with that?"

Not once in their three years together had Kelsey gone with Dillon to Wales. They'd spent holidays separate—Kelsey with her family, and Dillon with hers.

"She'll love you, Kam-Kameryn."

"It's settled, then." Kam paused. "There is one more thing, however."

The sudden nervousness in her voice worried Dillon.

"It's about London," Kam continued. "I'd like you there."

"Smashing coincidence," Dillon tried to tease, despite having an uncomfortable feeling she knew what direction this was heading. "I just so happen to live here."

"I want you to come to my premiere."

Quiet, Dillon stood from her sofa, crossing to look out the window at the London Eye. The city was lit for Christmas, brimming with the bokeh of holiday lights. She ran a fingertip along the frosted glass, tracing the river's outline.

"Is that a good idea?"

"Probably not. But do this for me—please? It's going to be one of the most monumental nights of my life. Sam could go with you. There would be nothing unusual about her attending the premiere. And you're her best friend—no one will think twice." Dillon could hear her swallow on the other end of the line. "Please, Dillon. I just want to know you're there."

Beads of condensation trickled down the windowpane, distorting the starbursts of light.

She sighed. She didn't know how to tell her no. Not after everything Kam had been willing to do for her. To protect her. She owed her this. And in truth—she *wanted* to be there. To support her. To see her shine. Even if it was just from afar.

"Is Carter coming?" She didn't know why she asked. She already knew. Kam had invited her mother to the opening premiere taking place in Hollywood, and thirty-six hours later, Carter would walk her down the red carpet in London, serving as her date.

"Yes." Kam was unapologetically matter of fact. "It's exactly why this works. All the attention will be on him." She softened. "And then he'll fly home the next morning and I'll go with you to Wales."

It was ridiculous, Dillon knew, to find herself battling a twinge of jealousy. All this had been done for her. If Kam had had her way, Dillon would have been the one beside her at the premiere.

She turned from the skyline. "Okay. But I'll have to talk to Sam."

"I already have. She said it was up to you." Thirty five hundred miles away, she could hear a smile creep into Kam's voice. "She did say something about canceling your friendship if you said no. Just so you're aware."

"Clever girl," Dillon smiled in return. "I see what you've done here. No way I'd ever be able to fend off the pair of you."

"Mates before dates—isn't that what you like to say?"

"Mates before dates didn't mean I wanted to take my mate *on* a date, just so we're clear."

"Good thing," Kam said archly, "because as soon as the night is over, I want you all to myself."

"I'll check my schedule. See if I can fit you in."

"Your *schedule*," she mocked Dillon's pronunciation of the word, "better be clear until the end of January. That's not an option."

"I'll have my people call your people."

"Aren't you hilarious?" Kam scoffed. "But really—you'll come?"

"I'll come."

A man's voice sounded in the background. *We'll be arriving at Teterboro Airport in nine minutes, Miss Kingsbury.*

"Thanks, Mark," Kam said, and Dillon could hear her sigh on the other end of the line. "I should probably go."

"Yeah."

"I really miss you."

Dillon dropped back onto her sofa. "Six more days."

"They can't go by fast enough."

Silence lingered, neither wanting to hang up.

"Okay," Kam finally resigned. "I'll text you when I land."

"I'll be counting the minutes."

"You'll be sleeping."

"All the better—I'll see you in my dreams."

In the middle of the night, long after Kam had texted her safe arrival in Chicago, Dillon lay awake scrolling her phone. It wasn't a habit of hers, but Sam had been flooding her with links on *What to Wear to a Red Carpet Event* and articles boasting what A-List celebrities would be attending the European launch ceremony.

It was impossible to escape the *Sand Seekers* headlines. Every ad, promo, and browser banner seemed to be covering the London premiere. Kam's face was everywhere. Smiling alongside Elliott Fleming and Grady Dunn outside a Hollywood theatre. Posing on the cover of Vogue. Staring into the lens on a snow-capped glacier dressed as Addison Riley. Laughing with Carter cheek-to-cheek in a photo she'd posted on Instagram as the pair watched fireworks on the 4th of July.

*The perfect couple*, read one of the top comments with several thousand likes.

*Gorgeous together*, read another.

*Aww, to have what they have*. And on and on.

Dillon couldn't help but wonder how different the feed would be if it was her in the photos instead of Carter.

Only she didn't have to wonder. She knew exactly what they'd say. She'd seen it all with Kelsey.

*Tell me its not trueeeeeee, Kelsey! Wasted on a dyke.*

*They just need a man to show them how to fill that void ha ha.*

*The wrath of God descend upon you and the man-vagina beside you.*

*Kelsey, I loved you as footballer, but this disgust me. It not natural, against laws of nature, what children will the two you make together?*

Early in their relationship, Kelsey had learned to laugh at the hateful comments, with she and Dillon occasionally turning them into a drinking game. A sip for every time the word *hell* appeared. A chug whenever one of them was called "a man."

Of all the things Dillon was ashamed of in her life, being gay was not one of them. It was simply who she was.

She clicked out of the photo of Kam and Carter, and swiping to her text messages, found another link from Sam. *Black Tie Duds for the Modern Queer.*

She texted back.

*David Beckham wore jeans to the Star Wars premiere.*

There was an immediate reply.

*Newsflash, Sinc: you're not David Beckham. I'll pick you up at ten. We're going shopping. Any more lip from you and I'll put you in heels.*

# Scene 37

Fifty feet ahead of me, I gazed with mounting envy at the sensibility of Margaret Gilles' low kitten heels. One would have thought I'd have learned two days earlier in Hollywood that skyscraping stilettos made for a miserable stroll down the red carpet…

But no.

Here I was, twenty feet into the quarter-mile trek through Leicester Square, with my toes already threatening to file a formal complaint with the union.

"Kameryn!"

"Kameryn!"

"Miss Kingsbury!"

The clamor of my name in stereo from a sea of strangers' lips still felt like I was waking in a dream. Thousands of people leaned against the railings, waving movie posters and memorabilia, begging for autographs as I walked by. I signed as many as I could get to, knowing most of these people had been waiting more than seventy-two hours to secure their place in line.

"Now, the burning question," the red carpet host, Matt Siker, a charismatic London comedian, greeted as I reached the first stage of interviews on my way to the Empire Theatre. "How would you compare tonight's event with that of Los Angeles?"

I wondered what he'd say if I leaned into his mic and said *I couldn't really give you a fair comparison, Matt. I don't remember much of the Hollywood premiere. I spent the majority of the evening trying not to lose my lunch on my borrowed Óscar de la Renta gown.*

Somehow, I didn't imagine my PR team would appreciate me admitting I'd been so nervous about my red carpet debut, that as soon as I'd made it through the doors of the Dolby Theatre, I'd stowed myself away in the backstage greenroom.

In my defense, I hadn't been the only one overwhelmed by the enormity of the occasion. I'd been kept company by Grady Dunn, who'd sat at the private bar, his tie dangling loose around his neck, face perspiring, as he waited out the showing of the film. In one of my passing trips to the bathroom, he told me he couldn't stand seeing himself on screen. And then tipped back another drink.

Those anecdotes, I was certain, weren't the ones my English host was looking for.

I played it safe. "The reception has been incredible. Both cities have made us feel extraordinarily welcome."

"And deservedly so," he beamed, "but tell me honestly, Kameryn," he lowered his voice conspiratorially, "no one can beat the way we do it here in London, don't you think?"

An impulsive side of me wanted to tell him he was absolutely right, but not for the reasons he believed. Because despite the magnitude of the Hollywood premiere—the largest the world had ever seen—on a personal level, London had the clear advantage by a mile. There was nothing Hollywood could offer that could outweigh my growing anticipation, knowing by the time the night was over, it was Dillon who'd be unlacing the silk ties on this Versace gown.

"London certainly holds a special piece of my heart." I offered him a broad smile as the flashbulbs continued to burst, creating a wall of chaotic light in every direction.

Somewhere behind us, by the rising decibel of the roar of the fans, I knew either Elliott or Grady had arrived. There was a certain magnetism that followed them—a kind of high voltage that electrified the crowd every time their names were announced.

It turned out to be Grady.

He smiled as he approached, and bent to kiss my cheek. "You look radiant, Kam. The true belle of the ball."

It still seemed surreal, somehow, to find myself at one of the most anticipated movie premieres in the world, with my name tumbling off Grady Dunn's tongue. Two days earlier, my mom had accompanied me to the Hollywood launch, and her bewilderment had nearly trumped my own.

"Pinch me, Kam," she'd whispered when Julia Roberts walked by and asked me for a selfie. For once, I don't think UCLA crossed her mind. Every time one of the screens towering above the entrance to the theatres rolled footage of me combating the elements of a cataclysmal winter or staving off scavengers in an apocalyptic wasteland, she squeezed my hand, gazing around us with a euphoric, glassy stare.

It had brought me a lot of joy, watching her grow starstruck posing for a photo with Margaret Gilles, and I'd laughed when her tanned cheeks had flushed floridly after Elliott made a point to introduce himself and kiss her hand.

For all of the differences we'd undergone over the past few years, I'd been undeniably grateful she was there. Her enthusiasm, her excitement, her unquestionable pride in being my mother had helped ground me when a moment began to feel too big to face on my own.

On the flight to London, I'd begun to second guess myself for having not asked her to come both nights. Her presence had felt so uncomplicated, so unobtrusive beside me.

It wasn't the same with Carter.

Now, to be clear—he'd been nothing short of wonderful these last few months in which I'd engaged him to take on a role that wasn't fair. I'd known it was selfish to ask for his help when our feelings for each other had been so convoluted for so many years. I knew he still loved me. But I also knew, despite the complexity of the situation, his ringside view of my relationship with Dillon had begun to help him find a closure we'd been lacking. No longer did he question any chance of our future. He knew I loved her in a way I hadn't been able to love him.

But even with complete transparency, and the awareness we were both in on this with full disclosure, it didn't wholly alleviate the awkwardness that arose.

As I left Grady to his interview, and rejoined Carter in my slow procession toward the Empire, I became acutely aware each time his hand rested at the small of my back, comfortable there from habit after so many years. And when we reached the step and repeat banner, posing for photos that would be viewed across the globe, I struggled to smile as he dutifully tucked me into the crook of his arm and kissed my temple, a familiar action he'd done so many times before.

The deception felt more stifling here, not because it was on display in front of the whole world, but because tonight I knew Dillon would be watching.

Yet even then, I couldn't bring myself to regret inviting her. It mattered too much to me to have her there—to share firsthand with her this thing I'd helped create, this film I was so proud of. The same way she'd wanted me present to watch her cross the finish line in Leeds.

Finishing with the official photo op, I lingered outside the entrance to the theatre. Grady swept by, signing a handful of last minute autographs, and then disappeared into the privacy of the Empire. I knew I should follow suit. I'd spent more than enough time smiling for selfies and signing Addison Riley bobbleheads and plastic quarterstaffs. Tomorrow, *Entertainment Weekly* would give me a five-star rating for my fan interactions. Not a kudos I'd intentionally been trying to earn. I just wasn't ready to disappear inside yet. I was still listening to the names of the guests arriving.

*Sir Ian McKellen. Helen Mirren. Harry Kane. Gordon Ramsay. Cate Blanchett. Dame Judi Dench. Princess Anne.*

*Sam Huntley.*

There.

I paused with a sharpie hovered over an 8X10 print of me locking lips with Grady in front of a snowy backdrop. In my peripheral, I could see Sam making her way along the cordoned path. She was impossible to miss, dressed to the nines in an outlandish suit of fuchsia, pausing to take photos and banter with the crowd.

I turned further away but continued to watch in the reflection of a lens thrust in my face until Dillon appeared beside her. I knew it was her, not just by the unaffected stroll of her relaxed gait, or the flare of her white sailor pants Sam had convinced her were worthy of the red carpet, but because of the meteoric way my heart responded.

She had come, just as she'd promised.

With my breath still hitched, I scrawled my signature across the photo of me and Grady—nearly misspelling my name in the process—and made one final wave to the fans before turning my attention to navigating the stairs of the theatre, determined to survive the nose-bleed height of my imbecilic choice in footwear.

Compared to the chaos of Leicester Square, it was quiet inside the theatre. Unlike my experience in Los Angeles, I felt calm, and even excited, about the unveiling of the European film launch. It seemed hard to believe after fourteen months of madness, that in less than twenty-four hours, *Sand Seekers* would be viewed in cinemas across the world.

In a glowing review from *Forbes* following the Hollywood debut, the business magazine predicted the film would have the highest-grossing weekend on record. The night before, on my flight to London, Aaron sent me a screenshot with the following sentence highlighted:

*It was a five-star electric performance from newcomer Kameryn Kingsbury, who showed thrilling chemistry with Dunn and Fleming, making it impossible to pull your eyes from the screen.*

And another, from *Entertainment Weekly:*

*Kingsbury proves she's not just another pretty face, delivering a nuanced, riveting performance as the indisputable star of the most anticipated film of the decade.*

Overcome with stress… relief… excitement… and the reality of it all coming to fruition, I'd pulled my hoodie over my head and cried half way across the Atlantic.

"Looking for someone in particular?"

Interrupted from where I'd found a moment of privacy along the outskirts of the lobby foyer, I startled at the whispered voice near my ear.

I turned to give Elliott a frosty glare. There was something in his cat-who-ate-the-canary grin that promised I wouldn't appreciate the tenor of his jesting.

"Carter," I answered coolly, knowing I'd been caught scanning every face in the crowd. "He went to get us a drink."

Elliott's hazel eyes gleamed. It was almost gross, how handsome he was dressed up in a tux with tails. And equally annoying how deftly he saw right through me.

"For someone almost certain to find herself shortlisted for an Oscar, it's almost astonishing what a miserable liar you are."

"I wasn't aware the two went hand in hand," I responded tartly.

We'd built an odd friendship, ever since his whistleblowing phone call. He'd never mentioned the conversation again, and when I'd tried to thank him for his help, he'd abruptly blown me off.

"We look out for each other, Kingsbury," was all he'd said, before making it clear the topic was off-limits. But over the following months, it was he who'd gotten me through the grueling stress and helped me survive our globe-traversing press tour.

"Acting, lying," he shrugged, "both forms of deception."

"Elliott—Kameryn!" It was L.R.'s wife, Rebecca. "Photo?"

Elliott draped his arm over my shoulders and we smiled obediently before she went on her way.

"Do you ever hate this?" I asked beneath my breath as he waved at another tuxedoed stranger.

We posed for another photo. And another.

"Every single day." His lips never moved as he spoke through his grin.

Alone again, he leaned closer. "So—point her out."

Not a hundred percent certain of his implication, I chose to remain coy. "Who?"

"C'mon, Kingsbury," he stopped a passing waiter, swiping two flutes of champagne, and handed me one while he downed the other. "Show me yours and I'll show you mine."

Apparently here, with the most prominent figures of English society surrounding us, he'd decided to lift the ban on our taboo.

"You've already seen mine," I said, hiding behind a sip of champagne.

"Give me a little credit, Kameryn. I'm an asshole, not a creep. I wrote a check and left the details of your personal life to my lawyer."

Oddly, I actually believed him.

"I haven't seen her," I said, still wavering on if I was willing to share Dillon with anyone else. He fixed me with a look. I supposed twenty grand bought him the right to an insider's scoop. "Not in here, at least."

His lips curled. "But I was right? She is here?"

I offered an indiscernible wag of my eyebrows.

Another waiter passed and he collected two more flutes. I shook my head, thinking he meant to hand one to me, but instead he pounded the first, and set the glass on the ground, before settling in to work on the other.

"At your eleven o'clock," he said, wiping bubbles from his upper lip with a cuff-linked wrist. "Glasses. Red tie."

I turned a slow gaze in the appointed direction. A slender redhead was talking to Rebecca Sims. He turned his head at something she said and I realized it was our 2nd Unit Director of Photography.

"Wesley Arthur?!" I said the name too loud and Elliott stabbed me with a thumb on the pretense of fixing a wrinkle in the satin of my gown. "Isn't he married?" I continued, correcting my volume to a whisper.

He shrugged. "Welcome to La La Land. His wife's sleeping with one of last year's nominees for Best Actress." I couldn't think fast enough to remember who had made the shortlist. "Now, come on," he returned to scanning the crowd, "let me guess your type."

I huffed. "Like you'd know anything about my type."

"Oh, please—I pegged you your first audition."

"Liar. When I started auditioning, I'd never so much as glanced at a woman."

"Trust me, darling, you can lie to yourself, but I can spot a girl-kisser from half a mile away. Repression doesn't make me wrong."

I rolled my eyes. "Have you always been a bastard, or did Hollywood do you in?"

He smirked. "Oh no, definitely since the day I was born. My mother's been trying to give me away since birth."

From over his shoulder, I spotted the bright hues of Sam Huntley's suit near the bar. To her left was Dillon. As my gaze swept to her face, she looked up and caught my eye. I realized she'd been keeping tabs on me from across the room.

I considered pointing her out to Elliott. Giving in to the temptation to tell him how to spot her—the unruliness of her sandy blonde hair, the keenness of her sea green eyes, the perfection of her physique showing through her unbuttoned blazer. I wondered what she'd do if I texted her? If I asked her to meet me in the bathroom? I contemplated the possibilities of reenacting Andrew Garfield's scene from *The Social Network*, taking a moment to allow the fantasy of that reel to run through my mind.

But unfortunately my newfound professional persona convinced me college shenanigans at a premiere with some of the most prominent VIPs in the entertainment industry wasn't the brightest idea. So I peeled my eyes away from her, and feigned another survey of the room.

"Well?" Elliott prodded, leaning so close to me I could feel the condensation of his breath on my cheek.

"Keep gazing at me like that and people are going to think it's us sleeping together."

"All the better," he smiled.

"Speak for yourself." I took a step back, giving one more cursory glance of the room. "She must still be outside."

From the brightness in his eyes, I knew he didn't believe me.

"Maybe she got cold feet. Not everyone wants to see their lover naked on the big screen." He lowered his voice. "At least not with seventeen hundred other people watching."

My face must have betrayed me. I'd been so anxious about a million other things, I hadn't even had a chance to worry about the revealing of my intimate scenes. But Elliott misunderstood my horror. It wasn't strangers I was worried about seeing it. I mean, even Judi Dench had once had whipped cream licked off her nipples—and that was back in the seventies!

But… my *mom*!

I was suddenly grateful I'd spent the Hollywood premiere praying to the porcelain gods, and hadn't been there to see her reaction to my nudity.

"She should have given you away," I glared at him.

"Who?"

"Your mother." I tipped my drink back. "Excuse me—I see my date."

His eyes snapped up, intrigued, before he was disappointed to find it was Carter walking our direction. "Not fair, Kingsbury. I showed you mine."

"Entirely unsolicited." I kissed his cheek, pressing my empty glass into his hand. "Thanks for the drink."

# Scene 38

"Smashing! Everything I hoped for and more!"

Up in her cups on free champagne, Sam was practically levitating down the pavement of Leicester Square. She'd not quit raving about the film since they'd been funneled out the double doors of the Empire, where an endless line of black sedans and limousines waited to whisk away their superstar clientele. "And Kam!" Sam continued, her voice hoarse with excitement. "Howay, man! A tour de force!"

Dillon was quiet, grateful that in the afterglow of her exhilaration, Sam didn't seem to notice.

She needed a moment to settle herself, to take it all in.

Sam was right. Kam *was* superb. Even if there had been any question as to the magnificence of her performance, one needn't have been a connoisseur of cinema to judge the reaction from the crowd. The standing ovation she'd received during the credits confirmed everything Dillon already knew. This wasn't a fleeting act of brilliance. Kam had just flung open the doors to a titanic career destined to be storied in success.

It had all felt a little overwhelming. A little more than Dillon had bargained for. She'd not expected to find herself intimidated by the woman on the screen. To feel like she hardly knew this enigmatic person with whom the world had just fallen in love.

She knew it was an asinine departure from reasoning. Kam was still Kam. Whether she was the standout star of the premiere or the girl who'd texted her half a dozen times the night before, deliberating how to properly address her mother—*Jacqueline or Mrs. Sinclair*—she was still the same person.

But when the fanatical crowd at the end of the square erupted in applause, and Dillon turned to find it wasn't Elliott or Grady they were cheering—but instead, Kameryn—she could feel her pulse quicken, along with the familiar wash of discomfort she'd once experienced with Kelsey.

She dismissed the reaction, forcing herself to look away from where Kam climbed with Carter into the back of a limousine and returned her attention to Sam, who hadn't stopped talking.

"That scene—with the wolves—you know the one I mean? She made me cry! I can't remember the last time I cried in a movie!" In her drunken rambling, Sam hardly drew a breath before her focus changed. "Are you sure we have to skip the do? The Beckhams are going. I could still text Victoria and ask her to save us a couple of seats?"

She meant the afterparty at Tate Britain, an exclusive event held for cast and crew, with an invitation extended to London's most prominent elite.

"Sam," Dillon began, making no effort to curb her warning, "you agreed—"

"Alright, alright," Sam waved her off, "keep your hair on—I was just checking that you hadn't changed your mind."

It had been part of their deal. Dillon would go with Sam to the premiere so long as Sam understood, under no circumstances, would they be going to the after party. The venue was smaller, the setting more intimate, and Dillon wanted Kam to be able to enjoy her evening without distraction.

"I'm going to order you an Uber," Dillon said, steering Sam through the hordes of people camped out in the square. The first public showing of *Sand Seekers* wouldn't play in the cinemas for another twenty-four hours, but already the queue exceeded the preplanned barriers. The Tube in any direction was bound to be a nightmare.

"Nah, I'm too hopped up to head straight home. Think I'll stop in for a pint. Keep me company?"

It was the last thing Dillon wanted to do. She was ready to get back to her flat. Even though she knew Kam's hopes of arriving any time before morning would likely be dashed by the after party, she didn't want to risk not being there. Just in case.

Sam laughed, quick to read her thoughts. "Come now, marra! As much as I now understand your urgency to get home—I mean, that opening scene, those…" she glanced at Dillon with a wicked smile, "*assets*," she chose the word carefully, "wowza!—you'll be lucky if she gets out of there before dawn. You can spare me an hour." She looped her arm through Dillon's, who reluctantly allowed herself to be dragged past the statue of Mary Poppins and onto the narrower alley running behind the Odeon. "Besides," continued Sam, "I still have to write Seren her Christmas poem so I can send it to Swansea with you in the morning."

Dillon groaned. What had started as a joke had become annual tradition.

The first time Sam met Seren, the footballer had been so taken by the older Sinclair, a week later she'd penned her a drunken rhyme in a London pub, and insisted Dillon hand it over to her sister when she went home for Christmas.

At the time, Seren had laughed and almost been flattered. Now, a decade later, the poems were a source of exaggerated eye rolls, despite Dillon knowing her sister secretly looked forward to them every year.

"Still holding out hope one of your miserable haikus will win her over?"

"I won't give up on her—she's too canny a lass to stay a spinster forever."

"Right. Because at almost thirty-three, she's practically got one foot in the grave."

Sam ignored her sarcasm. "I think I'm going to change it up this year. Skip the haiku and try something different. Maybe I'll go for a limerick."

They'd walked west, away from the pandemonium of the entertainment epicenter, and crossed Piccadilly toward St. James Square, where the streets grew quieter and the pubs less crowded.

"What do you think of this?" Sam asked as they waited at a traffic signal.

*"There once was a bonnie lass, Seren*
*For whom my heart was yearnin'*
*So I wrote her this poem,*
*And sent it on home,*
*With an offer for some winin' and dinin'"*

"If that's the best you've got, it's no wonder you're single."

Sam's full eyebrows shot up in the amber glow of the caution light. "Oh, I can do better." She bounded with her uneven gait across the street, forcing Dillon to jog to catch up with her. "I was just trying to keep it PG for your sake. You won't like my next one."

"Dirty limericks about my sister? Correct. Stick with the haikus. Or better yet, skip the prose and just buy her a nice jumper."

"A jumper?" Sam stopped beneath a sign that said *Thorn and Thistle*. "That's a gift you give your nan, not something you give someone when you're trying to get inside their knickers."

"Jesus, Hunt—"

"Here, I've got another," Sam fielded her a brazen grin as she paused with her hand on the black-lacquered door.

*"There once was a hinny with long dark hair.*
*Her tits were ample with plenty to share."*

"Sam—" Dillon threatened.

*I considered it jammy—.*
*To sit on her fanny—"*

"Sam!"

*"And lovingly touch her down there,"* she rushed on, laughing as she ducked beneath the palm Dillon swiped at her head, before shouldering her way through the door.

Three pints later, when Sam was truly bladdered, she finally conceded to allow Dillon to tug her out of the pub.

"Okay, okay, for real this time," Sam laughed, stumbling over the threshold. "I think I've got it!"

Dillon steadied her with an arm around her waist, trying to work her phone out of her back pocket. The weather had turned with the late hour and the thin material of their suit jackets did little to keep out the frigid December air. The sooner she could bundle Sam into an Uber, the better.

"Ahem!" Sam cleared her throat, the steam of her breath disappearing into the festive lights hanging from the pub front windows.

*"My darling Seren, this verse is for you*
*'Tis time to cast out the lads and pay me my due*
*You'll find the love of a lass*
*Is truly first class*
*But right now I just need a loo."*

Dillon couldn't help but laugh. "You are bloody bevvied, mate." She checked the time. It was twenty 'til eleven. No texts from Kam. She couldn't help but look south, in the direction of the river, where less than a mile away, Tate Britain was holding host to some of the most glamorous people in Europe.

Dillon's thoughts were only on one of them.

No matter how tonight played out, no matter how late Kam reveled in the aftermath of her much-deserved laudation, by this time tomorrow, they'd have escaped the suffocation of the city to the quiet shores of her Welsh hometown just outside of Swansea. With traveling by train no longer a viable option, Dillon had arranged to pick up a hire car first thing in the morning. And then they'd have a month together, instead of stolen nights and short weekends.

"M'be I sh'ld try'a sonnet," Sam slurred, staggering to lean against a corner lamppost. "Fourt'n lines—gives m'more t'work with."

"Or," Dillon swiped open her Uber app, "maybe you should call it a night? Get a good rest and in the morning you can go all out and write her a ballad."

"A ballad!" Sam's eyes brightened. "Brill'nt!" She shivered, suddenly pawing at the buttons on her jacket. "F'ckin' 'ell, it's positiv'ly baltic!"

Reaching forward, Dillon began to work on fastening Sam's buttons, before an unfamiliar voice interrupted her progress.

"What we got here, lads?"

Dillon looked over her shoulder. A trio of men had rounded the corner, their faces unmistakably ruddy with liquor. University-age. Not overly dodgy.

She ignored them and went back to finish buttoning Sam's jacket. The Uber wasn't due to pick them up for another ten minutes.

"We interrupt date night, ladies?" The first man continued.

"Ladies?" The stouter of the three barked a laugh over the blue stripes of a Manchester City scarf. "I know a pair of fanny fiddlers when I see 'em."

"Sod off," Sam snarled, spinning to face the speaker and nearly losing her balance.

The man's lips curled. "Plucky bint, are you? You put that sharp tongue to good use?" He brought his fingers to his lips in the form of a V, making a vulgar gesture.

"Why don't you ring up your girlfriend and ask her?"

The retort brought a laugh from the third man, who instantly fell silent at his mate's darkening glare.

"You think you're funny, you little slag?" He took a step forward and Dillon was quick to catch Sam's arm, preventing her from answering his challenge.

"Leave it," she hissed, digging her fingers into her elbow. She didn't want any part of this. It was too cold, too late, and Sam was far too drunk. "Let's wait back inside the pub."

Sam shook her off. "Want to find out how funny I am, you fucking chav?"

Without time for Dillon to process a way to stop it, the man—twice Sam's weight, despite sharing a similar stature—lunged forward, taking a wild, off-target swing in her direction. Sam, too drunk to make a proper parry, took an awkward deflection off her forearm, and returned a glancing blow to his stubbled chin.

For a second, Dillon fostered a fleeting hope the altercation was over, but before she'd drawn a second breath, the bloke—who'd feigned to turn away—suddenly spun back toward Sam and slammed his fist into her face.

"No cunt calls me a chav!" he hurled, as Sam crumpled to the pavement. At once Dillon was between them, even as the bastard's two mates were at his side, cussing him for a fool and trying to restrain his flailing arms. But the man was feral, his temper entirely undone. Something in the skirmish caught Dillon's temple—an elbow, a fist, she couldn't have guessed—and nearly sent her to the ground, but she'd gotten a hold of the prick's scarf and saved her balance, clawing her way back between them as he plunged his loafer into Sam's side.

"Jesus Christ, what the fuck is wrong with you, Jerry?" the man who'd first approached them shouted, finally securing a hold on his mate's shoulder and hauling him backward. "You bloody idiot!"

The second man stood momentarily dazed, his eyes wide on Sam, who was groaning on her side, before turning to his comrades. "We need to go!" he hissed, shoving at the pair. "We need to get out of here!"

There was another cursed whisper, followed by the sound of feet retreating down the street, but Dillon didn't notice. She'd dropped to her knees to check on Sam, who was still barely moving.

Seconds passed, or maybe minutes—it felt impossible to tell—before Dillon was vaguely aware of a car pulling up to the curb. It was their Uber.

"You all right there?" said the driver, poking his head out the window, and then "oh, holy hell!" he continued, seeing Sam on the ground. A car door slammed and a moment later a silver-haired man joined her on the pavement. "I'll call an ambulance!"

Sam moaned a refusal, but when she wasn't able to keep a sitting position for more than a few seconds, Dillon took him up on the offer.

An hour later, Dillon found herself sitting in the waiting room of St. Thomas' Hospital emergency department, listening to a physician explain that while Sam had suffered a concussion, the CT came back negative, and other than a couple of bruised ribs, she was no worse for wear. They'd hooked her up to an IV to treat her inebriation and recommended she remain under watch for a few more hours until her nausea was under control.

"You could use a few stitches yourself," the physician commented, gesturing to Dillon's brow.

Dillon ran a hand across her tender temple. She'd known she was bleeding—evidenced by the scarlet splatter down her lapel—but hadn't thought much of it. Beginning to decline, she took a glance at her reflection in a stainless steel clipboard hanging on the wall, and changed her mind. Thirty minutes later she was back in the waiting room, five sutures tidier, still waiting on Sam.

A vibration from her phone dragged her from her contemplations of the hundred different ways she was going to kill her friend as soon as she could stand.

Of course it was Kam.

"Hey!" Kam sounded cheerful, if not a little tipsy herself. There was music in the background, an upbeat tempo jarringly contradictory to the cold, sterile atmosphere of the hospital waiting room. "You finally answered! I was worried you'd maybe run off with Kate Winslet and kicked me to the curb."

Dillon didn't realize she'd missed a call. Three of them, apparently, according to her notifications.

She tried to laugh, but it hurt more than was worth the effort. "Sorry. I—I guess I didn't hear my phone."

"Is everything all right?" Kam's gaiety dropped a peg.

Dillon hesitated. Somewhere close to Kam, there was laughter. She was still at the party and Dillon didn't want to dampen her night.

"All's good. I'm out with Sam." Again she paused. She didn't want to lie to her. "She—got in a little scuffle. We're at the hospital, but everything's okay."

"The hospital? What do you mean?"

"It's nothing, honestly. Sam got into it with a couple lads at a pub. An ambulance was called as a precaution—"

"She went by *ambulance*!? Dillon, what hospital?"

Dillon took a sweeping inventory of the brightly lit waiting room with its plastic chairs and buffed floors and curt triage staff assessing feverish babies and sniffling toddlers as anxious mothers picked at their cuticles. It wasn't a place for Kam. Not after tonight. She couldn't waltz in there and sit beside her, waiting for Sam to be discharged. Not as silent footage covering the *Sand Seekers* premiere played on the flat screen hanging above the sign indicating toilets were only for patients.

Not without a circus.

"It doesn't matter. You can't come here."

Kam was silent as the opening strains of a new melody struck up in the background. An Ed Sheeran song, Dillon recognized the track—and then realized it was actually a live performance.

The perks of a life with the rich and famous.

"I'm sorry, Kam." She sunk lower in the uncomfortable chair. "It's just…"

"No." Kam was deflated. "I know. You're right."

"We're okay. I promise." Dillon tipped her head back to stare at the flickering recessed lighting. "We'll be out of here in a few hours. I'm going to take Sam back to my flat to watch her until morning."

There was another long beat of silence.

This was not the night they'd planned.

Kam sighed. "Will you call me when you get home safely?"

"Of course. Hey," Dillon said, worried she was going to hang up. "You were superb tonight. I mean, just—extraordinary. The whole thing."

"Thanks. It meant a lot to have you there. I know movies aren't your thing."

"If you're in them, they're my thing."

"Oh, please. You just liked my nude scenes."

"Hands down my favorite of your costumes," Dillon teased. "Might have enjoyed it even more outside a group setting."

Kam finally laughed. "Perhaps I'll consider giving you an in-person private screening."

"First thing tomorrow?"

"Oh, you're going to have to work harder for it than that. You owe me, after tonight."

"Good thing I'm not afraid of hard work, then."

"Sinclair!" A nurse stood in the doorway with a clipboard. "Dillon Sinclair?"

Exhaling, Dillon pushed off the sticky arms of the chair to stand. "Is it still best for you to come to me, or should I pick you up?"

"I'll have my driver drop me first thing in the morning."

"I'll be waiting," said Dillon. "Unless, of course," she added, "I run into Kate Winslet in the meantime."

"Unlikely, since I'm currently watching her tip back martinis with Elton John."

Dillon laughed. "All the greater possibility she'll twist an ankle and turn up at the emergency department."

"Sinclair?" The nurse hollered louder.

Forced to rush through a goodbye, Dillon approached the door.

"Dillon Sinclair?" the woman checked her chart. "Miss Huntley's asking for you. She's looking a bit better. I imagine she'll have a raging headache for a while."

Deservedly so, was all Dillon could think.

A few minutes later, she dropped onto the foot of Sam's hospital bed, sending an aide scattering off after getting Sam's autograph.

"Gave as good as we got, yeah?" said Sam, through the swelling of a lopsided smile.

Dillon crossed her arms.

*"I once had a good mate named Hunt*
*Whose prowess was only a front.*
*She talked a big game,*
*To live up to her name,*
*But in reality was only a cunt."*

Sam's grin widened. "Look at you—a proper poet."

# Scene 39

I hadn't arrived at Dillon's apartment expecting to find her and Sam resembling a pair of battered MMA fighters. Dillon had neglected to mention her own involvement in the evening, and it alarmed me when she opened the door looking like she'd been made to sit for a makeup class on special effects.

"That's a little more than a *scuffle*." I paused en route to kiss her, surveying the half dozen stitches and darkening bruise creeping across her forehead.

"It looks worse than it is," she assured me, and when I pressed her on it, she told me she hadn't said anything because she didn't want to ruin my night. It upset me, her thinking I wouldn't want to know, and I was still a little mad an hour later after we'd dropped off Sam and pulled onto the highway heading west.

But it was hard to stay mad at someone you'd been counting down the months—the weeks, the days, the hours—to see again. Someone who took care of a friend the way she'd taken care of Sam. Getting her home, setting her up on her couch, insisting she call every few hours so she knew she wasn't dead. Someone who opened my door, carried my bags, and remained entirely unflustered by my backseat driving. Who ignored my growing agitation at the congestion crawling through the city, while all of London appeared to be leaving for the holiday on the same road we were on.

No. My anger was fleeting, and by the time we passed Swindon, I'd reached across the console of the Fiat 500—an amusing contrast to the last four months of luxury SUVs and limousines—and found her hand.

"I'm sorry," she said, interlacing her fingers in mine, "I should have been more forthcoming."

"I'm just glad neither of you were hurt worse." I hesitated, debating my next sentence, uncertain if it was something I should admit. I knew it made me sound insecure, but decided to continue all the same. "When you didn't answer last night, I worried you'd gotten cold feet. That the premiere might have scared you away."

From the tensing of her fingers, I knew she understood what I was asking, without actually framing the question.

"I'm not going to do that to you, Kam."

*That*, meaning what she'd done to Kelsey. The thing I'd had a lowkey anxiety about for the past few months of the rollercoaster I'd been on.

She glanced at me, giving my hand a squeeze, before turning her eyes back to the road. And with that, the topic was closed.

I must have found more relief in the simple reassurance than I'd realized, because the next thing I knew, I was waking several hours later to the sound of tires grinding across the gravel of a roadside turn-off.

I hadn't even known how exhausted I was, both my mind and body craving rest. Rest from the endless travel, the sleepless nights, the high of endorphins I'd been surviving on, and the inevitable crash after the close of the premieres. For the next month, there was no one dictating my schedule, demanding my time and attention. I was finally in a place where I felt safe, where I felt understood, where I could just be me.

"Where are we?" I blinked sleep from my eyes and looked out the window. We were on an unpaved road parked beside a livestock fence. Grassland pastures swayed with a gentle breeze, before disappearing into a sloping coast of sand. Beyond, a silver sea rolled out toward the horizon, covered by a gossamer blanket of fog.

"Somewhere between Eglwys Nunydd and Kenfig, I should think."

"Oh." I had no idea what she'd said. With names like those, I imagined it was a safe bet to assume we'd crossed into Wales. "It's so foggy." I tried the window, but the car was off, so fumbled with the locked door instead. Flinging it open, I was met with a wintry blast of sea air, heavy on the salt. "Are we near Swansea?"

"Not too far."

My gaze trailed down the desolate coastline until it came to a glow of lights illuminating through the mist. Miles away, a city was hidden beneath the dense cloud cover, but here on the backroad, we were entirely alone.

The sudden realization made my skin tingle.

"Care for a little hike?" she asked, her hand on the handle of the door.

It was cold, but not freezing. I doubted anything would ever feel freezing again after spending three months trudging across the ice sheets of Greenland.

"The last time you asked me that, I came home covered in mud and bug bites and bruises." But I was out of the car before she'd even opened her door. The idea of having a little time together before we got to her mother's house was intensely inviting.

She came around the car, helping me into my jacket. "Luck is in your favor." Her lips were against my ear, raising a row of goosebumps along the nape of my neck. "Not many bugs in winter in Wales." But just as abruptly, she stepped away, turning to stroll down the gravel road until she found a weak wire in the livestock fence loose enough to pry apart, allowing us to slip through.

What were the charges for trespassing in Wales, I wanted to know.

Execution without trial, she said.

I asked her if they would bury us together like the Lovers of Valdaro, united until the end of time.

She told me she thought she could have it arranged.

Then it was definitely worth the risk, I said, stepping onto the other side.

I followed her down an overgrown wildlife path strewn with cow patties and seashells until we reached the knolls of sand built up along the shale-covered shore. The breeze had intensified over the ocean, beginning to blow off the marine layer, revealing white-capped waters that lapped onto the sandbar.

Dillon stopped, taking a moment to survey the view, and then dropped into the willowy reed growing atop the dunes. I took a seat beside her, glad to find the ground dry, and surprised to discover the woven stalks of grass provided a welcome shelter from the wind.

"My mam can come across as standoffish," she said without preface, evidently picking up in the middle of a conversation she'd been holding in her head. "It's just her nature, as a solicitor. She can seem brittle. But I promise, beneath her formal English exterior, she's kind-natured at heart. She'll like you." Still not looking at me, she drew her knees to her chin. "She's a terrible cook. Every Christmas she insists on baking, and promptly burns every item she shoves in the oven to a char. My dad always claimed it was the driving force that made him fall in love with her—her dreadful kitchen talents. He said he worried, if left to her own devices, she'd have withered away and died." Her laugh was hapless. "It's one of the reasons Seren moved back home. To uphold Dad's promise to keep her fed."

Continuing to stare through the curtain of seagrass, Dillon absently ran her palm across the feathery seed blooms listing atop the reeds. "They both love Christmas carols, my mam and Seren. My sister will sit at the piano and play the same ones over and over again. Don't let on that you can sing or they'll try and cajole you to join them."

"And what if I want to sing with them?" I challenged pertly, tapping one of her tennis shoes with the toe of my slip-on Vans. "Not everyone is so Bah Humbug, you know?"

I didn't earn the laugh I'd been hoping for.

She went on, talking about the modesty of her mam's home—a two-story brick house overlooking Swansea Bay. Respectable. Orderly. But nothing too elaborate. Her room, she said, was unchanged from how it had been when she was a child, complete with posters of her idols and gold-painted plastic medals hanging on the walls. Her mam liked it that way, and Dillon admitted she didn't spend enough time there to care.

She plucked a plume from its golden stalk and rolled it between her fingers. "It's all just very—ordinary."

With a twinge of heartache, I realized she was nervous. Nervous about bringing me home.

Two days ago, she'd seemed to look forward to showing me where she grew up. To introducing me to her mom. But now there was an underlying hesitation. An embarrassment that hadn't been there before.

It wasn't difficult to guess what had happened.

"Hey." I leaned over, resting my shoulder against hers, drawing her attention back from wherever it had wandered. "I'm still me, Dillon. Yesterday didn't change anything. Not between us, at least. I'm still the same old Kam."

I could feel her unconvinced inhale. And the sigh that followed. "Of course."

"Then stop worrying, will you?" I collected her hand in mine, pressing our palms together. My nails, still meticulously manicured for the premiere, were a direct juxtaposition of hers—short and unpolished. I loved the strength of her fingers. The way endless hours in the sun brought out a hint of freckles across her knuckles. "Believe me, please, when I tell you this: I can't wait to meet your mom. And I love singing Christmas carols. I have a weird penchant for blackened bakery goods. And to be perfectly honest, I am really looking forward to seeing what posters teenage Dillon had hanging on her walls."

It was a relief to hear her laugh.

"Most importantly, however," I continued with pseudo-seriousness, "I can't wait to have the burning question answered: is it a single or double?"

Wise to my implication, she smiled, slowly, deliberately slipping her fingers between mine. It was embarrassing, almost, my physical response to the intimacy of the gesture. The way my breath caught. The way I could feel a shiver run the full length of my spine. With the simplest of touches, she'd set my body on fire, and based on the wicked gleam in her eyes, my reaction hadn't gone unnoticed.

"And which were you hoping for, Kam-Kameryn?"

Striving to restore my sense of poise, I matched her smugness with an arch smile of my own. "Anything other than a trundle."

It dawned on me, then, suddenly—I'd never clarified that she'd told her mom we were in a relationship. I mean, I'd assumed she had—Seren knew, after all—but I wasn't sure. For all I knew, Jacqueline Sinclair might think we were just friends. That Dillon had told her the same bullshit story I'd told the Hallwells the previous year. That I happened to be in town for work over the holidays. That I had nowhere else to go.

"Your mom," I faltered, "she knows…?"

The dimples on Dillon's cheeks deepened. "Knows?"

"That we…"

"That we…?" She raised her stitched eyebrow. "That we, what?" she prodded, feigning misunderstanding. "Met in Hawaii? That you're a terrible driver and nearly ran me over? That I took pity on you and invited you to dinner—?"

"Hey—" I made to swat at her, but she was faster than me, securing my wrist in her grip.

"That by the end of that first night I was entirely besotted?" Her teasing tone slipped away as her expression grew serious. "That I've spent fourteen months falling ridiculously, hopelessly, madly head-over-heels in love with you? That you're so far out of my league, it terrifies me, but every day I keep hoping you won't notice?" She took a shaky breath, the pulse in her fingers pounding against my wrist. "Were you wondering if she knew all that?"

I stared at her, my mind spinning. I knew she loved me. It wasn't the first time she'd told me. But she wasn't one to wax poetic. And this time, there was something about the intensity with which she said it—the meaning behind it. I found it hard to breathe. When I swallowed, I felt like I was barely keeping tears at bay, and I wasn't even sure why. Maybe it was because I'd spent the entire past year worried I was in over my head. That the depth of my feelings for her wasn't entirely reciprocated. That I was bound to find myself hurt in an unbalanced, one-sided relationship.

And now, hearing her say that... knowing everything I felt was requited...

I managed a slow exhale, trying to drum up a smile. "I was actually just wondering if she knew we'd be running late to dinner?"

My teasing fell flat and I didn't care. The only thing I wanted—*needed*—suddenly, was to close the gap of the last six months of distance between us. I couldn't wait another second to remember the taste of her mouth, to breathe in the scent of her skin. To bury my fingers in her hair. To feel her against me. I didn't care that we were a hundred paces off a public hiking trail, overlooking a beach in a cow pasture. I didn't care that it was cold. That, as dusk arrived, the wind had found new vigor. I didn't care about the sand that found its way into my shoes, or the reeds that caught in my hair.

I no longer cared that *Sand Seekers* was being shown in theaters across the world even as we sat there. I no longer cared about the premieres, or the reviews, or the lingering apprehension that in two short months I'd already be back to filming—that once again I'd have to go through all the stress, the pressure, the highs, the lows, and the anxiety that came with it.

All of that disappeared with the setting sun on the languid Welsh coastline.

The only thing I cared about was that she said she was in love with me. And I desperately needed her to know I was in love with her, too.


In the aftermath of our beachside tryst, the magical insulation to the cold had eloped, lost somewhere along the way with my hair tie and one of my earrings.

"Tributes to the Welsh God of the Sea," Dillon teased when we gave up combing through the sand in search of the silver hoop. "Did you know his name is Dylan ail Don?"

I laughed through chattering teeth. "Of course you were named after a Welsh God."

"Or perhaps it was the other way around?" she goaded, earning an eye roll and poke to her ribcage.

We trudged our way back toward the car in the dark, at some point losing track of the wildlife trail we'd wandered in on. My pinky linked through hers, I followed behind Dillon as we waded into the waist-high grass, laughing each time I clipped her heels, and shuddering to think what kind of spiders might be hitchhiking home on my disheveled clothing.

I'd grown so cold I hadn't even had the decency to deny her chivalry when she offered her sweatshirt, leaving Dillon in her shirt sleeves and me bundled in the hoodie and my jacket, zipped all the way to my chin. When we got to the car, I was relieved to find my bra was still tucked safely into Dillon's back pocket, having survived the offroad trek and scramble beneath the livestock fence.

"You and your hikes," I chided, hooking my thumb through a satin strap and stealing back the black Victoria's Secret lace number I'd chosen in anticipation of tonight. I hadn't planned on a roadside detour, or a rendezvous involving salt and sand.

"Um, excuse me," said Dillon, holding the door as I climbed in, and then jogging to the driver's side, "my only intention was to stop for a beachside chat. *You* are the one who had other plans in mind." She yanked her door shut and flipped on the ignition, turning the heater on high.

I humphed, knowing I was on the losing end of this battle, but clawing to keep the high ground all the same. "As if you can claim you chose this secluded spot with anything else in mind."

She laughed. "Well, when last we spoke, I believe you told me I was going to have to work harder for it than that—so I didn't assume a roadside shag was on the menu. If I'd known you were going to be that easy," she brushed sand off my thigh, "I'd have chosen a tidier location."

With a pretense of petulance, I pulled my leg away from her, retreating the entire two-and-a-half inches the cab of the Fiat permitted. "I'm not *that* easy—"

"Care to wager?" she whispered through a smile, leaning across the console to ease the zipper of my jacket down below my chin. Her lips brushed my earlobe. "I've got a hundred pounds that say I could convince you of a reprise before I ever throw this car in drive."

"Game on," I challenged, without any actual conviction. The joke was on her if she thought I wouldn't willingly shell out a hundred bucks to keep her doing what she was doing. This was one bet I didn't mind losing. But as I leaned my head back to give her better access to my neck, I caught sight of my appearance in the sideview mirror, and bolted upright in a panic.

"Oh my God—I can't meet your mother like this!"

I looked feral. My hair resembled something out of an Eighties music video, wild with humidity and glistening with sand and seashells. The minimal makeup I'd applied before leaving my hotel was smudged or missing. My cheeks were flushed from far more than the chill, and my lips—I had to take a second glance—were swollen and… tinged almost blue? That was from the cold, surely…

"I look like…like…"

"Like we haven't seen each other in six months?" she shrugged, unperturbed.

I unzipped my jacket further, pulling the neck of Dillon's hoodie lower to examine a red mark along my clavicle. "I think I've got reed rash on my shoulder…"

"Amongst other places," Dillon smirked at me through her lopsided smile, dropping her hand to the gearshift and disengaging it from park. "I'll let you win this bet. It's worth the hundred knowing Hollywood's paragon of virtue is going to have to greet my mother with seaweed in her hair."

# Scene 40

Seren casually leaned against the kitchen bar, going out of her way to chop the peeled potatoes into not-quite-even cubes. It was driving Dillon crazy. The nonconformity. The haphazard use of the chef's blade.

Reaching across the counter, she swiped the knife from her sister's hand. "You peel, I'll cut."

"They taste the same either way."

"Do not." Dillon halved the tuber, and then sliced it in thirds, before tossing the equal parts into a waiting pot of cold water.

Disinterested in peeling, Seren moved on to combining ingredients for fresh bread, taking care to leave a trail of flour across the spotless granite. Given her otherwise extraordinary proclivity for fastidiousness, Dillon knew the act was deliberate, done to inflate her sister's joy of needling her.

"You're such a muppet." Dillon dropped another potato in the pot.

"Take's one to know one." Smiling through her meticulous application of modest lip gloss, Seren leaned down and blew the fine white powder in Dillon's direction, quickly retreating to the sink to avoid retaliation.

Dillon didn't pursue her.

"What's wrong, Dill Pickle?"

At that, Dillon's head jerked up, casting her sister a withering glare. *Dilly* was one thing. *Dill Pickle* was a no-go.

Seren didn't flinch. "What's on your mind?"

In Wales less than twenty-four hours, and already Seren was analyzing her.

*Welcome home.*

Still, Dillon couldn't help but rise to the bait. "Why doesn't she like her?"

"Hmm?" Seren turned to scrubbing vegetables.

"Come on," Dillon dropped the last potato into the water and paused a moment, listening for any signs of movement in the house. Their mam had run to the market and Kam, still exhausted, had gone to take a nap upstairs. Satisfied they were alone, she continued. "Why doesn't Mam like her?"

"What are you talking about? She was perfectly polite."

"Right. That's the problem."

"Dillon—"

"Spare me the bullshit—I know you know what I mean."

Tossing a carrot into the colander, Seren turned to face her. "Fine. It has nothing to do with *liking* her. I think she's just… worried, is all."

"About?"

"She watched the red carpet thing." Seren busied herself drying her hands on a dish towel. "I don't think she realized…"

"What? That she's a big deal?" Annoyed, Dillon dragged a sponge through the spilled flour.

"She doesn't want to see you get hurt—"

"—so it would have been better if she was just some bit player, is that it? Something a little more my level?"

"Don't be obtuse!" Seren snapped, flinging the towel back onto the oven handle. "No one's above you, Dillon—Mam's just concerned she's turned your head."

"Of course she's bloody turned my head—I love her! Is there a problem with that?"

"You know that's not what I'm saying." Resigned, Seren's shoulders sagged with her deep exhale, her ramrod posture deflating. "She's just worried you're not quite yourself. That you seem a little distracted."

"And she's reached that conclusion in the whole twelve hours I've been here, has she?"

"I don't think she's ever seen you skip a workout—"

Dillon hurled the sponge into the sink, rounding on her sister. "So that's what this is about? I sleep in one morning of the year, instead of going on a run, and Mam's decided I'm no longer focused? And somehow that's Kam's fault?" She laughed, angry.

"You're being deliberately petulant! You know Mam would love nothing more than for you to retire! But she knows you won't—so of course it worries her to see you put your training on a back burner. We all know what happens when you aren't at the top of your game—"

"I can't win with you two! I'm damned if I do, damned if I don't. If I train every day, I'm obsessed. If I skip a day, I'm no longer committed—"

"Don't you dare drag me into this! You asked about Mam, so I told you!"

"Are you really expecting me to believe you don't share her opinion?"

"I don't know what to think yet, Dillon! But I do think you can cut Mam some slack—she only wants the best for you."

"Then she should be glad that I'm happy!" Dillon slammed her palm onto the counter, nearly upsetting the bowl of rising dough. "For once I feel like I have something more than just—just—" she threw her hands in the air, frustrated. How could she ever expect Seren to understand? Everything her perfect sister did was balanced. Seren had never battled the highs and the lows. Her entire life was even keel, steady and categorically stable. It would be impossible for her to know what it felt like to have nothing beyond her training. She was far too practical to allow her sport to consume the entirety of her existence.

So how could Dillon explain that for the first time, she felt like she'd begun to find a glimpse of that normalcy? That her life wasn't just her career as an athlete.

The medals. The podiums. The prize money.

That she finally felt like more than just rankings and results. More than what the sum of her life had tallied.

That a future with Kam made her feel like maybe one day there'd be more to life than just winning.

"Forget it. It's not something you could ever understand."

"Try me." Seren reached to touch her arm, but Dillon pulled away, wiping her floured palm off on her joggers.

"I'm just happy, all right? Maybe you can relay that to Mam."

"Maybe she can relay what to me?"

The two sisters spun toward the voice to find their mother standing in the entry arch of the kitchen. She had a sack of groceries in one hand and the *South Wales Evening Post* in the other.

It never failed to startle Dillon, how much of Seren she could see in their mother. Or, rather, the other way around. They were two congruous beings cut from the same cloth. From the way they stood, perfectly poised, ever in command of their emotions, to their style of dress—sharp, modest, practical. Even their long dark hair seemed inclined to part in harmonious echo of one another, falling to the same place beneath their slender shoulders.

Seren would be the exact replica of Jacqueline Sinclair in another twenty years. Ever elegant. Ever refined. Ever with all the answers—their lives mapped out in impeccable, straight lines.

"Nothing." Taking the long way around the kitchen bar, Dillon skirted past her mother into the hall. "It doesn't matter."

"*Dillon*," her mother commanded, ever the executive, the word almost convincing Dillon to slow on her way to the door.

*Almost*. But not quite.

"Where are you going?"

She paused with her hand on the brass knob. "A run."

"Dillon—"

"Sorry Mam, couldn't possibly miss a day of training." And she was out the door, into the brisk coastal air.


Dillon ran until her calves cramped and her fingers lost all their feeling. Down the two-lane road, past the familiar pubs and restaurants, through the sleepy town of Mumbles unfolding along the waterfront. She slowed to a walk when she reached the ice cream parlor where Seren used to drag her every Sunday, and turned onto the pier. The boardwalk had been decorated for the holiday, festive in green and red and gold.

Taking a moment to catch her breath, she leaned against the railing.

The tide was high. Across the narrow strait of water, two small islands directly off the headland rose out of the fog. The previous evening, she'd pointed them out to Kam during their drive to her mother's, explaining how the suggestively-shaped islets had given the village its name.

"Mumbles is a derivative of the French word, *mamelles*—which means breasts. A nickname courtesy of imaginative medieval sailors arriving from France."

Kam had laughed, surveying the two sunset-silhouetted mounds. "Proof that men stuck at sea too long can sexualize just about anything."

Now, Dillon watched the waves crash against the sprawling bed of rocks that made up the base of the furthest island. At its highest point, several hundred feet above sea level, the stark outline of the Mumbles lighthouse flickered its caution through the mist.

As a child, Dillon often skirted across the beach at low tide, navigating the exposed causeway, and climbed the steep stone staircase leading to the eighteenth-century landmark. It had been a favorite escape of hers, a place she had often gone with her dad—fishing, tide pool-wading, ship-watching. She was glad today the tide was high, making the trek to the lighthouse impossible. It wasn't a place she cared to visit any longer.

Her lungs still burning from the exertion of the run, she sank onto a wooden bench to stretch her hamstrings.

She'd been unfair to Seren. She knew that. Her sister had nothing to do with the rift between her and their mam. If anything, she was the thread that kept their small family tethered together.

But Dillon was tired of her mam's endless scrutinization. Her ceaseless worry. She just wanted to be able to live her life without being analyzed for every move she made.

Snugging up her laces, she dragged herself to her feet. She knew she needed to go home, to try to set things straight. Her mam simply didn't know Kam. She couldn't judge her off what she saw on TV.

Dillon just didn't look forward to the conversation. No matter her intentions, when it came to heart-to-hearts with her mother, she always failed to say the right things.

It was almost dark by the time she jogged up the three stone steps to the front door. She'd cut her arrival dangerously close to dinner, and knew she would have to wait to talk to her mam later in the evening.

But instead of stepping into a quiet house, disturbed only by the routine sounds of meal preparation in the kitchen, she was greeted by laughter coming from the lounge. She peeked around the threshold to find Kam on top of one of her mother's portable file boxes, clinging to Seren's shoulder for balance with one hand, while stretching with the other to straighten the star on top of a towering Fraser fir. The tree had been bare when Dillon left earlier in the afternoon, but now glowed with lights and tinsel, its branches covered with hand-carved ornaments that had been passed down through four generations.

"A little to the left—no, no, your *other* left." Her mam was issuing directions from the comfort of the sofa, a cheerful headiness in her voice, no doubt in direct correlation to the half-empty wassailing bowl steaming on the coffee table. The flushed cheeks on all three women promised none were on their first round.

With more laughter, Kam and Seren managed to get the star set to Jacqueline's standards, before returning to the punch bowl to fill their glasses. From the door, Dillon could smell the strong aroma of the rum, combined with the fruity fragrance of the cider. She waited a moment, still concealed within the shadows of the hall, as the conversation resumed.

"So Kameryn, you were saying—your parents weren't approving of your decision to pursue the art of acting?"

Dillon leaned against the wall. Of course, her mother would interrogate Kam, digging into every corner of her life as if she were one of her clients heading to the courtroom.

"No." Kam laughed. "They definitely weren't."

"I hope you'll forgive me for saying so," said Jacqueline, in her no-nonsense, truth-can-hurt manner, and from her hiding place in the hallway, Dillon braced herself for what she knew would follow. "But I can sympathize with your parents. I imagine it's hard not to be concerned when your child chooses a profession many consider just a step above prostitution."

Before Dillon could intervene—to tell her mam how out of line she was—she saw Kam smile, entirely unperturbed by the insult. She waited.

"I can't argue that. I believe there's only one profession in Hollywood most consider to be less reputable than either acting or street-walking."

"And that is?"

Kam took a calculated sip of her cider, her smile never wavering. "Being a lawyer, Mrs. Sinclair."

The room went silent. After a beat, her mother laughed, her amusement genuine. "Touché, Kameryn. And please, call me Jacqueline."

Dillon exhaled. Kam didn't need her defense. She was doing just fine on her own.

# Scene 41

I woke to an empty bed.

Every morning since arriving in Mumbles, I'd risen with Dillon at dawn, and together we'd walk to the waterfront, where I'd sit on the seawall and watch her swim from the boat launch to the pier and back again.

After, once I'd helped peel her out of her wetsuit, and snuck a kiss as we climbed the stone steps to the pedestrian path running along the main road, we'd stop in at Dunn's Coffee Shop, just around the corner from her mam's.

Dillon would order a breakfast bap and I'd discovered the wonder of freshly made Welsh cakes, and the two of us would chat as her hair dripped salt water into her tea and I silently contemplated vanishing from the limelight of Hollywood and moving to a one-horse town in Wales.

But when I opened my eyes this morning, Dillon was already gone.

There was a note on her pillow.

*It's cold this morning. Thought you might want to sleep in.*

I tossed the note aside. I knew it was neither the weather nor my beauty rest that prompted Dillon to rise without me.

Yesterday, while we'd been at the coffee shop, someone recognized me. I'd been too absorbed in conversation with Dillon to notice—too blissfully secure in the anonymity of my surroundings in the quiet seaside village. Mumbles, despite being a favored tourist spot along the south coast of Wales, wasn't exactly a place one would have their eyes peeled for celebrity sightings.

But a few hours later, as I'd been helping Seren oil her saddles in the tack room of her barn, I'd gotten a text from Aaron.

A photo had been posted on Twitter.

It was nothing damaging—just a picture of me holding my latte, my attention fully committed across the table. Dillon's right arm was the only thing that had made it into the image, thank God. But the user—*firebrat2009*, just a kid, no doubt—had tagged @famousfacealert and

@star_spotter, with the caption *Kameryn Kingsbury!!! Eeeeeek*! Along with a bunch of hashtags. #SouthWales #Mumbles #kamking #sand-seekersightings #addisonriley #superheroesdrinkoatmilklattes. As with all of the accounts dedicated to celebrity tracking, the post quickly went viral, with thousands of comments speculating on what I was doing in Wales, and where would be the most probable locations to sight me.

Just like that, the security I'd found in feeling invisible in the tranquil little town was stripped away. And though Dillon hadn't said much, her absence this morning said everything.

While I was dressing, my phone buzzed on Dillon's nightstand. I scooped it up, hoping it would be her, asking if I wanted to come and meet her for coffee. But it wasn't.

I stared at the caller ID.

Dani.

Of course. It was Christmas Eve.

We'd hardly spoken in months. The last time she called, the entirety of the conversation had revolved around her rebuking me for not getting back to her in a timely manner. I'd been in the middle of the promotional tour for *Sand Seekers*, flying to a new city, state, or country nearly every day. Interview after interview after miserable cheeks-hurt-from-smiling, laugh-at-their-unfunny-jokes-interview. Over and over again.

That didn't matter to Dani. All she cared about was that I hadn't called her back in a week.

"Well, I guess it's like they say, fame really does change a person, Kam." Then she'd hung up.

In some ways, she was right. Fame did change a person.

It made them paranoid. Anxious. Lonely. Vulnerable. Isolated. Sad.

Or at least those were some of the things I'd begun to experience in my newly minted career as it burst into the public eye.

I couldn't deny that in a few short months—weeks, days, even—fame had altered my existence. But not for the reasons she thought. Not for the parties or the money or the esteem. Not because I was someone different than I had been. Or at least not because I wanted to be. More than anything, I just wanted to be me. To exist in a world where my girlfriend wasn't afraid to ask me to join her for coffee.

I let the phone vibrate dangerously close to voicemail, then finally swiped to answer.

"Hey," I hoped I sounded cheery. "Merry Christmas Eve."

"Wow." The word didn't sound condescending, or even sarcastic. I waited for her to go on, to see where this was leading. "Just *wow*, Kam." In the background there was chatter interspersed with Christmas music. It would be afternoon in Palo Alto. They'd be preparing for the annual Hallwell dinner. "We saw your show last night."

"Is that her??!" Marcus's voice interrupted. "Oh my God! Tell her —"

"Shut up, Marcus! Jesus. Go jerk off to her photo on the cover of *Vogue* or something. Sorry," Dani returned to the conversation, "he's obsessed—he's seen it like six times. Anyhow—Tom and mom and I went to the IMAX last night in the city. Kam. You were a-maze-ing."

It wasn't what I'd expected her to say. Praise wasn't something I thought I'd hear from her. Ever.

"I mean, of course I knew you'd be good, but Kam… and oh my God, Elliott Fleming! That scene—that *scene*! How does Carter stand it? How do *you* stand it? He's so insanely hot. Was he a good kisser?"

"Um, I don't know. It wasn't really something I was thinking about. It's pretty rehearsed, and—" *And I hated his guts at the time*, I wanted to say, but it wasn't something her overcharged heterosexual ovaries would comprehend.

"Oh, come *on!* The chemistry between you two was absolutely fire! That can't have all been fake!"

*Wild how acting works*. I bit my tongue, sticking to the safety of "I'm really glad you liked it."

"No, *loved* it. Mom even wants Dad to see it when it goes streaming."

*Gee. What an honor*. "Cool," I said.

"So where do the rich and famous spend their holidays?"

There it was, the subtle twinge of condescension—mixed with a dash of jealousy for flavor.

"I'm still in the UK, actually."

"Oh." She hadn't known. Which meant she must not have gotten anything out of Carter. I owed him big time. "Are you still filming?"

"Yeah."

It wasn't a total lie. It was the same thing I'd told my parents. The bulk of the second film's principal photography would begin in late winter, but I *had* spent two weeks in Germany shooting last month, so technically, filming had begun. I was just on a very long holiday break.

And it was none of her business.

"Dinner won't be the same without you tonight, you know?" Her voice carried a wistfulness to it, a sincerity uncommon of her. "I miss you, Kam."

It was odd. Despite the careless way she'd treated me throughout our friendship, the reality was, I missed her, too. Dani wasn't like any of my other friends. For everything that she was—her vanity, her hubris, her selfishness—she was still the person who knew me best. The details of my life may not have ever borne importance to her, but she was the one person who knew me behind my every facade.

And now, aside from only a handful of people—namely Dillon, Sophie and, oddly, Elliott—it felt like the rest of the world viewed me through a veneer. I was the face on the cover of *Glamour Magazine*, the smiling actress interviewed in *The Hollywood Reporter*, the girl from the movie poster—radiant, perfect, incorporeal.

I was no longer Kam, who'd wet her pants in the sandbox in preschool, and glued her hands to the fishtank in Ms. Coombe's third-grade class. I wasn't the girl who got her braces stuck to Cody Harvey's jacket zipper in PE as a freshman, or the klutz who broke a stem off her stilettos during the first dance of prom.

Only Dani knew that Kam. And it was a Kam I didn't want forgotten. A person I didn't want lost. And it was so easy to get lost in this world—to forget who you were.

"I'm back in LA at the end of January. Maybe we could get together?"

"Think you could squeeze me in?" She laughed to soften the tone. "Maybe a girls' weekend at SenSpa? For old times' sake?"

"I'd love it." It didn't dawn on me right then that my carefree days at our favorite spa were over.

We chatted a while longer, reminiscing on past Christmas Eves, and then Dani was summoned by her mother and we closed the conversation with the promise to talk again soon.

Slipping into a pair of Dillon's slides, I tugged my bedhead into a bun and wandered downstairs. Pots and pans were clanging in the kitchen.

I peeked around the threshold. "Good morning."

Jacqueline poked her head out of the pantry. "Oh, Kameryn." She still wouldn't call me Kam, and I continued to struggle to call her anything other than *Mrs. Sinclair*. But despite the formalities, she'd been a generous host and made it clear I was welcome under her rooftop.

"I assumed you were off with Dillon."

"She thought I might want to sleep in this morning."

The arch of her eyebrows assured me I hadn't done an admirable job disguising my disappointment. But if Jacqueline knew about the snowballing drama of yesterday's photo, she didn't let on.

"I see," she said instead, once again disappearing into her pantry.

I knew she blamed herself for Dillon's ardent recommitment to her training. Yesterday afternoon I'd heard her say as much to Seren. They hadn't realized I was in the kitchen, and Jacqueline had gone on, lamenting a comment she'd made about Dillon's focus.

Not wanting to be caught eavesdropping, I tiptoed with my glass of water into the hallway and up half a dozen stairs, before turning around and making a production of tromping down each step to announce my presence. The conversation in the lounge abruptly turned to plans for dinner, and what vegetables should be prepared.

Part of me had wanted to find a way to casually mention the article I'd seen pulled up on Dillon's laptop a few days earlier, the headline announcing Elyna Laurent's bold return to competition. She'd come up with an offseason win in Mexico City—a race Dillon had won the previous year.

It was that, I felt certain, that drove her from her bed before dawn each morning and into the ice-cold water of the bay. That which sent her on hours-long runs and cycles through the hills. Entire half-days spent at the aquatic center in the pool. But I left it alone.

Reappearing from the pantry, Jacqueline handed me four boxes of sugar. "Hold these, will you?" she said, before rifling through her fridge. She returned with several sticks of butter. "Tonight is Noson Gyflaith—*toffee evening*."

Consulting a spiral index of cards, she pursed her lips, clearly flustered. "This was always Bedwyr's thing. I don't know why, after all these years, I keep trying to hang onto his traditions." Not looking for an answer, she plucked a brass pan from the overhead rack and turned on a burner. "Water first? Or butter? I can never remember." The recipe card was given a second glance, to which she only shook her head. "I've lived in Wales longer than I ever lived in England, and I still can't read the bloody language." Tossing the butter into the heating pan, she turned to me. "I would be lying, Kameryn, if I said you were what I'd hoped for for Dillon."

The unheralded switch from toffee-making to matchmaking jarred me, and I lost my grip on the box I was opening, spilling the contents across the floor.

"Oh God, I'm sorry." Embarrassed, I dropped to my knees, trying to recover the remainder of unspoiled sugar, along with the remnants of my bruised pride. So much for my misconception of her affability.

Welcome under her rooftop, my ass.

Jacqueline knelt beside me, calmly sweeping the fine white grains onto a paper plate. "After what happened with Kelsey, it didn't elate me to learn about your very promulgated career. I'd been hoping her next relationship would be a little less—ambitious, for lack of a better word."

I stared at the glistening granules sticking to my hands. What exactly was I supposed to say to that?

"But I was wrong, Kameryn—to judge you without knowing you." She touched my forearm, prompting me to look at her. "You are nothing of what I expected. You are a treasure. And any parent should be so fortunate to find their child in love with someone as kind, as genuine and lovely, as you are."

Before I could fully appreciate her unexpected words of laudation, she leaped up, cursing. "Damn it!" The pan on the stove had begun to smoke, the melted butter blackened on the bottom. She tossed it into the sink, flipping on the cold water as a hiss of steam rose to fog the bay window.

For a moment, her aimless gaze turned melancholy, but just as quickly, the sentimentality vanished, and she huffed a dry laugh, tipping her chin toward the trash can. "You know, just toss it," she said of the salvaged sugar. "I don't even like toffee." Busying herself with a bristle brush on the soiled pan, she continued with her forthright candor. "Tell me about your parents, Kameryn. Have they met Dillon?"

"They—" I hesitated, "well, yes, last Christmas."

Her umber eyes flicked up from the sink, settling on me for further clarification. After three decades in law, I was certain she could read me far better than she could read the blurred writing on her toffee recipe. "But they don't know about her?"

I couldn't help but look at the floor. "They don't know about me."

"Ah," said Jacqueline. The single syllable made me feel like a coward. Uncomfortable under her scrutiny, I stepped too hard on the trash can lever to dump the spoiled sugar, sending the lid clanging against the wall.

Jacqueline didn't flinch like I did. "Are you concerned how they will receive that information?"

"I…"

I didn't know how to answer. I wasn't honestly sure. On one hand, my parents were some of the most open-minded people I knew. Vocal on equal rights, fair housing, the gender pay gap. My dad had driven around with a faded bumper sticker on his work truck that read *Feminism is for Everybody* until the old Ford finally quit turning over. Most of my mom's friends in the horse industry were gay men.

But when it came to me?

I didn't know.

"Isn't everyone?" I finally said, drying my hands on a dish towel. I risked a glance at her. "Wasn't Dillon?"

The subtle crease in her otherwise flawless brow was the only indication my question surprised her.

"It was never a conversation with Dillon." Setting the pan in the dish strainer, she turned back to face me. "It was just who she was."

"You just knew?"

Jacqueline shrugged. "She just knew. It wasn't a question. When she was thirteen and brought home a girl named Cambrie who she introduced as her girlfriend, I don't think any of us blinked an eye." She flipped the recipe Rolodex closed and shoved it to the corner of the counter. "That was the thing that infuriated Bedwyr most about Henrik. Aside from the reprehensible ethical dilemma of him being her coach and the morally abhorrent truth that she was only a child—it was made a hundred times worse knowing it was so completely against her grain. I think it was that which my husband could forgive himself the least. But anyhow," she said, picking up a soap bar and bumping the faucet on with her elbow, "that's neither here nor there. Grab the sack of potatoes out of the pantry, will you?" And just like that, the whirlwind of the conversation was closed, swirling down the drain with the sudsy water.

Late that night, long after Dillon returned from her workout and Seren came back from the barn, after the evening had been spent wrapping presents while Jacqueline gave in and attempted a second round of toffee, well after Seren had begged her sister to sit at their grand piano —I was shocked to discover Dillon played beautifully—when the house was finally dark, and my body was slack with sleep and content from lovemaking, I lay awake, staring into the dark.

My mind was back on the conversation with Jacqueline in the kitchen. On the way she and Dillon's father had so easily accepted Dillon for who she was. The way we were able to stay here, under her roof, sleeping in Dillon's childhood bed—a double, for the record— without any hint of discomfort or judgment.

It made me want to call my parents. To come clean with them and unburden myself of secrets.

But I couldn't. And not because I was overly concerned with their reaction. I imagined they would be surprised, but when the shock wore off, I anticipated they would be accepting.

The problem was—they'd both been over the moon when I'd put on a pretense of having reconnected with Carter. They adored him. They always had. When we first started dating, my dad joked about putting me up for adoption and keeping Carter if I ever broke up with him. Since rekindling our supposed relationship, I had no doubt my mom had once again been fantasizing about a wedding, and scoping out what future horse shows she could attend as a grandma.

So while *Marriage to Carter* may have been sitting in the *Things Never Going to Happen* category for $2000, until I found a way to let my parents down easy, I'd have to allow them to keep smoking that pipe dream.

Which meant there would be no late-night "Merry Christmas, by the way, I'm gay" call to Palo Alto.

Beside me, Dillon groaned in her sleep, and I could feel a muscle in her back quiver with a cramp. I'd noticed she'd gotten more of them since increasing the distance of her afternoon bike rides, but she never mentioned it. Nor did she ever complain about the blisters on her feet, or the chaffing rash from her wet suit, or the endless sunburn on the back of her neck and ears, no matter how much sunblock she applied.

*I've experienced worse* was her shrugged response whenever I would point out an injury. Enduring it all in silence seemed to be her steadfast motto.

Over the shadow of the uniformed stitches slowly healing across her brow, the moonlight from the garden window illuminated a sign hanging above her trophy shelf. The plaque was cut in the shape of a dragon, with the words *Bydd gryf, Ddraig Fach* painted in sweeping calligraphy.

When I asked about the sign the first morning we woke in Wales, she told me it had been a gift from her father. He'd hand-carved it for her fifteenth birthday.

And what did it mean? I'd asked, not even attempting the pronunciation.

*Be strong, Little Dragon.* A pet name he'd given her as a child.

In a house haunted by the absence of her father, I found the spirit of the words disheartening. Even ten years later, his presence—or lack thereof—was palpable. It could be felt in the empty space beside Jacqueline on the sofa. The chair left vacant at the head of the dining room table. The study door that never opened at the end of the hall.

There were no photos of him throughout the household. The first night in her bedroom, Dillon must have sensed I was looking for one as I scanned the various snapshots pinned on her wall.

"When my mam's grief eventually transitioned to anger, she put all the photos of my dad away," she said, unprompted, pulling out an unframed 5x7 from her desk drawer. In the picture, Dillon was in a race bib, her t-shirt plastered to her skin, her dad beside her with his arm around her shoulders. The two of them shared the same pale blonde hair and dimpled smile.

When I handed it back to her, she returned the photo to the drawer.

Somewhere in the house, a clock chimed the hour. Twelve strokes. Midnight. It was officially Christmas morning.

Careful not to wake her, I gently massaged the tense muscle in her back, kneading my knuckles into the fiery wings of the phoenix spanning her shoulders.

It had been exactly a year since I first slept beside her. Since the small hours of a misty bay morning had catapulted my world into the clouds. At the time, I'd had no sense of the future. No clue of what we were doing or the direction things would go. I'd known only that—when the holidays were over—I hoped to find a way to see her again.

So much had changed in a single rotation of the sun.

But nothing more so than how much I loved her—how much I could no longer imagine my life without her.

As her breathing deepened once more, I eased my body against hers, soaking in the comfort of her warmth, drifting to sleep with the smell of salt and sea, sunscreen and chlorine that never left her skin.

I woke the following morning with a start.

The fragments of an unpleasant dream faded with my return to cognition.

Dillon was up already, dressing in the dark.

My heart sank. Again, she meant to leave without me.

Last night, when she'd reached for me between the sheets, finding my mouth with hers, I promised myself to let that be enough. I'd known from the beginning our relationship was better off in shadows. The debacle with the photo had clearly shaken her—but it hadn't scared her away. I knew if I wanted to keep her, I needed to give her her space. To be content with whatever parts of her she would give me.

But still, this morning I was disappointed. I wanted to tell her I could be more careful. I could wear my glasses. Change my clothes. Blend in better with the crowd. Hell, I could even shave my head—*Britney circa 2007* was fine with me—whatever it took. Just please don't cut me out.

But as I heard her zip her jacket, I kept my eyes closed, not wanting to make it more awkward than it already was.

Instead of tiptoeing out the door, however, I felt the mattress shift beneath her weight as she sat on the edge of the bed.

"Happy Christmas." The scent of Banana Boat sunblock filled my nostrils before she pressed her lips against my ear. "I know you're not sleeping."

"Nadolig Llawen," I whispered, botching the impossible pronunciation of *Merry Christmas* in Welsh, despite having practiced it for the past three days.

I felt her smile. "Your butchery of my language is charming, but it still doesn't get you out of coming with me this morning."

My eyes flew open. Without another word, I was out of bed, into the previous day's discarded clothing, and stumbling into my Uggs before she'd retrieved her backpack from the closet.

I wasn't being left behind.

It didn't bother me that she walked a little further away from me on the sidewalk, or resurveyed our surroundings before kissing me as I unzipped her wetsuit, or that she changed our coffee spot to Valdi's, all the way out by the pier.

She wanted me with her enough to risk the chance of another photo. Another fan post. Another chink in the armor safeguarding her from the world's prying eyes.

It was the most meaningful gift she could give me.

*Nadolig Llawen*—however the hell it was pronounced—indeed.

# Scene 42

"So, is this what turning thirty does to a girl?"

Through the orange haze of her polarized lens, Dillon caught a glimpse of the stars and stripes plastered across the side of Alecia Finch's tri-suit. They were on the final lap of the bike leg, five of six hairpin turns executed, and less than two kilometers from the start of the run.

Dillon knew the breakaway group had been gaining on her. A cramp had threatened her calf over the past few kilometers, and when she'd risked a backward glance coming off the last 180° curve, she'd counted five cyclists pushing toward an attack. Alecia'd led the pack, but not by much, which meant the others were right behind her.

Elyna Laurent amongst them.

Dillon made the choice to let them catch her. She'd pulled off early as the solo leader, but with the headwind as brutal as it was, it was in her best interest to join the group and find some relief from the draft. She could retake the lead after the transition.

It was the strategy that had worked at the Olympic Qualifying race held the month prior. Elyna had caught her on the bike, but Dillon managed to wear her down by strategically surging during the run, breaking the Frenchwoman's rhythm and outpacing her in the final kilometer. The massive win stamped Dillon's ticket to a guaranteed spot on Team GB in Los Angeles.

The rest of the season's results varied. Early in the year, Dillon won Yokohama. Alecia ran away with Cagliari. A Spanish former middle-distance competitor pulled off a surprising gold in her hometown of Pontevedra. Elyna claimed Abu Dhabi—but only three-tenths of a second ahead of Dillon, Sam was constant to remind her.

Dillon didn't need to win today. Nor was it crucial to podium. In the worst possible outcome, even a DNF wouldn't change her qualification for the Olympic Games next summer.

It was the last race of the year. Any finish above fifth place earned her enough points to claim another world title.

But it wasn't a world title Dillon was after.

For the first time in the history of the sport, the championship final was being held in Hamburg.

Dillon couldn't stand the thought of losing to Henrik in the charming German city she'd come to loathe. *A weakling*, he had called her. *An embarrassment.*

As soon as she'd hit the once-familiar ice-cold water of the Elbe, she knew this was her chance to send Henrik a message: His turf, her turf, it didn't matter. Elyna Laurent may have been fast, but Dillon Sinclair was faster.

"Don't break a hip there, Grandma," Georgina joined in the banter, pulling alongside Dillon as Alecia moved to the lead. The teasing about her age had started a couple months ago when she'd finally crossed the threshold into her thirties.

Entering the new decade hadn't been as bad as Dillon expected, after dreading it for so many years. It helped that she was in the best shape of her life. At no point in her twenties had her form been as fit as it was this season. Apparently being set on a path for vengeance turned out to be a blessing.

Better even, however, had been the fact that she'd gotten to spend it with Kam, the two of them disappearing to the white sand beaches of Saint Barthélemy for the weekend. Since Christmas, they'd managed only stray nights in passing—Dillon always en route to race on yet another continent while Kam continued crossing the globe to finalize filming on the second installment of *Sand Seekers*. Which made the four uninterrupted days in Grady Dunn's private beach house in the French Caribbean all the more amazing. Not to mention, the island getaway successfully deterred Sam from throwing Dillon the surprise party she'd been threatening.

So if this was truly Henrik's so-called *twilight* of her career, she'd take it. Because in ten short months, she meant to come home with an Olympic gold—the only hardware she was missing.

"Thought I might share the view from the front since you haven't seen it in a while," she called to Georgina. "I don't want to be accused of being greedy."

The Englishwoman grinned beneath her mirrored sunglasses and flipped Dillon the bird as she followed behind Alecia, making a deliberate move to give Dillon relief from the westerly blowing in from the North Sea.

A few seconds later, Elyna nosed past without looking in her direction, followed by two Canadians and a Dutch rider.

Sitting on the rear of the group's left flank, Dillon slowed her pace as they came to the turnaround going into the final kilometer of the cycle. The tarmac was damp—it having rained in Hamburg that morning—and the cyclists were forced to be careful. Dillon leaned her bike into the turn, keeping her body upright, and waited to pedal again until she exited wide off the apex. Ahead of her, Elyna began to make a move for the front.

*Let them*, she could hear Alistair's startline reminder. The wind was strongest on this final stretch. Let Elyna burn herself out trying to break away.

The spectators were loud as they neared the transition. In Dillon's peripheral, she saw a young woman dressed in the colors of Great Britain, waving a sign that said *Sinclair Squared,* with two gold medals drawn beneath it.

If her calf hadn't still been cramping, the sign would have made her smile.

*Sinclair Squared*—she and Seren.

Seren, who punched her ticket to Los Angeles after a dream win at Badminton—a five-star horse trial considered by many to be the most prestigious equestrian event in the world.

Dillon had flown ten thousand miles to be there. She'd watched her sister's flawless dressage test, followed by an intrepid cross-country run that put her in the top-five horse and rider pairs leading into the final round of stadium jumping.

On the third day, Dillon sat with their mother and Sam, holding her breath as she watched Épée fly around the arena, giving Seren everything she had. Thirteen fences in less than seventy-five seconds. On the final oxer, when it was evident Seren was going to jump clear within the allotted time—clenching the biggest five-star win of her career—Dillon launched over the arena wall, evading a pair of white-jacketed ring stewards, and ran to meet her sister.

The photo headlining the sports page of *The Times* the following day—above *Liverpool's* win over *Manchester United*—was of the two Sinclairs embracing, with Épée's long, lean neck wrapped around them, searching Dillon's back pocket for carrots.

*South Wales Sisters Olympic Bound* read the title. The article had gone on to compare three-day eventing as the horse equivalent to triathlon. *Only cooler*, Seren teased Dillon.

Coming onto the straightaway, Dillon unclipped her left foot, stretching her heel down to try and ease the muscle tension. They were on a mild downhill slope, allowing a fast pace without increased exertion.

Using the momentum of the decline, Elyna and Alecia were a dozen yards ahead, battling for the lead, with Georgina right behind them. A few yards back, directly in front of Dillon, the Dutch rider was attempting to overtake the two Canadians.

Dillon ignored the jockeying. Her focus was on the dismount line several hundred yards ahead. She flexed her calf, mentally rehearsing the transition.

*Flying dismount. Rack bike. Helmet off. Running shoes on.*

Her mind was on the number of gels she should down when she heard the unmistakable sound of rubber hitting rubber. Ahead of her, she saw the Dutch rider waver. Her front tire had come in contact with the rear tire of one of the Canadians. For a split second, Dillon thought the woman might recover, but in her effort to stabilize, the athlete overcorrected, again colliding with the Canadian, taking the pair of them to the tarmac.

Dillon knew she was going down. With the riders tangled just feet in front of her, there was no space to avoid the collision, and she was moving too fast to stop. Her only options revolved around what she would hit—cyclists or barricade—and how she would fall.

It was preferable to slide. Despite road rash and embedded gravel, a slide offered fewer risks of more serious injuries. If a rider had time and space, it was best to go down on a side, keeping feet clipped in, and hands on the handlebars. Let the bike take the impact.

But Dillon didn't have the time or space to make those kinds of decisions. Instead, her only option was to run over the Dutch rider, or turn and hit the barricade at over twenty miles an hour.

Second nature forced her to choose the latter.

She closed her eyes.

The sound of the impact was smothered by screams from the crowd. She could feel the grind of metal as her wheel buckled, the carbon frame of her bike crumpling beneath her. A moment of weightlessness followed as she was launched over the handlebars.

It occurred to her in that fleeting interval of suspension that only her right foot was clipped to the pedal. Had both feet been secured, she would have likely stayed in the saddle, flipping forward over the barricade, taking the bike with her. Instead, the loose leg allowed the force of the collision to cast her off like a rag doll, leaving the mangled frame on one side of the barrier and catapulting her body onto the other.

She slid—five feet? Ten feet?—she couldn't tell. She only knew that the scent of burning flesh was coming from her shoulder, as her right leg dragged her bike along on the other side of the barrier. Then all at once, the inertia of her slide stopped. The fork of her bike had caught on a stanchion, ceasing her forward momentum and torquing her body backward.

For a heartbeat… two… three… four… she lay, half on her back, dangling by her leg, staring up at the Landungsbrücken clock tower. Inanely, she wondered if Alecia had beaten Elyna to the transition? If she had, with enough of a headstart, could she hold the Frenchwoman's pace on the fast course?

And then there were no more thoughts of the race. Of the strangers staring down at her. Of her detached awareness of Hamburg's landmark buildings casting the pavement into shadow. It was as if a switch had flipped, igniting every pain receptor in her body. A white, searing excruciation, followed by a vignette of black, as the mercy of unconsciousness took over.

The physician was young. Too young. His English heavily accented.

He cleared his throat too much. Said her name too often.

*Unlucky fall, Miss Sinclair.*

*Be grateful things were not worse, Miss Sinclair.*

As if she had something for which to be grateful.

He stood at the end of the hospital bed, gesturing at a computer screen, explaining that she'd shattered her clavicle. Hit the ground so hard she'd cracked her helmet. Dislocated the bones of her elbow. Broken four ribs. Fractured her tibia. Damaged a part of her knee he didn't know the word for in English.

It didn't occur to Dillon to tell him she spoke German. To try to clarify what he was saying.

She just lay immobilized on her back, washed in a haze of pain which made it difficult to focus.

"How long will her recovery be?"

It was Seren's voice, out of her field of vision.

The physician cleared his throat, thumbing the stethoscope dangling over his shoulders. "Miss Sinclair is fortunate to be alive."

"That was not my question."

"Seren!" Her mam was there, scolding.

*When had they arrived in Hamburg?*

Seren ignored their mother. "Will she race by summer?"

Again, another clearing of the throat.

Dillon felt consciousness drifting from her, slipping through her fingers like the white sands of St. Barthélemy, her limbs warm—was it the Caribbean sun or the morphine?

She didn't hear the doctor's answer.

When she woke again, she was in a different room.

The writing on the whiteboard—*patient name, nurse, care plan*— had changed to English. There was a pastel mural painted on the wall by the door, colorful silhouettes of children playing netball.

Beside the bed a body was slumped in an armchair and despite the hospital blanket drawn to her ears, and the ball cap tipped down to block out the light, Dillon knew it was Kam.

She tried to sit up but found the action impossible as a torrent of pain flashed from the numbness of her toes to the scalding ache of her shoulders. Her involuntary gasp woke Kam, who sat up, blinking the room into focus.

"Hey." She swept the hat off her head, unfurling her legs that had been tucked up beneath her. "You're awake."

"I think I'd rather not be." Dillon closed her eyes. Something was pinning her left arm to her side. Her right leg felt immobilized. When she tried to draw a deeper breath, she found a new sensation of pain stabbing beneath her ribcage. "What time is it?" The last thing she remembered was staring up at the clock in Landungsbrücken. It had been seven-thirty.

"About ten."

Dillon opened her eyes, verifying she'd seen light glowing around the edges of the drawn curtain. It couldn't possibly have only been a few hours.

"How'd you get to Hamburg so fast?" Kam should have been in Beijing. She'd been at a promotional event in correlation with the trailer release for her second film.

"You're back in England." Kam stood, allowing the coarse hospital blanket to slip to the ground, and settled on the edge of Dillon's bed. "Last night they transferred you to the Royal National Orthopaedic Hospital in London."

Dillon wanted to close her eyes and reopen them. To find herself waking in the hours before the race. Anything to shake her free of this nightmare.

"What day is it?"

"Monday."

*Two days*. The race had been Saturday morning.

"Who won?"

Kam didn't answer.

"Elyna, then." Dillon tried to suck in a deep breath but radiating pain immediately cut the action short. "And Alecia?"

"I don't know." Kam reached for her hand. "I'm sorry."

The halogen lamps flickered on the ceiling. Above the headboard, a monitor ticked out the slow beat of her heart. On the whiteboard, in bubbly print, a nurse had written her name—*Candice*—with a smiley face.

"You didn't have to come."

"Of course I did!" Kam's tone was sharp, her fingers tensing around Dillon's. "I was on a plane before the ambulance had gotten you off the race course."

"You're so dramatic," Dillon tried to smile, only to find her face hurt with the effort. She ran her tongue along her upper teeth, relieved to find she still had all of them. "I think I dreamt Seren was there?"

"She was. And your mom."

For the first time since Dillon woke, a tendril of fear pierced through the numbness, settling uncomfortably in the pit of her stomach. "Looked that bad, did it?" Her voice wasn't as light as she would have liked it, the question no longer feeling rhetorical.

"It *was* bad, Dillon."

There was something about the way Kam said it.

Behind them, the persistent beep of the heart rate monitor ticked upward as Dillon formed her next question.

"What exactly is the damage?"

Kam glanced toward the door. "I should get the doctor. She can explain it—"

Dillon dug her fingernails into Kam's palm, preventing her from pulling away. "Kam!" The coil of fear was unraveling. "What is it you don't want to tell me?" She could account for the obvious. Her elbow. Her shoulder. Something in her shinbone. The pounding in her head indicative of a concussion. She forced herself to wiggle her toes, her fingers. All of that was working. "Is it my ACL?" she asked, suddenly nauseous. "Please say it's not my ACL."

She tallied the timeline. It was late September. The Olympics were in August. Was a little more than ten months enough? It had taken her the better part of a year to return to competition when she'd ruptured the ligament as a teenager.

She ran through the early season lineup. She would have to race before summer. Something to prove to *British Triathlon* that she was still a contender.

Bermuda was in March. Andalucia in April. Weihai in May. Worst case, there was always Leeds in July.

If she finished any of those races in the top twenty, they couldn't deny her after her auto-qualifier.

"It's not your ACL."

The statement derailed her premature problem-solving, temporarily swinging the pendulum of her anxiety in an arc toward relief until she glanced over and caught Kam's expression. The monotone chirp of the monitor continued to accelerate.

"Okay." Dillon found it difficult to produce enough air to make the word audible. She couldn't bear the look on Kam's face. The way she could only meet her eyes in glancing intervals. "What then?"

Again, Kam looked toward the door. Whether she was seeking an escape, or hoping for reinforcements, Dillon couldn't decide. In either case, Kam finally took a deep breath, evidently surrendering to the awareness that she could not free herself from the situation.

"You damaged something in the cartilage, Dillon. The surgeon called it a—an osteochondral defect." She hesitated. "She said it was like a pothole in your knee."

"How long, then?" It was the only thing Dillon could think to say. There were just over three hundred days until the gun went off in Los Angeles. "How long, Kam?" she persisted.

"The doctor said she wouldn't know anything for certain until she got a scope in there. You'll be going in for surgery this evening." Kam attempted to shift her tone, to paint the future with a coat of possibility.

But Dillon already knew. She'd known it since Kam's first staggered breath. Perhaps she'd known it already while lying on the pavement in Hamburg.

And late that night, when the head of orthopedics came to see her after she'd woken from the attempted reconstruction surgery, she'd known before the woman ever opened her mouth what she would say:

She was very sorry.

She'd taken a career-ending fall.

She'd never race again.

# Scene 43

The plane banked, circling for landing. Somewhere beneath us, Cardiff was hidden by the thick November marine layer. My thoughts had been so far away, I'd hardly noticed the miles traveled, but now, as the luggage rattled overhead, I buried my nails into the fabric of the first-class armrests.

"Not a fan," said the woman beside me. They were the first words she'd spoken since we boarded the plane.

"Same," I managed, trying not to jump as the landing gear lowered, the engines whining in their acceleration. "I hate the wind."

She didn't look up from the book she was reading. "No. Of you, I mean."

It took me a moment to understand it wasn't turbulence she was referring to. "Oh." I said. Because how do you respond to that?

*I'm sorry? My bad? Fuck off?*

I'd have preferred the latter, but my press agent wouldn't. Contrary to popular opinion, *all* press was *not* good press.

"You give girls unrealistic expectations of what it is to be beautiful. My daughters want to look just like you—no matter how often I tell them your look isn't natural."

I sat silent, stunned by her accusation. Women came in all shapes and sizes. All bodies were beautiful. Living in the fishbowl of public scrutiny left me damned if I did, and damned if I didn't. I wanted to ask her if she had any idea what it felt like, being judged by millions of strangers based solely off appearance? If she had any other advice for me, aside from the recommendation to eat a cheeseburger?

But I stayed quiet. I'd long since learned that trying to get the public to view you as a person—flesh and blood, thoughts and feelings—was impossible.

The pilot came over the loudspeaker, announcing that it was a balmy 6°C in the Welsh capital and reminding everyone to remain seated and keep their seatbelts on.

I checked my belt twice. Ten more minutes and we'd be on the ground.

Well, unless the engines suddenly cut out.

Or a wing fell off.

Or the wind blew us out of the sky.

Then the landing would come a bit faster.

I closed my eyes, uncertain which was worse: reflecting over the events of the last two months or worrying about cataclysmic engine failure. My mind chose to focus on the former, though it would have been more tolerable to dwell on the latter.

Dillon had been through three surgeries since her accident in Hamburg. The most heralded surgeons in Europe had examined her case, each offering a glimmer of hope, before reaching the same conclusion: in time, she'd heal. Probably even be able to bike and swim. But she wouldn't run again. Her days as a professional triathlete were over. No amount of patching, of trimming, of reconstructing would get her back to an elite level of competition.

I'd stayed with her at her mom's the first week after she'd been discharged from the hospital. My emergency hiatus forced the studio to reschedule more than a dozen interviews in three countries.

*Did I know how that looked?* I could hear Waylon MacArthur's muffled shouting when my unexplained absence had been upgraded to a call from his personal assistant.

I didn't care. *So fire me* I snapped into the line as the producer's rants turned to threats of recasting the final film if I wasn't back in Los Angeles, prepared for wheels-up by the following weekend.

Ten minutes later, I received a backpedaling text from the same assistant, assuring me everything was fine. To take as much personal time as I needed.

I didn't bother to reply. I had far too many other things on my mind.

Like how to deal with Dillon.

I would have known how to handle it better if she'd cried. If she'd cussed and punched walls. If she'd pointed accusatory fingers, turning her anger toward God, toward Elyna, hell, even toward me. I could have been the reassuring voice, the steady hand she could hold. I could have googled articles on *how to soothe someone who is mad at the world*.

But she did none of that. Instead, she just receded, shutting everybody out. She sat for endless hours in her upstairs bedroom, saying nothing, staring out the window. When she did talk to me, it was trivial. A turn in the weather. What book I was reading. What her mom would burn for dinner.

I sat helpless on the end of her bed, listening when the final specialist called, informing her he did not feel she was a candidate for further treatment.

I was sitting in the same place the following day when *British Triathlon* phoned to say they were withdrawing her qualification, replacing her with the next highest-ranked athlete.

*We're sorry, Miss Sinclair*—the formal voice droned—*it's an unfortunate situation. Our best wishes for the future.*

When Dillon hung up, I waited, willing her to say something—anything. Include me in her hurt. Let me bear some of the load she was carrying. But she didn't. And I didn't know the right words to say. I didn't know how to ease her pain.

At the end of the week, when I kissed her goodbye, forced to return to the life I'd put on hold, she no longer bore that subtle scent of chlorine. Her lips were soft, unmarred by the sun and the sea. The freckles on her cheeks had faded into pallor.

I crossed the Atlantic feeling more despondent than I had ever felt. And terribly, achingly alone.

I had no one I could talk to. No one with whom I could share my grief. Because there was something different about saying, "Oh, my good friend just had a serious accident," and "The person I love most in all the world has just lost everything that matters to her." They are not the same thing.

So when I landed at LAX, I texted my manager, Charlie—a new acquisition to my team—and told her I'd had a change of plans. I didn't care if I drove her nuts trying to rearrange my schedule. Waylon MacArthur could wait. I hopped on the first departing flight to San Jose. I couldn't bear the idea of waking another morning under the guise I'd been living. I'd had enough of the Carter charade. I didn't need to dangle my personal life out for all to see—but I needed those closest to me to know. To understand the real me.

I walked into my parents' home unannounced at six AM. The Uber driver had been too consumed with rocking out to *Pink Pony Club* to ever take a glance in his rearview mirror. And even if he had, what would he have seen? A red-eyed, depressed, exhausted girl who hadn't brushed her teeth in twenty-four hours.

Before my mom had the chance to set her half-sipped coffee and riding crop on the counter, or my dad fully registered my presence over the top of the *San Francisco Chronicle*, I stood in the kitchen and said "I'm in love with a woman. I have been since the day I met her. The one you met at Darlene's. And if you don't like it, I don't care."

And then promptly burst into tears.

Had I approached the topic with more finesse, maybe their response would have been different. Maybe they would have had time to be surprised. To dwell on the information, to suggest to me that I was just confused—after all, I'd had plenty of boyfriends.

But instead, in the ambush of information, and my immediate meltdown following, they were left with no choice other than to be consoling as I sobbed out my heartache over Dillon's accident and the devastating end of her career.

They both hugged me. My dad said he'd briefly wondered about our relationship at the Hallwells. The way I'd watched Dillon eating her cassoulet had reminded him of how he felt when he'd first met my mother. But then, I'd been so suddenly recommitted to Carter, so seemingly in love, he'd brushed the thought aside.

My mother told me her only disappointment was in herself—that she regretted any part she may have played in making me feel like I couldn't tell them. That it hurt her to think I had worried my relationship with Dillon could have changed her love for me in any way.

When I calmed down, when my mother produced a spare toothbrush and combed my hair at the kitchen island the way she had when I was a child, when I had drained two cups of coffee and was working on a third, life as I'd once known it resumed its practical course. My mom asked me to help her muck box stalls while offering advice on my IRA, and my dad dragged me to the garage to show off the remote-controlled model sailboat he planned on racing the following spring.

I left their home that afternoon feeling like a snake that had shed its skin. It wasn't exactly a revolutionary coming-out parade, but simply unburdening myself to my parents had lifted a taxing yoke off my shoulders. For the first time in years, I bid my parents farewell, and genuinely meant it when I said I looked forward to seeing them again.

Intent on completing the mission of my trip to Palo Alto, I called Dani and asked if we could meet for dinner. Grab take-out, head to one of our favorite spots along the bay where we could be alone. I'd seen her a handful of times over the course of the year, and the strain in our friendship had begun to feel as if it had self-repaired.

Still, with her, I chose to be more delicate. To attempt to handle the situation with kid gloves. She wasn't my parents. To Dani, image meant everything.

"I'm sorry?" she blinked through her eyelash extensions after I'd explained for the second time that my relationship with Carter was a sham. "What exactly are you trying to say?"

I kind of felt like: *I haven't been honest with you about my personal life; I've been using Carter as a beard* was pretty self-explanatory.

Apparently not.

I tried again. "Do you remember the woman I brought to Christmas Eve? She and I are dating."

Dani's mouth opened and closed once—twice—before any sound came out. "You—can't seriously be trying to tell me you're a lesbian?"

It was a fair assumption. That was generally what it meant when a woman was in love with another woman. But I hadn't really labeled it. Was I bisexual? Pansexual? I didn't actually know. I just knew I loved Dillon. But it wasn't something I was about to analyze with Dani, so I said yes.

"That—that *girl*?" She uttered the word with such paramount disgust, she may as well have said dyke or fag or homo. "That runner? The blonde woman—with the hair?"

My sashimi lay untouched in its to-go container on the side of the bench where we sat—a place I imagined it would remain, given the direction the conversation was headed.

"Yes." I held Dani's stare without shrinking. "That's the one." After all, Dillon had hair. She was blonde. She was—had been—a runner. No disputing that.

"You're telling me you've been—been—," she waved her chopsticks in the air, directing an agitated symphony of exasperation, "*sleeping* with her? Like…like…!"

Like sex was the only part of a relationship Dani could comprehend.

She couldn't fathom the efforts we made to be together. The thousands of miles traveled with short clandestine hours our only reward. She had no understanding of being so in love with someone that their hurts and heartaches became paramount to your own.

But in an attempt to connect with her surface-level grasp of our relationship, I shrugged the affirmative: yes, I was having sex with Dillon.

Her microbladed eyebrows continued to climb up her forehead. "I—I don't understand. You're not gay. I mean, you got caught by my mom giving Carter a handjob in the jacuzzi."

*On second thought, maybe it was better to have friends who didn't know you when you were sixteen.*

Dani stabbed a chopstick into her unagi. "How, even? Why?"

I skipped the *how*—I didn't imagine she actually wanted to know—and focused on the *why*. Because Dillon made me laugh. Because the dimples in her smile made my legs weak. Because she was uniquely brilliant. Endlessly talented. Charming. Witty.

Because in two short years, with oceans dividing us in every direction, she'd taken the time to learn everything about me. She loved me for exactly who I was, with every fault and idiosyncrasy. And because when I was with her, my world felt complete.

Dani didn't hear any of that.

"You've seen me naked," she blurted instead, as if she'd stumbled across some deep epiphany. "Did you—have you ever—did you have the hots for me?"

"What?!" I jerked backward. Was she even fucking serious? That was her concern? That I'd been jonesing for her since we started changing in the PE locker rooms in 7th grade? "No, Dani." The words ground through my clamped teeth. "I certainly did not."

She shook her head, still not hearing me. "I just don't get it. How do you even have sex with a woman?"

Clearly, I'd been wrong. The *why?*—not important. The *how?*—everything.

How did a woman have sex with a woman? I daydreamed about the answers I could give her. I could clear my throat, channel my inner Elizabeth Barrett Browning: Ahem, *Let me count the ways*:

Wholly. Completely. Consumedly. Passionately. Sometimes fast. Sometimes slow. In the middle of the night with the Celtic moon shining through a childhood bedroom window. In the afternoon sun amongst the reeds of the sea. Laughing, smothered against the steering wheel in a crowded underground Los Angeles parking structure. Quietly, on a riverfront balcony, soaking in the glow of the London Eye.

They were things she would never understand. Feelings she would never know. I would have felt sorry for her if she hadn't still been gawking at me like I'd escaped the confines of a freak show.

In my silence, Dani continued. "I mean, just—," she shuddered, "gross. I couldn't do it. I know it's in vogue with your set, but still."

I stood, gathering my untouched tray of sashimi. "I think it's about time for me to get back to LA."

"Oh, come on, Kameryn. You're overreacting. It's fine. Whatever. Love whoever you want and all that. It's just not my thing."

I dumped my dinner in the trash can, feeling guilty about the wasted fish. "I wasn't actually seeking your approval, Daniella," I returned the favor of her full name. "I just..." Just, what? Hoped she'd be someone different than she was? It was my fault, expecting her to change. "Look—I hope you respect me enough not to betray my confidence. It's not something I'm ready to share with the world. But if you just can't help yourself, so be it. I can't stop you."

"I'm not going to say anything!" For a moment, she looked hurt, and I almost felt bad, but then her upper lip curled. "I mean, it's obviously just a phase you're going through."

I stared at her, turning over the dozen friendship-ending words that flew to my tongue, and then decided she wasn't worth it. I kept my mouth shut and walked away. Back to life under the bright lights of Hollywood. To flashing cameras and waiting cars. To private airline terminals and last boarded, first disembarked. Back to being managed in and out of public spaces. To twenty-hour days on set and lonely trailers marked *VIP*.

And then, finally, a few days of respite, allowing me to get back to Mumbles. Back to Dillon.

And back to the bitch in the seat beside me.

I gave my seatbelt one final tug and held my breath until the wheels touched the runway.

And then my anxieties drifted in a new direction.

I wondered how I would find Dillon. What mood she would be in.

These last two weeks there'd been a change. Over the phone, I began to notice some of her anger, her sullenness, her hopelessness was waning. For the first time since her accident, she made the effort to reach out to me, instead of me always contacting her. Her conversation expanded from one-word answers to some of the humor and teasing I loved. The future began to exist again. *When we did this. If we did that.* She almost sounded content.

It gave me pause about the pitstop I'd made in New York City on my way to Wales. About the surgeon's personal number I now had stored in my phone.

I didn't know if it was the right thing to do for her—to offer hope that might not pan out. I'd sought the consultation with the innovative specialist without telling her. After listening to what I had to say, he said felt he had a procedure that might help.

But now, with her brightening attitude, part of me wondered if I should have left well enough alone.

Stepping onto the passenger boarding bridge, I came to the conclusion it wasn't my choice to make. It was her life. Her future. I may have been the one to open this can of worms, but it was now up to Dillon to decide.

# Scene 44

"Did you figure out what we're ordering for dinner?"

Startled by Seren's head craning over her shoulder, Dillon shoved her phone beneath the hotel duvet and swatted her sister away from her. "Don't be a creeper."

"What—are you sexting?" Seren teased, flicking the back of Dillon's neck.

"It revolts me to even hear you use that word."

Huffing, Seren flopped down beside her. "I'm single, not dead, thank you very much."

"Still… yuck. You're my sister. I prefer to think of you living a life of celibacy."

"Yeah, well, sorry to disappoint you, but—"

"La-la-la, I don't want to hear this!" Dillon made a show of sticking her fingers in her ears.

Taking advantage of her unguarded ribcage, Seren poked her in the side, and then dove for the phone tucked beneath the covers. Slowed by her limited mobility—her collarbone still healing and leg locked in a knee immobilizer—Dillon wasn't fast enough to block her.

"Alright, Romeo," Seren held the phone aloft, "let's see what Kam…" her voice trailed off as she realized there would be no golden opportunity to embarrass her sister. The screen was left on an Instagram account for Dr. Robert Monaghan.

*Surgeon to the Stars* was the handle.

"Do they really call him that?" Seren rolled her eyes, handing the mobile back to Dillon.

Dillon shrugged. Outside, snow began to cling to the seventeenth-story hotel window, the tops of the trees covering Central Park dusted in white. She turned her attention back to the phone.

The surgeon's profile photo had to be at least a decade old. The man she met this morning had wrinkles and a bad spray-on tan. But his handshake was firm and his confidence even firmer, his office littered with signed photos of his former patients. Tiger Woods. Tom Brady. Harrison Ford. Bill Clinton. That sort.

Three weeks ago, Kam sat cross-legged on Dillon's bed and explained how she'd met with a surgeon renowned for taking on cases others found unsolvable. A specialist who focused on bio-medicine.

"He thinks you could run again."

Dillon had looked over the material Kam brought with her from NYC. *Paste grafting and stem cell cartilage repair.*

As his moniker suggested, he dealt primarily with celebrity clientele, cherry-picking his patients. He was out of Dillon's league, but that was no longer the case for Kam. A call to a friend-of-a-friend and she had been granted his full attention.

Dillon had set the pamphlet aside.

"You know I can't afford this." His practice worked outside the parameters of insurance—a cash-only basis which provided him the ability to pursue unconventional treatments.

"Please don't insult me." Kam's jaw tightened. "I would give every penny I have if it meant you would be able to race again—if that's what you want. If the tables were turned, I know you would do the same for me."

The tables *had* turned. It had once been Dillon who was at the height of her career. Dillon who'd traveled the world. Who'd earned the better living. Kam was lightyears ahead of her now—the disparity between them only broadening.

But if she could race again? If she could make it to Los Angeles? If she could etch her name in stone—in *gold*—to solidify her place in Sports History?

Maybe her story wasn't finished.

*If that's what you want* Kam had said.

There should have been no question.

Dillon's entire world had collapsed with her wreck back in Hamburg. Everything she'd pushed for. Everything she'd fought for, suffered through, year after year, mile after mile, clawing tooth and nail to achieve. Gone in the fraction of a second—the clipping, or unclipping, of a cleat.

So why had she hesitated to jump on the opportunity? Why, in the last couple weeks, had a contentment crept in, whispering to her the promise of peace?

It didn't belong there. She was born to compete.

Dropping her head into Kam's lap, she'd closed her eyes to the familiar comfort of the fingers trailing through her hair and nodded her agreement. She would meet with Dr. Monaghan. See what magic he could weave.

And today, three weeks later, he'd stood in his office and assured Dillon eighty percent of patients who underwent this specific type of surgery returned to competition. If all went well, by the end of the week, she'd be on her way home with a different forecast for her knee. A month non-weight bearing. Another month in a brace.

After that, only time would tell.

Could she run by spring?

His pepper-gray brows had knit, wrinkling his bronzed forehead. He was not so arrogant as to guarantee a timeline. Every injury healed at a different speed. But at the door he'd stopped, clapping her on the shoulder. "A long shot is better than a final whistle." He'd drawn his arm back to throw an imaginary ball. "After all, sometimes a Hail Mary finds the end zone."

Dillon forced herself to sign on the dotted line—she wasn't a quitter —and Kam wired over more money than Dillon made in an entire year.

"Are you sure you want to do this?"

Shifting her attention off the headshot of the doctor, Dillon's thoughts returned to her sister. "Of course I am." She tossed her phone on the bedside table. "What a stupid question."

"It's not, though, is it?" Seren set a tentative hand on her leg. "You know you don't have to do this."

Frustration building, Dillon shoved the hand away, angry at herself for wavering on her conviction, and angry at Seren for always seeing through her.

"Tell me, if something happened and you were told you would never ride again—but then an opportunity arose that offered you a second chance, would you not jump on it without ever looking back?"

"I think it's a little different for me. Aside from you, from Mam, riding is what I love most in the world."

"And you think I don't feel the same about racing?" Dillon snapped, defensive.

Seren's composure remained infuriatingly intact. "I wouldn't know, because you won't talk to me. You won't tell me how you're feeling. The best I can do is try to read behind the words you aren't saying.

And maybe I'm wrong, but I think, as hard as these last couple of months have been, part of you has embraced the outcome. You've had a remarkable career. There's no shame in hanging up your boots. Thirteen years. Three Olympics. Countless world championships. You have nothing left to prove—"

"Sam won the Ballon d'Or. Competed in three World Cups. Was twice voted FIFA's Best. Do you think for a single second she wouldn't give everything in her power to lace up her boots again? To feel the lights of Wembley on her back?"

"You're not Sam—"

"And you're not *me*! So stop thinking you can psychoanalyze everything!" The brace felt too tight on Dillon's leg, the sling pinning her elbow to her chest too confining. She wanted to get out of the hotel. To disappear beneath the blanketed canopy of trees. To run from questions she didn't know how to answer.

How could she put it into words? The fear of trying versus the fear of doing nothing?

"Alistair called," she said after the silence in the room had grown too stifling. "*British Triathlon's* holding the third quota open. They've given me until Leeds to qualify."

The fine lines around Seren's mouth deepened. "You don't have to do this for Team GB. You don't owe the BOA a thing."

Dillon's laugh was dry. "Do you know what kind of investment they've made in me? The time? The money?"

"And yet, the moment you were no longer useful to them, they tossed you aside. Don't fool yourself into thinking they care about you or your career, Dillon. The only reason they're holding that spot is because they know, if there's a possibility you can run, you're still their best chance at a medal."

"Exactly. The *gold* medal. I'm their best shot to do what no British woman has ever done. You think Georgina's going to bring it home?"

"I don't care—don't you get that?" Seren's equilibrium was finally cracking. It brought an odd sense of satisfaction to see her imperturbable sister angry. To see the whites on her knuckles as she slammed her fist into the duvet. "I don't care about medals. Or breaking records. I don't care about what hasn't been done before! The only thing I care about is *you*! I want the best for *you*!"

Dillon lay back and stared at the ceiling. The best for her? She didn't even know what that was anymore.

But it didn't matter. It was too late to change her mind. Too many people were counting on her. Too much was invested.

"I'm going to do this. And I'm going to run. It's what I do." She closed her eyes. "And I need you to support me."

She felt Seren move closer, pressing her cheek against her chest. "I have supported you—and will continue to support you—with every fiber of my being, Dillon Sinclair. You're my little sister. It's what *I* do."

Dillon had to pass the back of her free hand across her eyes, swallowing away an unwelcome lump in her throat. On another day she would have given Seren grief about her shower-damp hair soaking through her shirt. She would have brushed her off, telling her to save her affection for Épée, who had no choice but to endure it. But today she welcomed the weight of her sister's comfort. She'd loved these last few days spent together, just the two of them. The slow, ambling afternoons exploring the city. The drowsy late nights watching American talk shows. The morning tea from the street vendor who didn't know the difference between matcha and Earl Grey. The friendship, the closeness between them. How it had once been when they were children.

But the respite would soon be over. Seren put her life on hold to travel with Dillon to New York, but when they got home, she'd be off to Italy to compete in Verona. And Dillon would be stuck home with her mam, waiting to see if fate had any compassion. Then would come Christmas. Kam. Holidays spent together.

And after? Would *Sinclair Squared* still be a thing, or would only one of them see Los Angeles?

It was the unknown that felt the heaviest.

She opened her eyes to find Seren watching her.

"Promise me one thing, Dill?"

She hiked a noncommittal shoulder, feeling the ache in her clavicle.

"If it gets to be too much, you'll walk away?"

"Seren—"

"I mean it, Dillon. If it's not working, if things aren't going as planned, promise me you'll let it go?"

How easily that was said from someone sitting at the top of her sport, with the Olympic Games steady in her crosshairs. All Seren had to do was pull the trigger.

But Dillon didn't want to fight. Instead, she eased herself upright and scooted to sit against the headboard. "Fine. But I hate to break it to you, one way or another, I'll be in Los Angeles." She nudged her sister with her toe. "Because even if I'm not racing, you're going to need a groom. And it goes against the Equality Act not to hire someone just because they're a cripple."

Seren finally smiled. "What about not hiring someone because they suck at grooming?"

Dillon shrugged. "I'm your sister. You don't get to say no."

# Scene 45

The reviews were polarized. Half the critics hailed the second film as revolutionary, the other half were scathing.

Elliott, like always, took a sick satisfaction in homing in on the condemnatory.

"*The New York Times* called it 'Cinema Suicide.' Oh," he cooed, his voice trailing one beat behind on the transatlantic phone call to where I sat in Jacqueline Sinclair's living room, "but here's my favorite! The cover of *Empire Magazine*," he cleared his throat, "*Sand Seekers Sinks: No Bulkheads High Enough to Keep this Billion Dollar Barge Afloat.* Jesus. Who writes this shit?"

I tapped out an impatient rhythm on the arm of the couch. "It also broke the opening weekend record as the highest-grossing film in box office history, so I somehow doubt we'll find our heads underwater any time soon."

Elliott scoffed. "Why you gotta be such a little ray of sunshine? Let me sulk."

"Well, you're going to have to sulk alone. We're about to make toffee." I was anxious to get on with Christmas Eve. Dillon would be home soon from physical therapy and Seren would be back from the barn. I was ready to drink wassail and forget about life in Hollywood as I soaked in the serenity of the nineteenth-century stone home. I'd been on the road for seven weeks, transversing five continents, more countries than I could remember, and four premieres—the last of which had taken place five days earlier in Japan. I'd drank too much. Slept too little. Existed on a diet of caffeine pills, airplane snacks, whiskey, and Gatorade.

I'd begun to forget what it felt like to exist in a world where you weren't on exhibit every waking second of the day. How it felt to live the sort of life where you could stop in at the Farmer's Market to pick up asparagus on sale or hit a WeHo nightclub without having to call ahead, arrange security, and devise an entrance and exit plan. To not have every angle of your life scrutinized, criticized, or glamorized by strangers across the globe.

A life devoid of fan accounts. Fan fiction. Shipping. Stanning. Stalking.

Two weeks earlier, I'd ended the farce with Carter. He'd met a girl I could tell he really liked. A set designer who'd been at our wrap party. I would have liked her, too, if I hadn't known she was sleeping with him thinking it was behind my back. It provided me the motive I needed, however, to call things off. I wanted him to be able to pursue a relationship out in the open, and it got me out of staging holiday photos that made me feel like a schmuck.

I called him, thanked him eternally, and then deleted all our photos together from my Instagram.

Celebrity code for *Trouble in Paradise*.

Hollywood gossip was still obsessing over it, with entire articles speculating on what went wrong, who I might be dating, if I was or wasn't a slut. For months, rumor had circulated that I'd been carrying on an affair with Elliott, stemming from the inconceivable notion that a man and a woman couldn't possibly be friends without fucking. A scandal that likely would have petered out the next time Elliott showed up at an event with one of his blonde armpieces sporting stilettos longer than my inseam, but instead, the idiot decided to fling fuel on the fire, choosing to kiss me on the red carpet at the European premiere.

"That's for the billing," he'd whispered in my ear, referring to my name that appeared on the marquis above his. I'd pinched the inside of his arm hard enough to leave a bruise, and he'd strolled away, offering me a wink as he disappeared into the theatre. The next day every entertainment news site ran with the photo.

But despite his endless impertinence, I'd come to consider him one of my best friends. He'd proven to be a pillar of support as I navigated the unknown territory of turning into an overnight celebrity, and the rocky waters of life on the A-list. He'd become my ally. My confidant. We understood each other. We had the same secrets to protect.

He talked me through the hype of being nominated for a dozen different awards following the first film release—MTV Movie Awards, BAFTA, Empire, EDA, SAG—and the disappointment of losing the majority of them. He reminded me my worth wasn't tallied by Roger Ebert's great-great-granddaughter's opinion or the sweatpant-wearing, forty-year-old keyboard warrior still living in his mother's basement with his hands down his pants.

He consoled me through Dillon's accident. It was his networking that got the consultation with Dr. Monaghan. Every day he'd checked in to inquire about her progress, and how I was holding up.

And the thing with him was—he meant it. Beneath his cocky veneer, his arrogant playboy exterior, he was kind. He was generous. And I loved him for that.

It still didn't change the fact that I was glad when he got another phone call and was forced to hang up.

I texted my parents, sent Sophie a requested toffee recipe, and then helped Jacqueline in the kitchen until I heard Dillon come through the front door. Her gait was unmistakable, the click of her crutches and pad of her single tennis shoe soft as she moved across the tile.

She'd been in good spirits over the seventy-two hours that I'd been there. Her mood had been generally optimistic, Seren told me, since she'd come home from surgery, but her fixation with recovery seemed to double by the day.

I'd hoped my presence might alleviate her blinkered obsession with speeding up Mother Nature's *Laws of Healing*, but it hadn't made much difference. She was still up before dawn, but instead of us going to the bay for her morning swim, she left for the Swansea Aquatic Center, where she pushed the limits of Dr. Monaghan's instructions for non-weight-bearing activities. In the afternoons she attended physical therapy, and at night, as she reviewed race results across the various federations, she stretched the painful muscles that threatened to constrict.

There were three more weeks before she was permitted to cycle. Two months before she could test out jogging. And an undetermined length of time before Dr. Monaghan would entertain anything more aggressive.

Dillon ignored this last part.

"I can do Bermuda," I'd heard her tell Seren the previous morning.

"Science says you can't." Seren had not sounded thrilled about her sister's eagerness to fast-track her return to competition.

"It's fifteen weeks away. The run is mostly flat."

"You won't even be at five months!"

"Seren, I can do it—"

"You promised me!"

Dillon remained pragmatic. "I promised if it became too much. How can I know what is too much if I don't even try?"

My eavesdropping had been interrupted by Jacqueline, who'd appeared behind me at the top of the stairs. Before I'd worked out an excuse for my lingering, she smiled tightly and made a noisy descent to where her girls had grown silent in the kitchen. She'd undoubtedly heard the exchange, and her opinion on Dillon's desire to expedite her healing appeared on par with Seren's.

A little part of me had begun to feel like I'd overstepped my bounds by recommending Dr. Monaghan—by finding someone to tell Dillon yes, there was still a chance.

But certainly, the alternative had been worse. Hadn't it?

Christmas afternoon, after we'd opened presents and I'd neutralized my hangover with Dillon's twice-baked Welshman's cheese soufflé, I asked if we could go for a walk along the bay. I wanted to be alone with her—just the two of us.

"Seren said she'd be happy to drop us off. It should be quiet due to the holiday." I'd already outlined my argument in preparation for any excuse she might make. I wanted desperately to get out of the house. To have some time together. I needed to feel like it mattered I was there. That I wasn't just in her way.

To my surprise, she willingly agreed. I tried not to allow it to slip into my head that her resistance may have been greater if the Aquatic Center hadn't been closed for the day.

"Where'd you have in mind?"

"Mumbles Head?" I loved the scenic views from the peninsula.

She nodded. "Alright. We can walk down to Limeslade Beach."

I didn't bother questioning if she felt up to tackling the coastal terrain. She was more agile on crutches than I was on my own two feet.

As hoped, the picturesque cliffside was deserted, the usual hikers home with their families.

"Take care along the edge," Dillon warned after we'd turned off the main trail and woven our way along one of the narrow paths leading to the highest point of the headland. "It's slippery."

In the distance, the lighthouse atop the furthest islet blinked through the low-lying fog, heeding ships we couldn't see.

"Would you jump in to save me?" I taunted, leaning over the ledge to look at the frigid water crashing against the rock face. I could tell she was uneasy about the height, but it didn't stop me from wanting to get a rise out of her. To slip beneath her skin. Anything to gain her attention.

"I'd jump in after you," her expression remained neutral as she gave an unfazed shrug. "But neither of us would survive the fall."

"Modern-day Romeo and Juliet? Thelma and Louise?"

"You've been reading too much Tolstoy."

It wasn't an unfair assessment. I'd been cast in a contemporary retelling of Anna Karenina set to begin filming the following summer, and in preparation for the role, had filled countless travel hours poring over the Russian's tragic prose.

"Better than the fluff of Margaret Gilles—isn't that what you said?"

"I didn't call it fluff."

"But that's what you meant, right?"

I'm not sure why I wanted to pick a fight with her so badly. I think I just needed to feel like she still saw me. To know I still mattered. With her single-minded fixation on her rehabilitation, it had become difficult to tell where I fit into her life.

"Don't be thick," she chided, resuming her one-legged travel along the ridge, "I called it light reading. Not everything has to be Joyce and Faulkner. You're making something of nothing."

Justly scolded, I watched three more signals from the lighthouse lantern before trotting to catch up.

"Dillon." I caught her arm just as she reached the Y that split the trail's further destinations: right, the parking lot, left, Limeslade Beach. I had to get it off my chest. "Are you still happy? With me, I mean."

Her look of unmistakable astonishment simultaneously filled me with embarrassment and relief.

"Happy with you?" The crease of her brow deepened. "Whatever are you going on about?"

"I… I don't know." I tried to brush it off. It was ridiculous to have worried. Naturally her focus would be on her training. She was living under the colossal pressure of a question mark, the entire path of her future dependent on her recovery. The last thing she needed was to deal with me and my insecurities. "Come on." I pressed my hand against her back. "Let's go to the beach."

"No," she studied me a moment, and then my heart sank as she swung a few steps up the trail leading away from the water.

"Dillon, come on. Please." I didn't move. I would have given anything to take the question back. I couldn't stand the idea that I'd ruined the outing. "Forget I said anything."

"Impossible." She paused, looking over her shoulder. "I remember everything you say. And even the things you don't say." The ghost of a smile graced her lips. "Now come on, Kam-Kameryn."

I hesitated. "Where are we going?"

"I'm going to take you on a proper hike." She resumed her trek toward the main road. "After all, it's tradition."

The twelfth-century castle cast an ominous shadow across the acres of parkland as the sun settled behind the ruin of its western walls. I'd seen the crumbling stone structure plenty of times from a distance. It was impossible to miss, sitting atop its hill less than a mile from the heart of the village, but this was the first time I'd had the opportunity to see the landmark up close.

I would have found it charming. I never grew tired of the way ancient fortresses seemingly popped up from nowhere across Great Britain. But today we'd come in through the back side of town, which meant we'd spent the last ten minutes weaving through the massive Swansea cemetery.

It had been my mistake, mentioning to Dillon how the centuries-old tombstones and obliquely protruding grave patches gave me the creeps.

Especially at dusk.

Suddenly, despite having led the entire way at a pace I'd nearly had to jog to keep up with, Dillon became a hobbling invalid, limping along through the most tenebrous sections, taking time to tell me about Lady Alina, the mistress of Oystermouth. Dead these last seven hundred years, her spirit was said to haunt the castle grounds.

"Especially at night."

"And why exactly would we want to come here, then?" I asked as her swiftness returned up the final grass hill leading to the castle entrance. My cowardly soul found a moment of triumph when I saw the thick chain wrapped around the iron gates. "Oh, what a shame. It's closed."

She never gave the entry a second glance, instead continuing around the side of the towering walls, further into shadow.

"Dillon?" I followed for no reason other than I refused to be left alone with a mysterious ghost in the quickly burgeoning darkness.

Coming to a stop beneath a narrow slot vaguely resembling a window, Dillon turned to face me. "Want to go in?"

I glanced at the window in question. It was less than a foot wide and at least ten feet above us—and, to my relief, had a bar running down the middle to keep idiots out who might be stupid enough to trespass.

"I'm assuming this question is rhetorical."

I was rewarded with a lopsided smile. "Are you afraid?" She glanced higher. Another dozen feet above the first window was a second—this one without a bar.

"You think *I'm* climbing that?" I laughed, relieved, because I knew there wasn't a snowball's chance in hell that was ever going to happen. "You think *you're* climbing that?" I gave a pointed glance toward her non-weight-bearing leg. "You're a regular comedian."

"You think I can't get inside these walls?" There was something in the timbre of her voice that made me wish I hadn't challenged her. "Tell me, what do I get if I prove you wrong?"

"The satisfaction of being right." I was still doubtful, but I knew better than to put anything past her. "As well as the opportunity to spend a lonely night inside a haunted castle."

"Who said anything about being lonely?" She gave me an arch glance before sweeping aside the knee-high grass with her crutch, prodding for something along the stone. "I'll have Lady Alina to keep me company."

Her crutch clanked against something that sounded hollow. With a smug smile, she smoothly dropped to the ground—despite her straight-locked knee—and a second later her legs disappeared into the wall.

*A drainage pipe*, I realized. One that was too dark. Too narrow. And —with little doubt—too full of spiders.

"Enjoy your transcendental tryst." I stepped back. "I'm sure you'll give Ol' Alina a thrill." The last glacier in Antarctica was going to melt before she convinced me to crawl into that hole.

"I'm calling your bluff, Kam-Kameryn. You'd get jealous." Her body vanished up to her shoulders.

"I'd be more jealous of catching the flu."

"Suit yourself." Her dimples creased as the last glow of sunset turned her hair to amber. "I would have made it worth your while."

Then she was gone, crutches and all.

I stood alone in the unfolding blackness.

I absolutely was not going. I didn't care if she'd smiled at me in a way she hadn't smiled at me in months. I didn't care if the thought of being locked alone with her behind two-foot solid stone walls ignited a blaze in every fiber of my body. I refused to be the substantiating proof that even the highest form of intelligence could be undermined by corporeal desires.

And then I was down on my belly in the wet grass—because who was I actually kidding?—and army crawling after her.

By the time I wormed my way out the opposite side, Dillon was up on her feet, crutching across the vacant courtyard.

"Oh, no you don't," I laughed, springing after her. "You owe me. Big time!"

Faster than should have been possible, she disappeared into a narrow stairwell, taking the spiraled steps two by two in a manner suggesting she knew every nook and cranny, turret and alcove of the tattered castle. I followed to the upper level, guided only by the click of her gait and brush of my fingers across the moss-covered walls.

I'd nearly caught her when I stumbled through the highest threshold and suddenly found myself suspended in the air, the waxing moonlight through the demolished roof revealing the ground forty feet below. Dillon laughed at my moment of panic as I tried to determine why we weren't falling, but before it had fully processed that we were standing on the transparent floor of a glass viewing platform, her mouth was on mine, and I no longer cared.

Fall. Float. Fracture into fragments absorbed by the surrounding stone—it didn't matter. I could think of nothing beyond the way she grabbed me, the intensity with which I knew she wanted me. The ferocity with which I needed her.

She walked me backward until my body collided with rough-edged Sutton stone, my hands finding the intricate tracery of a majestic Gothic window. It occurred to me, as I helped strip layers of winter clothing, that the unforgiving earth of the outer courtyard lay an unreasonable distance below us. I didn't know how admirably the stone mullions of eight-hundred-year-old architecture withstood the elements of time, but I couldn't bring myself to worry. So be it if tomorrow morning headlines across the globe read *Sand Seekers actress; dead at 25. Found mostly nude*—mostly, only due to the fact that my jeans were caught around my ankles, one tennis shoe still in place—*after rapturous rendezvous resulted in apparent fall from haunted castle window. Details to follow.*

When it came to the inevitability of dying, at least this way led the current list of choices.

Impatient, she turned me away from her, tangling one hand in my hair while the other sought the remaining inconvenience of clasps and buttons. I could feel her mouth against my ear, the staggered rasp of both our breathing, the weight of her healing body supported against me.

There was nothing gentle in her touch. Nothing delicate. No lingering kisses or trailing fingertips. In the darkness, with our bodies pressed against the window alcove, it was little more than the pent-up exchange of heartache. The expulsion of months of frustration. A sharing of hurts. Of healing. Of longing. Of yearning.

I fought the urge to close my eyes, finding the caressing breeze from the bay erotic against my exposed body. It was entirely prurient, knowing we were somewhere we were not meant to be, aware that a stone's throw from the dark parklands, the glowing homes of Mumbles were preparing to sit down for Christmas dinner. All one had to do was look up, to scan their eyes to the highest window in the castle. Would they see the shadows, find the desperate silhouettes searching for cathartic absolution, lost in one another?

Relenting to the feel of her traveling mouth and urgency of her persistent hands, I finally closed my eyes, giving up all thoughts of Mumbles, of castles, of the past and future. I found myself only in the present. Only in the throes of desire. Of the shedding of uncertainty that she still wanted me.


Later, Dillon laughed when I wondered aloud how many women had been fucked in that exact spot throughout the centuries. We were lying on the renovated glass floor, surrounded by the remnants of stately Gothic architecture, the stars burning overhead through the collapsed ceiling.

"Probably fewer than you think. For one, I imagine an altar once took up the majority of this space. And two, I believe sex in a chapel was deemed an explicit act of blasphemy."

I side-eyed her. "An entire castle at our disposal and you chose to lead me to the chapel?"

She shrugged. "There's no better view than from Alina's window."

"Alina?" Scanning our surroundings, I noticed for the first time the stone-cut aumbry and well-preserved piscina, the obvious hallmarks of a Catholic place of worship. "Alina—as in Castle Ghost Alina?"

"One in the same."

I wasn't religious. What I knew about Catholicism stemmed from playing Aldonza in a high school production of *Man of la Mancha*. I wouldn't have thought twice about putting a confessional booth to good use in the modern world. But igniting the wrath of a devotional medieval spirit? No thanks.

I started to push onto my elbow, but Dillon dropped an arm across my waist, barring me from rising. "Relax. You said to give the ol' girl a thrill. Who knows—maybe she liked watching?"

"If you're listening to this, Alina," I teased in a stage whisper, "please remember, it's her soul you want, not mine."

"She was imprisoned in the Tower of London while her husband was drawn and quartered by Edward II—I imagine we're low on her list when it comes to revenge."

"Your pillow talk is a bit rusty." I flipped on my side, flinching as my bare skin found the glass platform beneath our discarded pile of clothing. It was getting colder, the breeze picking up from the water, stirring the Welsh flag that flew atop the gatehouse. "Why do you know so much about this place?"

"I volunteered here a few summers when I was in school."

"Ah ha," I gave her a knowing smile, "so Lady Alina's no stranger to your late-night dalliances."

Her laugh was tighter than I expected as she brushed my teasing off, sitting up to rifle her jeans pockets. "I have something for you. I wanted to give it to you when we were alone."

I sat up, curious. Earlier that morning, she and Seren had given me a joint gift—a hardbound first edition of the *Sand Seekers* trilogy. The set had to have cost a fortune—a near-impossible collector's item to find, especially now, with the frenzy of the movies. I'd been thrilled with the thoughtfulness behind the present. In turn, I'd given her an out-of-print signed copy of *Sports Illustrated* with her all-time favorite triathlete, Michellie Jones, on the cover. I'd hunted the magazine down on eBay and spent a week stalking the auction lot, finally waking up at two AM in Japan to be certain I was the highest bidder.

In the end, the decades-old publication cost me a whopping twelve dollars—two dollars for the magazine and ten dollars for shipping. The paltry price had made me feel guilty. But the look on Dillon's face when she opened the package reassured me the value of a gift was rarely in the cost of the purchase.

"It's, um…" She fished a tiny tissue-wrapped parcel into the palm of her hand, tugging on a bow of hemp twine. "Maybe it's weird. I don't know. I…" Struggling to get the knot undone, she grew more flustered, until I reached out and swept it from her hand.

"It's my gift. I get to open it." I pulled out my phone and turned on its flashlight, undoing the string handily.

Inside the tissue, I found a delicate pendant of silver. A spoon, less than an inch in length, with a series of intricate designs crafted along its handle.

"It's a… a kind of promise. A gift given to someone you love. They're usually carved from wood, but I didn't think you'd have much need for that, so…" She flicked a finger toward the charm. "I asked the silversmith to make it with two hearts, because—"

"Because two hearts mean the love is reciprocated." I looked up from examining the flawless cast, taken by the design's beautiful complexity. "I know what a lovespoon is, Dillon."

Her smile was half surprise, half relief.

"And why would a girl from Hollywood know about an old Welsh tradition?"

"Because she fell in love with a girl from Wales." I rubbed the smooth silver between my thumb and forefinger before catching her eye and smiling. "Well, that, and they have an exhibit of them in the lounge at the Cardiff airport." Sweeping my hair over a bare shoulder, I unclasped the chain and held it out to her. "Will you?"

"Don't feel like you have to wear it." She hesitated. "It was just something I wanted you to have—to know."

"For someone remarkably intelligent, you really are an idiot." I tipped my head forward, exposing the nape of my neck. "I'm never taking it off."

She smiled—the slow, perfect, beautiful smile I loved—the one I could feel without even looking at her—and slipped the fragile chain into place. "Are you going to write it into your next nudity clause?"

She fastened the clasp, pausing to kiss the top of my shoulder. "*All clothing negotiable except for my tiny comfort spoon?*"

"I think I'll phrase it exactly like that," I sassed, twisting to make a grab for her wrists, but finding her superior strength turned the tables against me. Her counterattack immediately left me flat on my back.

It wasn't a defeat I minded.

"And your premieres?" She held herself aloft above me.

"I'm wearing it."

"Golden Globes?" Her lips moved to the hollow of my throat.

"Still wearing it."

"BAFTA?"

"Wearing it." The words came out through clenched teeth as her mouth made a slow procession to my hip bone.

"What about the Met Gala?" She spoke into the ticklish crease of my thigh.

I laughed. "They're never going to invite me to the Met Gala."

"Fair enough. That would require a sense of fashion."

"Hey!" I pressed my palms against the wall of stone, trying to keep myself from squirming. "Be nice!"

"I think I'm nice." She eased my legs apart, sliding her hands down the slope of my calves to my ankles. Unlike earlier, with the frantic rush, the impatient desire leaving no room for lingering, she was now torturously slow, going to great efforts to tease me. "You think any of Alina's husbands were this nice?"

I didn't answer.

"I bet not." She dipped her head, trailing her lips against me, before abruptly sitting up again. "Not that I can blame them. She probably spent more time kneeling at the altar, exalting the virtues of agape, than she did practicing eros on her knees in the bedroom. Not very *nice*, if you ask me."

"*Dillon!*" I covered my face with my hands to prevent me from going with my first inclination—which was to strangle her. "Fine! You win! You're *nice*!"

"How nice?"

"*Very* nice." Her lips brushed me again, and this time, when I raised my hips to meet her, she didn't pull away. "*Exceedingly* nice." Whatever it took to get her back on track. "*Tremendously* nice." To stop her from waxing philosophical with her head between my legs.

She smiled. "See—that wasn't hard."

I bit back a cutting retort—willing to forfeit this battle to win the war—but my treaty was interrupted by the grating sound of metal striking metal, and the shriek of an angry hinge.

Flying upright, I clipped Dillon's head with my chin, and then paused, trying to hear over the drubbing of my heart.

"Who's up there?"

A gate slammed closed.

*Holy fuck.* I looked at Dillon.

"Oh, fuck me!" she hissed.

*Yeah, the time for that had clearly departed.*

Not needing any additional motivation, I lunged to my feet, grabbing for my clothes—her clothes—whatever threads of fiber I could find to tug on.

She was still half dressed—courtesy of her knee brace—and was on her feet and ready to run before I'd even pulled up my pants.

"Turn off your torch!"

In my current state of turmoil, it took too long to register her meaning. She reached out and snatched my phone, flicking off the flashlight.

"Okay, come on, we can go through the south keep."

Again, I struggled to keep pace with her, my shoulders colliding with ninety-degree turns and toes stumbling over jagged steps. Down a pitch-black staircase into an even darker hall, I caught hold of the tail of her t-shirt as we burst out a cockeyed doorway and ran for the west curtain wall.

"Hey!" A man's voice bellowed, his shadowy shape moving across the courtyard lawn. "Stop!"

*Had yelling* stop *ever actually worked in the history of crime?*

Dillon threw on the brakes as we reached the drainage pipe, waiting to shove me head-first to the other side.

"Head for the wood," she whispered as her crutches preceded her through the pipe.

Inside the castle, the man's curses rang off the stone, but we were already halfway across the open parkland, making for the shelter of the trees.

"Oh, my God," I panted when we'd finally waded through waist-high foliage to find the woodland hiking trail leading to the main road. "What the fuck, Dil—?" My words were cut short as I stumbled over an exposed tree root and a low-lying branch smacked me in the face.

The perfect abridged synopsis of the way my evening was going.

Dillon was still laughing as she caught my elbow, steadying me. "Mr. Roberts—the groundskeeper. He must have seen your light."

"You didn't mention a groundskeeper!"

"I wasn't expecting him to be around. He lives off property."

As we picked our way out of the last of the trees and onto Mumbles Road, I paused to take inventory of what I was wearing:

Dillon's jacket. My unbuttoned pants. Underwear on one leg. Both shoes.

Which meant my bra, t-shirt, sweatshirt, jacket, scarf, beanie, sunglasses, and dignity had been lost to the holy chapel of Oystermouth.

*Sorry, Alina.*

But whatever. Centuries of ladies left alone while their lords went off to war—no one was going to convince me Dillon and I were the first pair of women to find pleasure within those walls. *Against* those walls. However you wanted to look at it.

"Uber will be here in three minutes," Dillon said, looking up from her phone.

An older couple passed us as we waited on the corner for our ride. I struggled not to laugh from behind the upturned collar of Dillon's jacket as they gave us a wide berth, no doubt assuming we were a pair of derelicts wandered out from the pub. Dillon's hair was wild, slick with sweat and dusted in cobwebs. Her elbows and thighs were streaked with grass and mud from our belly crawl through the drainage pipe, and half the foliage in Mumbles was stuck to the velcro of her knee brace.

"Happy Christmas," she said cheerfully, prompting the pair to pick up their pace.

The Uber driver gave us a long glance in her rearview mirror, and then Dillon turned the chat to the latest Wrexham football match until we reached her front door.

"Longer coastal walk than anticipated?" Seren called as the two of us tried to tiptoe across the hardwood floor. She and her mom were playing a game of chess in the living room and had both looked up from the board.

I froze midstep, feeling like a rabbit caught in the crosshairs.

There was a walk of shame, and then there was *a walk of shame.* This certainly fell under the category of the latter.

Dillon struck a casual pose, leaning against the doorway. "Nah. Cut a little short, if you ask me."

The burn of my cheeks rivaled the glow of Christmas lights on the Fraser fir.

Jacqueline gave us a calculating once-over, tapping a black rook thoughtfully against the table. "Where's your hat, Dillon?"

Code for: *why is Kam half-dressed and wearing your coat?*

Dillon was unperturbed. "Somewhere in Oystermouth."

The way she said it was a challenge and from the hardening line of Jacqueline's lips, appeared to be received the same. I'd expected Seren to laugh, but she didn't even smile.

"You went to the castle?" Jacqueline set the rook down.

"Yeah—til Old Roberts came around."

"I see," said her mother, returning her gaze to the game. "Well, the two of you should go tidy up. We've been holding dinner."

"What was that?" I asked once we were behind the closed door of Dillon's bedroom.

She took a seat at the end of her bed, working a thorn out of her t-shirt. "She's not fond of the castle."

"Yeah. I got that."

To my surprise, she didn't make me ask her to elaborate.

"It's where I started to meet Henrik." She flicked the thorn onto her nightstand. "Outside of training."

I paused my efforts to eliminate my hair of forest debris, looking into her dresser mirror to catch her reflection.

"Okay." I held her gaze. "Then why bring me there?"

She didn't look away. "Because I want it back. The things he took from me."

I nodded, waiting to see if there was more she wanted to say. She made it easy to forget, sometimes, armored behind her bravado— behind her humor, her bold confidence, her endless drive—that she hurt in ways I couldn't see. In ways I didn't know how to fix.

But instead, she stood, coming to lean over my shoulder, still holding my gaze in the mirror. A wryness in her smile said she was done with the conversation, wanting to set it aside. "Come on, Kam-Kameryn," she pressed her lips against my ear, "if you join me for a shower, maybe I'll finish being nice."

# Scene 46

"She's canny blinding, I tell you! Poetry in motion. And those white pants—"

"*Sam.*" Dillon wasn't about to listen to Sam express her thoughts on her sister's skintight breeches. They were on their way back from watching Seren compete in a 4-star in Windsor, where she'd come within half a point of sweeping the tournament. It was late on a Sunday night, and the train was nearly vacant.

"She should have won! It ought to be illegal to look that good and come in second!"

"Wild how the riders win for their performance instead of their fashion."

"Exactly what I'm saying! The bloke who bagged it certainly didn't send my heart galloping."

Dillon decided it probably wasn't the time to tell Sam she was pretty certain that same bloke *definitely* sent Seren's heart galloping. The American rider, Jeremy Hartman, had been spending more and more time in her sister's company. But there was no reason to bring Sam down off her high.

The train pulled to a stop at *Hayes and Harlington* and a group of rowdy, inebriated kids piled into the empty carriage, cussing one another and pelting a football off the windows and ceiling.

"Sod off," a dark-haired boy shouted when the ball collided with his forehead. A roughhousing scuffle ensued that sent a second boy sprawling in the aisle at their feet.

"Sweet kicks," he said by way of apology for landing on Sam's custom *Nikes*. Climbing to his feet, he cast a quick look at Dillon, and then returned for a doubletake. "Aren't you…?"

"Will you kindly fuck off?" Dillon didn't give him a chance to finish his sentence. She knew where it was leading and wasn't in the mood for it.

The kid was taken aback but didn't push the situation, and instead scurried to where his mates had resumed their horseplay at the other end of the carriage.

"You might want to reel it in a bit," Sam cautioned once they were alone again. "Can't go on snapping at every person who casts a glance at you."

"That's where you're wrong." Dillon pressed herself closer to the vibration of the wall. "I'll snap at whoever the bloody hell I want." She'd been irritable all day, uncomfortable making an appearance in public. For three months, she'd been holed up in Wales, hiding with her head in the sand.

Ever since photos of her and Kam had turned up on the internet.

It had been the middle of January, three days after Kam flew home to Los Angeles. She'd called Dillon that morning in tears to warn her about the tabloids. The driver who'd picked them up after their escapade at the castle had evidently not been entirely oblivious.

According to Kam's lawyer, the woman sat on the dashcam photos for almost two weeks, battling an ethical dilemma, but in the end, each photo she sold made her more than an entire year's wages driving for Uber. The payout neutralized the sting of being terminated for her violation of privacy toward their patrons.

"You never could do anything on a mediocre level," Sam had mulled, sipping Jack in her coffee while poring over the internet carnage in Jaqueline Sinclair's kitchen. She'd taken the first train to Wales after Dillon texted her about the images going viral. "Leave it to you to get caught post-shag with the hottest movie star on the planet. I guess there's not much room to deny it?" She let out a low whistle, zooming in to view the unmistakable smear of lipstick on Dillon's collar. The stills were wide-angle, high definition, a clear representation of exactly what had transpired.

"Of course we're going to deny it!" Dillon hadn't quit pacing the kitchen. "Kam's on her way to Morocco to finalize filming. The last thing she needs is this rubbish trailing her to the Middle East!"

"The last thing she needs or the last thing you need?"

Dillon stabbed a finger onto the counter. "The last thing *either* of us needs. Don't lay this all on me, Sam. You know this will affect her career."

"I also know she's made it clear to you she doesn't care—"

"She was crying, for fuck's sake—"

"I got a fiver that says she was crying because she's terrified history is going to repeat itself," Sam said coldly, distant from the empathetic ear Dillon had desired. "After Kelsey—"

Dillon cut her off. "I'm not running away from this, alright? I love Kam. I'm not leaving her. I just..." she glanced at Sam's iPad, where half a dozen browsers hung open, the top headlines flashing across the LED screen.

*Out Athlete Identified With Kameryn Kingsbury—Is Love In The Air?*

*Questions Arise for Sand Seekers Star Caught On Camera With Former Girlfriend of Kelsey Evans*

A third, featuring her Team GB headshot, read in bold: *Everything We Know About Dillon Sinclair* and then wrapped her life into a series of bullet points.

She slumped into a chair. "You're right. It's not her I'm protecting. I just—I don't know how to deal with this level of scrutiny, Sam. I can't handle the press. The attention. Maybe..." She leaned against the island bar, taking in the quiet surroundings of her mother's kitchen. "Maybe when Los Angeles is over. Just not now. Not while I'm feeling so much pressure."

Sam said nothing. They both knew *not now* was just another variation of *not ever*.

And so while Kam faced an initial barrage of homophobic hate while filming in a country famous for its intolerance, Dillon had hidden away in Wales, insulated from the outside world. She focused on her training, steered clear of all social media, and let Kam's PR team do what they did best—quell the rampant rumors.

*A night out with friends.*

*A proud ally of the LGBTQ community.*

All the implications she was still straight as an arrow.

It was doubtful many people believed it, but as was the habit with celebrity gossip, when the next A-lister took a misstep—in this case, thanks were to be offered to J Lo for divorce rumors #4—the hyperfocus of the zoom lenses turned another direction.

And for the most part, life went on. Dillon ignored the sidelong glances at the aquatics center, performed batch deletes of emails and messages, and tried to let the intrusive comments roll off her shoulders.

Especially when they came to her by way of strangers—like today at the horse show, when a Dutch rider she'd never met stopped to ask if she would introduce her to Kameryn at the Olympics. Or the creepiness of an American spectator who'd trailed her through the barn aisles to the stands, where she spent Seren's entire dressage test surreptitiously clicking photos of Dillon with her mobile.

"So—you just planning on being a tosser from now until the end of forever?" Sam queried as the train started moving again.

At the other end of the coach, the boys were passing around a bottle of cheap whiskey.

Dillon watched the station disappear out the window. "I wouldn't want to deviate from my status quo."

Sam ran her fingers through her short hair, unsmiling. "Tell me— how are the rest of things going, marra? You've been quiet since your last appointment."

Quiet—because she had nothing to report. It had been five months since her surgery. She'd been back to cycling for nearly eight weeks, but still, Dr. Monaghan wouldn't release her for running. The thickness of the cartilage had yet to meet his requirements.

"Time," he kept telling her.

Time she didn't have. Already, she'd watched Bermuda from the unwelcome comforts of her mam's lounge, staring at the live footage as Elyna Laurent breezed to an easy win on the blue carpet. Now, there were less than four weeks before she was in danger of viewing Yokohama in the same position.

Discomfitted beneath Sam's scrutinizing glance, she self-consciously rubbed at her knee, aware of the way the joint shifted and clicked in its new, uncomfortable pattern. "It's going."

"Yeah?" Sam lifted a brow. "Which direction?"

"Better every day," Dillon lied, trying to force aside her growing agitation. For months she'd tried to focus on the positive. To follow the advice of her sports psychologist, who reminded her setbacks led to comebacks—and all that other fustian nonsense he was paid to say. But each day that passed drew her nearer to a desperation that was getting harder to keep beneath the surface.

Sam steepled her fingers. "What's the word on Yokohama?"

Dillon shrugged. "He thinks I have a chance."

Only, that wasn't what he'd said. A week earlier, over a tele-appointment, Dr. Monaghan had reviewed her latest x-rays and advised her—

unless her body miraculously grew two millimeters of cartilage over the next twenty-five days—the Japanese race was out of the question.

*Take it slow, wait another month, and we'll reconvene.*

As if she had another month to sit around and do nothing. Leeds—her final opportunity to qualify for Los Angeles—was in eighty-seven days. She couldn't cut it that close. She couldn't leave that much to chance.

"Well, that's good, innit?" Sam tapped out an enthusiastic drum roll on the hard plastic of the seat in front of her. "A chance beats a sharp stick in the eye!"

Before Dillon could muster her canned optimism—*sure thing, one day at a time*—the boy from earlier staggered down the aisle.

"I know you told me to piss off," he planted himself in front of them, "but my sister's a huge fan of yours, and she's not going to forgive me if I don't ask you for your autograph."

Out of habit, Sam made a move to take the pen he'd pulled from his school bag, but he shook his head. "Sorry, I mean her." He chucked his newly stubbled chin at Dillon. "My sister came in top ten in juniors at last year's WTCS championship and you're basically her idol."

The kid wasn't lying. You didn't throw out the acronym for the governing body of triathlon without knowing what you were talking about.

"Alright." Dillon felt a twinge of regret for her earlier beratement. His interest in her had nothing to do with Kam. "What's her name?"

"Olivia."

She signed the back of a Costa Coffee pastry wrapper. *Olivia, Keep Racing.*

"Ta." The boy pocketed the wax paper.

Another lad from the group appeared over his shoulder, waving the half-empty bottle of whiskey. "Ladies care for a swig?"

For too long, Dillon stared at the Jameson label. She hadn't had a drink in—she didn't even know when. Sometime before she broke up with Kelsey. She and alcohol made poor choices together. Ones that didn't bear repeating. But tonight, it felt tempting.

"No," she finally said, aware of Sam's side-eye at her delay. "My best to your sister, mate."

"Cheers. She'll be rooting for you this summer."

Sam waited until the pair had woven their way back to the opposite end of the carriage before leaning in toward Dillon.

"You sure everything's all right, Sinc?"

"Ace." Dillon brushed off her concern. "Knackered, is all."

"You know I'm here, yeah, if you ever need a chat?"

Dillon waved her off. "It's all good, Sam, really. Every day's forward progress."

*More headshrinker rhetoric.*

Sam bumped her shin with her toe. "I ever tell you you're a piss poor fibber?" But she let it go.

Two stops later, they parted at Paddington, promising to get together soon. Dillon was staying back at her flat in London, scheduled to meet with a new physiotherapist, and assured Sam she'd call her in the next couple of days. They'd get dinner. Maybe she'd even allow Sam to drag her from hiding to catch an Arsenal match the following weekend.

Something both of them knew wasn't going to happen.

After Sam disappeared on the underground, Dillon skirted the turnstiles to the *Bakerloo Line* and took the stairs to the street exit. She could feel her knee with every step, the subtle grind that never seemed to vanish.

*Another month.*

The words rattled around her head. How easy it was for Dr. Monaghan to sit in his plush corner office and say that. To nod like he understood and then tap his pen against the screen and tell her to be patient.

*We knew from the start a summer recovery would be a long shot.*

She stepped off the curb, fishing her vibrating phone out of her pocket.

Kam was calling.

Behind her, a cabbie honked, hustling her along the crosswalk. Dillon flashed him a two-finger salute and sent Kam to voicemail. It was late in Morocco. She would call her in the morning.

Tentative, she jogged a few steps onto the pavement.

*You're basically her idol,* the kid on the train had said. *She'll be rooting for you this summer.*

Her gait felt stiff, her steps heavy beneath the staccato rhythm of her trainers.

Quickening her pace, she continued down the street, past the off-license advertising bottles of Smirnoff in the window.

There were twenty-five days until Yokohama.

She lengthened her stride, ignoring the protests from her weakened knee, and disappeared into the darkness of Hyde Park.
Twenty five days.
*Fuck Dr. Monaghan.*

# Scene 47

I stood on the balcony of my seventeenth-floor high-rise, holding my modem up in an offering to the gods of WiFi. Briefly, my computer—perched haphazardly on a Balencia chaise lounge—chimed its connection, before promptly losing signal. I cussed, tempted to fling the device over the railing onto Pacific Coast Highway.

It was bullshit to live where I lived and still have sketchy service. I would have had more luck connecting to *Tico's Taco Shop* but the owner had gotten wise and applied a password.

Sweeping through the wide French doors, I reset the router and pulled a bottle of Château Lafite out of the wine cooler. As I waited for the box to reset, I tipped the chilled red into a Waterford crystal goblet Dani had sent as a housewarming gift. Her version of a peace offering. The sight of the glass suddenly intensified my loathing for the superfluous opulence around me. The walls of windows. The high beam ceilings. The travertine and hand-carved crown molding and Miele dishwasher larger than my first refrigerator.

I'd moved to the oceanfront penthouse six months earlier. It was my second move in as many years, and though I'd instantly hated the extravagance of the suite and the maddening drive from the studio during rush hour, the building served its purpose. It was private. It was secure. And it was designed for people like me: people who lived high-profile careers and didn't care how much they had to pay to buy their little piece of freedom.

But it didn't stop me from missing my six-hundred-square-foot, run-down one-bedroom in WeHo.

I loved that apartment. I missed the bohemian vibe of the community. The tree-lined walk to the farmer's market. The neighbor's cat who used to sit in my screened window and yowl the song of her people.

And more than anything, in my present predicament, I missed the steadfast reliability of the internet.

Dillon's start time in Yokohama was in less than twenty minutes.

The router signal turned green, so I collected my glass and returned to the panoramic view from the balcony.

As I waited for the *World Triathlon* livestream to load, I sipped the heady Rothschild and watched a flock of pelicans dip their wings into the golden shimmer of the Pacific.

I knew when the leasing agent showed me the luxury apartment, she felt it was her mention of the in-house five-star restaurant and rooftop infinity pool that tipped me over the edge to sign the contract. Little did she know, it was actually the view of the Santa Monica Pier—the sight of the pilings where I'd shared that kiss with Dillon—that sealed the deal on my new residence.

This evening, the distant murmur of the landmark carnival provided a background ambiance as I silently pleaded to any deity who would listen to help see Dillon across the finish line. All she had to do was place in the top twenty. It shouldn't have been a concern. Aside from her single DNF, she had never come in lower than fifth on the Japanese course in the eight times she had run it.

But it *was* a concern.

For the last three weeks, she'd returned to full training despite lacking medical clearance. I hadn't known until a few days ago that Dr. Monaghan had seen her name on the start list for Yokohama and dropped her as a patient. She'd brushed off my immediate alarm and told me not to worry.

"I feel good, Kam. Better than I did before Hamburg."

Every fiber of my being wanted to believe her.

But I also knew her.

I knew she would do anything… give up anything… fight through anything… to have a shot at another Olympic medal. The long-term consequences weren't her priority.

Her mom, Seren, Sam, even her coach, Alistair, had begged her not to push it. But she'd refused to listen.

So, in the end, what choice did I have but to show her support when everyone else was against her? She had enough people telling her she would fail. I couldn't bring myself to join them.

The livefeed clicked over and a commentator's voice funneled through my speakers. I wasn't surprised to see the cameras on Dillon as she stretched out her hamstrings. The media coverage of her return to triathlon had been relentless. We'd known, after the uproar of her name getting linked with mine, she'd be unable to avoid the spotlight.

It had been expected. But I'd hoped, after four months, the obsession from the press would have dwindled.

*Wishful thinking.*

Everyone loved a comeback story. Combine it with rumors of a scandalous affair, and the added pressure of the upcoming Olympics, and it was a plot practically scripted for Hollywood.

Dillon had taken it in stride, never once blaming me for the unwanted publicity. We stuck to our narrative—we were friends—and instead of me flying to watch her in Japan—where I wanted to be—I'd spent the previous evening out with Elliott and his circle, providing fodder for the paparazzi.

Apparently, it hadn't helped, because Dillon was still the race day headliner.

"No question all eyes this morning are on Great Britain's most decorated triathlete," the American pundit said as the footage zoomed in on Dillon's sunburnt cheeks, hollow beneath her goggles. She did a couple of jumping jacks and dumped a bottle of water into the neckline of her wetsuit. "The big question today is—after an eight-month hiatus from competition, following what was nearly a career-ending accident—does Dillon Sinclair have what it takes to punch her ticket to her fourth Olympics?"

"You know, Mike, if it were anyone other than Sinclair," an English commentator answered, "I'd stack the odds against her. But I've watched the Welshwoman compete for over ten years, and I'll be the first to say, if anyone can do this—she can. I don't think the world of endurance sports has ever seen a grittier competitor."

The two men went back and forth, chatting stats and rankings, as the camera panned out to reveal the sixty-nine women stepping to their marks on the swim pontoon. I skimmed over the faces I'd come to know well—Alecia Finch, Georgina Potter, Elyna Laurent—and focused only on Dillon, whose gaze was on the water. She looked calm. She looked confident.

I, on the other hand, felt like I was going to throw up.

The horn blew, and a split second later the swimmers were crashing through the churning tide of Tokyo Bay. A washing machine cycle of kicking legs and swinging arms obscured all visibility of individual athletes, but as the strongest swimmers separated from the group, I could pick out Dillon's neon orange cap edging toward the lead.

There was no question she would be first out of the water. The commentators agreed. The swim and cycle were her opportunity to get ahead of her competition before backing off on the run. Despite it going against everything in her nature, it wasn't in her strategy to podium. Today, it was only about qualifying. Then she would sit out Leeds and turn her full attention to Los Angeles.

I paced, unable to keep seated, unable to stand still. Twice I looped my balcony, returning to peek over the lounge at my laptop, feeling like a child viewing a scary movie through splayed fingers and covered ears. I hated to watch but had to know.

Dillon was out of the swim and onto the bike, making a clean transition. Behind her, A breakaway group of eleven women chased in pursuit. I immediately took note that Elyna Laurent was amongst them.

"Sinclair's done an admirable job of giving herself some breathing room," the English commentator observed as Dillon moved into the third and final loop of the bike course. The drone footage showed a sizeable lead—but not enough for my comfort.

My phone chimed, and I swiped a sweaty palm across the lock screen. It was a text from Sam Huntley.

*She's bloody got this!*

I tried to send a heart, but my shaking fingers clicked on an emoji of a duck instead. I didn't bother to correct it.

The footage turned grainy, my internet threatening to freeze, and in the stupidity of my frustration I snapped the laptop closed. It took an eternity to reconnect, and by the time the livestream rebooted, the athletes were out of T2 and into the run.

I scanned to the real-time rankings at the bottom of the screen. Dillon had fallen to fourteenth place.

*Fuck.*

It was okay, I schooled myself. Even in her prerace interview, she'd made it clear she would allow herself leeway in the run. Today was about conservation.

I closed my eyes, chorusing a silent mantra. *Top twenty. Top twenty. Top twenty.*

"Oh, that is unfortunate," the American commentator said, interrupting my meditation. "It appears Dillon Sinclair has incurred a time penalty."

My eyes flew open.

*This couldn't be happening.*

Dillon was stopped in front of an official holding up a stopwatch. Her head was tilted to the sky, her frustration evident.

The American continued, "Word's just come in the British athlete is being penalized for dropping her goggles outside her swim bin."

"It's truly some hard luck," the English commentator lamented. "Sixty seconds is a steep punishment for an inadvertent equipment violation."

"I think we've all been there, Andy—moving too fast through transition."

I held my breath the entire time she was sidelined, internally screaming as runners continued to pass her.

*Fifteen.*

*Seventeen.*

*Twenty-one.*

I pummeled my palm into the cushion of the chaise lounge. "Come on, you bastard! It's been sixty seconds!"

Finally, the official clicked the stopwatch and Dillon bolted into the fray of runners. She was in twenty-sixth place.

The English pundit groaned. "It's a bit of a sticky wicket now for Sinclair—having to play catch-up. There's no question this is exactly *not* what she wanted."

"I wish I could say that stride looked more comfortable, Andy. If I were a betting man, I'd wager that knee—just six months out of surgery—isn't prepared for heavy sprinting."

I studied Dillon's face. Her jaw was tight, the subtle crow's feet at the corner of her eyes deepening. Having been forced to increase her pace, there was no question she was hurting.

The pair continued their banter as I tore apart my cuticles, the minutes ticking by with excruciating slowness. Dillon overcame a runner. And then another.

*Twenty-fourth place.*

I sat. Sipped wine. Stood. Paced. Sat again. I tried not to notice her shortening stride. Her noticeable grimace.

My attention was suddenly returned to the commentary when I heard my name mentioned by the American.

"I don't know, Andy—if there was a chance Kameryn Kingsbury was waiting for me at the finish line, I'd probably give it a go, too, even if I had to do it one-legged."

Was he even kidding? They were there to report on a professional race and this clown managed to slip in my name?

*Hard fucking pass, Grandpa.*

The English analyst offered an uncomfortable laugh before steering his cohost back to a more appropriate narrative.

"It looks like it's going to be a good day for France. Elyna Laurent's pulled well into the lead, with her French teammate, Josephine Durand, not far behind her."

They were on the final lap of the run, less than a kilometer from the finish.

*Fall,* was all I could think as I stared at the Frenchwoman's graceful stride soaring across the pavement. Trip. Stumble. Faceplant. Whatever it took to keep her from winning.

It wasn't fair, I knew, rooting for an injury. Dillon wouldn't approve. I'd never once heard her wish ill on a competitor. The only way she wanted to win was to beat them at their best—because if they weren't at their best, was she beating them at all?

*Whatever.*

I'd leave the righteousness to Dillon. I wasn't that noble. I would have traded an ungodly sum of money to see her run down by a wild pack of tanukis. Or waylaid by a snow monkey. Maybe slip on a banana peel. Anything to see the Frenchwoman eat shit—to avoid the misery of watching her draped with another medal.

It was a hope born in cloud-cuckoo-land, as a few minutes later, the lean, leggy bitch set a new course record.

I hated her. I didn't care if my anger was displaced. If she wasn't the one who deserved my contempt. I couldn't stand the sight of her demure, awkward smile.

As the cameras focused on the athletes beginning to cross the finish line, I stared at the bottom of my screen, watching Dillon's ranking.

Twenty-third place.

Twenty-second.

"Please," I breathed, casting the word to the sea breeze fanning my burning cheeks. "Please let her do this." Every ounce of energy I could muster, I channeled across the ocean.

"Oh, this has become nailbiting!" the American chimed as Dillon reached the straightaway amidst a pack of five runners. "It doesn't get more exciting than this! Sinclair's entered a footrace on the final two hundred meters."

I flicked the sound off. I couldn't take it. I watched in unbearable silence as Dillon overcame a Spaniard, and then fought, stride for stride, with an Australian runner. The pair were at the lead of the small group, jockeying for position. Dillon's gait looked stiff. Her cadence was uneven. Sweat was streaming down her face, her breathing forced between clenched teeth.

*Please, God.*

They were a hundred feet from the tape.

Fifty.

Twenty.

Two yards from the finish line, the Australian pulled ahead, hurdling herself across the timer. Dillon crossed a half second behind her.

I sat, stunned, watching her drop to the ground on the sideline. A medical staff member knelt beside her, but she brushed him away.

*Twenty-first.*

A news alert flashed at the bottom of my screen.

*Legendary Welsh Athlete Fails to Qualify for Olympic Team*

In a fit of disbelief, I swept my arm across the patio end table, sending the Waterford crystal shattering against the sandstone tile. Wine pooled at my feet before the rivulet of red slowly made its way to drip over the side of the glass railing. I choked back a sob. Never had I imagined she wouldn't do it. That was the magic of Dillon Sinclair—she could do anything she put her mind to.

I stared emptily at my screen as athletes continued to finish the race, thrilled with their top-third placing.

How strange it felt—to see people smiling.

With the footage still on mute, I watched Elyna Laurent's post-race interview. I watched her nod. I watched her lips move with robotic, one-word answers. And then I watched her walk away without an ounce of joy or celebration.

I should have felt sorry for her. I didn't doubt her story varied much from Dillon's. She was just another pawn, the two of them sharing the same loathsome denominator.

But at present, she meant nothing to me. I could think only of Dillon. What I would say when she called. How I would help her move forward.

There was still Leeds. Seven weeks away, she had another chance.

But I'd seen the look on her face. The pain she'd been in.

On my lap, my phone buzzed. It was a text from Seren.

*Please, Kam. You have to convince her not to race again.*

I sat on my balcony until the sun disappeared beneath the silvery waters of the horizon. Until the traffic waned on the boulevard. Until the lights dimmed on the pier. My body ached when I finally dragged myself to my feet, my muscles stiff and heart heavy.

Standing at the railing, I replied to Seren.

*I can't, I'm sorry. I have to support her.*

# Scene 48

A stoop-shouldered woman in an Uncle Sam hat swung a hemp cord necklace toward Dillon.

"Name on grain of rice? Unique gift for special boyfriend."

Dillon would have ignored her, having already managed to avoid the other hundred clamoring Venice Beach street vendors, but the word *boyfriend* made her laugh.

"Not today, thanks."

The woman's smirk turned wry. "Perhaps for pretty girlfriend? I have all names. If not your spelling, I make you one."

Dillon paused in front of her table. The last thing she needed was a cheap boardwalk trinket, but it was Kam's birthday. They'd agreed on no presents, just time spent together, but she thought the chintzy tourist souvenir might make her smile. A token reminiscent of the stuffed dolphin won on the pier in what felt like a lifetime prior.

"Alright." She leaned against the cart. "You'll make one custom?"

"Anything you like."

She sorted through the hollow glass charms, choosing a sea turtle. "Can you put two grains in there?"

The woman shrugged. "Ten dollar more."

"Deal." Dillon told her her name, and then spelled out Kam-Kameryn.

"Ohhh, with *K*, like big movie star." The woman's eyes grew to a disproportionate size behind her magnifying glass as she printed the letters with impossibly steady hands. "She live near here, you know? Not far."

"Oh yeah?" Dillon cocked a disinterested hip, running her fingers through a box of beads. "Smashing."

"Must be nice. Live in big glass tower. Another fifteen dollar—I show you where."

Pulling a pair of twenties from her pocket, Dillon politely passed on the tour. Wouldn't the woman have been disappointed to learn that same *big movie star* had already given her the backstage, VIP, full-benefits package entirely free of charge?

Kam's flat was only a few blocks away, just past the Santa Monica Pier.

It was as excessive as Kam had warned her it would be. A grandiose rooftop suite screaming with all the amenities of the Hollywood elite. There was no semblance to the life of the girl who'd felt her luck had peaked when she signed her first blockbuster contract for less than a tenth of what her male co-stars made. Recently, a headline had run in the *Daily Mail* reporting the final *Sand Seekers* film had landed Kameryn Kingsbury one of the most lucrative deals in cinema history.

The luxuriant penthouse overlooking the ocean was a glaring confirmation.

"It's okay, you can tell me you hate it," Kam had said a week prior when Dillon first arrived. "I know it's ridiculous, especially for how little time I spend here."

Dillon had given a cursory glance through the chef's kitchen, before stopping in the palatial living room surrounded by walls of glass. "I mean, it is a bit cramped," she'd teased, "but it's got you—and a kettle—so it'll do in a pinch."

"Well, I'm glad I got billing above the kettle."

"Who's to say I listed my necessities in order of priority?"

Kam rolled her eyes. "You're an ass—" but the rebuke was cut off in a shrill of laughter as Dillon caught her belt loop and dragged her to her.

"An arse who's glad to be here," she whispered against her temple, and realized she meant it.

For the first time since her failure to qualify for Los Angeles, the world felt a little brighter. A little less daunting. Simply being with Kam restored a glimmer of hope for a future she'd no longer been able to see clearly.

Three weeks earlier, her defeat in Yokohama had felt paralyzing. It had taken something out of Dillon she didn't know how to reawaken.

The loss had left the upcoming race in Leeds a question mark—one she still wasn't sure how to answer. She no longer knew if she had what it took to drag herself back to the starting line.

She'd failed by *two-tenths* of a second.

Her knee was giving her trouble—unquestionable damage done from pushing too hard, too fast—but it wasn't her fitness that left her uncertain. Had it been her body that let her down, or even the unexpected derailment of the penalty, she would have accepted the loss more easily. Injuries, time faults—they were the unavoidable variables of competing.

But it was her mind that hadn't felt right. Her conviction that went slipping.

Coming off the bike in a near-perfect transition, she'd found the first steps of her run plagued with unwelcome thoughts that snaked their way to the surface. Thoughts she hadn't known how to silence.

If she qualified—even at the time, with a strong lead, her mind had been set on *if*, not *when*—what came next?

There were two scenarios at the Olympics.

One: she won.

The other: she didn't.

It should have only been the latter that frightened her. The concern that, if she lost, she still wouldn't know how to concede. She'd promised Seren if it got to be too much—and it *had* gotten to be too much—she'd hang up her ambitions and walk away. She knew she didn't have another season in her, let alone a four-year campaign. But if a loss was what it came to, would she really be able to let it go and give up on her gold medal dreams?

She didn't know. And it bothered her even more that the alternative outcome came with its own set of worries.

What happened if she won and it still wasn't enough? If she still felt this hollow? This incomplete? What purpose did she have if there was nothing left to prove?

It was that idea that scared her more than anything.

Over and over, she'd replayed the events of Yokohama. She'd asked herself a thousand times if she'd been careless with her goggles, purposely flirting with the possibility of a penalty? When it came to the footrace at the finish, could she swear to herself she'd truly given everything? Or had she held back, justifying the loss on the pain in her knee?

The truth was, she wasn't sure.

And still today, three weeks later, her future felt unclear.

However, of one thing she was certain, being there with Kam—spending the days cloistered behind the walls of the laughably lavish suite, lounging in the rooftop pool, swimming at dawn in the sea—had made her failure of Yokohama more bearable, and alleviated her all-consuming thoughts on the upcoming decision on Leeds.

Dillon pocketed the sea turtle and told the old street vendor to keep the change.

On a different morning, she would have walked the long way back to Kam's flat via the water. The cushion of the sand had proven good for her recovery after a run. But there wasn't time for that. Tonight, Kam was hosting a small party in celebration of her twenty-sixth birthday. It was something she'd been planning ever since returning from her on-location filming in the Middle East.

Dillon wasn't looking forward to it. Despite knowing the people coming were Kam's most intimate friends—all of which were privy to her relationship with Dillon—the thought of socializing with them made her uneasy. She wasn't sure how she'd fit in.

But today wasn't about her, and she wanted nothing more than for Kam to have the perfect evening.

"The secret to good fondue," Dani Hallwell gave a practiced flip of her hair over the strapless neckline crossing her shoulders, "is in the amount of wine added. The more, the merrier."

Dillon watched from the corner of her eye as Kam's co-star, Elliott, the target of Dani's attention—and ill-advised cooking counsel—glanced up from the hors-d'oeuvres table. "Is it? Well, my compliments to the chef. This is truly epicurean."

Misconstruing his polite acknowledgment for interest, Dani slapped on an air of authority. All evening she'd been attempting to engage the actor in conversation, and apparently decided this was her golden opportunity. "If I were to guess, I'd say a 1959 Latour was used in this specific dish. I tend to have a good palate for these things."

Elliott paused with a roasted Brussels sprout midway to his mouth. "A red wine? In fondue?"

Dillon had to hand it to Dani—the ignorant twit covered her blunder with a convincing wave of her hand. "A little kitchen secret. It's what makes the cheese so creamy."

"Huh." He popped the sprout into his mouth and looked to where Dillon was setting out flatware in the kitchen, offering her a subtle this-chick-is-full-of-shit wag of his brow. "How odd."

Dillon had to look away to cover her smile.

She'd been surprised how much she liked him. Despite everything Kam told her, she'd still half expected him to be the suave, self-preening Lothario he presented to the media. But he was far from it. She found him amusingly self-deprecating. Unexpectedly cultured. When he asked her questions about herself, his interest seemed genuine.

"Aren't you an accomplished culinarian, Dillon?" he said now, spearing a prawn off the table. "I think Kam mentioned that."

"I don't know about accomplished, but I know my way around a kitchen."

"I'm curious," he darted a glance toward Dani, before returning his attention to Dillon, "what's your go-to for fondue? I'd always heard white wine or vodka."

Dillon wasn't thrilled to be dragged into the conversation. Dani's distaste for her was evident; she'd been making digs at her all night. But out of respect for Kam, she'd ignored them. She knew the turbulent friendship was already on the rocks and had no wish to contribute to its downfall.

"Most recipes tend to call for a dry white, but I'm sure there's a lot of room for variation."

"At least we can all acknowledge the most important thing is alcohol," snapped Dani.

Dillon should have let it go. The woman was a petulant socialite with less than two brain cells. But it was wearing, the way she glared at her for no reason. The way she felt she was an expert on everything.

"Not in this particular dish," she muttered, closing the cutlery drawer.

Dani's eyes flashed to her. "And how would you know?"

"Because I substituted apple cider."

"Don't break my heart and tell me you made all this, Dillon," said Grady Dunn, arriving with a martini in hand. "I was hoping to beg Kam for the name of her caterer."

"Now you know to refuse an invitation to Dunn's poker game on Thursday nights," Elliott teased. "He'll be trying to trade you a buy-in for an appetizer."

Dillon didn't have the time to laugh before Dani had once again turned herself into the center of attention.

"Oh, my God!" She dramatically covered her mouth, staring at Dillon. "I wasn't thinking when I mentioned the wine in the fondue. Of course, you would substitute." She lowered her voice into a pseudo-whisper. "I forgot you were… well, you know, that you had a… um, drinking problem." She cringed.

Blindsided by the comment, Dillon didn't know what to say. The way Dani made it sound—that's not how it had been. Had Kam really told her that?

"Are you an idiot?" Elliott hissed behind her back, his vehemence directed at Dani.

Dillon's entire body tensed as she laid out the remainder of the cutlery. It wasn't like her to find herself embarrassed. Who cared what the little bitch thought? But it was Elliott's defense, and Grady's sympathetic glance, that brought an unwelcome rush of heat to her cheeks.

"I don't know where you heard that," she said, managing to keep her voice indifferent, "but you're mistaken. I skipped the wine because *Trader Joe's* didn't carry an unoaked chardonnay with high enough acidity to keep the gruyère from stringing together. So I chose a better alternative." She turned, crossing the kitchen to the wet bar, her heart pounding an angry meter.

There was a bottle of Beluga Gold and dry vermouth sitting on the counter, left over from where she'd stirred Kam her favorite vodka martini.

"I don't drink during race season because it makes it harder to recover." She pulled a glass from the hanging rack. It wasn't the entire truth, but it was none of anyone else's business. She wasn't willing to accept a label for something she hadn't struggled with in many years.

So fuck Dani Hallwell for trying to humiliate her.

She uncorked the vodka. "But you know what, it's Kam's birthday —what better reason to make an exception?"

Dillon didn't look up from stirring her third martini. She'd known Kam would seize the opportunity to interrogate her the moment she was alone, so it was no surprise when the familiar scent of *Miss Dior* cut through the aroma of vermouth.

"Hey." Fingertips brushed her elbow. "Is everything okay?"

"Cracking." Dillon drew a paring knife through the rind of a lemon. "Never better."

"Dillon." In response to the sarcasm, Kam pressed her fingers firmly against her arm. "What's going on?"

"Did you really tell her I was an alcoholic?" Dillon finally turned. Her gaze flicked to where Dani was standing on the threshold of the balcony, holding Grady's wife hostage to another *me*-centered soliloquy. "Is that what you tell everyone?"

"What?" Stung, Kam dropped her hand. "I've never said *anything* like that." She lowered her voice, aware of the way her words carried across the open floor plan. "When she asked me what alcohol to bring, I told her you didn't drink. That's the only thing I said."

"But apparently that's what you think?"

It was a cheap shot. She knew it the moment she saw the hurt sweep across Kam's face.

She knew Dani had only come looking for trouble. She should have turned the other cheek.

But if Dillon was honest with herself, she knew she'd just been waiting for an excuse. Whatever reason she could find to palliate the guilt of taking that first sip.

"How would I know what to think, Dillon?" Kam stepped back. Her friend Sophie called her name from the dining room; they were ready to light the candles. "You never tell me anything."

Leaning against the wet bar, Dillon set the glass to her lips, watching her walk away.

She was borderline drunk—she knew that. Half a decade without alcohol followed by back-to-back-to-back martinis tended to have that effect.

But she couldn't bring herself to care.

She'd forgotten what it felt like—the rush of endorphins delivering all the highs of a win without the struggle or work it took to get there. The way the burn of vodka crept into all the hollow places, filling her with temporary peace.

She watched as Grady carried out the two-tier cake and they all sang *Happy Birthday*. For a moment, Kam's eyes found hers as she made her wish, but by the time Dillon convinced her lips into a smile, Kam had already looked away.

The night slogged on. There was a toast to Kam, parlor games, a competitive round of movie trivia Dillon used as justification to get another drink.

By midnight, the small group had dwindled. From her place by the window, Dillon saw Elliott check his watch. Grady and his wife shifted in their seats. Dillon was tired, the effects of the alcohol waning. She was ready to be alone with Kam. She owed her an apology.

But Dani appeared to have no intention of leaving.

Unlike the other guests, who'd made little fanfare of their exotic gifts—ranging from L.R. Sims' bestowal of a photography session with Annie Leibovitz, to Elliott's ten-day excursion on the exclusive atoll of Tetiaroa, or even the diamond-encrusted bottle of *Glenfiddich* Waylon MacArthur had discreetly sent over via courier—Dani seized on the opportunity of the captive audience, commanding attention to the center of the room.

"Oh," she exclaimed loudly, as if an afterthought had struck her, digging a palm-size navy blue parcel out of her Louis Vuitton purse. The glance she cast toward Dillon held the hint of a challenge. "I almost forgot!" She handed the box to Kam. "It's just a little thing, but I did have it made custom…"

Caught off guard at the interruption from her conversation with Grady, Kam tugged the filigree ribbon loose, flipping the box open.

"I—" The word hung in the abrupt silence. "It's… wow, Dani."

From the reflection in the vase beside Kameryn, Dillon could see it was a necklace. A heavy chain of yellow gold hung with an emerald-studded star pendant. It amazed Dillon, after so many years, that Dani still knew Kam so little. That her own love of showy flamboyance blinded her to Kam's preference for the understated. Delicate chains. Petite charms. Her fondness for silver…

Impatient at Kam's hesitation, Dani snatched up the necklace to display it to the room.

"Twenty-two emeralds—your birthstone, of course—to celebrate every year of our friendship. And the star goes without saying. It's pure gold, so I took the liberty of including an insurance policy."

"'*It's just a little thing*,'" Elliott mimicked Dani's voice with surprising accuracy. "Says the woman handing out bespoke *Harry Winston* as she goes out of her way to pretend it's nothing." He rattled the ice cubes around his glass before tipping back its contents. The remnants of his limited filter had vanished, down the hatch with the whiskey. "That's the kind of gift I typically reserve when I'm trying to get someone to sleep with me. Look out, Dillon," he winked in her direction, "you might have some competition."

Dani shot him a hostile glare. She was noticeably drunk, but not so drunk as to mistake his taunting for playful banter. All evening he'd called her out on her showboating. There was no question he didn't like her.

She ruffled herself, clinging to her air of superiority. "It's hardly surprising a guy like you has to buy his way into a woman's bed. Indisputable proof money can't buy good breeding."

"Ironic, coming from the woman gasconading a thirty-thousand-dollar hunk of metal while trying to pass it off for anything other than what it is—a last-ditch-effort buy-in."

"It's almost like you're jealous. Perhaps I'm not the one with my eye on Kameryn?"

"'A hit. A very palpable hit,'" Elliott covered his heart with dramatic flare, entirely amused at the irony of her accusations. It was evident Dani wasn't privy to his secrets. "'False face must hide what the false heart doth know.'"

"Oh please," Dani huffed, "take your Bible verses elsewhere."

"Methinks you've mistaken *MacBeth* for *Matthew*."

Oblivious to the reference, and furious at his uncensored—however warranted—roasting, Dani spun her focus back to Kameryn.

"As I was saying," her knuckles were white where she clutched the medallion, "as the friend who knows you better than anyone—I wanted to give you something personal. Something a little more intimate than, oh, say a trip to French Polynesia." She cast Elliott another withering glare.

Elliott mimed a tennis serve, tossing a balled-up napkin onto the floor. "Game, set, match. All that blustering and you're still falling one point short of a victory. Because something tells me—if bequeathing the most *intimate* gift is the killshot of the evening—it's Dillon who's got the one-up on all of us."

"Okay," Grady—who'd remained silent through the back-and-forth exchange—laughed, clapping his hands to his knees while shooting his wife the universal let's-get-out-of-here signal. "On that note, I think it's time—"

"And what exactly would that be, Elliott?" Dani challenged, ignoring Grady's attempt to break the tension. She was unwilling to let it go. Unwilling to accept that Kam's life no longer revolved around her. "I mean, honestly," she shifted her gaze and, with it, the focus of her anger, across the room to Dillon. "I'm trying to understand: what exactly does *she* have to offer?"

"Dani!" Kam warned. All playful raillery had departed, and what had started with Elliott's flippant spar of words had turned into something darker. But heedless of Kam's sharp rebuke, the woman plowed ahead with all her pent-up fury.

"Cheap costume jewelry?" she waved her hand toward the lovespoon hanging in the shadow of Kam's throat. "The thrill of an illicit relationship? Oh, let me guess: the promise of a gold medal?" She laughed, her caustic words rattling like gravel. "What a joke. I mean, let's just call a spade a spade—she's got you wrapped around her little finger, Kam. All that money spent on her medical bills and the truth is, she's just a washed-up has-been!"

Kam was immediately on her feet. "What the fuck is wrong with you, Dani!?"

Somewhere behind the cannonade of blood rushing between her ears, Dillon was aware of Kam's outrage. Aware of angry voices. The breaking of a glass. The slamming of a door.

But it was little more than background noise, like the static of a radio submerged in water.

She found herself on the balcony, her flaming cheeks little soothed by the breeze creeping up from the sea.

Had her mind been clear—had she not plunged headfirst into a bottle of self-pity—she wouldn't have left it to Kam to defend her. She could hold her own against an imbecile like Dani. But tonight, she'd only wanted to get away. To escape into the shadows.

She stood leaning over the glass railing, trying to catch her breath. Her anger went so much deeper than the vitriol spewed by Dani. It was so much more than just one night... one month... one race... one injury... one rollercoaster of a year.

She hurt in ways she couldn't describe. Ways that had nothing to do with the injuries, the surgeries, the wear and tear on her body. There was part of her that had begun to forget how to push back the hollowness threatening to rise. And another part—a more frightening part—that no longer cared.

Reaching into her pocket, she pulled out the little glass sea turtle with its two grains of rice tucked neatly in its shell. The gift seemed so ridiculous now.

*What exactly does she have to offer?*

The insult had been flung right through her—as if she wasn't even there.

Behind her, footsteps sounded on the tile. Slow. Tentative. She didn't have to look to know they belonged to Kam.

"Dillon?"

Quickly curling her fingers, she hid the turtle in the palm of her hand.

"I…" Kam's voice trailed off as she stepped beside her. Their shadows touched, the misshapen lines blurring into a single silhouette, but the physical distance between them felt unsettling.

A long silence passed. Below them, the lights of the pier continued to glitter, a spectacle of bokeh splashed across the black backdrop of the shore.

"I'm sorry," Kam finally whispered through a shaky breath. "You know none of what she said is true."

Dillon watched a couple walk hand-in-hand across the sand, disappearing beneath the pilings. "I know."

"She's a jealous bitch. She always has been. And I'm sorry I ever let her—"

"Kam." Dillon interrupted her. She didn't want to talk about Dani. "I think I'm going to go home for a while."

From her peripheral, she could see Kam's entire body stiffen. See her fingers grip the salt-crusted rail. "Please." The word hung on the verge of tears. "Please, don't. What happened tonight—"

Dillon couldn't bring herself to look at her. "It's not you, Kam. Or even her. Or honestly anything to do with tonight at all. It's…"

How could she explain? It was so many things she didn't know how to talk about. Feelings she had to sort through.

It wasn't new. It was how she felt after her DNF in Yokohama. The same as it had been the Christmas morning she found out Kam would be a Hollywood star. It was the feeling of being told she would never race again after her accident. And the way she felt the day she learned her dad had died.

"I just need a little time."

She needed to get back to training. She couldn't focus here. Being with Kam made it too comfortable to forget what she wanted. Too easy to quit on herself.

*She's just a washed-up nobody.*

Leeds was five weeks away. At whatever cost, she was going to qualify.

Dani could go fuck herself.

"Are you coming back?" Kam's voice was carefully neutral. The question felt so loaded, so much more implied than what was asked.

"Yeah," she said after a long pause.

Kam passed the back of her hand across her eyes, her face hidden in shadow. "Is that a promise, Dillon?"

"Yes." She breathed the word through a strained smile, adding it to the long list of promises getting harder to keep. "You can't get rid of me that easily."

Kam struggled through a deep breath before turning to face her, a trail of mascara darkening her cheeks. "You know I love you, right? More than all of this."

She didn't need to define *this*. They were standing on a glass balcony a dozen floors above the Pacific Ocean. Kam's face was plastered on every bus that lumbered down the street. Taylor Swift had left a voicemail singing her happy birthday. The *Cartier* diamonds hanging from her ears could have put a deposit on a Lamborghini.

Dillon wanted to reach out. To touch her. To smooth the tear streaks from her face. Stains that never should have been there, especially tonight.

But, she didn't.

"You're daft, Kam-Kameryn," she forced another smile instead.

This time, Kam smiled back, but it didn't quite reach her eyes. "I'm going to make us a cup of coffee. Will you come inside?"

"I'll be right behind you."

When she had gone, Dillon released a deep exhale, feeling her entire body sag. Her knee ached, the mercy of the alcohol long faded, and an unfamiliar sting came from her palm. It was the sea turtle, she realized, unclenching her fist. She looked at the little creature for a long minute —at the incongruity of the names trapped inside—and then allowed the figurine to slip from her fingers, disappearing over the railing into the dark.

# Scene 49

It was the fourth day Dillon hadn't returned my calls.

I knew she was okay—earlier in the afternoon, I'd watched a livestream from *British Triathlon* featuring her and Georgina Potter. They'd filmed an open-water training session to promote the upcoming race in Leeds. I recognized the bright bobbing buoys of Serpentine Lido, the swimming club where Dillon often swam. It was a glorious spot in the middle of Hyde Park, only a few miles from her apartment in South Bank. We'd walked there together a handful of times that first blissful week I stayed with her in the city—the week we had ridden the London Eye.

Days that seemed to belong to someone else, now, as I once again sat on my balcony, cloistered away from everything resembling real life.

I hit redial.

I needed her to answer. I needed to hear her voice.

The woman I watched on the livestream had seemed almost foreign to me. Someone I didn't know. I mean, it was Dillon alright, with her sunbleached hair hanging damp in her eyes, and dusting of freckles beneath exertion-pinked cheeks. But it somehow felt like the hollow version of her. Like a knockoff replica or poorly cast body double for daytime TV.

She said all the right things in the post-swim interview, answering questions with Georgina in all the appropriate places. She acknowledged her only option for Leeds was a podium finish after her missed top-twenty in Yokohama. It would be the only way to prove to the *BOA* that she was medal-contender-worthy.

Visibly annoyed, she brushed off the reporter's queries when he asked about the improbability of her comeback story. *Did she think she had a chance on Saturday?*

"You think I'd really be out here freezing my arse off before the sun pipped the horizon just for a bit of a lark?" Her smile had been tight, the green of her eyes unblinking.

The man backpedaled, circling around to the excitement leading up to the race, and emphasizing that the entirety of Great Britain was behind her. With her storied success on the podium, it was unquestionable, he emphasized with a thump on her back, she would make their nation proud.

I'd watched, analyzing every detail of her expression, trying to get a glimpse behind her facade. Wanting to find some indication in the stone-faced, glassy-eyed competitor on auto-pilot that told me it was just her typical race mode—that it was her armor of hyperfocus I was struggling to see through.

But I couldn't reconcile the woman on my screen with the woman who'd once kissed me so soundly on those same stone steps leading into the lake, we'd ended up turning her pre-dawn workout into a ridiculously risky—yet wildly passionate—tryst in the swim club's empty changing room. I could still smell the baby powder she'd sprinkled on her skin, hear the way she'd laughed as I clumsily struggled with the zipper on her wetsuit.

The woman today didn't resemble that woman at all.

She was a dimmer, more stripped-down version of the woman who'd left my apartment a month earlier, two days after my birthday.

I'd initially been relieved, the morning after my party, when she told me she'd decided to race Leeds. It allowed me to accept her abrupt decision to return to the UK. It gave me hope the uncomfortable distance newly come between us was less to do with Dani and her idiocy, and instead, was Dillon's switch to competitive mode. That making a firm decision on the upcoming race had toggled her into hyperdrive.

But it was different this time, and I could feel it immediately. She didn't text me for two days after she'd landed back at Heathrow. When I finally got a hold of her, the conversation was brief. *Yes*, she'd arrived safely. *Yes*, she was fine. *Yes,* she'd call me again in a few days. It had ended with a curt *love you* without enough time for me to respond.

The next time she called, it was in the middle of her night. I'd answered, terrified something had happened, but she'd shrugged off my alarm. "Just couldn't sleep." She'd sounded dull. Tired. Part of me had wondered if she was drunk, but I didn't have the heart to ask.

Instead, I'd committed a far greater blunder. I'd voiced the question gnawing at me ever since she left.

"You're not doing this because of what Dani said, right? You know you don't have to prove anything to—"

"You really think I care what that cunt said?" she cut me off, and I knew at once I'd made a mistake. "You realize this is what I do, Kam, right? It's what I did, way before I met you, and it's what I'll continue to do, until…" She didn't define a deadline.

"I'm sorry," I tried to recover, "I didn't—I didn't mean it like that. I just—you're so hard on yourself. I worry about you."

"Yeah, well, join the fucking queue with Seren and everyone else."

It was so unlike her to snap at me, I hadn't known what to say. I chalked it up to stress and let it go. I didn't want her to shut me out completely. More than she already had.

The next day she apologized, and had called nearly every day since. Things almost felt normal.

Until this week.

Without warning, I'd been given complete radio silence.

With no explanation.

The previous weekend, I'd texted her, floating on cloud nine.

*I've got incredible news!!!! Call me when you can!!!*

I had a meeting with Steven Spielberg about a project kept entirely under wraps. A few months earlier, I'd tested to play the role of soccer legend, Mia Hamm, in an upcoming film about her life. I hadn't said anything to anyone, uncertain if it would pan out, but over a steaming pot of mint tea on the courtyard of Chateau Marmont, I'd finally gotten the green light from Mr. Spielberg himself.

There was no one I wanted to tell more than Dillon. It was the first role I'd landed that I thought she might find impressive.

It wouldn't be *Sand Seekers*, Spielberg warned me, acknowledging the drama was on the more low budget scale, but I hadn't cared. Dillon loved the American athlete. She used her as a frequent example of grit and tenacity. It was a part I knew I could play, and one I knew I could do well. For once, I felt, Dillon would be thrilled.

But a day went by, and then another, and she still didn't call. I left a couple voicemails. Another few texts. I'd started to panic last night, deciding to reach out to Seren this morning, but then I came across the livestream.

First, I'd been relieved, and then furious. Because there she was—home in London, alive and—despite the gauntness of her cheeks and darkened circles under her eyes—apparently well, just without the courtesy of three seconds to text me back.

Once again, I punched *call* on her contact, and once again, the phone rang—this time four rings before being sent to voicemail. *Sent* —as in, deliberately.

I left a final message. "Listen, I know you're getting ready to race, but do you think you could spare half a moment to call me? If I don't hear from you by this evening, I'm going to fly to London." I hung up and texted her the same thing. It wasn't an idle threat—and we both knew it.

She called a couple hours later.

"I'm glad you could finally squeeze me in," I answered, unable to hide my anger boiling over.

"I'm sorry." The words were toneless.

"Where have you been?"

"Home."

I waited, needing more than a single syllable. I needed an explanation. A reason why it took the threat of flying there to get her to respond.

"That's all you have to say?" I finally snapped, when the line remained silent. I hadn't planned to pick a fight with her. I'd just wanted her to call. But I thought she'd at least have an excuse—some kind of reason.

*I've been training.*

*I've been focused.*

*I've been drunk.*

I would have accepted any of those. Anything at all.

"Did it ever occur to you that I might worry?"

"I'm sorry, Kam."

*Those fucking words again.*

"Yeah, I can tell!" I hated that my voice wavered. And I hated it even more that I didn't have the guts to ask what I really wanted to know.

I needed her to tell me if we were finished. If it wasn't the race, or the disaster of my party, or my so-called friends, or this fucked up existence I lived in… But instead, if it was me—plain and simple. And if we were done.

But I couldn't bring myself to voice the concern. Not today, with Leeds in less than forty-eight hours. As angry as I was, I didn't want to burden her with any added stress. Any more additional pressure than she was already going through. After the race, whichever way it went… I'd ask her then.

For now, I needed to be supportive. To try and understand.

I took a deep breath. "I know you've got a lot on your mind—and when you're in this mood, you can't think about anyone but yourself —" okay, so I threw in one last dig. I couldn't help myself. "But please remember—there are a lot of people who love and care about you. Please don't close us out."

She was quiet.

"Well, okay, then. Good talk. I guess I'll hear from you when I hear from you—"

"Kam?"

I quieted. And waited.

And waited.

She didn't continue.

"Was there anything else?"

There was a longer silence. I could hear her swallow on the other end of the line. "Sorry, no. I'll call you after the race, okay?"

"You promise?" I tried to keep the bitterness out of my voice.

"Yeah."

So much of me wanted to tell her everything would be alright. She was going to make it. If there was one thing I knew about her, it was she could do anything she put her mind to. After all: she was Dillon Fucking Sinclair.

But I didn't say any of it. I don't know why. Instead, I just said goodnight. She told me goodnight. And we hung up.

It was the first time in longer than I could remember that I hadn't told her I loved her when we said goodbye.

I wanted to hit redial. To tell her I was sorry. To beg her to let me come and support her. I didn't have to come to the race—the headlines about the two of us had finally subsided—I could just be there. Be near. In whatever capacity she'd allow me to be.

But I didn't call her back. I knew what she would say. It would be easier for her to focus without me there. Just give her until Saturday.

I got up and poured a glass of wine, deciding to bring the whole bottle back to the balcony.

I'd forgotten to tell her about Mia Hamm. Steven Spielberg.
It didn't matter. I'd tell her after she qualified.
Because she *would* qualify. She *had* to.
And after that, everything would be okay.
*We* were okay. She wasn't done with me. I knew that in my heart.
She was just being Dillon. And I was just being dramatic.

Friday night, I got a text from her while I was up pacing my apartment.
I double-checked my watch. It was almost midnight in Los Angeles,
which meant it was early morning in Leeds. In less than half an hour,
she would dive headfirst into the most important race of her life.

I swiped the text open, anxious. It was so unlike her to have her
phone on—especially this close to the time of the start.

*I'm sorry. I love you.*

I breathed a sigh of relief, promptly texting her back.

*I'm sorry, too. I was just worried. I love you. So much. You'll do
great today. I'll be thinking about you the whole time. XOXO*

The message went unread.
I set my phone on the kitchen counter and headed to the balcony.
Just a few more hours and this would be over.
This part, at least.
Then…
*Too far ahead.*
I turned my focus to today—and today, only.
She could do this. She *would* do this.

# Scene 50

Dillon stood in the body marking station as a chattering Scottish woman meticulously applied the number *3* across her clean-shaven skin: first her upper arms, then her thighs, and lastly, her calves.

"Braw number, that. Good omen, if you ask me." The woman continued to hum away as she checked the ankle strap on Dillon's timing chip and gave her the thumbs up. "Alright, lass, get out there and give it laldy!"

Dillon said nothing, just walked away.

Roundhay Park was teeming with activity, spectators already lining the barriers to stake their claim on the best places to view the race. Somewhere in the crowd would be Seren. Sam. Her mam.

She didn't look that direction.

Instead, her attention turned to the gleaming surface of Waterloo Lake, where the swim course marshals were preparing to enter the water.

The race start was in less than an hour.

Scattered across the gentle slope of trampled grass, athletes were stretching, pulling on wetsuits, rubbing their faces with sunscreen and dusting their bodies with talcum powder.

Dillon knew she needed to join them. It was time to double-check her gear. To go through her race-day rituals to get fired up for the horn.

But it wasn't there—the rush of adrenaline, the unrelenting obsession that had fueled her ruthless ambition since the first time her dad pinned her with a competitor's number when she was twelve-years-old. There was no start line anxiety. No pre-race jitters. Her heart was beating too slowly, her palms dry, and fingers steady, with none of the charged energy needed to hone her focus onto the start.

Stepping off the damp grass onto the pavement, the bones in her knee made a familiar grind.

It hadn't taken the results of her latest MRI to know she'd fucked up, ignoring Dr. Monaghan's advice.

*Patience*, he'd preached. *Slow and steady wins the race.*

But slow and steady had never been how Dillon lived her life.

And it didn't matter now—what was done was done.

She stabbed her toe into the ground, seeking the sensation of the pain. Trying to find the ache all the handfuls of ibuprofen and expired bottles of OxyContin had been unable to hide. For the past month, it had become a hurt she had come to rely on—the defense of endorphins creating some kind of warped high.

But this morning there was nothing. All she felt was numb.

And overwhelmingly, despairingly tired.

"You're looking a little pale there, Sinclair. Come to add another loss to your collection?"

Dillon turned. It should have been Henrik; it would have been fitting. But instead, it was just that tosser, Isaac Fortin. His wife's race bag was slung over his shoulder, his shorts rolled up too high.

"I have to admit, I never thought I'd see the day when you turned up simply to be a field filler. I'm beginning to think you just like viewing that pretty little French ass from behind." He leaned closer, the smell of cheap aftershave sending Dillon's empty stomach into turmoil. "I'm right, aren't I?" His lips parted to reveal a row of too-small teeth as he ran a palm over his greased black hair. "Well, don't you worry—it'll stay our little secret. No reason you can't keep your American girl and have a sweet French bit on the side."

She should have felt angry—she was certain of it—but the effort of the emotion took energy she didn't know how to find.

Issac's eyes shifted over the top of her head as an elongated shadow darkened the grass between them. It was Kyle, the weight of his protective arm draping over her shoulders.

"Hello, Wood." Issac straightened. "You joining the women's race today?"

"Take a long walk off a short pier, ya shitlark. The volunteer tent is over by the portaloos."

Elevating his weak chin, Isaac's lips curled as he regarded Dillon down the barrel of his nose. "As I was saying, good luck, Sinclair. God knows you'll need it just to finish."

She stared through him as he walked away, finding no part of herself that cared enough to reply.

"That prick is such a waste of oxygen. He really—" Kyle paused when he saw her face. "You alright, Sinc?"

Dillon didn't know how to answer. Her mind felt caught in a riptide, her sense of reality disjointed. It was as if she were watching the world from eyes not her own. As if she were just the husk of someone else.

"Tired," she managed, realizing he was still waiting for a response. She couldn't remember the last time she'd slept. The last time she'd eaten.

"I feel you, mate," he squeezed her arm, not understanding. "But we're on the home stretch now. Just stick to the plan and let Georgina carry the load." He lowered his face to hers. "You've got this, Sinc. Leeds has always been yours." His fingers pressed into the bare flesh of her arm hard enough to make her flinch. To jolt her back to the present.

"Yeah," she nodded. "I'm good."

"Okay." He straightened. "I'm going to look in on Georgina. I'll see you in a couple hours—on that podium, you hear? And then we're packing our bags for Los Angeles."

He gave her a final clap on the back, and then was off, disappearing into the throng of arriving volunteers.

Uncertain how she got there, Dillon found herself back in the transition zone, assessing her equipment. Everything was in order— her bike, her shoes, her gels and chapstick. All she had to do was step into her wetsuit. One foot, and then the other. Dump in baby powder. Zip and velcro. Pull on her swim cap.

She stared at her pile of swim gear, repeating the steps to herself over and over.

Outside the transition barrier, she could feel the cameras—the click of their lenses, the commentary of the race-day reporters. A dozen different languages clashed in high and low tones, filled with the nervous energy of her surrounding competitors.

Dillon hooked her goggles over her elbow and picked up her wetsuit.

To her right, a Spanish athlete slammed her bike into the rack after a last-minute inspection, the sharp clang of metal jarring Dillon. The neoprene slipped from her fingers.

"Lo siento," the woman apologized, offering a quick smile before spraying on her sunscreen.

Dillon couldn't bring herself to return the smile. She couldn't bring herself to do anything.

Floating through a maelstrom of unnavigable emotion, she stepped over the fallen wetsuit and picked up her backpack waiting to be delivered to the bag drop.

She couldn't do this. Not for another second. Not today. Not again. Not ever.

She flung her goggles into the nearest rubbish bin and weaved her way out of the transition zone. Away from the chaos. The mounting pressure. The anxiety. She bypassed the arrow indicating the *swim start* and turned onto one of the quiet trails leading away from the vortex of activity.

Sitting at the bus stop, she pulled out her mobile. She needed to text Kam. To try to explain. But what words were there to ever make her understand? To tell her how she was feeling?

Uncertain how to express herself, she finally typed:

*I'm sorry. I love you.*

And shut off her phone.

As she stepped onto the bus, she heard the start horn blow. Leeds was underway, with one less swimmer in the water.

# Scene 51

The soundscape of the tranquil Polynesian coast faded as the buzz of a motorboat engine grew louder.

I groaned, trying to block out the noise. The breeze was so fresh, the warmth of Dillon's body beside me so comforting. I wasn't ready to wake up. I pressed my face into the nape of her neck, inhaling her essence. Wanting to live in the peacefulness of it forever.

But the buzz grew louder. What was a motorboat doing so close to the shore? Or was it the hymn of the island cicadas?

I was no longer sure.

Reluctant, I pried open an eye. It was dark. The birdsong vanished, taking with it the rustle of palm trees and distant hum of music from the resort. I wasn't on a tropical island. Dillon wasn't lying alongside me in the warm white sands of Tetiaroa.

I was home—whatever that word meant—lying on the chaise lounge of my balcony, and it was the middle of the night. I rummaged for my phone to check the time and realized it was still sitting on the kitchen counter. The vibration against the tiles had woken me.

Stumbling over an empty bottle of wine, I lunged to my feet, quickly forced to steady myself against the glass door as dizziness threatened to upheave my equilibrium. I couldn't believe I'd fallen asleep. It had to be late. Judging by the moon in the cloudless sky, I imagined it was at least two—I dragged myself to the kitchen, swiping up my phone—*three* in the morning. *3:19* to be exact.

The race would have been over for more than an hour.

I hadn't been able to bring myself to watch. My heart couldn't take it. She'd told me she felt strong enough—healthy enough—she felt she had a shot to win it. Even her coach, Alistair, had echoed the sentiment.

"Sinc's fitness is on par with her pre-injury results. I expect her to put in a strong standing," he said in an interview earlier in the week.

So instead of tearing my hair out, agonizing over her every footfall, analyzing her every grimace, I washed down a Xanax with a bottle of

Château Margaux (Hollywood had stamped its firm imprint on me) and took sentry on my balcony to channel all my positive energy to the north of England.

That had been more than three hours ago.

*God damn it.*

Without allowing myself to look at the notifications on my screen, I staggered through the dark back to my balcony. Whatever the results, I wanted the salty sea air, the ocean of stars, the unfettering pull of the tide to surround me.

Part of my consciousness was still lingering in the tropical buoyancy of my dream. In the way I'd felt Dillon's presence. Warm. Soothing.

It was a good omen, surely.

Settled at the glass railing, with one final plea to the moon to let the results be what she—what *we*—needed, I swiped open my screen.

*Seven missed calls.* Not one of them from Dillon. My heart plummeted.

*Fuck.*

*12:03: Seren Sinclair*
*12:17: Sam Huntley*
*12:25: Sam Huntley*
*12:37: Seren Sinclair*
*01:01: Jacqueline Sinclair*
*02:21: Kyle Wood*
*03:17: Seren Sinclair*

Four voicemails.
One text.
I felt sick.
I tapped the text. It was from Sam.

*Call me ASAP!*

My fingers were shaking as I thumbed to my inbox. The first voicemail was from Seren.

*Hi Kam, I'm sorry it's so late. It's Seren. Have you talked to Dillon? Her start is in twelve minutes and no one can find her. Please call me.*

The next message was from Sam.

*Howay, Kam—it's Hunt. Sinc's missed her start. Ring me back, like. Ta!"*

Then Jacqueline.

*Hello Kameryn, it's Jacqueline Sinclair. I was hoping you might have talked to Dillon. Will you please call me or Seren when you get this? Thank you.*

The last message was Seren again.

*I'm sorry to keep calling, Kam, but we can't find my sister. Her mobile has been shut off. She didn't scratch and she didn't start. Please call me.*

My legs felt weak as I hung my elbows over the railing to support myself.
*She didn't scratch and she didn't start…*
It made no sense. She'd never *not* start. There was some miscommunication. She wouldn't walk away. That simply wasn't her. She didn't back down from anything.
They had to have found her by now.
I checked the time of Seren's last call. Just a few minutes ago…
A wave of nausea made it difficult to breathe. Difficult to speak when Seren answered my call.
"Kam—?"
"Have you found her?"
Seren's sigh was long, deflated. "You haven't spoken to her, then?"
"No. Not since before the race. She texted me…" I pulled the phone away from my ear to open my messages, unable to recall exactly what she'd said. I read it again.

*I'm sorry. I love you.*

Had she meant something different? Had I misinterpreted the context?
"Kam?" Seren queried in my silence.
I stared at the words, reading them over and over.

I thought she meant about the day before… About our fight on the phone…

"Kam—"

"I have to call you back." I abruptly hung up, my voice tasting like bile.

This was all just a misunderstanding. There was an explanation, I was certain of it.

I tried to take a deep breath, but my lungs reviled against the bitterness of the salt in the breeze, the sound of the gentle breakers deafening in my nightmare.

Because that *was* what this was—a nightmare—nothing more. I was going to wake up. I was going to find I'd simply had too much to drink. I would open my eyes back on the beaches of Tetiaroa.

I stood for what felt like an eternity, knowing none of that was true. Knowing I had to pull myself together.

I finally looked at my phone. It was only 3:33.

I opened favorites and selected the first contact, input playfully as *DFS.* A photo of her popped up, sunburnt and covered in sand, which I'd told her I found 'exceptionally hot' at the time I took it.

The light of the moon dimmed as it slipped behind a newly formed cloud, the call going directly to voicemail.

> *You've reached Sinc. You know what to do. Hang up. Text. Don't call. Cheers!*

I still called nineteen times in a row, swearing each time she'd pick up if I just tried once more. I listened to the voicemail every time, hanging up before the beep. Finally, on the twentieth redial, I left a message.

"Dillon. I know you're going to get this. As soon as you do, please call me." I hung up. Then dialed straight back. "P.S. I love you." My voice wavered, my breathing staggered. "I really, really, *really* love you. Please call me."

All the warmth had left my hands, and it took a half dozen stabs from my index finger to end the call.

I watched the screen turn black and wanted to chuck it over the balcony.

But I couldn't.

She *would* call. She'd promised. She wouldn't do this to me.

Overcome with a wave of despair, I slipped down the misted glass of the railing, and sat cross-legged on the cold tile, staring at nothing.

# Scene 52: Take 1

The tide was rising.

Dillon pulled herself out of the waist-deep water onto the moss-covered landing. The first step of the steep stone staircase was already submerged beneath the rolling sea swell lapping against the island. Two hundred feet above her, the Mumbles Lighthouse flashed its brilliance, the lantern abrasive against the midday sun.

She didn't linger. For the first time since stepping onto the train in Leeds, she was confronted with an unsettling clarity. Like the mantle enveloping her for the past few days had finally lifted, revealing the world in the vivid starkness of her new reality.

It was over.

She'd destroyed everything. Everything she'd worked for, everything she'd fought to achieve. Thrown it all away. In one stupid, blinding moment of weakness, she'd shattered her career. Her life. Her dreams.

And now—she was nothing.

Behind her, the advancing tide flooded the foreshore, cutting the two tidal islets off from the headland, leaving no navigable return. She didn't care. She didn't look back.

One foot in front of the other, she worked her way up the winding staircase. She didn't count each weatherworn step as she'd once done as a child, her dad whistling behind her with an armload of fishing gear and lunch packed for two. Nor did she stop to peek into the long-abandoned keeper's cottage, or admire the cormorants and razorbills nesting on the cliffside.

Her mind was back in Leeds, in Roundhay Park. Back on the race, which would have been over for hours. Back on the people she'd let down.

Her teammates. Her country. Kyle. Alistair. Her sponsors. Her fans.

Sam. Who'd been through so much worse, yet was still stronger, braver, more deserving than she had ever been.

Seren. Who had begged her to bow out while she could still take the high road. Who had understood her better than she'd understood herself. Who had been right. Who had known.

And Kam. How did she explain it to Kam? The one person who had believed in her when everyone else told her to quit. After all the money she had spent… the boundless encouragement… the unwavering support she had shown her… Dillon owed her so much more. Had failed her so gravely.

Cresting the isolated summit, she allowed her pace to slow as she navigated the eroding pathway paralleling the shadow of the light-house. To her left, the Mumbles Pier stretched into the distance, the jetty quiet, save for a pair of silhouettes fishing near the lifeboat station.

How often had she and her dad watched a boat launch down the slipway to save a wayward seafarer or retrieve an unsuspecting tourist stranded at high tide on the island? It wasn't swimmable, the narrow channel back to the mainland. The current was too strong, and any person fool enough to enter the water at flood tide would be swept out to sea.

"Even you, Ddraig Fach," her dad had razzed when her swimming prowess had gotten too big for her boots. "Get caught in that, and I'd be scooping you up in England." Dillon had rolled her eyes, her twelve-year-old ego blustering that she could swim anything.

Turning her attention to the south, where the horizon disappeared across the Bristol Channel, Dillon ventured off the pathway onto the jagged cliff edge. It was her favorite part of the island, the steep rockface giving way to the gaping mouth of a colossal cave stretching deep beneath the ocean's surface.

*The Dragon's Lair*, her father pointed out on her first trek to the lighthouse. He'd spent the afternoon spinning a tale of a fierce sea dragon—the protector of Wales—who preyed on poaching fishermen sailing too close to the Gower.

"What's his name?" Dillon had worried a loose tooth with one hand while clutching the safety of her father's arm in the other. Anxious to catch a glimpse of translucent scales, she'd risked a glance over the edge to stare into the black opening of the cavern.

She could still feel the warmth of her father's strong forearm. See the way he had smiled. "Who said it was a he?" He ruffled her hair. "It's well known the bravest hunters are female."

Banishing the memory, Dillon picked her way onto a rocky crag jutting over the water. The wind had risen, stirring the ocean into a canvas of white caps, the spindrift misting her sea-soaked trainers.

Uncomfortable with the height, she dropped to sit amongst the pink blossoms of long-stemmed Sea Thrift and yellow clusters of Bird's-foot trefoil sprouting from the sparse soil. In a nearby thicket, a joyful birdsong chafed against her unraveling nerves.

She wanted to scream. To curse the boundless beauty all around her.

Angry, she plucked the tender white petal off a bindweed corolla and flicked it over the edge, watching the flower drift into the abyss of the cave's mouth.

She'd given up. When it mattered most, she'd done what she did best—she'd run away. She'd buckled.

She could blame it on her knee. She could blame it on the agonizing toll the months of recovery and return to form had taken on her body. Or point to the fatigue she'd been battling.

But it was none of that. If she had raced, she could have won. Even hurting. Even tired.

The truth was, she'd simply not been strong enough to handle the pressure.

*If the mind is willing, the body will follow.* Had that not been the mantra she'd risen to every morning? The proverb that filled her dreams at night? The creed she had lived by? It had gotten her through thousands and thousands of exhausting miles. Through injury. Through burnout. Through sheer moments of misery.

But this time it had failed her.

This time she'd been—she *was*—weak. Weak in ways that had nothing to do with her physically.

The media would be on a feeding frenzy. All the doubters, all the haters, all those who'd been waiting, willing her to fail—it was finally their moment of *I told you so*.

None more so than Henrik.

*Drückeberger*, he'd taunted. *Quitter. Coward.*

And all she'd done was prove him right.

Tearing another petal from the bindweed, she crumpled the delicate flower, bitter at its determination to blossom in the unforgiving terrain.

What did it matter now, any of it? She'd never race again.

For a long time, she sat looking across the channel, thinking about her mam. About the way she fought to hide her quiet disappointment.

Her unspoken resentment. And Seren, who was always there to lift her up, never asking anything in return. How tired she must be of catching someone always one step away from a fall.

And then, of course, there was Kam. Kam, who had changed her life, making it all feel worthwhile. Kam, who had gifted her her generous heart, her selflessness, her unending capacity for love—receiving so little in exchange.

But also Kam, who lived in the shelter of her ivory tower, where she could hide behind her optimistic naivety, pretending there were no disparities, no adversities, no unscalable obstacles driving them apart.

Dillon pressed her palms against her temples, trying to clear her mind.

It wasn't real. A fleeting part of her—distant, stifled, smothered beneath her sinking despair—cried to be heard. These thoughts were invasive. Untrue.

Her mam didn't blame her.

Seren was strong, capable of supporting the weight of two.

And Kam?—Kam loved her. *For* their differences. *For* the circumstances that made their relationship unique. She didn't care about anything else. She just loved her—for *her*.

But the cry was too faint, the noise in her head too persistent. And she was so tired—tired of treading water, trying to stay afloat. All she wanted was to disappear. To hide. To sleep. To escape the perpetual cycle of pain.

Restless, she got to her feet.

The afternoon breeze had welled, driving the swift-moving current against the base of the island, slamming the waves into the rocky outcrop guarding the entrance to the cave.

A scattering of pebbles slipped beneath the shift in her weight, and her heart raced as she watched them plunge into the dizzying drop to the sea.

Her hand went to her pocket, fingers shaking. She needed to turn on her phone. She needed to call Kam.

But she didn't. She couldn't.

She knew why she was up here. She knew why, after so many years, she'd finally ascended that staircase.

How many times had she felt the pull, yearning to give in?

First, the temptation back in Hamburg, on the cold mornings waking in Henrik's bed. And then, more loudly, more frighteningly, in the days, the months, the year that followed her dad's death. And again, after Kelsey. After Yokohama. After… after…

Her heart pounded, crescendoing the rush of blood in her head.

It was a losing battle. One she could never win.

She pulled out her phone. Thumbed the power button. She could turn it on. Call Seren.

*No.*

A wash of uncanny stillness overcame her as she flung the last of her lifelines over the edge. She watched the phone spiral, violently dashing against the rocks, before being taken by the sea.

It was too late. There was no place to run. She'd stumbled down the wrong path one too many times.

It was no one else's burden to bail her out this time.

# Scene 53: Take 1

I couldn't sleep.

On the fourth day, Seren called in the middle of the night. I was lying in bed, still fully dressed, staring at my ceiling.

I knew, before I answered my phone, why she was calling—what she would say.

I'd known since that first morning. I'd felt it in my soul.

It didn't stop me from clinging to a fraying thread of hope as I answered my phone.

"They found her. She's gone." It's all she said. All I could understand. And then the stoic, ever-poised, ever-proper sister of the woman I loved most in all the world was crying. Sobbing. Wailing on the other end of the line.

I must have said something. I don't think I just hung up. I don't know if I hung up at all.

I got up, walked across my bedroom, and collapsed in the hall.

I lay there on the cool marble tile, with my cheek pressed to the floor. I didn't cry. I didn't move. I didn't breathe. If my heart still beat, I no longer knew it. I simply felt nothing.

And then, as the seconds ticked away, as reality set in—it hit me: a sudden, crushing, turbulent cataclysm of emotion. A violent surge of hysteria ripping through the numbness. It swallowed me whole.

Somewhere, a high, wavering, desperate noise pierced the air, and it took a moment to realize the sound was coming from me. I pummeled the floor—screamed and screamed and screamed. I didn't care who heard me. I didn't care about anything.

My beautiful, extraordinary, perfectly imperfect Dillon Sinclair was gone, lost forever. Three days before her thirty-first birthday.

The truth struck me in searing, agonizing waves of pain—the dawning realization that I'd never see her again. Never kiss her chapped lips, never smell the sea in her hair, or hear the smile in her voice when she called me Kam-Kameryn. I had held her for the last time.

Our final conversation had been curt, my temper short, her voice distant. I hadn't understood. I hadn't begun to imagine…

An entire new cascade of anguish overcame me, a nauseating guilt racking my body.

*No!* It wasn't possible. I slammed the heels of my hands into the wall. Seren was wrong. *Wrong!*

It *couldn't* be Dillon. I needed to call her back. Ask if they were certain.

But I didn't. Because deep down, I knew.

She'd bought a train ticket to Swansea on her credit card that morning, then taken a cab to Mumbles Head. A fisherman had seen a woman climbing the stairs toward the lighthouse shortly after high tide.

They'd searched for her for days and found nothing.

And now they had.

Afraid I was going to vomit, I rolled onto my side and curled into a ball, hugging my knees. As if I could hold myself together. As if I weren't coming unglued at the seams.

Fuck her. *Fuck her.* FUCK HER! How could she do it? Leave me like this? Like she'd never loved me at all.

At some point, I crawled to the balcony. The sun had risen. A sun that had no right to rise. I lay there, half-in, half-out of the open glass doors, listening to the sounds of the city waking beneath me. How could the world keep on turning when my life was falling apart?

I couldn't bring myself to get up. On hand and knee, I pleaded with a God I no longer believed in to let me sleep, to wake, to find it was all just a dream—the continuation of a neverending nightmare. That I would open my eyes and find it was four days earlier. That I would have a text from Dillon, saying she'd won Leeds. Saying she was on her way home.

But each time I dozed off, exhausted from insurmountable heartache, I'd wake once more, only to relive the stabbing, undeniable actuality that this was real—and lose her over and over again.

And so the cycle went—for hours. Days. Weeks.

My mom came and stayed with me. She brewed tea that grew cold on my end table, held my hand when I would let her, called my agent and manager. She made meals I never touched, and comforted me as I wailed with grief in the middle of the night, or broke down in sobs at my breakfast counter.

My manager rescheduled my studio pick-ups, citing 'a death in the family.' I wanted to come clean, to explain Dillon, but she convinced me to keep it vague.

*It wasn't the time. I wasn't in the right frame of mind. Later, maybe.*

I was in no condition to fight her. And she wasn't wrong. I couldn't function. I could hardly brush my hair—dress myself.

On more than one occasion, I stood leaning over my balcony railing, staring at the courtyard thirteen stories below. I thought about jumping. I mean, I thought about it in the way any disconsolate, bereft, heartbroken lover might think about it: not with any real intent (I didn't have the nerve for that), but with the wish that I could. Anything to relieve all the hurt, all the pain I was suffering.

I'd sit and watch our piling beneath the pier for hours, desperate to remember every detail of that night: our first "real" kiss, the water lapping at our feet, the way she'd lit my world on fire. I could feel the warmth of her fingers pressed against the small of my back, taste the mint tea on her tongue. I fantasized details I couldn't remember, preventing myself from turning to hysterics when I couldn't recall things that didn't matter—the color of her shoes, the way I'd worn my hair, the location of the North Star.

I'd play little head games with myself, making negotiations with the universe: if I could count fifteen hundred waves break on the shore without blinking, if I could hold my breath for one hundred revolutions of the Ferris Wheel, if I could trace the path of a falling star all the way to the horizon—a portal would appear on my balcony, something I could step through, allowing me access to join her—wherever that might be. They were always unachievable tasks, impossible victories —games that I could never win.

I knew it was all bogus. I wasn't actually crazy. And when I grew tired of torturing myself, I'd slip to my knees, press my forehead against the glass railing, and cry.

Countless days I spent trying to figure out what I could have done better for Dillon—and even longer nights dwelling on the ever-pressing, impossible question: *why?*

Why had she done it?

She never left a note, never explained herself. The text I received that morning was the last thing she ever sent—my response permanently unread.

Her bike sat in the corner of my living room; I couldn't bear to move it. Some days, I'd pour whiskey over a glass of ice, and by the time I shifted to drinking straight from the bottle, I'd talk to the bike as if it were a conduit allowing conversation between the living and the dead. *I'm sorry*, I'd tell it, over and over—for failing her, for not doing enough to make her feel like life was worth sticking around. And then again, as the contents of the bottle emptied, my focus would inevitably shift to seeking resolution it would never find.

Why, why, *why?*

I wanted to imagine she was drunk when she jumped. That an outside influence forced her to believe having no life was better than the life she left behind. But her toxicology report had been clean, without a single drop of substance in her body. She'd stood on that ledge, clear-headed and sober, and made her last decision with a sound mind.

Had she planned it on the seven-hour train ride to Wales? Had she climbed the steps to the lighthouse knowing she'd never walk down? Or had it been a rash decision, a shortcut to a palliative end?

Alone, just her bike and me, I'd tip back the bottle, drowning in my sorrow, and wonder if she tried to swim… if she regretted jumping in? If she'd ever given a single thought to the hurt I would feel, the loneliness I'd face being the one left behind?

They were answers that died with her in the wild seas of the Gower.

When I finally returned to the studio to finish pick-ups for *Sand Seekers*, everyone gave me a wide berth. I looked like hell; my skin was ashen, I'd chopped my hair above my shoulders with a pair of kitchen scissors, and all my costumes were too big. Hair and makeup had their work cut out for them, but I didn't care.

No one mentioned Dillon. The rumors circulated—I wasn't unaware —but the subject remained taboo. I wanted desperately to publicly grieve my loss, but under the advice of my PR team, and gentle, yet insistent persuasion from Elliott, I remained slammed in a closet I had never wanted to be in. *It was for the best*, everyone kept telling me. *For who*, they never said.

Somehow, by the grace of the Gods of Entertainment—along with a healthy dose of *get-your-shit-together* from L.R. and MacArthur—I got through the final photography and completed the film.

It should have felt monumental—the closure of an era in my life I would never experience again. The trilogy was finished; my journey as

Addison Riley complete. Tears should have flowed freely at the wrap party, with hugs and toasts for the cast and crew who I'd learned to love like family.

Instead, I spent the night nodding through an unconvincing smile beside one of the soaring atrium windows of the Ritz-Carlton, silently contemplating how long it would take to get home through traffic on the Santa Monica Freeway.

I ended up leaving in the middle of a blooper reel documenting hilarious moments of the three-year odyssey. I couldn't stand the footage of me laughing, reminders of how happy I'd once been. On the way home, I got a phone call from Dani. I canceled it to voicemail. We hadn't spoken since my party. But as the car turned onto PCH, I was overtaken by an abrupt explosion of fury. I asked my driver to stop, and stepped into a sea of taillights, crossing the highway to the beach. And there, amongst the littered wash of Venice sand, I hit redial, and proceeded to tell my once-best friend exactly how I felt about her. When I hung up, I knew we'd never speak again. It was cathartic, I guess, cutting out a cancer in my life. But as I cried myself to sleep that night, it still didn't return Dillon to my side.

Later in the summer, when the Olympics came to town, I tried desperately to hide in a fog of oblivion. But all the whiskey in the world, the shuttered blinds, the hum of self-guided meditation, the glow of Netflix, and the mind-numbing sting of scorching showers failed to permit me to escape the sight of those five interlocking rings. The city pulsed in blue, black, red, yellow, and green.

Seren called the Thursday before the start of the equestrian competition. We'd spoken little since Dillon's passing, neither of us having much to say. We were both wading through our own personal hells—ironically less than a hundred miles apart. I knew she and Épée had arrived in Los Angeles. I'd seen a headline: *Seren Sinclair elects to remain on Team GB after the death of famed Olympic sister.*

She asked if I would come to watch her. If I would sit with her mam.

I don't know why it felt so important. Dillon wasn't there. And I wasn't a Sinclair.

I wanted to say no. If I'm honest, after attending Dillon's private funeral, I wasn't sure I wanted to see Seren or Jacqueline again. A shamefaced, self-condemning side of me worried they might blame me for the loss of Dillon. I was the one, after all, who had found Dr.

Monaghan. The one who had supported her in her quest to qualify, and encouraged her to compete again. I was the last person she texted. The one who hadn't read the signs. If I hadn't been so blind, perhaps Dillon would be alive.

But neither woman had ever given any indication that was true. It was just my guilty conscience talking, playing tricks on my mind.

So I told her yes.

I had no excuse to say no. I wasn't working. I'd had to buy my way out of my contract for *Anna Karenina*. The Tolstoy film felt too dark, too painful in my present emotional deterioration. I wouldn't begin filming the *Mia Hamm* project until winter. Until then, outside my obligation for the press tour for *Sand Seekers*, I was taking time off, trying to pull myself together. Trying to find a way to feel whole—no, not whole. I didn't imagine *whole* was in my future. That would be like trying to put Humpty Dumpty back together again. Operational, maybe. Functional, at best.

But I owed it to Dillon to be there for her sister. Despite my professional stance that she and I had never engaged in a romantic relationship, I'd never denied we were friends. Going in support of the Sinclair family felt like a satisfying *fuck you* to my publicist, my agent, my manager. Every person who continued to pressure me to live in hiding.

So I went to the competition.

I was glad to be a hundred miles away from LA at the equestrian grounds when Elyna Laurent won the women's triathlon. The bike leg of the race had taken a course down PCH, traveling through Santa Monica. It would have dismantled me to stand on my balcony watching the triathletes cycle past without Dillon.

Still, sitting in the crowded stands awaiting Seren's dressage test, I'd been unable to scroll past Elyna's photo on the podium. I stared at her stiff smile, Dillon's gold medal around her neck, Henrik's ever-present shadow blurred in the background.

I wanted to excuse myself, to go puke in the VIP bathrooms.

Instead, I forced my thumb to click *unfollow* on *World Triathlon* and turned my focus back to Seren.

*Baby steps*. I could practically hear my therapist applauding.

My mom flew down to stay for the weekend, joining me to sit with Jacqueline. While the two of them made polite small talk, I daydreamed of an alternate reality, and stared at the leaderboard.

*Sinclair: #1*

On the third day, going into stadium jumping, Seren was sitting in a position to win the individual gold.

But it was the wrong Sinclair. Another should have been there in her stead.

Seren must have felt the same. Because when she did win—when the President of the *FEI* placed the medal around her neck—she sank to her knees and covered her face with her white-gloved hands. Cameras panned-in, international footage rolling as an instrumental of *God Save the King* played in the background, Seren Sinclair sat on the podium and sobbed.

I had to leave. I didn't wait for my mom, or say goodbye to Jacqueline, or alert the team of security surrounding me. I simply got up, shoved my way to the aisle, and ran down the stairs. I didn't care if the press caught my hasty exit—if they photographed the mascara running down my cheeks. I only wanted to escape. Back to the prison of my apartment. Back to the comfort of Dillon's bike and analgesic influence of the whiskey. Back to the seclusion of my misery.

A few weeks later, Sam called. We'd kept up a tentative friendship, the two of us needing one another, both hurting in equal, horrible, dissimilar ways. She told me she'd talked to Seren. After the Olympics, Seren had gone home and left the medal on Dillon's grave.

Sam said the next day when Seren went to the cemetery, the medal was gone. She hadn't cared. She said it never belonged to her in the first place.

The gold medal ambitions had always been her sister's. And now they were all lost—Dillon, the medal, the dream.

It took me a long time to understand I didn't kill Dillon Sinclair.

Years, if I'm honest. A journey through unconquerable heartache. Hours upon hours of endless therapy. Midnight calls to my parents. Unannounced drop-ins on my friends. It was a one-step-forward, two-steps-back, nonlinear kind of healing.

It was only when I finally came to terms with the acceptance that I could not have saved Dillon without her willingness to save herself, that I was able to let go of some of my guilt. There would always be things I could have done better—but the blame wasn't solely on me.

My therapist allowed me to explore my *what-ifs*—what if I had done this, what if I had done that—and then bade me put them to rest.

I had done the best I could with the information Dillon made privy. Some things were out of my control, and always would be.

With the lessening of my guilt, a more uncomfortable emotion came to pass: anger. I didn't know how to forgive her. Forgive her for the hurt she put me through. Forgive her for the future she stole from us, without ever giving me a choice in the matter.

I grew obsessed trying to understand suicide, trying to understand the darkest places depression lured a person. Trying to understand how someone could see no other way out, no other relief from a pain so visceral, they felt there was no alternative. *See the person, not the act*, my therapist drummed into me. She reminded me I needed to remember Dillon for who she was, not for the decision she made during a time of intense emotional suffering.

Compassion was imperative—both for her and for me.

But even still, even as I grew to accept it—even if I knew I would never fully understand—the truth remained: I lost someone I wasn't prepared to live without, and the despair of that will never go away.

It's been two years now, and I still cry. Probably more often than I should. Certainly more often than I'd admit to anyone. But not as often as I used to. It's when the sun hits just right—when a breath of chlorine and sunscreen touch the air—I can feel her, somewhere near me. Never close enough. Forever out of reach. And when that happens, wherever I'm at, I have to sit down—to try to catch my breath. To try to keep myself from crumbling.

I fail, frequently. *All the king's horses and all the king's men...* But I've learned to continue. To get up, dust myself off, and try again.

I still wear the necklace she gave me. Aside from filming, I've yet to take it off. Dillon was right; I haven't been invited to the Met Gala— but I did get nominated for an Oscar for my portrayal of Mia Hamm. And win or lose, I'll be wearing my Welsh lovespoon in front of the Academy.

Elliott keeps telling me it will get better. Maybe he's right. He says one day I'll find someone—that I'll look up, when I least expect it, and catch a smile that makes my head spin and my heart feel things that currently no longer seem possible.

I like to think that's true.

But it probably won't be on a Hawaiian island. I probably—*hopefully*—won't run them over with a rented Jeep. Our first kiss is unlikely to taste of pineapple.

I just know, whoever it is, they won't be Dillon Sinclair. And I'll never be their Kam-Kameryn.

Because the truth is, life isn't fair. Not every love story has a Hollywood ending.

But here's the thing: that hasn't stopped me from feeling like our story was an unfinished line—like someone hit pause before the credits were rolling.

And it makes me wonder: what might have happened if a different choice had been made? If life were more like a movie, where a director could call 'cut' when a shot wasn't working? Where the actors could go back to firsts, the crew could reset, and we could rewrite the scene. How different would our future be if we could film the take again?

*Quiet on set!*
*Take two.*
*Roll sound!*
*Roll camera!*
*Action!*

# Scene 52: Take 2

The tide was rising.

Dillon hesitated on the landing of the staircase.

Just one foot, and then the other. One hundred eighty-three stairs to climb. She knew the way. And she knew the decision that awaited her at the top.

But the first step felt so daunting.

Two hundred feet above her, a Herring gull sang its guttural song as it circled the lighthouse. She watched the bird, temporarily transfixed as the pounding in her heart accelerated. It was now or never. Behind her, the foreshore to Mumbles Head was disappearing, and soon, a return trek to the mainland would be impossible.

Which was what she wanted.

Wasn't it?

She had felt so certain, wading through the water. Ever since walking out of *Roundhay Park*, she'd known what she had to do.

But now that she was here, she felt her conviction falter.

She snapped her eyes away from the bird. Nothing had changed. She just needed a minute to catch her breath—to find her bearing.

Her thoughts seemed so disjointed.

Careless of the burgeoning current, she dropped to sit on the landing.

A crab skittered across the first stone step, before vanishing into a crevice. She didn't allow herself to think about Kam, about the way she'd stop to point out the crustacean. How she'd know its scientific name, and ramble off a list of facts, a testament to her love of all things aquatic.

No, she couldn't think about that now. The time for that had passed.

Drawing her knees to her chest, she tried to slow her breathing.

Her life was over.

Henrik had been right. She was nothing but a coward. A coward who ran away from everything.

Across the narrow strait, the Mumbles Pier glistered in the sunlight. She scanned the quiet jetty to where a pair of silhouettes stood, their fishing rods cast over the railing: a man and a child. How many afternoons had she and her dad stood on that same platform? It was where he'd taught her to tie a clinch knot, to bait a hook, to reel in a lurking flounder.

Her gaze trailed to her thumb, where she still had a fine white scar from mishandling a knife while prying open the shell of a blue mussel.

"Bydd gryf!" her dad had gently reprimanded when the crimson well of blood had threatened to spring a gush of tears. "A dragon does not cry."

*Bydd gryf*—be strong.

So many times she'd repeated the phrase, his voice an echo in her mind.

*At the start of a race. In the last steps before the finish line. On long, exhausting training rides.*

And today she had failed him.

She squeezed her eyes closed, trying to shut out the carousel of voices. Her father. Henrik. Kam. Seren.

*Ddraig Fach.*

*Drückeberger.*

*You can't think about anyone but yourself.*

*You promised me, Dillon!*

Desperate for silence, she slammed her fist against the jagged stone of the landing, sending a blaze of pain up her forearm, the white heat startling her, dragging her back to reality.

Everything that had seemed so clear before no longer felt certain.

She stared at the blood dripping down her knuckles.

How could one moment of weakness truly discount a lifetime of courage?

It wasn't fair. And it wasn't true.

Somewhere, a voice of rationale—a voice of reason—begged to be heard, fighting to reassure her: she wasn't a coward. She'd given everything she had. Over and over.

Forcing herself to her feet, her bounding pulse returned. Water was washing over the landing, the rock pools at the base of the island beginning to overflow. She had to act, one way or the other—up the stairs or return to the safety of the shore.

On the pier, she could see the fisherman's rod bending, his line taut with tension. The child beside him was jumping up and down in anticipation.

Dillon turned away. Her heart felt like it was going to beat out of her chest. Above her, the gull cried again, still circling. She took one step up the staircase, glancing at the lighthouse, and then looked back to the mainland.

Her father had once told her the flood tide was unswimmable.

But he'd been gone so long, he'd never really had a chance to know her.

She turned—away from the lighthouse, away from the stairs—and dove headfirst into the water.

The brass knob turned reluctantly as the door creaked open, twelve years of dust weighing on its hinges.

Dillon froze. The room was musty: salt, brine, and wood rot hanging thick in the air. And somewhere beneath it, the subtle scent of cologne —an aroma she'd almost forgotten. Her skin pricked with gooseflesh underneath her sea-soaked clothing.

She took a breath. It was time to face this.

For the first time in more than half her life, she stepped across the threshold of her father's study.

It was smaller than she remembered it. The rosewood desk seemed less majestic, the wall of books less imposing. But it was otherwise unchanged. The evening of his funeral, her mam had closed the door, and the room was never mentioned between the three Sinclairs again. A well-preserved time capsule oblivious to the life that had continued on around it.

Her damp trainers left a trail of footprints as she slowly took inventory of the once-familiar surroundings. There was the antique turntable beside the radiator and his Beaufort jacket hanging on the wall. She stopped in front of an end table. A weathered copy of *Theory of Elasticity* lay open, his glasses propped between the pages, marking a passage that no longer mattered.

Closing the book, she ran her fingers along the broken spine, before crossing the room to his wingback chair. The scent of his cologne was strongest here. She could still see the indent of his elbow on the leather of the armrest. It was the same chair where he'd been sitting when, at four years old, she burst into his study to show him she'd learned how to whistle. Despite his maze of blueprints and ongoing business call, he'd tugged her onto his lap and listened with pride to the shrill, breathy warble. All these years later, and she could still feel the scratch of his five o'clock whiskers, and hear the smile in his voice as he told her he'd never been prouder.

There was nothing she wouldn't give to hear those words again.

Setting the memory aside, she leaned over his desk, pausing to look at a faded calendar. Beneath a layer of dust, the final month of his life was frozen in time.

Her breath hitched.

July, the 27th was circled in red, the word DILLON written in capital letters.

Unsteady, she sank into the empty chair to keep her knees from buckling. He'd marked the day of her Olympic debut, twelve years earlier.

For a long time, she sat in silence and stared at her dad's handwriting, before eventually allowing her gaze to drift to the shadows of the open beams in the ceiling.

She didn't know how he had done it, putting their mam through that. Did he know she'd be the one to find him?

Or, had he ever considered Seren would feel obligated to move back home, that she'd spend her life trying to fill the hole he'd left in their family?

The tightness in her chest shifted, her sorrow disintegrating to anger.

And what about *her*? Had he realized the effect his death would have on her? The darkness that would follow?

Lunging to her feet, she swept the calendar to the floor, suddenly finding the emptiness of the room suffocating. She threw open a long-rusted window.

Along the shore, the moored sailboats bobbed in the high tide, their masts reflecting the late afternoon sun as it slipped toward the horizon.

She closed her eyes, allowing the fresh air to fan her burning cheeks and listened to the waves break against the headland.

Her resentment was misplaced. She knew she couldn't blame him.

Because, deep down, she understood. His hurt. His need to escape it.

But she also knew what it was like to be the one left behind, to carry that guilt on her shoulders.

It wasn't something she could do to the people she loved—to the people who loved her.

The coastal breeze stirred the long-stationary curtains, unearthing a paper trapped beneath them. Dillon bent to retrieve it. Flattening out the folds, a recumbent ray of sunlight illuminated its yellowing creases.

It was a photo of her above a faded headline: *Olympic Dream: Swansea Star Dillon Sinclair Makes History as Team GB's Youngest Triathlete.*

The paper was brittle, the small columns of text no longer legible, but the image remained clear. She was nineteen years old, standing on the podium in Bermuda. She'd outraced an entire field of seasoned competitors to earn her place as a rookie at the upcoming London Games.

Dillon slid to the floor. She thought about the letter her father wrote her, how he had been so proud. He must have clipped the article from his daily paper.

And a week later, they buried him.

Tears she didn't bother to wipe away dripped off her chin.

She studied the grainy image. The girl on the podium was smiling, her hair drenched with champagne, but there was a joylessness in her expression.

She'd expected to find the selfish woman who'd caused her father's death. A woman who'd put her own ambitions above everything else.

But all she saw was a child.

A child who'd been manipulated.

A child who'd been controlled.

And a child who'd assumed a burden that wasn't entirely hers.

She crumpled the article, allowing the fragments to slip through her fingers.

She wasn't that child anymore.

She'd spent a lifetime trying to atone for her mistakes, always chasing resolutions to an outcome that couldn't be changed. There was no record she could break to show him how sorry she was. No medal she could win that would ever bring him back.

And it was time to let it go.

Her dad had taught her to be strong. Henrik taught her to be ruthless. But no one ever taught her the value of knowing when to walk away.

That quitting wasn't always weakness.

She leaned against the wall. A weariness washed over her, brought on by the setting sun. She couldn't remember the last time she'd ever felt this tired. But with the fatigue also came a sense of relief. A feeling of closure.

She didn't know what she'd do next, but for the first time in longer than she could remember, she felt like things might be okay, like she could start to see a future.

The light shifted over the windowsill. It was late.

She pulled out her phone. She needed to text Seren.

But first, there was another promise she had to keep.

Staring at the lovespoon on her father's mantel—one he had once carved for their mam—she hit the first number in her contacts.

She drew a deep breath.

The call was answered on the first ring.

Exhaling, she closed her eyes.

"Hey, Kam."

# Scene 53: Take 2

I couldn't sleep.

In less than twelve hours, I'd be arriving on the red carpet, attending the Oscars for the first time as a nominee. That alone would have been anxiety-inducing, but tonight, Dillon was coming as my date.

I'm not really sure what we were thinking. Our first official public outing as a couple probably would have been better served a little more low-key. For instance, we could have had a quiet dinner at *Nobu Malibu* or maybe attended a soccer match to watch *Angel City*. But no, straight to the Academy Awards. Go big or go home, right? Or, as Elliott liked to say: *lights, camera, action—or cut!*

Despite it being her decision to come, I was concerned about how she would handle the press and the massive amount of publicity we would receive. But my sympathy was quickly abated when I glanced over from my midnight turmoil and found her peacefully asleep. I considered bumping her, or tugging off the duvet, 'accidentally' forcing her awake to join me in my worry, but begrudgingly, took the high road, and chose to leave her to her halcyon dreams. It did little good for both of us to lie here, staring at the ceiling.

Instead, sacrificing what little time was left in the small hours of the morning, my thoughts wandered, replaying the journey of the last two years, and what had led us here.

Three weeks after walking away from Leeds—after officially announcing her retirement as a professional triathlete—she returned to LA.

We needed to talk, she told me.

My heart sank. I thought she was coming to end things.

So needless to say, I was stunned when we walked down to the Santa Monica pier in the quiet hours of early morning, and she told me she didn't want to hide anymore. That she was ready for us to live openly, if that was still what I wanted.

I told her I needed a couple of days to think about it—I didn't—but I wanted to give her a chance to change her mind. I didn't want her to feel pressured into believing the only way we'd have a future together was if she stepped outside her comfort zone. But this time, she was adamant.

What had changed, I wanted to know?

She wasn't able to give me a pinpoint answer. In some ways, *nothing*. In other ways, *everything*.

Part of it, I think, was that she'd been seeing a new therapist. Someone different than the sports psychologist she'd relied on throughout her career. And though she didn't talk to me about everything she was going through, I understood a lot of her healing centered on building a new sense of self and finding ways to address her fears.

The media was going to be relentless, I warned her.

I was worth it, she assured me.

So it was settled.

The next big question was how we were going to handle it. Did I want to wait until we'd wrapped on *Sand Seekers*? Did I need to warn the studio? Did I want my PR team to curate an announcement?

No. And no. And no.

I didn't want to ask permission. I didn't want to be managed. I didn't want a 'coming out statement' handcrafted to mitigate backlash and keep my image 'on brand.' I just wanted to be able to post the occasional stupid selfie with my girlfriend—to end the speculation on what guy *Entertainment Weekly* currently thought I was blowing.

So, we came up with a plan, and a week later, to the horror of my unprepared manager, and utter delight of the media frenzy, we posted a photo on my Instagram.

Amusing myself, and tolerated—with numerous good-natured eye-rolls—by Dillon, I restaged the viral photo the Uber driver had taken off her dashcam: Dillon—her hair askew, cheeks flushed, and clothing disheveled—and me—wearing her jacket, my lips swollen, the top button of my pants unfastened, looking exactly as if I'd just been freshly fucked in a castle cathedral on a whim. I completed the image with lipstick on Dillon's collar and a hickey—no makeup required—below my ear.

I captioned it: *OK, fine: I lied. More than 'just friends.' She's my person.* And then posted it to my 150 million followers on Instagram.

And you know what? The world didn't implode (the same could probably not be said of my manager's head). The studio didn't fire me (fat chance of that, anyway—no offense, but I was Kameryn Kingsbury). I wasn't even struck down by a bolt of lightning from the heavens.

I got some hate mail—but honestly, what celebrity didn't?—a few hundred marriage proposals, and an invite to speak at GLAAD. And that was pretty much that. I received over a hundred thousand *likes* when I changed my Facebook status from *it's complicated* to *in a relationship*, which I still find kind of wild.

Dillon had long since deleted all her social media, so other than having to put up with me posting the occasional *TikTok* video of her cooking French toast in my kitchen, her life as the now-acknowledged love of *my* life, didn't change. We dealt a little with the paparazzi—it was just a part of life for me—but for the little time we were seen in public together, it didn't bother her the way I think either of us had been afraid it might.

Life simply went on.

Three weeks later, I shot my final pick-up for *Sand Seekers*. It was an emotional, fulfilling moment for me. Two and a half years, tens of thousands of miles traveled, over a thousand hours of raw footage, and my journey as Addison Riley in Margaret Gilles' beloved trilogy was complete.

I went to the wrap party solo—Dillon was back in Wales, helping Seren prepare to fly Épée to Los Angeles—and at the end of the night, after endless hugs, probably one too many martinis, and a hitch in my side from laughing too hard at the blooper reel, I was surprised when Elliott strolled up to the podium and said he had an announcement.

The ballroom at the Ritz quieted, five hundred sets of eyes turning toward where he'd tapped the microphone. He wasn't drunk, I noted, and he wasn't quite smiling.

He told the room he'd be brief, promising this wasn't just another longwinded *goodbye, see you later* speech.

And then, without fanfare, without a joke or drumroll, he proceeded to announce that he was gay. He said he was tired of living a lie and that his press agent would be making an official statement the following afternoon. But he wanted us to hear it from him first.

My heart sped up when I found him looking directly at me.

Leaning over the mic, his brow glistening in a nervousness uncommon of him, he credited me for my bravery. He told me I was his best friend—not only the most beautiful woman he knew—inside and out—but also one of the most talented actors he'd ever had the pleasure to work with. He called me *authentic, brilliant, and obstinately hardheaded.* And said he wouldn't want me any other way. And then he stepped off the platform stage, kissed me on the cheek, and walked out of the room.

The next day, *Time Magazine* ran a story with him on the cover. The title—*Elliott Fleming: #loveislove.*

I texted him and gave him shit for upstaging me. He texted back that it was payback for landing top billing on the third movie. And we promised to catch up—a double date—soon.

Two weeks later, I flew to Venice to begin principal photography on the contemporary retelling of *Anna Karenina.* My only regret filming the tragic Tolstoy prose in the historically enchanting *Floating City,* was that I would miss the Olympics. I'd wanted to be there for Seren. And even more importantly—for Dillon.

My consolation, however, was that her mam and Sam were there for Dillon, and Dillon was there for Seren.

Over the three days that Seren competed, I would sprint to my trailer after being released from set. There, I would plant myself—still in full makeup and costume—in front of my iPad and watch the equestrian rounds.

Épée was on fire. Seren was crushing it.

When the president of the *FEI* finally placed the gold medal around her neck, I found myself unable to breathe as she stepped off the podium and went directly to Dillon. There had been a lot of media coverage over Dillon's retirement, with sympathized viewership lamenting her unfortunate end to her quest for gold. It was safe to say the sporting world had been rooting for *Sinclair Squared,* which meant a lot of heartstrings were given a firm tug as the two sisters embraced over the railing. With Dillon's lips pressed against Seren's ear, I couldn't tell what was said between them, but it was Seren who was crying. I watched through blurry vision as Dillon leaned back and shook her head, tapping first the medal, and then Seren's heart. *This is yours,* she seemed to be saying. And then, more clearly: *I'm okay.* It was she who reached up to wipe the tears off her sister's cheeks.

The following weekend I sat on break in the glorious mezzanine of *Teatro La Fenice* and watched Elyna Laurent decimate her competition. *Superhuman*, the commentators raged as the Frenchwoman sprinted to a blazing finish. *Unstoppable*, they called her. *The next great generation.*

My heart thrummed when I answered Dillon's call that night. I wasn't sure how the day would affect her. How she would handle Elyna's unquestionable dominance. Her shattering of the Olympic course record.

It hurt, she admitted over the long-distance line. I could hear the melancholiness in her voice, and my soul ached to hold her. She told me Elyna would have beaten her anyway, even if she had never been injured. That she was, without question, the superior athlete.

I didn't argue. She wasn't looking for sympathy or wanting me to dispute her. She just wanted to talk. And so we did, well into the hours of the Italian morning. I didn't care that I had an early call time. We spoke until sunrise, and when I hung up, I sent her a photo of the mist rising over the canals.

A month or so earlier, not long after Leeds, she'd reached out to Elyna. I'm not sure if it was on the advice of her therapist, or if it was just something she felt compelled to do, but I know the topic of conversation revolved around Henrik. Dillon never told me what the two of them talked about. Even on the long, heartfelt chat we'd had the night Elyna won the gold medal, she kept the dialogue between them private. What I did know was, three weeks prior to the Summer Games, Elyna terminated Henrik and attended the Los Angeles Olympics as a self-coached competitor.

The more shocking news hit the triathlon community a week after Elyna returned to France a national hero. *World Triathlon* announced that Henrik Fischer was permanently suspended from the organization. The German, French, and British Federations followed suit with lifetime bans on coaching. Multiple charges had been brought against him in a joint indictment on the allegations of abuse of position of trust, sexual coercion, and child exploitation—a case framed by Elyna, Dillon, and seven other female athletes.

I'd known it was coming—Dillon hadn't left me in the dark—but I was still awestruck by the sheer volume of women affected and the heinousness of offenses. I was proud of her. Proud of Elyna, who I didn't even know. It was going to be a long legal battle—years, likely

—and would drudge into the spotlight things I was certain none of the victims wished to face in public. But it would stop the cycle of abuse —and that was what Dillon told me finally forced her to action.

In late fall after the Olympics, when I met Dillon in Tetiaroa after completing *Anna Karenina*, Dillon asked what I thought about her selling her flat in London.

We'd been lying on the private beach looking out over the turquoise lagoon. I asked about her mam—about Seren?

She told me Seren had sprung the news on them that the American rider she'd been dating, Jeremy Hartman, had asked her to marry him. And that she said yes. She would be moving her training business and horses to his facility in Woodside—ironically, less than half an hour from my parents.

I, too, was stunned. And selfishly thrilled. Because I knew it meant Dillon was serious about moving here. About living permanently in the US.

I was still polite and—despite the awkwardness of the conversation while wearing as little clothing as we were—worried about her mother.

Dillon laughed and assured me she was ready to live her life sans the meddling headache of her adult children. And so it was decided— after three years of struggling to keep our long-distance relationship afloat—we finally shared the same bed. The same closet. The same kettle every morning. Her presence in the ridiculousness of that overblown, grossly grandiose apartment finally made the place feel like a home.

The following spring, Dillon took the first steps toward a new career. She'd continued her long-term sponsorship with *Nike* and joined the company in an ad-based campaign promoting athlete mental health, but she wanted more than that when it came to an enduring shift in vocation.

Around the same time, photography had started on my next movie —*The Perfect Strike*—based on Mia Hamm. We needed to hire a sports consultant for the film, and I mentioned it to Dillon. A week later, her profession as a freelance athletic advisor for film and television was born. And aside from her telling me I was hopeless when it came to perfecting my form on sprinting, and quipping that I'd have been better cast as the clumsy extra who broke her ankle tripping over the ball, I loved having her connected to my world of Hollywood.

Looking back, there's no question it's been a long transition. The journey has had its shares of ups and downs. I still worry about her when she is late to call. I don't think I'll ever get over the anxiety of how I felt those sickening hours when she walked away from Leeds—when I hadn't known if I'd ever see her again. But she's more open now about her feelings. She tells me when she's low. She usually lets me in. And she's yet to break a promise to me—and I keep that, for comfort, in my back pocket. I give her space knowing parts of her are —and maybe always will be—healing.

We are sometimes like ships in the night, passing reluctantly, both of us ferried along by our careers. But so far, we've made time for the important things—just the way she had, by flying in on a redeye to make it to the Academy Awards.

So I guess I couldn't begrudge her the few hours of sleep she'd gained over me while I lay there, rehashing the last two years.

My thoughts gradually shifted to the day ahead—the cameras, the press, the interviews that cared less about the work I'd come to represent and more about what I was wearing.

But, what did it matter?

I already knew I wasn't going to win. I was up against Cate Blanchett, who was nominated for playing the role of some English billionaire businesswoman. How was I supposed to compete with that? It annoyed me that I'd even taken the time to jot down keynotes on a longshot acceptance speech, knowing it would never come to pass.

The truth was, however, it really *didn't* matter. Because I didn't care about the awards. I only cared that the person I loved was going to be by my side—that we'd managed to navigate a path allowing us to share our lives together. And that she loved me enough to sit beside me, even when I knew the glam and glitz of Tinseltown really wasn't her thing.

As I stood in my ensuite, having forgone the Hollywood norm of a fashion crew, and opted instead to dress myself, Dillon sat on the edge of our infinity tub overlooking PCH. She watched me apply my makeup in the vanity mirror, far calmer than I was.

"Nervous?" she asked, languidly rising to her feet.

I found her eyes in the mirror, deja vu of another time and place.

"Have you seen the woman I'm arriving with?" I fed back the words she'd once handed me, smiling as she reached to straighten the lovespoon pendant hanging at the hollow of my throat. "I have nothing to be nervous over—I've already won."

She bent to kiss my shoulder. "You're daft, Kam-Kameryn."


And that's how our scene should have been written.

# Author's End Note

I started writing *The Unfinished Line* in late 2020. I'd had Dillon and Kam in mind for a while, and knew I wanted to explore their love story, but wasn't certain where it would lead.

As the story progressed, and their journey took shape, I began to see what felt like the most organic ending. And it broke my heart.

But from it, *Take 1* was born.

It wasn't the story I wanted to write, but it was one that resonated with me deeply.

Having spent my life surrounded by elite athletes (first as a collegiate softball player and later as a professional equestrian), I've witnessed firsthand the pressure many of these athletes are under—not only from external sources but also from themselves. The drive to compete, to win, to live their sport to perfection, is exactly what puts them at the top of their game—but it is also what pushes many to the edge, both physically and emotionally.

There has been a heartbreaking increase in the number of athletes lost to suicide over the last two decades—particularly among women. The rise has been attributed to various factors including intense performance pressure, injury, and mental health challenges, which are frequently left untreated or overlooked. Combined with the individual nature of many sports, particularly those without strong team support (such as triathlon), the feelings of failure and isolation can be exacerbated.

For years, I debated whether I should put Dillon's story out in the world. The subject is a personal one to me. I've lost family and friends to mental health struggles and faced many of these same challenges myself.

When I finally picked the book up again, I knew I wanted to do things a little differently.

While I still felt *Take 1* was the authentic ending, I needed to write *Take 2*—to show a different option and emphasize another path. I wanted *The Unfinished Line* and its alternate endings to pave the way for ongoing conversation surrounding mental health.

Because this is something we need to destigmatize. It's something we need to be able to talk about openly.

We all struggle in one way or another, and it's not something we should be ashamed of.

Life can be so overwhelming, we need to find ways to show ourselves more compassion and more grace.

I know it may not always feel like it, but change is possible. And with support, healing can happen.

Just hang in there—one day, one step at a time.

Because there's room in every story for a *Take 2*.

Xoxo,
Jen

If you or someone you know is struggling, help is available. Call or text 988 for the Suicide & Crisis Lifeline.

# Acknowledgments

There truly aren't enough blank pages to properly thank everyone who helped this book reach completion. But as always, I have to begin by thanking my tremendously supportive, endlessly patient wife, Donna. Without her unfailing encouragement, this book would not have come to fruition. But from the moment she leafed through my miserable first draft, she believed in it and has been its champion ever since. It simply wouldn't be here without her. But then again, none of my books would.

I owe my sister, Lara, a huge shout-out for being my "first reader" and guinea pig. I am always grateful for her honesty and enthusiasm.

Thank you, Dad and Mom, for constantly reminding me how proud you are of everything I do—it keeps me going.

Piper, Josey, and Daisy—you're the best company in what would otherwise be a lonely profession.

Charlie and Jules, once again, thank you for alternating between motivation and well-deserved kicks in the pants. I can always count on you both to deliver whichever one I am due.

Erika—thank you for your continued words of encouragement and all the love you show indie authors.

Abby Craden—I will forever be grateful for your truly incomparable talent that has brought these characters to life. You never cease to amaze me.

And to my fellow writers, many of whom have become wonderful friends over these last two years—Sharon, Alaina, J.E., D.A., Alicia, to name only a few—thank you, thank you, for the warm welcome into this community, and all the kindnesses you've shown me.

# Other books by Jen Lyon

The Senator's Wife
Caught Sleeping
Whistleblower

## Coming soon

The fourth title in The Senator's Wife series
The Curse of Queens
Let Them Burn